# Flight of the Nighthawks

## The Darkwar Book One

## Raymond E. Feist

W F HOWES LTD

This large print edition published in 2007 by
W F Howes Ltd
Unit 4, Rearsby Business Park, Gaddesby Lane,
Rearsby, Leicester LE7 4YH

1 3 5 7 9 10 8 6 4 2

First published in the United Kingdom in 2005
by Voyager, an imprint of HarperCollins*Publishers*

A CIP catalogue record for this book is available
from the British Library

ISBN 978 1 40740 151 5

Typeset by Palimpsest Book Production Limited,
Grangemouth, Stirlingshire
Printed and bound in Great Britain
by Antony Rowe Ltd, Chippenham, Wilts.

# ACKNOWLEDGEMENTS

As I have done in the past and will continue to until Midkemia is no more, my thanks everlasting to the mothers and fathers of Midkemia for giving me a wonderful sandbox in which to play. From Thursday to Friday nights, for thirty years your voices echo in my ear each time I sit down to spin a yarn on our world.

To Jonathon Matson, as always, my thanks for friendship and wise counsel.

To my editors, for always trying hard no matter how crazy the circumstances.

To my mother, for always inspiring me through sheer endurance and unqalified love.

To my children, for giving me a reason for existing beyond mere self-gratification and personal goals.

To those ladies with whom I dine, thanks for the amusement, the affection, the drama, and the glimpse into a world I barely understand.

To new friends and to enterprises that keep things interesting.

Again to my readers, who let me keep doing this.

Without any of the above mentioned, and some

I'm leaving out, life would not be worth enduring, let alone living.

Raymond E. Feist
San Diego, CA July, 2005

*For Andy and Rich,*

*long overdue thanks for stepping in and being there at the right time*

# CONTENTS

Fate will bring together those a thousand miles apart;
Without fate, they will miss each other though they come face to face.

Chinese proverb

# PROLOGUE

# HARBINGER

The storm had broken.

Pug danced along the edge of the rocks, his feet finding scant purchase as he made his way among the tide pools. His dark eyes darted about as he peered into each pool under the cliff face, seeking the spiny creatures driven into the shallows by the recently passed storm.

His boyish muscles bunched under his light shirt as he shifted the sack of sandcrawlers, rockclaws, and crabs plucked from this water garden. The afternoon sun sent sparkles through the sea spray swirling around him, as the west wind blew his sun-streaked brown hair about. Pug set his sack down, checked to make sure it was securely tied, then squatted on a clear patch of sand. The sack was not quite full, but Pug relished the extra hour or so that he could relax. Megar the cook wouldn't trouble him about the time as long as the sack was almost full. Resting with his back against a large rock, Pug settled in to relax. He opened his eyes suddenly. He had fallen asleep, or at least he knew he had fallen asleep here once . . . He sat up.

A cool wet spray struck him in the face. Without

having closed his eyes, somehow time had passed. Fear rose up within his chest, and he knew he had stayed much too long. Westward, over the sea, dark thunderheads were forming above the black outline of the Six Sisters, the small islands on the horizon. The roiling, surging clouds, with rain trailing below like some sooty veil, heralded another of the sudden storms common to this part of the coast in early summer. The winds drove the clouds with unnatural fury and distant thunder grew louder by the moment.

Pug turned and looked in all directions. Something was terribly wrong. He knew he had been here many times before, but . . . He had been here before! Not just in this place, but living this very moment!

To the south, the high bluffs of Sailor's Grief reared up against the sky, as waves crashed against the base of that rocky pinnacle. Whitecaps started to form behind the breakers, a sure sign the storm would quickly strike. Pug knew he was in danger, for the storms of summer could drown anyone on the beaches, or if severe enough, on the low ground beyond. He picked up his sack and started north, towards the castle. As he moved among the pools, he felt the coolness in the wind turn to a deeper, wetter cold. The day began to be broken by a patchwork of shadows as the first clouds passed before the sun, bright colours fading to shades of grey. Out to sea, lightning flashed against the blackness of the clouds, and the boom of onrushing thunder rode over the noise of the waves. Pug picked up speed when he came to the first stretch of open beach.

The storm was coming in faster than he would have thought possible, driving the rising tide before it. By the time he reached the second stretch of tide pools, there was barely ten feet of dry sand between water's edge and cliffs. Pug hurried as fast as was safe across the rocks, twice nearly catching his foot. As he reached the next expanse of sand, he mistimed his jump from the last rock and landed . . . poorly. He had twisted his ankle!

He had been here before, and when he had jumped he had twisted his ankle and a moment later the waves had washed over him.

Pug turned to look at the sea and instead of the surge of water that would wash over him, the water was pulling back! The sea gathered in on itself and as it pulled away, it climbed higher and higher: a wall of water reaching angrily to the heavens. An explosion of thunder erupted over his head and he ducked, crouching to avoid the threat from above. Pug risked an upwards glance and wondered how the clouds had gathered so quickly. Where had the sun gone?

The roiling breakers continued to mount the sky, and as Pug watched in dread, he could see figures moving within the liquid wall. It resembled a barrier of sea-green glass, clouded with sandy imperfections and explosions of bubbles, but transparent enough to make out the shapes moving within it.

Armed creatures stood in ranks, poised and

waiting to invade Crydee, and a word came to Pug's mind: Dasati.

He turned, letting go of the sack in his hand as he attempted to reach higher ground. He must warn Duke Borric! He would know what to do! But the Duke is dead, over a century now.

Panic-stricken, the boy clambered up the low rise, his hands unable to find a firm grip, his feet denied solid purchase. He felt tears of frustration rise in his eyes and he glanced over his shoulder.

The black figures stirred within the mounting wall of water. As they stepped forward the wave rose to impossible height, blackening out the already storm-grey skies. Above and behind the massive wave a thing of dark anger revealed itself – a murk without form and feature, yet coherent – a powerful presence with purpose and mind. From it poured pure evil, a miasma of malevolence so vast that it caused the boy to fall over backwards, sitting helpless as he waited.

Pug saw the dark army of the Dasati marching towards him, emerging from waves turned black by the hateful thing in the sky. He slowly rose, balled his fists and stood defiantly, yet he knew he was helpless. He should be able to do something, but he was only a boy, not yet fourteen summers old, not even chosen for a craft, a keep-boy without family or name.

Then as the nearest Dasati warrior raised its sword, a malevolent cry of triumph sounded, a bell-like clarion that brought the child to his knees.

4

Expecting the blade to fall, Pug watched the Dasati hesitate. Behind it, the wave – now taller than the tallest tower in the keep at Crydee – also seemed to pause for a moment, then it came crashing towards him, sweeping up the Dasati before bearing down upon the boy.

'Ah!' said Pug, sitting up in bed, his body drenched with perspiration.

'What is it?' asked the woman at his side.

Pug turned towards his wife, sensing more than seeing her features in the darkness of their sleeping chamber. He calmed himself and said, 'A dream. Nothing more.'

Miranda sat up and put a hand on his shoulder. With the briefest gesture she brought every candle in the bed chamber to life. In the soft glow from the candles, she saw the sheen of moisture on his skin reflecting the flickering light. 'It must have been quite a dream,' she said softly. 'You're drenched.'

Pug turned to regard her in the warm glow. He had been married to Miranda for more than half his life now, yet he found her a constant mystery and occasionally a challenge. But at moments like this he was grateful she was close at hand.

Their bond was a strange one for they were two of the most powerful practitioners of magic on Midkemia and that alone made them unique to the other. Beyond that their histories had intersected before they had met. Pug's life had been manipulated by Miranda's father, Macros the Black, and even now as they lived together, they occasionally wondered if their marriage might not have been another of his clever plots. But whatever else, in each other they had found a person who could understand their burdens and challenges as no one else could.

He got out of bed. As he crossed to a washbasin, and soaked a cloth in the water, she said, 'Tell me of the dream, Pug.'

Pug began to clean himself off. 'I was a boy, again. I told you about the time I almost drowned on the beach, the day Kulgan's man Meecham saved me from the boar.

'This time I didn't get off the beach, and the Dasati rose from within the storm.'

Miranda sat up and moved back, resting her shoulders against an ornate headboard Pug had given her years before. She said, 'The dream is understandable. You're feeling overwhelmed.'

He nodded, and for a brief instant in the soft light of the candles she glimpsed the boy he must have been. Those moments were rare. Miranda was older than her husband – more than fifty years his senior, but Pug carried more responsibility than anyone else in the Conclave of Shadows. He rarely spoke of it, but she knew something had happened to him during the war with the Emerald Queen years before, during the time he had lingered between life and death, his body a mass of burns from a mighty demon's magic. Since that time he had changed, he had become more humble and less sure of himself.

It was something only those closest to Pug saw, and then only rarely, but it was there.

Pug said, 'Yes, I feel overwhelmed. The scope of things . . . makes me feel . . . insignificant at times.'

She smiled, got out of bed and came up behind her husband. Over a hundred years old, Pug looked no more than forty years of age – his body was still trim and athletic, though there was a touch of grey in his hair. He had already lived two lifetimes, and while Miranda was older, Pug had suffered more during his years. He had been held captive as a Tsurani slave for four years, and had then risen to become one of the most powerful men of that empire – a Great One, a Black Robe – a magician of the Assembly.

His first wife, Katala, had left him to return home and die among her people, succumbing to a disease that no priest or healer could cure. Then Pug had lost his children, something no parent should ever have to endure. Of his oldest friends, only Tomas abided still, for the others had only been allotted a mortal's span. Some, Miranda had known briefly, but most were merely names she recalled from his stories: Prince Arutha, who Pug still held in awe even after all these years; the Prince's father, Lord Borric, who had given Pug a family name; Princess Carline, the object of his boyish infatuation; Kulgan, his first teacher, and Meecham, Kulgan's companion.

The list of names went on, but they were all dead. Laurie, his companion in the slave swamps on

Kelewan, Squire Roland, so many of his students over the years, Katala . . . his children, William and Gamina, their children. For a moment he thought of his two surviving sons. 'I'm worried about Magnus and Caleb,' he said softly, his tone betraying his concern as much as the words.

She hugged him tightly from behind. His skin felt cool and clammy. 'Magnus is hard at work with the magicians of the Assembly on Kelewan and Caleb should reach Stardock Town tomorrow. Now come back to bed and let me comfort you.'

'You are always a comfort,' he said softly. He turned slowly in the circle of her arms. Facing her, he again marvelled at his wife's appearance. Beautiful, but strong. The planes of her face were softened by a high forehead and a delicate chin, and her eyes were dark and piercing. 'There are times when I feel I barely know you, given your penchant for secrets, my love. But then there are also times when I know you better than anyone, even myself. And I am certain that no one understands me better than you do.' He held her tightly for a moment, then whispered, 'What are we to do?'

'What we must, my love,' she whispered in his ear. 'Come, back to bed. Dawn is still hours away.'

With a wave of her hand Miranda extinguished the candles, and the room was plunged back into darkness. Pug followed his wife to bed and they nestled down together, seeking comfort in each other's arms.

Pug's mind wrestled with the images from his

dream but he pushed them aside. He knew what was troubling him: once again circumstances were forcing him to act against improbable odds, and that he must again deal with the repercussions of events that had taken place long before his birth.

*Why*, he thought, *must I spend my life cleaning up after other people?* But even as he framed the question, he knew the answer. He had made peace with his gifts years ago, and with such power came responsibility. Try as he might, it was in his nature to be responsible.

*Still*, he thought as sleep returned, *it would be lovely to return* – even if only for one day – to the time when he and Tomas were boys, filled with the hopes and ambitions of youth, when the world had been a much simpler place.

# CHAPTER 1

# BROTHERS

The boys burst through the door.

Chickens scattered; one moment they had been peacefully pecking the ground, seeking spilled grain and the occasional insect, the next they were squawking in protest, and scurrying in all directions as the two boys hurtled past and landed in the village street with loud grunts.

To passersby the boys appeared as a flurry of fists, elbows and knees rolling on the ground pecked clean by the chickens. Thrashing about, their blows were ineffective but heartfelt as each boy sought enough leverage to land a winning strike, while at the same time prevent his opponent from punching back effectively. The result appeared to be more of a pointless wrestling match than a serious fight.

The boys appeared to be roughly the same size and age – about sixteen summers old. The dark-haired youth wore a maroon-coloured tunic and leather trousers. He was slightly shorter, but possessed broader shoulders and was arguably the stronger of the two. The boy with dark-blond hair was dressed in a blue tunic and leather trousers. He possessed a longer reach, and was arguably faster.

They had been raised as brothers for almost their entire lives and, like brothers everywhere, were prone to conflict in an instant. Both were handsome after a rough fashion: sunburned and possessing the lean strength gained from long hours of hard work and barely adequate food. Neither boy was stupid, but at this moment they were not behaving particularly brightly.

The cause of their current conflict hurried out of the door after them, shouting angrily. 'Tad! Zane! Stop this right now or I won't go to the festival with either of you.'

The struggling combatants appeared oblivious to her warning as they rolled in the dust. 'He started it!' shouted the dark-haired boy.

'No I didn't!' countered the other.

The girl was the same age as the rivals. She had brown hair like Zane, and green eyes like Tad, was smarter than both of them put together, and was arguably the prettiest girl in Stardock Town.

An older woman followed Ellie from the house carrying a bucket of well water and she unceremoniously tipped it over the boys.

Shouting at their sudden drenching, the lads released each other and sat up. 'Ma!' shouted the blond boy. 'What'd you do that for? I've got mud all over me now.'

'Then go clean yourself up, Tad.' The woman was tall and regal looking, despite her plain homespun dress. Her light brown hair had some grey, and her face was sunburned and creased, but her expression was youthful. Looking at the darker lad, she added, 'You too, Zane.' Her brown eyes were merry though her expression was stern. 'Caleb will be here soon and then we're leaving with or without you two hooligans.'

The two boys stood up, dusting themselves off as best they could, as the woman threw a large cloth at them. 'Get the mud off with this, and then go to the well and rinse it out!' she admonished the two boys. 'It's one of my good kitchen rags.'

Ellie stood looking at the hesitant brawlers. 'You idiots. I said I'd go with both of you.'

'But you said it to me, first,' said Tad. 'That means you'll dance with me first.'

'No it doesn't,' said Zane, ready to resume the fisticuffs.

'Stop this before it starts again!' shouted the older woman. 'Now get out and clean yourselves up!' Grumbling, the two boys complied.

'Marie, why are they always fighting?' asked Ellie.

'They're just bored.' Then she looked at the younger girl. 'When are you going to tell them?'

'Tell them?' said Ellie, feigning ignorance.

Marie laughed. 'You'd better tell them soon, girl. It's a poorly kept secret and they might hear about it at the festival.'

The girl's brow creased and her eyebrows raised as she made an expression of exasperation. 'We used to be like family, you know?'

'All things change.' The older woman looked

around the town. 'When my family first came here, Stardock Town was still a small place. Now it's twice the size. The Academy was only half finished, now look at it.'

Ellie nodded as they both stared at the distant island across the lake. 'I see it every day, Marie. Just like you do.'

The massive building dominated the island in the middle of the Great Star Lake, rising like a dark mountain. The village that rested at the Academy's edge now engulfed the entire northeastern end of the island. Only those who served in the Academy of Magicians lived there. Stardock Town had grown around the ferry station to the island – at first just a simple trading stop, but now a bustling centre for commerce in the region.

'Well, if Grame Hodover's anything like his pa, he'll start yakkin' as soon as he has some ale in him.'

'And Tad and Zane will be throwing punches before anyone can talk sense into them,' finished Ellie.

'So, best sooner than later,' said Marie as she motioned for Ellie to follow her back into the house. They entered a large, single-roomed building, with just enough room for a hearth, a table, and bedding for three. Once inside she said, 'The boys are your best friends, though they don't realize it right now. Each thinks himself in love with you, but that's born from competition rather than for any serious reason I can see.'

Ellie nodded. 'I do love them, but like brothers.

Besides, even if I wished to marry one of them, father –'

'I know. Your father is the wealthiest shipper in Stardock Town and Grame's pa is the only miller, so it's a natural match.'

'I do love Grame,' said Ellie. 'At least enough to live with him.'

'Love is not the simple romance that the tales make it out to be,' cautioned Marie. 'Tad's father was a good enough man, but we had our moments. Zane's pa treated his mother well enough, though he had a sore temper when he drank. Marriage is mostly about taking the good and the bad together, Ellie. Zane's ma loved her family no matter what trouble they brought and, as she was my best friend, it was natural to take Zane in when they died.' She put out her hand and gently gripped Ellie's arm. 'As I would have taken you in, had your pa not survived.'

Zane's parents and Ellie's mother had died during the last troll raid in the region. The bloody attack had cost the lives of dozens of townspeople before the magicians across the water had reacted and driven the monsters away.

'I know, Marie,' said the girl. 'You've been like a ma to me for most of my life. I mean, I do remember my ma, at least bits about her, like her voice and the way she'd hum melodies while she cooked and I played on the floor. I remember her holding me.' Ellie's eyes became distant for a moment, then she looked back at Marie. 'But in truth, you're the only

14

ma I've really had.' She laughed. 'My pa has certainly never said anything about how to deal with boys, 'cept to stay away from them!'

Marie smiled and hugged the girl. 'And you've been the daughter I didn't have.'

The two boys returned and Tad's mother inspected them. 'You'll dry out before the fun starts,' she said. 'Now, I want you to promise there'll be no more fighting today.'

'All right, Ma,' said Tad.

'Yes'um,' added Zane.

'Why don't the three of you make your way to the square now. I'm sure all the other boys and girls are doing the same.'

'What about you, Ma?' asked Zane, his face betraying his eagerness to be off.

'I'm waiting for Caleb. He should be here soon.'

Zane and Ellie said they'd see Marie later and left, but Tad lingered. He seemed to choke on his words, but finally said, 'Ma, are you going to wed Caleb?'

Marie laughed. 'What brought that up?'

'Well, he's been here three times in the last two months, is all, and you see him a lot.'

'His father built Stardock, if you remember what I told you.' She shook her head. 'Are you worried I might or that I won't?'

The boy shrugged, his lanky frame suddenly appearing more man-like to his mother. He said, 'I don't know. Caleb's a good man, I suppose. But it's just—'

15

'He's not your pa,' she finished.

'That's not what I meant,' said Tad. 'It's just . . . well, he's gone so much.'

With a wry smile, Marie said, 'There's more than one woman who'd count her husband being away a blessing, boy.' She put her hands on his shoulders and turned him around. 'Now, catch up with the others. I'll be along soon.'

Tad ran off after the others, and Marie turned her attention to her small home. Everything was neat and dusted; she might be poor, but she had pride in an orderly house. Keeping it tidy was difficult with two boys underfoot, but they usually obeyed her without question.

Marie then inspected the soup simmering over the hearth and judged it to be ready. Everyone in the town was expected to contribute to the harvest festival, and while her soup was simple fare, it was delicious and welcomed, even by those who contributed far more.

Glancing at the door, she half-expected to see a tall man silhouetted against the light, and for a brief, bitter moment she realized she wasn't sure who it was she wished for more to be the one to see – her late husband, or Caleb. Pushing aside such irrelevant thoughts, she reminded herself that aching for what you couldn't have was pointless. She was a farmer's wife, and knew the nature of life: it rarely gave you choices, and to survive you looked forward, not back.

★　　★　　★

A short while later, Marie heard someone approach and turned to find Caleb at the door. Wearing half a smile, he said, 'Expecting someone?'

She crossed her arms and gave him an appraising look. Only a few years younger than Marie, a clean-shaven chin and a long, unlined face gave Caleb a youthful look, despite the grey creeping into his shoulder-length brown hair. His eyes were also brown and fixed on her like a hunter's. He wore well-made but plain-cut garb, fit for a woodsman, a large floppy hat of black felt, a dark-green wool tunic cut snugly over his broad shoulders, and leather breeches tucked into buckskin boots around his calves. He had a long face, but she thought him handsome, for he carried himself proudly. He always spoke calmly and thoughtfully and he wasn't afraid of silence. But the main reason she was drawn to him was because when he looked at her, she felt that he saw something of value there. Caleb smiled. 'I'm late?'

'As usual,' she answered with a slight smile. Then her expression bloomed as she laughed. 'But not too late,' she crossed the room to stand before him. Kissing and hugging him, she said, 'The boys left a few minutes ago.'

He returned the hug, then said, 'How much time do we have?'

Marie looked askance at him and said, 'Not enough, if I read your mood correctly.' She tilted her head towards the hearth. 'Help me with the kettle.' She moved to the hearth and picked up a long oak pole leaning beside the stonework chimney.

Caleb unslung his bow, hip quiver and backpack, and stored them in the corner. As Marie slipped the pole through the iron handle of the large kettle, he took the opposite end.

They lifted it from the iron hook which held it above the flames and started towards the door. 'You first,' he said.

Once outside, Caleb swung around so they could walk side-by-side with the kettle between them. 'How was your journey?' Marie asked him.

'Uneventful,' he answered.

She had learned not to ask about his business or where he had been, for she knew he was working on his father's behalf. Some claimed that Caleb's father had been the Duke of Stardock once, but at present no one claimed dominion over the island or its town on the opposite shore. Patrols from the Kingdom garrison at Shamata would occasionally spend a day or two at the local inn, or Keshian patrols might ride up from the border fortress in Nar Ayab, but neither side claimed the Great Star Lake or the surrounding countryside. This region was under the control of the Academy of Magicians on the island, and no one disputed their authority.

But Pug was no longer in control of the Academy, and like all those who lived in Stardock Town, Marie was unsure how that had come to pass. Yet, his sons – Caleb and his older brother Magnus – were still occasional visitors to the Academy. Whatever the relationship between Pug and the ruling council of the city of magicians, it was an enduring one, no matter what estrangements might have occurred in the past.

Marie had met Caleb when she was a young girl and he little more than a scruffy woods-boy. They had played together from time to time, but then he had vanished. Some said he had gone to live on an island in the Bitter Sea, while others said he stayed with the elves. They had been reunited when Caleb was Tad and Zane's age, and Marie just four years older. Though her parents disapproved of them spending time together, they said nothing because of who Caleb's father was.

But, after the summer during which they had become lovers, he vanished once more. His last words explained that he had to leave on his father's business, but he promised to return. Marie had waited more than a year before bowing to family pressure. She married young Brendan, a man she eventually came to care for deeply, but who could never set her heart racing the way Caleb had. Years went by and Caleb didn't return.

But whatever the reason for his long absence, Marie had wed, and birthed two sons – one who had died as a baby before Caleb had appeared again – without warning, three years ago at the Midsummer's festival of Banapis.

Her heart had soared at the sight of him, and while she chided herself for allowing the memories of a silly girl to overwhelm her, she had still sought him out as soon as she knew of his arrival.

That night she had indulged in far too much wine and dancing, and it had been the most fun she could remember since before her husband's death. After the boys were sound asleep, she had slept in Caleb's arms.

And the next day he was gone once more.

Since then she had grown used to his ways – appearing without notice and then vanishing. He had made no promises and she had asked for none. Yet they had formed a bond and she was certain that no other woman waited for him. Why she felt so certain she couldn't say, but she was sure.

'Staying long?'

'That depends.'

'On what?' she asked.

'A number of things. I have a message to deliver to the ruling council, and they may take a while to consider their answer. So, a few days, perhaps a week.'

'Anything you can talk about?'

He smiled. 'Not really. Let's just say it's another of my father's very important missives.'

'Yet you delay to come to the festival with me?' She wore a knowing smile on her lips.

'A day will make no difference.' He grinned at her. 'Besides, I have my own business here.'

'Oh, do you now?'

'Yes,' he laughed. 'As you well know.'

As they approached the town square, several

people greeted Marie. 'Well,' she whispered after returning their greetings, 'we can discuss that *business*, later.'

Caleb looked at the unusually large crowd gathering and asked, 'More people have arrived?'

'Some,' she answered. 'A shipping concern out of Shamata has put up a building on the edge of the south road, near the old stone bridge. They have three new families and some single men from town working for them. They're making Ellie's pa real nervous. I think that's half of the reason he's marrying her off to Miller Hodover's boy, Grame. He wants to make sure that he's secured the grain shipment contracts up to Land's End and Krondor.'

'As good enough reason for a marriage as any, I guess,' said Caleb, 'if you ignore love.'

She glanced at him to see if he was being serious and found that once more she couldn't quite read his mood. Sometimes Caleb was as easy to read as a child. At other times she had no idea what he was thinking, and disappointingly this was one of those times.

They carried the kettle over to one of the large wooden tables borrowed from a nearby inn and placed it on the spot indicated by one of the women overseeing the feast. One of the other women looked up, 'Marie, Caleb,' she said, smiling a thin welcome.

'Tessa,' returned Marie.

The woman, florid-faced with ale-bloom cheeks as if she was a heavy drinker, had a jowly face set in a painful smile. 'Brought another kettle of your nice little soup,' she remarked, her tone condescending. Tessa was the miller's wife, and soon-to-be mother-in-law of Ellie. She was well attired and took Marie's hand disdainfully, patting it softly, and giving a slight nod. 'We understand, dear.' Her tone couldn't have been more patronizing.

Caleb's smile didn't falter, but there was a slight tightening around his eyes. He said, 'That's just the start.' He pointed to a fire-pit set burning at the opposite edge of the square. 'We've also brought that ox being roasted.' He winked sidewise at Marie so Tessa couldn't see. 'And that wagon,' he added, indicating the wagon that was rolling into view. 'It carries two barrels of dwarven ale from Dorgin, as well as six cases of Ravensburg wine.'

Tessa blinked like a barn owl caught in lantern light. 'Really?' she said.

Caleb said nothing, merely inclining his head with a slight smile. The now-flustered miller's wife muttered something under her breath, gave a pained smile, and hurried off.

Marie turned to Caleb and said, 'Why did you do that?'

Caleb shrugged. 'I remember how she annoyed you at the last Banapis festival. Besides, last year all I contributed was a brace of partridges and some rabbits.'

'No, I meant why did you say *we* when *you* were the one who brought the ox and the wagon?'

Caleb said, 'Well, because I brought them for you.'

Marie was silent for a moment before a small smile

crossed her lips, but her eyes showed no humour. 'I thank you for the gesture, Caleb.'

'It was my pleasure,' he said. 'Now, shall I fetch bowls and a ladle?'

'No,' said Marie, her tone neutral. 'I'll return to the house and fetch them myself. You find the boys and make sure that they're staying out of trouble, will you? I'm worried about them.'

He nodded, and moved away from the table. Making his way through the quickly gathering crowd, Caleb found himself both amused and surprised at the changes he had seen in the town since his childhood. Though his family had never lived in Stardock Town, they had visited it frequently.

Caleb's father's relationship with the ruling council of the Academy was strained, at best. Caleb had heard Pug complain about them frequently enough to fully understand the reasons behind the estrangement, but they were his father's reasons, not his own. Magnus, his older brother, was a magician like their parents, but Caleb had been the odd child out – the one who possessed no magical ability at all.

The rest of his family viewed Stardock through a haze of political strife, but Caleb saw it simply as the place where he used to have fun as a child. In Stardock he had found children like himself – ordinary boys and girls who were concerned with ordinary things like growing up, learning to love, to hate and to forgive, trying to avoid work and finding playmates. All the day-in, day-out things that Caleb had never encountered before.

Caleb had benefited from his unusual upbringing in many ways. Much of Caleb's childhood had been spent attending tedious classes designed for students with magical ability. Only now could he see the wisdom in this, for unlike most people without ability, he could at least sense the presence of magic. And, as the most powerful enemies facing the Conclave of Shadows were magicians, Caleb counted this ability as a good thing.

The children of Sorcerer's Isle, and even those he lived with on the island in the Great Star Lake, were caught up in magic – even their play involved it, often to the annoyance of their teachers. For most of his childhood, Caleb had been a solitary child. While he was a good runner and as adept with a ball as any boy his age, he often stood alone, watching others play the games of illusion in which he could never partake, except as the object of a cruel child's joke. His possessions often moved away when he reached for them, or items suddenly appeared to trip him up without warning.

The wounds of childhood were, at times, the deepest. As he grew, Caleb became less isolated from the other children, as their interests shifted from one thing to another. But even when he was at the heart of the mischief, he still felt different.

There had been only two places where Caleb had felt free and at peace as a child. In his tenth summer, he had been taken to Elvandar, where he lived with the elves for five years.

Caleb had learnt as much as he could of elven

ways, and had been tutored in the sword by the Queen's consort, Lord Tomas, Warleader of Elvandar, and was taught the use of the bow by Prince Calin and his half-brother Prince Calis. Although Caleb lacked the natural skill of Talwin Hawkins with the sword, he excelled as an archer. Both Tomas and Prince Calin had often remarked that Caleb was the equal of a man named Martin Longbow, who they claimed had been the finest human archer ever known to the elves.

Caleb knew the elves were not prone to flattery, so he took the compliment as a mark of his achievement for long, hard hours of practice. It had taught him that even an impossible goal could be reached if enough effort and sacrifice was made. He also realized ruefully that the elves had never seen Talwin Hawkins shoot; he was undoubtedly Caleb's equal, if not his better. Though, being the second finest human archer was still no mean feat.

Caleb held deep affection for the elves and their magical home in Elvandar, and he could speak their language well. But it was in Stardock that he had learnt his first lessons about being ordinary.

He made his way through the bustling town square. If previous festivals were any indication, the boys would now be with the other youngsters near the fountain.

He acknowledged greetings from many of those he passed, for they were the same children he had played with thirty years earlier. Some of the men had grown stout and others had grey in their hair – if they still had hair. The women whom he had known when they were girls had matured, and those who hadn't got fat, had the gaunt, lean look of too much hard work and not enough rest. A few, like Marie, had kept their looks despite the rigours of parenthood and farming.

But today they all looked reasonably happy, for it was the harvest festival, and if what adorned the table was any indication, it had been a bountiful year. Grain wagons would creak up the roads towards the Bitter Sea and barges would make their way from the great Star Lake downriver to the Sea of Dreams and the trading docks at Shamata or Landreth. Cattle in the field were fat for the winter and the sheep looked healthy as their new wool grew in for the colder season. Everywhere he looked, Caleb saw signs of bounty: barrels of freshly picked apples, baskets of berries, cherries, and figs, all manner of vegetable, and at every farm he had passed, he had seen more chickens and pigs than he could imagine.

He remembered other years when the harvest had been poor, or the times after the troll raids and he acknowledged silently to himself that these people were entitled to a little celebration of their good fortune. Winters were mild in the Vale of Dreams, snow having fallen only once in fifty years, and already farmers were planting winter crops that would grow nowhere else. By the time the autumn traders returned from the Kingdom and Great Kesh, with wagons of tools and other necessary items, the second crop would be ready to feed the demand for fresh food in the frozen north. Compared to most farming communities, Stardock was wealthy, but even here a farmer's lot was not an easy one. Caleb pushed his musings aside as he turned the corner and spotted the boys. He had taken only one step before he realized trouble was about to erupt.

Ellie stood up and said, 'If you two don't stop this right now, I'm leaving.'

The two to whom she referred were Tad and Zane, who stood confronting one another, ready to resume the brawling. The lithe girl positioned herself between them and started pushing them apart with surprising determination. This caused both boys to hesitate and gave Caleb just enough time to reach them and ask, 'What is the problem?'

Both boys glanced at Caleb, then locked gazes again. Ellie gave them a final shove. She said, 'These idiots have decided that it's important which one of them has the first dance with me.'

'You promised me!' shouted Tad, only a half-second before Zane echoed the claim.

Caleb lost his smile. The musicians had gathered near the ale casks and were tuning their instruments. In a moment they'd start playing, and the boys would start fighting. 'Your mother asked me to keep an eye on you.' Both boys regarded him, Zane's expression only slightly more belligerent than Tad's.

'It seems there was good cause,' Caleb added. He reached into his belt-purse, fished out a large copper coin and showed it to the two boys. 'This is the head and this is the tail. Head is Tad, tail is Zane.' Tossing the coin into the air, he let it fall to the ground. The boys followed its descent closely.

It landed on tails and Zane shouted triumphantly, 'I get the first dance!' just as the musicians struck the first notes of the dance.

Tad started to complain, but thought better of it as he noticed the dark expression on Zane's face. Caleb had led Ellie out among the dancers and shouted back at them, 'Winner gets the second dance!'

Ellie laughed as Caleb escorted her through the steps of a traditional farmer's reel. Even those not dancing were clapping their hands. When it came time for him to take Ellie's hands and lead her in a series of turns, she said, 'That was quick thinking, Caleb.'

'They're getting as bad as two young bucks with green horns. What are you going to do?'

She lowered her voice a little and said, 'I'm going to marry Grame.'

'That'll start a dust-up,' said Caleb with a laugh. 'Still, you can't very well marry both of them.'

'I wouldn't marry either,' said Ellie. 'They're like brothers to me.'

As he moved behind her, placing his hands on her waist and then following her steps, he said, 'They obviously don't think of you like a sister.'

'Oh, they would if there were more girls around,' she said, turning to face him before standing still as he bowed before her, ending the dance. She slipped her arm through his and said, 'It's just not fair, the other girls are already spoken for, or too young.'

Caleb knew what she was thinking. Many children their age had been killed during the last troll raid. There was still ill feeling from the parents of those lost children towards the magicians for not acting sooner. Caleb had been up in the Eastern Kingdoms, working on behalf of the Conclave at the time of the raid. It had occurred nine years ago, when Ellie, Zane and Tad had been little more than babies.

Caleb walked Ellie back to the boys slowly, reaching them just as the second song commenced. He planted a strong hand in the middle of Tad's chest as the blond boy began to protest again, and said, 'Son, don't spoil a perfectly fine festival. You'll get your turn.'

Tad seemed ready to argue, but seeing Caleb's serious expression, he simply let out a slight sigh and nodded. 'Yes, Caleb.'

Caleb was glad it had been Zane who had won, for he was the more hot-tempered of the two and would possibly have ignored Caleb and forced him to do something the older man didn't want to do: stop him physically.

He studied Tad while Ellie and Zane danced, and watched the boy seethe. Ellie was right; they were acting contrary to their nature.

When the song was over, Ellie returned and it was Tad's turn to dance. As he had before, Caleb watched the boy not dancing with Ellie. Zane could barely contain his jealousy.

When the third song had ended, Caleb said, 'I'm in the mood for something to drink, why don't you three come along?'

Ellie readily agreed for all of them, and slipped her arm through Caleb's, leaving the boys to follow. They went to the table where four men were filling flagons of ale and then passing them out as fast as possible. Ellie declined the strong drink, instead she accepted Zane's offer to fetch her a fruit-scented water. Tad volunteered to bring her something to eat, and she declined until she saw him wilt, so said, 'Perhaps something light, until we all sit down to eat?'

He ran off, and Caleb sighed, 'What are we going to do with those two?'

'I don't know, but something. They sit around all day with little to do. They're not the sort to take to strong drink . . . yet.'

Caleb understood. Stardock Town was big enough to support a fair amount of commerce and a little bit of industry – a blacksmith had opened a shop the year before, working ore brought down from the foothills – but most of the work was done by family members. There were always more men than work to be done, and without fathers to teach them a craft, Tad and Zane were growing up without skills. They were becoming wild and feckless.

He knew them both to be bright, able young men,

but without a direction to their lives, they were in danger of becoming lost. More than one younger son without a craft had ended up as a bandit, or working hand-to-mouth in the city.

Caleb was pondering the matter when Marie re-appeared. He nodded to her and moved away from where Zane was anxiously awaiting Ellie's favour. He kept his voice low so that the boy couldn't over-hear, and said to Marie, 'I mistook your meaning, before. I thought you meant that you were worried about the boys today. I see what you mean now.'

She studied his face, then said, 'Do you?'

He nodded. 'Let's keep an eye on them for now and try to have some fun. We'll speak of this later, tonight.'

She nodded, then forced a smile. 'Dance?'

He took her by the hand and said, 'It would be my pleasure.'

They danced to several tunes then fell upon the heavily laden tables. After filling their platters with food, they found a quiet corner on the steps of a shop closed for the festival. Caleb set down the platters and left Marie for a moment to fetch two flagons of ale. When he returned, she said, 'Where are the boys?'

'Over there,' he said, pointing to a spot on the other side of the town square. 'I've not let them out of my sight.'

'How do you do that?'

He smiled. 'I'm a hunter. Besides, they're hard to miss.'

She nodded, and spoke with a mouth full of food. 'I know, just look for the trouble.'

He laughed. 'No, just those two tunics.'

They ate quietly, with little conversation, and for the next hour the festivities continued uneventfully. Then a stout man mounted one of the wagons being used to dispense ale and started shouting, 'My friends!'

Marie said, 'Here comes trouble.'

Caleb said, 'Yup,' and put aside his plate to move towards the wagon. Marie followed.

The man was Miller Hodover, and standing next to him was a young man, roughly twenty years old. The resemblance was obvious, though the man had run to fat years ago and the boy was young and fit, his shoulders still broader than his belt.

Grame Hodover was a sturdy lad, and seemed thoughtful and bright – it was often thought a miracle that his parents could have produced such a well-liked young man.

Caleb made straight for Tad and Zane who were standing on either side of Ellie. She looked at Caleb with relief in her eyes – she knew what was coming next.

'My friends,' repeated Miller Hodover, 'I have an announcement to make. Today, I am a very happy man.' He positively beamed as he looked around the crowd.

One of the townsmen – under the influence of too much ale – shouted, 'Why, you raising prices again, Miller?'

There was a ripple of laughter, and Hodover looked irked for a moment, but let his smile return. 'No, Bram Connor, I'm not . . . yet.'

Another round of laughter followed his retort and everyone relaxed as they realized that the miller was in a particularly good mood. His well-known parsimony and love of gold were constant subjects of ridicule.

'No, my friends,' said the miller. 'I have an announcement to make. This day, after one of the most bountiful harvests in memory, at a time when everyone seems to be doing so well, I wish to add to the joy of the moment by sharing wonderful news with you all.'

'Out with it, then,' shouted another voice from the crowd. 'You're making me thirsty!'

Throwing the speaker a black look, the miller smiled again. 'I would like you all to know that this year my son, Grame, will be wed to Ellie Rankin.'

He motioned to where Ellie stood between the two boys, who looked as if they had just been poleaxed. Zane stood with a furrowed brow, as if he couldn't quite understand what had just been said, and Tad stood open-mouthed, obviously unwilling to believe it.

Ellie was halfway to the wagon when the boys started after her. Caleb reached out and grabbed each by their collar and hauled them back. 'Don't go making a fuss now,' he said in a low, menacing tone.

Tad threw him an angry look and Zane drew back

his fist, but Caleb merely pulled upwards, lifting the boys onto their toes. 'Don't even think about it.'

Zane reconsidered, and let his hand fall to his side. Marie said, 'If you stoneheads really care about Ellie, you'll be happy for her. Now, the first one to start a fight will have to answer to me. Is that clear?'

Both lads said, 'Yes, Ma,' nodded and Caleb let them go.

The townsfolk had gathered to congratulate the engaged couple, while Tad and Zane continued to pout. Caleb indicated that Marie should join the throng, and said, 'Come with me, boys. I've got something special for an occasion such as this.'

The boys looked like they were about to argue, but one glance from their mother caused them to nod and follow Caleb obediently.

He led them to a wagon behind the one which had carried the ale casks. Night was fast approaching and the festival was becoming more raucous. One of the teamsters sat on a buckboard, watching the town bestow its best wishes on the newly betrothed. The man was not a local, so he felt no need to join in, and remained contented with eating and drinking ale.

'Thomas,' said Caleb, greeting him.

'Evening,' said the wagoner.

'You have that box up there?'

'It's under that tarp, Caleb.'

Caleb found the box and pulled it towards the rear of the wagon. Drawing out his large hunting knife, he used the stout blade to pry open the lid, exposing a dozen bottles of amber liquid. He picked one out and held it up to the lantern light.

'What is it?' asked Tad.

'Something I discovered on my travels down in Kinnoch Country.'

'Looks like brandy,' said Zane. 'The colour, I mean.'

'Not brandy, but you've a good eye.' Caleb turned, and sat on the back of the wagon, letting his feet dangle. 'Brandy's just boiled wine, this is something else.

'In Kinnoch they have a way to distil a mash of grain, slowly cooking it over fires fed by peat, and then the brew is aged in casks. When it's made badly, it can peel the paint off a warship's hull, but when it's made well—' He bit the cork and pulled it out.

With his free hand he felt around in the box and produced a small cup of glass. 'You can't drink this out of clay or metal, boys. It'll foul the taste.'

'What is it?' asked Tad.

'They call it whiskey,' said Caleb, filling the small glass to the top.

'That's not very much.' Zane's eyes narrowed as he regarded the tiny vessel which held no more than two or three ounces of liquid.

'A little is more than enough,' said Caleb, tipping the contents of the glass into his mouth and swallowing. 'Ah,' he said. 'You try it.'

He produced another glass and filled them both. 'You can learn to sip this later, boys. Just toss it back and swallow for now.'

The boys did as instructed, and an instant later both were coughing furiously, with their eyes watering. Zane said in a hoarse voice, 'Damn me, Caleb, are you trying to poison us?'

'It takes a little getting used to, Zane, but you'll grow to love it.'

'It burns like a hot coal,' said Tad, whipping at his eyes with the sleeve of his tunic.

'Give it a minute,' said Caleb. 'It'll warm your gut.'

Zane smacked his lips. 'Not that I think it's good, but let me try another.'

Caleb poured again and the boys drank. This time there was no coughing, but their eyes continued to water.

'I think I'll stick to ale,' said Tad.

'I don't know,' said Zane. 'There's something about it I rather like.'

'You're a young man of promise, Zane Cafrrey,' said Caleb.

Laughing, Tad said, 'Whoa. I can feel it going to my head!'

'The Kinnoch men say it "has a kick", and they know of what they speak.'

'What are you going to do with it?' said Tad, indicating the other cases.

'I'm taking it to my father, as a gift. There's not a lot that's new to him, so I thought he might enjoy this.'

'Why are you giving us this?' asked Tad. 'I mean, thank you, but why?'

'To take your mind off an imagined slight,' said Caleb. 'If I let you drink alone two things would happen.' He held up a finger, while he poured them another drink. 'Firstly, you'd receive no end of teasing from the other men in town who know how you've been butting heads over Ellie for nearly a year. Secondly, you'd just pick a fight with Grame.'

The boys quickly drank the whiskey and seemed to be getting used to it. Caleb filled their glasses again. 'Here, have another.'

The boys finished their fourth drink, and Tad's eyes began to close. 'You're getting us drunk. I can feel it.'

Caleb filled the glasses yet again and said, 'One more should do it.'

Zane asked, 'Do what?' as his speech began to slur.

Caleb jumped down from the wagon bed. 'Get you too drunk to pick a fight.' He pushed Tad who wobbled as he tried to compensate for being slightly off balance.

'Come along,' said Caleb.

'Where?' asked Zane.

'Back to your ma's, and into your beds. You're going to pass out in five minutes and I don't want to carry you.'

The boys had never drunk anything as potent as the whiskey before, and they followed Caleb quietly. By the time they had reached their home, both boys were unsteady on their feet.

Caleb ushered them inside and when he had seen them onto their sleeping mats, he left and returned to the festival. It took only a few minutes to find Marie and when she saw him, she said, 'What did you do with them?'

'Got them very drunk.'

'As if they needed any help doing that.' She looked around anxiously. 'Where are they?'

'Back at your house, sleeping it off.'

Her gaze narrowed. 'They haven't had enough time to get that drunk.'

He held up the whiskey bottle. It was nearly empty. 'When they just tossed down five double portions each in fifteen minutes, they have.'

'Well, at least they won't be troubling Grame and Ellie,' said Marie.

'Or us.' Caleb said with a smile.

She said, 'I don't care how drunk they are, Caleb, if they're in the house, then you're not.'

He grinned. 'I already have a room at the inn. If we head over there now, no one will notice you come upstairs with me.'

She slipped her arm through his. 'As if I care what people think. I'm not a maiden trying to catch a young suitor, Caleb. I'll grab happiness where I can and if anyone cares, it doesn't matter.'

Caleb pulled her close to him and said, 'And those who do matter don't mind.'

They skirted the edge of the crowd and made for the inn.

Their lovemaking had an urgency to it that Caleb had not experienced before, and afterward, as they lay with her head on his shoulder, he asked, 'What troubles you?'

She knew that one of the reasons why they had been drawn to each other was his ability to read her mood so accurately. 'Tad asked me if we were going to wed.'

Caleb was silent for a moment, then he let out a long sigh. 'If I were the the marrying kind, Marie, it would be you.'

'I know,' she said. 'But if you won't stay, marry me, and be a real father to the boys, you have to take them with you.'

Caleb moved out from under her and levered himself up on his elbow. Looking down at her, he said, 'What?'

'You can see how it is for them, Caleb. They have no future, here. I had to sell the farm and that coin won't last forever, even if I grow most of my food in the garden. I can make do alone, but feeding growing boys . . . And they have no one to teach them farming, and no guild to teach them a craft. Every other lad was apprenticed to a farmer, trader, sailor, or guild two years ago at the Choosing, but my boys stood alone at the end. Everyone likes them, and had they means to help, Tad and Zane would be apprenticed by now, but there just isn't enough work here.

'If you don't take them with you, they'll become layabouts or worse. I'd rather lose them now than see them hanged for robbers in a few years.'

Caleb was silent for a long moment. 'What would you have me do with them, Marie?'

'You're a man of some stature, despite your home-spun garb and leather hunting togs, or at least your father is. You've seen the world. Take them with you as servants, or apprentices, or take them to Krondor and find them work there.

'They have no father, Caleb. When they were little a ma was all they needed – to wipe their noses and hold them when they were scared. We did a lot of that after Zane's folks were killed in the troll raid. But at this age they need a man to show them what to do and what not to do, to knock some sense into them if need be, and to praise them when they do well. So, if you won't wed me and stay here, then at least take them with you.'

Caleb turned, and sat with his back against the plastered wall. 'What you say makes sense, in a way.'

'Then you'll do it?'

'I'm not sure what I'm agreeing to, but yes, I'll take them with me. If my father doesn't know what to do with them, I'll take them to Krondor and see them apprenticed with a trader or placed in a guild.'

'They're like brothers now. It would be a crime to split them apart.'

'I'll keep them together. I promise.'

She nestled closer to him. 'You'll come back from time to time and tell me how they're doing?'

'Yes, Marie,' said Caleb. 'I'll make them write to you often.'

'That would be grand,' she whispered. 'No one has ever written to me before.' She sighed. 'Come to think of it, no one's ever written to anyone I know.'

'I'll see that they do.'

'That's lovely, but you'll have to teach them to write, of course.'

'They don't know their letters?' Caleb couldn't keep the surprise from his voice.

'Who would teach them?'

'Don't you . . . ?'

'No, never learned,' she said. 'I can make out word-signs a bit, because I've heard them at the shops, but I've never really had a need for them.'

'Then how will you read what they send you?'

'I'll find someone to read them to me, I just need to know that they're doing well somewhere.'

'You're a rare woman, Marie,' he said.

'No, I'm just a normal mother worried about her boys.'

Caleb settled back into bed and let her return to the crook of his shoulder. Silently he wondered what he had got himself into.

# CHAPTER 2

# COUNCIL

**P**ug held up his hand.

He was a short man who looked no more than forty years old. He was dressed, as always, in a simple black robe, and his dark eyes surveyed all the people who stood before him. His eyes were the one feature that betrayed the extent of his power. Otherwise he was, to all outward appearances, a very average looking man.

The cave on the north side of Sorcerer's Isle had become the traditional meeting place for the Conclave's leaders. It had a narrow entrance, with a low ceiling. It was dry, free of moss and lichen, and from time to time, it was dusted to provide a modicum of comfort for those who met there. The cave was almost bare, save for two stone shelves and a few rocks which offered the only resting places. Light was provided by a spell that Miranda employed – an enchantment which caused the walls themselves to glow faintly. Only one feature of the cave was unnatural: a bust of Sarig, the putative God of Magic rested upon a pedestal against a wall.

Over the years, Pug had slowly come to understand more about the way in which the gods 'died'.

Sarig was lost, and had been presumed dead since the Chaos Wars, yet Pug was coming to the conclusion that he still existed in some form and still had a hand in things. The bust flickered as the features of the icon shifted constantly, occasionally resembling Pug, or one of Pug's companions. Its changing countenance illustrated the theory that all magicians were avatars of the god in one manner or another.

Pug pushed his chronic curiosity over that artefact away, as he looked from face to face, seeing his most trusted advisors. All but two of them were former students. Those two – Miranda and Nakor – stood quietly to one side. Magnus, Pug and Miranda's son who had recently returned from the world of Kelewan, stood behind his mother. Pug caught a glimpse of resemblance between them in the faint light and smiled slightly. Magnus and Caleb were unmistakably brothers, save for their skin tone and hair colour – Magnus was pale with white hair while Caleb's skin was tanned and his hair dark brown – but neither looked especially like their parents. There were hints and glimpses of similarities from time to time, but Pug had wondered more than once whether the boys might carry the look of one of their paternal grandparents, neither of whom was known to him.

Miranda had not changed since Pug had first met her over fifty years before. Her dark hair held only a fleck of grey and her eyes changed colour with her mood – dark grey, to green, to brown-flecked hazel, to dark brown. She had high cheekbones and a determined set to her mouth that at times could undermine her regal beauty.

To Pug, she was always beautiful, even when he was angry enough to strangle her. It was her strength and passion that made him love her. Katala, his first wife, had possessed the same qualities in her youth. Pug's eyes locked with his wife's for a moment and they exchanged the silent communication they had shared for years.

Nakor settled down on a rocky ledge, and Pug wondered again if he would ever truly understand the strange little man. Nakor refused to accept the traditional concept of magic, always insisting that it was just tricks, the deft manipulation of some kind of mystical stuff that underpinned all things. There were moments when the bandy-legged little man drove Pug to distraction with his abstract musings on the nature of things, but at other times Nakor could provide insights into and had a grasp of magic that stunned Pug. The Isalani was also, to Pug's mind, potentially the most dangerous magician in the world.

The newcomers to the Conclave's inner circle sat waiting for Pug to speak. They were: Rosenvar, a middle-aged magician from Salmater and Uskavan, a mindmaster from the world of Salavan.

Uskavan looked human but his skin had a decidedly magenta hue if you were close enough to notice. Pug had made contact with his homeworld a decade before, via the Hall of Worlds, and had agreed to let him study with the Conclave in exchange for sharing knowledge of his mind-magic. Uskavan could produce illusions so vivid in the mind of a subject, that they could cause physical reactions – he could conjure phantom blades that could cut, or imaginary flames that could burn. Pug also found his alien perspective useful.

Uskavan had taken the place of Robert de Lyse, one of Pug's best students and a valuable servant of the Conclave of Shadows. Robert had died peacefully in his sleep the year before, though he had been less than seventy years old.

Pug began, 'I have spoken to each of you separately and now want to share some intelligence, so I've asked you to join me today to sum up what we know regarding two issues of great importance.

'The first is the matter of the Talnoy.' He glanced at Magnus, who stepped out from behind his mother.

Magnus' face was set in a concerned expression. 'The Tsurani magicians are as baffled as we are by the nature of the magic used to create these things.'

The Talnoy were artefacts from another circle of reality, created by a race called the Dasati and were extremely dangerous. They were suits of armour powered by the imprisoned souls, or spirits, of the Dasati, and as such they were almost impervious to damage, immune to pain, and mindless in their obedience. According to what

Kaspar of Olasko had told the Conclave about when he had brought the first Talnoy to their attention, 'Talnoy' was Dasati for 'very hard to kill'.

Magnus continued, 'They agree that any major incursion into our level of reality, for lack of a better term, would be catastrophic. As such, they are endeavouring to discover as much as possible about the wards we disturbed when we first discovered the Talnoy repository in the cave.'

He glanced at Nakor who said, 'Nothing new to report, I'm sorry to say.' The self-proclaimed gambler who refused to admit that he was a magician, paused as he considered his words. Finally, he continued, 'Our girls and boys' – he referred to all the younger magicians on Sorcerer's Island as girls and boys – 'are trying very hard to understand these things.

'The one good thing,' he said with a grin, 'is that I think we have found a way to ensure that only we can command them should it come to a confrontation with the Dasati.'

Pug said, 'That's something at least. Ten thousand Talnoy under our command is nothing to be taken lightly.' He ignored the impulse to add that against the hundreds of thousands of Talnoy controlled by the Dasati, that number would amount to very little. 'But I think our interests are best served if we can discover how they remained hidden for so long. In other words, if *we* can stay hidden from the Dasati, then we will have accomplished the most important task we have before us.

'Our other task is hunting down Leso Varen.'

Miranda said, 'Have we any idea to where he might have fled?'

'I have agents keeping alert for anything out of the ordinary concerning magic.'

Miranda's dark eyes narrowed. 'He's gone to ground for years at a time.'

Pug said, 'But this time I think he will be anxious to re-establish his presence. He knows something important is out there, even if he has no idea what the Talnoy represent or how he might use them to his advantage. If nothing else, he will want to deny us something that powerful.

'His attack on the island and Elvandar last year proved that he has grown bolder, and whatever tendency he had for stealth is gone. He re-manifested his powers quickly after his host was killed by Talwin Hawkins. I think it's safe to assume we'll hear from him again, and soon.'

Rosenvar said, 'Pug, what is it you've not told us?'

Pug smiled. He had chosen Rosenvar to join the inner circle because the man had keen insight and an almost intuitive ability to glean answers from very scant information. 'It is nothing specific, really. Just some troubling dreams, and bad feelings.'

Uskavan's black eyes were wide as he said, 'Never ignore dreams, Pug. My people believe that parts of our minds are always at work, always seeking to understand things. Dreams are often the means by which some parts of the mind communicate what is about to become conscious thought; especially when the emotions are strong. Our races are not that different; when it comes to the workings of our minds we have much in common.'

Magnus glanced at the alien magician and Pug could almost read his son's thoughts: few humans, including Pug, Miranda and Magnus, could even begin to approach the mind-discipline of a novice of Uskavan's order. Salavan minds were far more complex than human ones, despite Uskavan's insistence this was only because the Salavans were an older race and had been practising mental arts for thousands of years.

Pug nodded, a slight expression of resignation on his face. 'Indeed. I fear my dreams may be portends of coming disaster. Or, they may simply be a manifestation of my concerns over the Dasati.'

Magnus said, 'Father, we must prepare as if they are coming.'

'I know.' Pug looked at each member of the inner circle of the Conclave. 'Send word to our agents who are placed in all the royal courts. I want to know about every ambition, plot or intrigue, and any situation that could be turned to our advantage. If we must, we shall bribe and threaten to secure help in such a conflict.'

Pug fell silent for a minute. He remembered the Riftwar; for twelve years, while the Tsurani had fallen upon the Kingdom and the Free Cities, Queg, Great Kesh and the lesser kingdoms to the east had watched with keen anticipation, seeking any opportunity to advance their own cause at the Kingdom's expense. 'Should the Dasati come, we must have friends in high places who will argue that every nation needs to respond quickly, no matter where the invasion strikes.'

Magnus said, 'Father, that is all well and good should an attack happen in Triagia – all the monarchs on this continent have some sense of vulnerability – should aliens set foot on close by soil they would be equally vulnerable and will unite, but what if the beachhead is some deserted shore of the Sunset Islands, or down in the grasslands of Novindus, or the high plateau of Wynet?'

'A more difficult task, then,' said Pug. He looked at his council, pausing a moment to study each face. Miranda seemed as enigmatic as a stranger. She often kept her own counsel and took matters into her own hands. They had fought more than once over the years about her putting agents into the field without consulting him or giving orders that he disagreed with. He smiled slightly. As long as his wife was involved, Pug could never be accused of ruling the council of the Conclave of Shadows. She nodded slightly and returned his smile, and he knew this time she was in full agreement.

Rosenvar's lined face looked as if it was fashioned from sunburnt leather. His reddish hue was accentuated by a shock of unruly blond hair, now rapidly turning white. 'It seems to me,' he said, 'that we might be well served if we started leaking a rumour or two.'

Pug was silent for a moment. 'To what end?'

The magician from Salmater smiled and Pug recalled the first time he had met him, sitting in the corner of an ale house, dispensing sage advice, minor charms and outright lies with equal abandon to anyone who'd stand him the price of a drink. Since coming to the island, he had stayed relatively sober, and his drinking bouts were few and far between.

'Rumours are wonderful things, when employed correctly,' said Rosenvar. His voice tended to rumble as if it started somewhere deep within his bowels and slowly worked its way up through his throat. 'I've seen entire cities turned on their collective ear by the right rumour, Pug. Rulers distrust official reports and credible witnesses, but a juicy rumour . . . ah, that'll set them running around like turkeys in a storm, heads turned upwards with mouths agape, trying to drown themselves in the downpour.'

Pug chuckled. He enjoyed Rosenvar's turns of phrase. 'Very well, but what rumours?'

Rosenvar lost his smile. 'Word is Duke Erik is ill, perhaps dying, in Krondor.'

Pug nodded. 'So I have heard.'

Miranda said, 'He is the last.'

Pug knew what she meant. He was the last survivor of Calis' company of 'Desperate Men', those prisoners given their freedom in exchange for making the journey down to Novindus at the start of the Serpentwar, and the only man of rank still serving who had survived the conflict. Erik knew what distant dangers could mean. 'Then we start in Krondor?'

'It seems wise,' said Rosenvar. 'There are a couple of rumour-mongers who have various highly placed officials of the Western Realm among their clients. If we start something vague enough to not cause an immediate response, but something familiar enough to Lord Erik that he'll feel obliged to warn the Prince of Krondor . . . well, it's a start.'

Magnus said, 'And if the Kingdom of the Isles takes the warning seriously, so will Great Kesh.'

'And if Great Kesh and the Kingdom start to marshal their defences, so shall every other kingdom in their vicinity,' added Miranda.

'But we can only hold them alert for so long; we must not rush this,' said Rosenvar.

Pug said, 'We need Erik around long enough to make this work.'

Nakor said, 'I'll go to Krondor and visit the Duke. I'll make him well for a while.'

Pug nodded. Nakor had travelled with Erik, Calis on the journey to Novindus when they first encountered the Emerald Queen. The old duke would trust Nakor.

Pug said, 'Rosenvar, I need you to coordinate what rumours to start, where, and when. We have some well-placed agents in nearly every capital of importance on Midkemia. But I want to ensure it's a gradual discomfort and concern, not instant blind panic.'

'Understood,' he replied, standing. 'We'll draw up a list of ideas to put the rulers of the world on edge.' He smiled slightly. '*Slightly* on edge.'

To Uskavan, Pug said, 'If you would, I'd like the names of your very best students. We may need to dispatch them to work in the field soon.'

The alien magician nodded, rose, and departed with Rosenvar, leaving Pug, Miranda, Nakor, and Magnus alone in the cave. Pug looked at his older son and said, 'Where's your brother?'

'Down in Stardock, I believe. He should be delivering some supplies, but no doubt he lingered for the festival.'

Miranda said, 'Lingered to spend time with that widow, you mean.'

Pug shrugged. 'Let him grab whatever joy he can, beloved. We don't need him back here for anything special, and I expect he's enjoying himself.'

Magnus looked at his mother and asked, 'Shall I find him, or return to Kelewan?'

Miranda glanced at her husband. 'Which?'

'Neither. Go to Novindus and continue Nakor's work on the Talnoy. The Great Ones of the Assembly of Tsuranuanni can muddle along without you for a while. When Nakor returns from Krondor, I'll send him back to you and you can go back to Kelewan.'

Nakor smiled. 'Don't break anything before I get there.'

Magnus glanced with a wry smile at the little gambler, nodded, reached inside his robe and pulled out a golden orb. He clicked a switch and suddenly vanished.

Miranda came to stand behind her husband and put her arms around him. 'You're worried.'

'I'm always worried,' said Pug.

'No, this is something more.' She studied her husband's face. 'You sense something?'

Nakor said, 'I think I know what you're going to tell her. I will go to Krondor and see that Duke Erik stays alive long enough to help us.' He glanced at Pug and Miranda and said, 'You two really do need to talk to each other more often. Really,' he repeated, picking up his rucksack and staff, then vanishing from before their eyes.

Pug closed his eyes a long moment, then answered his wife's question. 'Yes, I do sense something. And it's growing. I don't know what to call it, but it feels more . . . intense than mere foreboding.'

'A premonition?'

'The dream troubles me, love. I think something is approaching and when it emerges, the struggle will be more fearful than anything we could ever imagine.'

'Given what we have seen, husband, that's quite a lot.'

'Once, during the time of the Great Uprising, Tomas and I faced a Master of the Dread. We bested the creature, though it took all of our magic and no little guile. Then at the end, in Sethanon, I beheld a Dreadlord – a Greater Dragon, with all her magic and might, could barely contain it.'

'But the Dread come from one of the lower planes, while these Dasati are from the second. Surely they are only slightly more dangerous than men?'

Pug held his wife's hand. 'You know more than I do on many subjects, Miranda, but scholarship has never been your first love.' She furrowed her brow but said nothing, acknowledging the truth in his words.

He sighed and lowered his voice. 'It's the nature of beings from the lower levels of creation to absorb the life force from those from the higher. Think of it as water running downhill; just the touch of a Dasati would cause damage after only a few moments.

'The Dread are the most fearful beings able to reach this level of reality and survive; creatures from the depths below them draw so much energy to themselves so fast that they are destroyed when they reach our plane, unless they employ powerful magic to keep themselves alive. No, it's the fact the Dasati are from but one level below us that makes them so fearful to contemplate, my love.' He sighed as if fatigued. 'Nakor understands, for he has spent more time studying the Talnoy than anyone else.' He glanced at the mouth of the cave. 'The others will discover what I'm telling you; no need to create any risk of panic.

'The Dasati are mortal like ourselves, but if they reach this level of reality, they will slowly draw life force from around them, from the very grass they tread upon, so that even should we establish

54

a military stalemate, as we did with the Tsurani during the first Riftwar, they would eventually wither us to defeat. Also, the flow of life force towards them makes them harder to kill and ourselves weaker. The longer we are locked in struggle, the more difficult victory will be. And we must remember the numbers; if Kaspar is correct and he saw a true vision of that world, they would not send thousands of warriors, but tens of thousands. If they find us, we must react and react quickly. We can't have the monarchs of Midkemia fully understanding what we must face, at least for a while, else fear might overwhelm their resolve.'

Miranda studied her husband's face for a while, then said, 'We shall do everything we can.'

'I know,' he said. 'Now, we both have work to do.'

'How are you going to return?'

He smiled. 'I'll walk. The fresh air clears my head and helps me think.'

She kissed his cheek. 'I'll see you at home.'

Before she could vanish, he said, 'Wait a minute! Did you see Nakor use an orb to leave?'

'Not that I noticed.'

He smiled. 'Another of his "tricks", I expect.'

She smiled in return and then was gone. No one could transport herself better than Miranda. She had been trying to teach Pug and some of the others how to do it without the aid of patterns or the Tsurani orbs, but few achieved it through mind alone, and then only to very familiar locations.

Pug concluded that Nakor must have studied with her. The wily little man was right, he and his wife did need to talk more.

Pug left the cavern and stopped at its mouth. It was late afternoon on Sorcerer's Isle and by the time he reached the Villa it would be almost suppertime. He took one more look around the cave and then started his walk home.

The Royal Chirurgeon shook his head and spoke softly to the attending squire. 'I fear he will not make it through the night.' The two figures were dwarfed by the enormous chamber in which the Duke of Krondor lay dying. A single candle burned on the table next to the bed.

'Shall I inform the senior squire, sir?' asked the young man, a blond-headed rail of a lad no more than fifteen years old. The senior squire served Prince Robert, ruler of Krondor these last eight years, and heir apparent to the Kingdom of the Isles.

'The hour is late. I shall check on the Duke again very soon. If his condition worsens, there should be time enough to wake the Prince.'

'Yes, sir. Shall I stay?'

'No need,' said the old healer, his face drawn with worry and fatigue. 'He'll not rouse and I have other patients to care for; the stomach flux has struck the royal nursery, and though it may not be fatal, the wrath of the Princess is sure to be if I can't get the children to rest through the night.'

The healer snuffed out the single candle next to the bed and he and the boy left the Duke's large sleeping chamber, closing the door quietly behind them.

A moment later a figure stepped out of the shadow behind a large curtain. He crossed the room to the bed and touched his fingertip to the still-warm candle wick, and the flame instantly reappeared. Glancing down at the recumbent figure, he softly said, 'Oh, Erik, you don't look so good.'

Nakor had known Duke Erik when he had been a boy, fresh from the smith's forge, tall, with huge shoulders and the strength of three men. He had also been born with a temper, which had almost got him hung for murder, but in the end he had served the Kingdom of the Isles well and had risen in rank to Knight-Marshal of the West, and held the title of the Duke of Krondor under young Prince Robert.

Nakor now looked down on an old man, past eighty years of age. His skin was like old parchment drawn tightly across his skull. His shoulders showed none of the massive strength of his youth, and were lost beneath the voluminous nightshirt he wore.

Nakor retrieved a vial from his rucksack and pulled out the stopper. He administered a single drop on the dying man's lips and waited. Erik's mouth moved, slightly, and Nakor poured in another drop. He repeated this application for almost fifteen minutes, a drop at a time, then sat back on the side of the bed and waited.

After a few more minutes, the Duke's eyes fluttered, then opened completely. He blinked, then said in a soft, hoarse whisper, 'Nakor?'

The little man grinned. 'You remember me?'

With a deep intake of breath followed by a long sigh, Erik von Darkmoor – once a sergeant in Calis' Crimson Eagles, veteran of the Serpentwar, hero of the Battle of Nightmare Ridge and now Duke of Krondor and Knight-Marshal of the Western Realm – sat up and said, 'You're damned hard to forget, old friend.'

'You look better,' said Nakor.

Erik moved his arms and said, 'I feel better. What did you do?'

Nakor held up the vial. 'I bought you some time. I need to talk to you.'

'Then hurry,' said the Duke sitting back. He chucked, a dry raspy laugh. 'By all accounts I don't have much time – wait, how did you get in here?'

Nakor waved the question away. 'I just waited until no one was looking then came in through the window.'

Erik smiled. 'Like old Duke James when he was a boy, then?'

'Something like that.'

'So why are you troubling a dying man?'

'I need you not to die for a while, Erik.'

'I'd be pleased to accommodate you, but I believe fate has other plans.'

'How do you feel?'

The Duke stretched out his hands before his face

and said, 'Surprisingly good, all things considered. I'll ask again, what did you do?'

'It's a potion, which I got from a priest who lives a great distance from here. It will . . . restore you.'

'Restore me?'

'It'll keep you alive for a while longer, or if you drink a lot, for a lot longer.'

The Duke shifted himself higher in the bed, so he could sit up. 'I'm not sure I'd like that, Nakor. My body has betrayed me and, to put it bluntly, it vexes me to be so dependent on others. It's hard not to be able to walk to the jakes and take a piss. Nothing humbles a man as much as waking in the morning, sopping wet like a baby. I think I'd rather die than have to spend more days in bed.'

'Well, you don't have to do either,' said Nakor with a grin. 'The potion will make you stronger, too.'

Erik's gaze fixed upon Nakor. 'I can see better; I've just realized.'

'Yes,' said Nakor. 'It's a pretty nice potion.'

'Is that how you've remained unchanged over the last fifty to sixty years?'

'No. I know some other tricks.'

'Very well, if you can get me out of this bed so I can protect the Kingdom a while longer, I'll stay around, but what is your reason for this?'

'Well, first of all, I like you.'

'Thank you, Nakor; I like you, too.'

'You are the last of the Desperate Men who went south with Calis and Bobby.'

'I was there; I remember. Now, I appreciate nostalgia as much as the next man, Nakor, but what's the real reason?'

'We need someone who is close to the Crown to listen and help when the time comes.'

'We?' asked the Duke. 'You mean the Black Sorcerer?'

'Yes, Pug.'

Erik sat back with a long exhalation of breath, shaking his head slightly. After the Serpentwar, Kesh had moved against and almost destroyed Krondor, seeking to an advantage itself in its seemingly never-ending struggle with its northern neighbour. Pug, who was Duke of Stardock at that time, and vassal to the Crown of the Kingdom of the Isles, had refused to use his powerful magic to destroy the invaders, but rather had ordered the Keshians home, while at the same time publicly humiliating Patrick, who was then the Prince of Krondor, and was now King of the Isles.

Erik said, 'Pug's been *persona non grata* since he defied Prince Patrick, after the Serpentwar. Robbie may be related to Patrick in name only – he's as thoughtful as Patrick is rash – but the collective royal memory is a long one. Pug pulled Stardock out of the Kingdom and set it up as an independent state; that looks like treason from the throne's point of view.'

'That's why we need you to persuade them otherwise. 'Something bad is coming, Erik.'

'How bad?'

'Very bad,' said Nakor.

'As bad as the Emerald Queen?'

'Worse,' said the short gambler.

Erik sat motionless for a moment, then said, 'Go over to that table, Nakor.' He pointed to a long table set against the wall. 'Open that box.'

Nakor did as requested and found the simple wooden box with a small brass hasp and ring latch. Inside it he found a black amulet. He pulled it out, letting it hang from the chain. 'Nighthawks?'

'We received that from one of our agents in Great Kesh. I suspect you and your companions have as many agents down there as we do.'

Nakor turned to regard the old Duke. Erik's blue eyes were now alight with energy and his voice was growing stronger by the moment. 'Oh, I have no problem with your . . . what do you call it? Your Conclave?'

Nakor said nothing, but smiled slightly.

'But you're not the only ones out there paying for information, my old friend,' said the Duke. 'I served with you and Calis long enough to have no doubt you only intend good, no matter what the Crown's official position on your activities may be. Truth to tell, Patrick needed the public spanking that Pug gave him when the Keshian army was outside the city walls. Just as much as the Keshians needed to be sent home with their tails between their legs.

'But if it ever comes down to choosing between your vision of a larger good and my duty to the Crown, you know what I will do.'

'I know, Erik.' Nakor understood if it ever came to a choice, Erik would put his oath and duty to the Crown ahead of anything Pug asked. He put the amulet back. 'How long have you had it?'

'A week. Some minor court officials and influential merchants are starting to turn up dead in the City of Kesh. It's a big place and the dead men are of marginal importance, so the Keshians don't appear to be taking note of it yet.'

Nakor was thoughtful. 'Or someone highly placed is ensuring they don't.'

'My thought, as well,' said the Duke. He looked at the window, and said, 'How long before dawn?'

'Four hours or so,' said Nakor.

'I think I will stick around a while longer, Nakor. If the approaching danger is worse than the Emerald Queen's army, I want to be fit enough to stand on the wall with my sword in my hand.'

Nakor grinned. 'You will.'

Erik smiled back and Nakor could see the health returning to his cheeks. When Nakor had seen him sleeping, Erik had looked like an eighty-year-old man, near death's door. He now seemed more like a vigorous man of seventy or less.

'I need to go. Drink the rest of that vial now.' Erik did so and handed the empty bottle back to Nakor. The skinny gambler pulled another and said, 'Hide this somewhere. Drink half of this one in a week's time if you don't feel as strong as you'd like to. And if you want to feel really wonderful, drink the rest a week after that.' He put in on the pillow next to the Duke. 'I'd leave more, but it would be difficult for you to explain to the Prince why you suddenly look younger than he does.' Grinning, he added, 'It's a good thing you were born blond, Erik, because people won't notice your hair isn't as grey as it used to be.'

The door at the far end of the room began to open. 'Got to go now, Erik,' said Nakor and he darted into the shadow behind the large curtain.

Erik knew that the window behind the curtain had stayed closed, but that if he rose and investigated it, Nakor would have vanished.

The Royal Chirurgeon and the Duke's squire entered the Duke's chamber and showed open astonishment at seeing the Duke sitting up in bed. 'Your Grace!' exclaimed the healer.

'Rossler,' said the Duke.

'Sir?' asked the squire with a near stammer.

'What are you two staring at?'

'Why, Your Grace . . . you, sir.'

'Well, you can stop it.'

'It's just that, well . . .'

'I know,' said Erik, interrupting the healer. 'You didn't think I'd make it through the night. Well, I've got better.'

'Apparently so, Your Grace. May I?' he indicated his desire to examine the Duke.

Erik patiently allowed the man to proceed, listening to his heart and breathing, and thumping on his back and chest. When he began examining the colour of his eyes, Erik pushed him away. Swinging his legs over the edge of the bed, he said, 'I need to go to the jakes.'

The squire said, 'Your Grace, I will fetch the chamber pot.'

'Not tonight, Samuel. I'm certain I can walk to the garderobe by myself.'

Both stood a moment in silent amazement as Erik stood and walked across the room to the door that led to his private garderobe and opened the door. When it closed behind the now revitalized Duke, the stunned healer and the grinning squire exchanged looks of wonder.

# CHAPTER 3

# JOURNEY

The boys groaned.

Caleb looked back over his shoulder from the driver's seat at the two slowly-waking boys. He had dumped them in the wagon, said goodbye to Marie, and left Stardock Town before dawn.

Zane was first to regain a semblance of consciousness and he blinked like a stunned owl as he tried to sit up. It proved a bitter mistake as his head throbbed and his stomach heaved. He barely got his face over the side of the wagon before the sour contents of his stomach reappeared.

Caleb slowed the horses, then halted them. By the time the wagon came to a complete stop, Tad had joined his foster brother in a painful display of morning-after distress.

Caleb jumped and with a rough grab, pulled Tad, then Zane out of the wagon and deposited them in a heap on the roadside. They were a portrait of misery. Both had pale complexions and perspiration dripped off their brows. Their eyes were red-rimmed and their clothing dishevelled and dirty.

'Stand up,' said Caleb, and the two lads did so. 'Follow me.'

Without turning to see if they complied, Caleb started walking down a gentle slope dotted with trees. From the sounds behind him, he judged that the two boys were following along grudgingly.

They reached a small gully thick with waist-high grass, and Caleb motioned for them to move ahead of him. The two miserable lads half-stumbled, half-walked through the grass. Zane trampled upon what was in front of him, while Tad parted the slightly waving foliage with his hands.

One minute they were trudging along and the next, Zane vanished from sight with a loud yelp of shock. Tad only just avoided stepping off the bank, some six feet above the river. As Zane's head appeared above the water, Tad felt Caleb's foot on his rump, and suddenly he was propelled through the air, landing backside-first in the water next to Zane.

'Clean yourselves up,' instructed Caleb. 'You smell like the floor of a tap room.' He threw down something which landed in the shallow water between them. Zane picked it up and saw it was a bar of milled soap. 'It won't take your skin off like that stuff your mother makes, boys, but it will get you clean – hair, bodies, clothing, everything. You can carry your clothing back to the wagon.'

Grudgingly the pair began to strip off their wet gear as Caleb watched. 'Drink some water, too, while you're at it. It'll help get you back amongst the living.' He turned back towards the wagon, then shouted, 'But try not to drink the soapy water.'

Caleb returned to the wagon and waited. In less than half an hour, a pair of dripping boys appeared, nude and carrying their clothing. Caleb pointed to the cart and said, 'Spread them out on the side of the wagon and let them dry in the sun.'

Both young men stood shivering in the cool morning. After a few minutes, Caleb pointed to a small chest nestled behind the driver's seat and said, 'You'll find dry clothing in there.'

As the boys dressed, Tad said, 'I've never felt this sick from drinking before.'

Caleb nodded. 'Whiskey has a terrible hangover, no doubt.'

'Why'd you do it?' asked Zane as he pulled on a fresh tunic.

'So I wouldn't have to beat you senseless to get you to leave Stardock.'

As if coming out of a sleepwalk, the boys looked around. 'Where are we?' asked Zane, his dark eyes narrowing. Caleb could see the anger rising.

'We're on the road to Yar-Rin, then we'll go on to Jonril.'

Tad's eyes also narrowed. 'Why Jonril?'

'Because your mother didn't like what was going on with you two in Stardock, and asked me to take you somewhere that you could find trades.' He motioned for them to finish dressing. 'You two have been aimless layabouts since the Choosing two years ago.'

Zane's eyes flashed angrily as he said, 'That's not true, Caleb!' Pulling on dry trousers, he glanced at his foster brother. 'We work when we can find it.'

'Unloading freight for a day or two every month is no craft,' said Caleb.

'We do more,' added Tad. 'We help during the harvest, we cart freight over to the island and we have found work as builders, too.'

Caleb smiled. 'I know you've tried. But there's precious little work now, and less when the new freight line sets up – they're bringing their own lads with them down from Landreth.

'No, your mother has the right of it. If you're to find your way in life, it has to be somewhere else besides Stardock.'

The boys finished dressing and Caleb motioned for them to climb back into the wagon. He mounted the driver's seat and took up the reins. As the horses obeyed his command and moved along, he continued. 'There's not much going on in the Kingdom, I'm sorry to say. I know people who could get you work, but no one who'd apprentice you. But things are looking up in Kesh and I've a few friends in Jonril who owe me a favour or two. We'll see if there's someone who'll take in two promising lads. Apprentice at a trade, learn your craft and in a dozen years or so you can return to Stardock as journeymen crafters, if you wish, but apprentice at a trade you will.'

The boys sat uncomfortably in the back of the jostling wagon, Zane with his knees drawn up to his chest and Tad with legs straight out. Both knew it would be a long ride.

The wagon bumped down the road, the horses kicking up small clouds of dust as the afternoon heat beat down. It was unusually hot for this time of year and the boys complained from time to time. They were restless and bored and the novelty of the journey had worn off. Caleb bore their complaints with good humour, for he understood their distress over the turn of events in their lives.

During the first day, they had expressed both anger and sadness at their mother's decision to send them away. They fully understood her reasoning; Stardock had not been a prosperous town for years and work was hard to come by. Their youthful optimism had always led them to believe that something would have worked out had they remained, but by the end of the day both had slowly come to the conclusion that their mother was probably right. They would eventually accept the change as a welcome one, but for the moment they felt ill-used. At least, to Caleb's relief, neither had mentioned Ellie and her part in Marie's desire to see them somewhere other than home.

Caleb had known the boys for most of their lives and he was very fond of them; they were as close to sons as he would ever have, and he knew that while they didn't consider him as a father, they did look upon him as a surrogate uncle and someone their mother cared for, even loved.

He had known Marie a little while her husband was alive, and had known even then that she had felt drawn to him, for he had seen it in her eyes, despite the fact that she was a dutiful wife who observed all the proprieties. Later, she had told him that even in those days she had found him compelling. He had noticed her too, but as with any other married women, he put any thoughts of attraction aside. Two years after the troll raid and the death of her husband, they had become lovers.

Caleb would have liked nothing better than to settle down with Marie, but he knew that with his duties, it would never be possible. His work for his father and the Conclave of Shadows called for constant travel and putting himself in harm's way. He was absent more than he was around, and Marie deserved better than that.

Yet she had never voiced any complaint nor showed any interest in another man, and Caleb secretly hoped that someday he might convince her to move to Sorcerer's Isle – the place he considered to be home – or perhaps he would return to Stardock and live there. He put those thoughts aside as he had many times before, for dwelling on them only put him in a dark mood.

As they drove into the wagon yard, Caleb said, 'When we get to Nab-Yar, we'll find a buyer for this rig and purchase some saddle horses.'

Zane turned and said, 'We don't ride, Caleb.'

Caleb said, 'You'll learn while we travel.'

The boys exchanged glances. Riding was something reserved for nobility, soldiers, rich merchants, and the occasional traveller, but farm hands and town boys got from place to place by shanks' mare or in the back of a wagon. Still it was something new to contemplate and anything that would break the tedium of this journey was welcome.

Tad shrugged then Zane grinned, his face lighting up as he said, 'Maybe we can become fast messengers?'

Caleb laughed. 'In that case you'll have to become very good riders, and how is your sword work?'

'Sword work?' asked Tad.

'Fast messengers get paid all that gold for getting their messages through in a hurry and safely. That means avoiding highwaymen, but also being able to fight to the death if attacked.'

The boys looked at each other again. Neither had touched a sword in their life and both thought it unlikely that they ever would. Zane remarked, 'Young Tom Sanderling went to soldier in Ab-Yar, and he learned to handle a sword.'

'Kesh trains all their dog soldiers to be swordsmen,' said Caleb, 'but, if memory serves, Old Tom wasn't happy about seeing his son go a-soldiering.'

'True, but what I'm saying, is that if he could learn, so could we,' said Zane.

Tad said, 'You could show us. You carry a sword, Caleb, so you must know how to use it.'

'Maybe,' said Caleb, realizing he'd probably have to teach them a few basics when they camped that evening.

Tad swung wildly at Caleb, who easily moved to the side and smacked the boy hard across the back of his hand with a long stick he had cut a few minutes before. The boy yelped and dropped Caleb's sword on the ground. 'The first rule,' said Caleb, bending down to retrieve the fallen weapon, 'is don't drop the sword.'

'That hurt,' said Tad, rubbing his right hand.

'Not as much as it would had I been using a blade,' said Caleb, 'though it wouldn't have hurt for as long, because I would have gutted you a few seconds later.' He reversed the sword and tossed it to Zane, who caught it deftly. 'Good,' said Caleb. 'You're quick and have a steady hand. Let's see if you can avoid repeating Tad's mistake.'

The sword felt as if it were alive and deadly in Zane's hand. It was heavier than he had expected and its balance felt odd. He moved it around a little and flexed his wrist one way and then the other.

'That's right,' said Caleb as he circled the fire to face Zane. 'Get used to how it feels. Let it become an extension of your arm.'

Suddenly he lashed out with his branch, intending to smack the boy on the hand as he had Tad, but Zane turned his wrist and caught the branch on his blade.

'Very good,' said Caleb, stepping back. 'You may have a knack for this. Where did you learn that?'

'I didn't,' said Zane with a grin, lowering the sword. 'I just tried to keep the stick from hitting me.'

Caleb turned to Tad. 'Did you see how he did that?'

Tad nodded.

Caleb motioned for Zane to drop the point of his blade, then stepped over to the boy and gripped his wrist. 'By turning your wrist, like you did, you achieve the most efficient use of your arm-strength and energy. You'll see men who use their entire arm, sometimes up to the shoulder, and sometimes you have to do that for a particular block, but the less strength you use early on, the more you'll have should the battle wear on.'

'Caleb, how long does a fight usually last?'

'Most are short, Tad. But if two men are evenly matched, it can continue for a long time and endurance becomes vital. And if you're in battle, as soon as you kill the man in front of you, another will take his place.'

'I don't know much about battles,' muttered Zane. 'Maybe I should get a really fast horse . . .'

Tad laughed and Caleb said, 'Not a bad way to look at it.'

After a few more minutes of sword practice, Caleb said, 'Time to turn in.' They had been sleeping under the wagon, so he motioned for them to take their usual places. 'I'm going to keep watch tonight. I'll wake Tad first, then he'll wake you, Zane.'

'Watch?' asked Tad, his face looking particularly ruddy in the firelight. 'Why? We haven't had one so far?'

'We were close in to Stardock.' He glanced around, as if trying to see something in the darkness beyond the fire's glow. 'From here to the village of Ya-Rin, things might be less civilized. We're heading deeper into the Vale.'

The Vale of Dreams was a lush series of rich farmlands, orchards, and villages benefiting from a seemingly endless series of streams that ran from the Pillars of the Stars Mountains to the Great Star Lake. The region had been the object of conflict between the Kingdom of the Isles and the Empire of Great Kesh for over a century. Both sides maintained claims, and both sides sent patrols into the Vale, but the Kingdom observed an unofficial accommodation with the Empire, and the Kingdom patrols did not venture too far south, and the Empire patrols did not wander too far north. As a result, the region had spawned a host of bandit gangs, mercenary companies, minor robber barons, and constant struggle. Finding a pillaged town or a burned-out village at any point was not unusual. If banditry got too out of hand, one nation would look the other way while the other sent troops deep into the Vale to punish the malefactors.

Zane looked around as if suddenly aware of a potential menace behind every tree bole. Tad seemed less convinced. 'What would bandits want with an empty wagon?'

Caleb's smile was indulgent. 'Anything that you can sell, they'd want to take. Now, get some sleep.'

The boys turned in and Caleb took the first watch. The night passed uneventfully, though Caleb roused himself twice to ensure the boys were not falling asleep while keeping watch. Both had, and he gently chided each, promising not to tell the other about the dereliction.

By the third night, both boys were keeping alert and Caleb felt comfortable sleeping until dawn.

The wagon bumped down the road and Caleb said, 'One more night under the wagon, boys. By mid-morning tomorrow, we'll be within sight of Yar-Rin.'

Both boys nodded with a lack of enthusiasm. Riding in the back of the wagon for days had taken its toll. Both boys were bruised and sore from the constant jostling over what passed for a road in these parts. Caleb had observed that with the constant strife in the region, neither nation was taking great pains to repair what passed for highways in the region. Occasionally a town or village might elect to send out a gang to repair a stretch that had fallen into such disrepair that it was impairing commerce, but unless a significant loss of income was involved, the locals tended to ignore the problem.

Which meant that at times the boys were thrown around the back of the wagon without mercy, hanging on to the sides to keep from bouncing right out of the wagon bed. Finally Tad said, 'Don't bother stopping to camp, Caleb. Just get us there. I'll sleep in the stable if it means not having to endure another day in this wagon.'

As Caleb suspected, the wagon journey had conspired to make the boys a great deal more amenable to learning how to ride. He knew he could probably find three saddle horses in the village and that after a couple of days the boys would be sore in a whole new array of places, but that eventually they would be happy to be travelling on horseback.

They were travelling slightly uphill, as the terrain rose from flat farmland and pastures and scattered woodlands, into a more heavily forested range of hills. Rising up to the south of them on their right hand was the Pillars of the Stars, the range of mountains that served as an absolute marker for the border of the Empire of Great Kesh. Yar-Rin was located in the foothills of the eastern terminus of those mountains, in a lovely valley that separated the mountains from the mammoth forest known as The Green Reaches.

But the most significant thing abut reaching Yar-Rin was they would at last be out of the no-man's land that was the Vale of Dreams and be in Great Kesh. Caleb was determined to begin inquiring about possible apprenticeships for the boys, for he was anxious to be done with this responsibility and get back to his family on Sorcerer's Isle. He really had no business taking the boys into Kesh, save there were little opportunities for boys their age without fathers in the Western Realm of the Kingdom these days. There was a general malaise of commerce that had been plaguing the region for over two years, giving rise to all manner of social ills: youth gangs in the larger cities, increased banditry and theft, prices for common goods soaring, and more than usual privations heaped upon the poor.

The wagon jostled more than usual when the wheels rode up over a large rock and the boys were thrown back and forth again. They were on the verge of voicing their displeasure when Caleb abruptly reined the horses in.

They had rounded a bend in the road and were now at a small crest before a long downhill run into a shallow dell. Trees now hugged the side of the road and the late afternoon shadows made the way look menacing.

'What is it?' asked Tad, standing up so he could look over Caleb's shoulder.

'Thought I saw something in the tree-line up at the top of that rise,' he said, indicating the top of the road where it rose up on the other side of the vale.

Zane stood up next to his foster brother and put his hands over his eyes.

'Lower your hands, Zane,' said Caleb. 'We don't want them seeing we know they're there.'

'Who?' asked Tad.

'Whoever it is who is waiting for us.'

'What are we going to do?' whispered Zane.

Dryly, Caleb said, 'I don't think they can hear us.'

'What if we just wait here?' asked Tad.

Urging the horses forwards, Caleb said, 'They'd just come here.'

Zane sounded worried. 'Why don't we turn around?'

'Because then they would be certain we have something of value we're hiding.' The horses picked up speed heading downhill, and Caleb said, 'Listen carefully. I'm a teamster and you're my helpers. We delivered a load of trade goods in Stardock from a trading concern called Mijes and Zagon.'

'Mijes and Zagon,' repeated Tad.

'The goods were paid for in advance and we are returning our wagon to our employers in Yadom.'

'Yadom,' echoed Zane.

'Why the story?'

'Because if they think we're hiding gold on us, they'll kill us before they look for it. If we're just teamsters, they'll maybe let us walk to Yar-Rin.'

'Walk?'

'They'll take the wagon and horses, and anything else they think is worthwhile.'

'You're going to let them?'

Caleb said, 'All I have to lose is my sword, and I can buy another.' The wagon reached the bottom of the dell, the road disappearing under a shallow wide rill strewn with rocks which caused the wagon to bounce the boys more than usual.

As they started to climb upwards to the next ridge, Zane said, 'What if they don't believe you?'

'Then I'll shout "run", and you two take off into the woods. As fast as you can, work your way back down into the dell behind us – you'll never elude them if you're trying to run uphill. When you get to the bottom, follow the creek to the south, then in the morning you'll find a game trail a mile south coming out of the foothills. It will lead back to this road about five miles outside the village of Yar-Rin. Go there and find a man named McGrudder at the sign of the Sleeping Rooster. Tell him what happened and do as he says.' Tad started to ask a question, but Caleb said, 'Now silence. Do not say anything. I will do the talking.'

As they mounted the rise Caleb slowed the wagon, and at the crest, halted the horses. The sun had set over the ridge behind Caleb and the boys, turning the forest ahead into a dark tunnel as shadows quickly deepened. Caleb waited. After a moment, a man emerged from behind a tree. 'Good day, traveller,' he said with a smile devoid of any hint of warmth. He spoke Keshian with a Kingdom accent.

He was a stocky man in dirty clothing, a mixture of buckskin pants, a once richly brocaded shirt, a heavy faded blue sash around his waist and a sleeveless overjacket of black leather. His hair was hidden under a red bandanna and two large golden earrings were visible. He wore a long sword at his right hip and a pair of daggers on the left.

His boots were frayed and down at the heel. When he smiled, the boys could see his two upper front teeth were missing. 'Late for travel, isn't it?'

Caleb's voice was calm. 'Just decided to push on a bit. There's a clearing about a mile up the road that's a nice campsite, near water.'

'You've been over this road before?'

Caleb nodded. 'Many times. It's why my employer hired me for this run. What can I do for you, stranger?'

The man smiled, then said, 'That's the question, isn't it? What can you do for me?'

Caleb sighed, as if he had been through this before. 'We're travelling empty. My apprentices and me just ran some trade goods into Stardock, prepaid, so we're not carrying any gold. I've got a purse with two silvers and a few coppers in it, and the rest is the clothes on my back.'

Other men began to appear from the trees, and the leader of the bandits said, 'Boy,' pointing at Zane, 'where'd you get your load?'

'Yadom,' Zane answered quietly as he watched four others, one armed with a crossbow, surround the wagon. 'At Mijes and Zagon's . . .' he was about to say, 'shop', but realized Caleb hadn't informed him just what sort of business that was, freight company, supplier, or merchant. He just let his words fall off as if he was frightened out of his wits, which he was.

Tad's hand closed on Zane's wrist, and Zane understood what it meant: be ready to jump and run. Tad glanced slightly behind him, and Zane recognized the bandits had left the rear of the wagon unguarded.

Caleb looked around and said, 'Look, there are five of you and I'm not inclined to fight over this wagon. You know this rig isn't worth much, so I'll not risk these boys and myself to keep it. I'm getting paid when I get back and Mijes and Zagon can afford to buy a new one. So, how about I just get down and walk away?'

'How do we know you're not hiding gold on you?' said the bandit leader, losing his smile. 'Maybe you have it tucked in a belt or under your tunic?'

Caleb stood, showing he was wearing only his tunic, trousers, boot and hat. His sword rested on the seat next to him. 'No gold belt, no pouch. Only spare clothes in the chest. You can search the wagon, but let me and the boys go.'

'There's something about you I don't like,' said the bandit, pulling his sword. 'You're no more a teamster than I am. Mercenary, maybe. No one hires a mercenary to drive a wagon unless there's something worth killing over.' He saw the small chest tucked under the wagon's seat. 'Maybe you have something valuable in that chest, huh?' He laughed and glanced first right, then left at his companions. 'Besides, I have no doubt should the situation arrive that you'd be happy to describe us in great detail to the local constables. That would make it hard to spend our booty!' He drew his sword with his left hand and said, 'Kill them!'

Caleb shouted, 'Run!' as he grabbed his sword, leaped to the right, putting the wagon between himself and three of the men, facing the two on his right first.

Without hesitation, Tad and Zane were off as instructed, stumbling and barely keeping control of themselves as they hit the ground and ran downhill, dodging trees and rocks.

Behind them came the sounds of struggle, and closer, the sounds of boots on the dirt as at least one of the bandits chased after them. Tad and Zane both possessed the reckless certainty of boys their age, that somehow they could navigate this rapidly darkening maze of trees and brush. Zane glanced backwards, almost losing his footing as he caught a glimpse of the man pursuing, and Tad stumbled.

They both crashed through thick underbrush and then came to a long stone ledge supporting a game trail that ran along the side of the hill. They hurried down the trail for a dozen yards, the downward slope on their right, then found a depression from runoff heading downward. Remembering Caleb's instructions on reaching the creek, they started down the hill again, hoping the trees hid them from view long enough to elude their pursuers.

Tad grabbed Zane's arm and pointed to his right. Zane didn't hesitate and both boys ran down what appeared to be another slight wash, a depression in the ground between the boles carved by years of rainwater.

The light was falling fast, but both boys knew they couldn't successfully hide for at least another half-hour. They almost ran off a ledge and barely avoided a nasty fall by grabbing a tree trunk. Tad motioned and Zane followed as they hurried along the lip of a deeper wash that cut downward at an angle to the floor of the dell.

The thick underbrush slowed the boys. They could hear the sound of pursuit growing louder behind them. Zane stopped at the base of a tree and glanced upwards. He fashioned a stirrup with his hands and motioned for Tad to climb. Tad stepped into his friend's hands and was boosted up to a branch four feet above their heads. Zane glanced around and saw a fallen tree branch roughly the size of his forearm that would serve as a club, so he picked it up and tossed it up to Tad.

Tad deftly caught it with one hand, then reached down with the other. Zane leapt, catching his friend's outstretched forearm and clambered up to rest upon the heavy branch with him. Both boys tried to calm their breathing, for they were gasping for breath. The boys spread out, lying sideways head to head, so that their feet wouldn't dangle down in plain sight.

A moment later two men appeared, running quickly through the woods. They stopped directly below the two silent boys. 'Damn!' said the first bandit, a tall, rangy man with dirty blond hair that hung limply to his collar. 'Where'd they go?'

'Gone to ground, I'll wager,' said the other, a

broad-shouldered man with a heavy black beard. 'Bloody brush hides the tracks. You go that way,' he pointed to a rough path along the edge of the rill that ran through the centre of the dell, 'and I'll work my way up. Let's see if I can flush 'em back to you.'

They moved off and the boys waited. Tad put his finger to his lips. His caution turned out providential, as a few minutes later the tall blond bandit returned down the path. Zane quietly took the club from Tad's hands and waited as the man hurried through the quickly darkening woodlands; he took no pains to hide his whereabouts. Muttering curses to himself, he was oblivious to the sudden movement above, as Zane twisted so his hips lay across the branch and swung down hard holding the wooden club in both hands. The man walked right into the blow, a loud, meaty crack that made Tad wince at the sound. It shattered the bandit's nose and knocked him backwards as his feet went out from under him.

The impact also had the effect of causing Zane to pitch forward and tumble to the ground on his back, knocking the air out of his lungs. Tad leapt down from the tree and knelt next to the groggy dark-haired boy. 'You all right?' whispered Tad.

'I'll live,' he said, standing on wobbly legs. 'How's he doing?'

Both boys turned their attentions to the fallen bandit. Kneeling next to him, Tad said, 'I think you killed him.'

The man's face was awash with blood from a pulped nose and a gash across his forehead. Zane leaned down and touched the man's chest. The man's eyes suddenly opened and he reached out, grabbing Zane's tunic. The boy yelped in fear and pulled away as the man tried to wipe the blood out of his eyes with his other hand. Half-blind, the bandit said something incoherent but his murderous intent was obvious.

Tad picked up the branch Zane had used as a club and with all his strength he hit the man in the back of the head, the blow providing another nasty sounding crack. The bandit released his hold on Zane and pitched over sideways. The man lay groaning, and Tad hit him again, this time causing the man's body to jerk and then lie still.

Zane had scuttled backwards when released and now he rose and came to stand next to Tad. After a moment, he whispered, 'He's not breathing.'

'I hope he's not,' said Tad.

'You killed him,' said Zane softly, in mixed admiration and shock.

'He would have killed us,' was Tad's reply.

'Hey!'

Both boys turned as one at the sound from below, the second man trudging back up the wash. 'Did you see them?'

Zane glanced at Tad, who nodded, and yelled back in a faux deep voice, 'Up here!'

Zane's eyes grew wide, but Tad pointed upwards, and put his hands together. Zane stepped into the stirrup Tad formed, and took the boost to reach the branch. 'I'll draw him here,' said Tad. 'You hit him!'

Zane said, 'Then give me the branch, you fool!'

Tad was just on the verge of tossing it up to Zane when the second bandit came hurrying up the gully. He was out of breath but the instant he saw Tad standing over his fallen comrade holding the makeshift bludgeon, he pointed his sword and ran towards the boy.

Tad stood rooted in terror for an instant, then at the last he ducked as the bandit tried to cut his head from his shoulders. The blade struck the tree trunk and cut deep, like an axe. The blade was wedged deep and the bandit yanked to free it. Tad thrust upwards into the man's face with the butt end of the dried branch, and the erstwhile club struck him square on the nose. 'Damn!' shouted the man as he threw up his left arm, knocking aside the branch while he staggered back. Tad could see the man had some small cuts on his face and a few embedded splinters, but the blow did nothing more than annoy him. Tad grabbed the hilt of the man's sword and yanked the blade free, then stood resolutely facing the bandit.

The man drew back his dagger. 'If you know how to use it, y'whelp, you'd best be about it, else I'll cut you from chin to crotch for what you did to Mathias.' He stepped forward, blade ready, as a pair of feet appeared directly over his head. Zane jumped from the branch above, one foot striking the side of the man's neck, the other landing on his shoulder. The boy's weight drove the bandit straight to his knees and Tad could see the wide-eyed, startled expression on his face as his head twisted impossibly to one side, and he could hear the loud crack as his neck broke.

Zane again tumbled hard to the ground and lay there uttering a groan. Tad looked downward, first at the bandit who now lay at his feet, his head bent at an unnatural angle, his vacant eyes staring up at the night sky. He then looked at Zane who lay on his back, also wide-eyed and motionless. Tad knelt next to his foster brother who took in a large gasp of air and softly said, 'I think my back is broken.'

Tad said, 'Are you serious?' with concern approaching panic in his voice.

'It hurts like it is,' said the shorter boy.

Tad stuck his thumbnail into his companion's leg and said, 'Can you feel that?'

'Ow!' said Zane, sitting up. 'That hurt.'

'Your back's not broken,' said Tad, standing and giving Zane a hand up as he did.

'How do you know?' said the ill-used boy.

'Jacob Stephenson told me that when Twomy Croom's father broke his back from that fall in their barn, the old man couldn't move his legs, couldn't even feel anything below the waist.'

'That's bad,' said Zane.

'Didn't matter,' offered Tad. 'The old man died a day later.'

'Feels like I broke it,' said Zane in a weak bid for sympathy.

'Get the other sword,' said Tad.

Zane took the one next to the first man they had killed. Tad hefted the other and the taller boy said, 'We should get back to the wagon.'

Zane said, 'But Caleb said not to come back?'

Tad's blood was up and he almost shouted, 'But he may need our help!'

'You think Caleb's all right?'

Fear and exultation mixed in equal measure as Tad said, 'If we can kill two of these bastards, I'm sure Caleb was the equal of the other three.'

Zane didn't look convinced, but he followed his foster brother.

They moved cautiously up the hillside towards the road. It was now full night and the way was difficult as they navigated their way through the underbrush and thick boles. As they reached the verge of the road, they stopped and listened for any hint of the bandits. The sounds of the forest at night was all they heard. A light evening breeze rustled leaves and the sound of night birds echoed from some distance away. All appeared peaceful.

They ventured onto the road and looked in both directions. 'Where's the wagon?' whispered Tad.

Zane shrugged, the gesture lost on his companion, so he said, 'I don't know. I don't know if this is where we were, or if we were that way' he pointed down the road to his left, 'or the other.'

Then they heard a horse's snort and the rattle

of traces coming from the left. They had climbed back to the road farther to the east than they had thought. The boys hurried along the edge of the road, ready to dart back into the trees should they encounter bandits.

In the gloom they barely saw the first body, sprawled on the far side of the road. It was the bandit who had first accosted them. Farther down the road the wagon was stationary on the other side of the road while the two horses attempted to crop whatever they could from the underbrush. Another bandit lay dead as they reached the end of the wagon.

The boys circled around and saw two figures, the last bandit, the one with the crossbow, lying dead next to the wagon's left front wheel and another figure slumped down beside him, back against the wheel of the wagon.

Caleb sat upright, but was unconscious, his body held in place by the wagon wheel and the dead bowman's corpse. Tad knelt next to him and said, 'He's breathing!'

Zane pulled the corpse of the last bandit aside, and Caleb fell over sideways. Tad examined him and found a deep gash in his side where a crossbow bolt had found its mark, as well as several sword cuts. 'We've got to do something!'

Zane said, 'Strip that man's shirt,' as he pointed to the nearest bandit. 'Cut bandages.'

Tad did as Zane said and pulled out Caleb's huge hunting knife, using it to cut bandages from the man's filthy shirt. Zane hurried to inspect the other two corpses and returned with two more swords and a small purse. 'They must have robbed before,' said Zane.

Throwing an impatient look at Zane, Tad said, 'You think?'

'I mean recently,' said Zane, holding up the purse. 'It's got some coins in it.'

'Well, we had better get Caleb into the wagon, because I don't know how long he's going to make it without help.'

Both boys picked up the injured man and deposited him in the back of the wagon. Tad said, 'You stay back there with him. I'll drive.'

Neither boy was an experienced teamster, but both had spelled Caleb on their journey, and Zane admitted Tad was a better driver. The horses were reluctant to leave their forage and head down the road. 'How far did he say that village was?' asked Tad.

'I don't remember,' said Zane. 'But hurry. I don't think we have much time.' Tad pulled to the right and got the horses pointed down the road and with a flick of the reins and a shout got them moving. With another flick and a louder shout, he got them up to a brisk trot, the fastest he could manage in the darkness without running themselves off the dark road.

Caleb lay motionless, his head resting on a bundle of empty sacks while Zane tried his best to halt the bleeding. Softly, Zane whispered, 'Don't die!'

Tad silently echoed his foster brother's request as he urged the horses down the dark and forbidding road.

The ride through the forest seemed to take forever. The boys alternated between an almost panic-stricken terror and a determined optimism that everything would turn out for the best.

They had no sense of time, as the minutes passed by and the road passed under the hooves of the horses. The animals had not been rested for hours before the ambush, and they were panting and the one on the left seemed to be favouring his left hind leg, but Tad ignored it; he'd kill both horses in their traces if it would save Caleb.

Both boys liked the tall, quiet hunter, as they thought of him. They knew he was related to the owners of Stardock, though the exact nature of the relationship was vague to them. They also knew that their mother was in love with Caleb and that he cared deeply for her. Resentful of his attentions at first, they had both come to appreciate how happy his visits made her. Tad's deepest fear was having to return to Stardock and seeing the look on his mother's face should he have to tell her of Caleb's death.

Suddenly they were in the village. Tad realized that he had been so focused on what he would have to tell his mother and that Zane had been tending Caleb so closely, neither had noticed they had left the forest and had been passing by farms for some time now. The large moon was up and in the shimmering light of its reflected glow they could see the village of Yar-Rin. A few huts lined the roadway into the village square, and three large buildings dominated. One was the mill, on the far side of the square, and the other two appeared to be a shop of some sort, and an inn. The inn showed a sign with a sleeping rooster ignoring a sunrise. Remembering Caleb's instructions, Tad pulled up before the inn and went to bang hard on the bolted door.

After a minute a voice from above sounded as a window was thrown open. 'What is it?' shouted an angry landlord as he thrust his head out the window.

'Are you McGrudder? We need help!' shouted Tad.

'Wait a minute,' said the man as he withdrew his head.

A moment later the door opened and a large man in a nightshirt appeared in the doorway holding a lantern. 'Now, who's *we* and what sort of *help*—' His questions died on his lips as he saw Zane kneeling next to the prone figure in the wagon bed. He held the lantern close and said, 'Gods of mercy!'

Looking at the two boys, both obviously exhausted and filthy, he said, 'Help me get him inside.'

Tad jumped up next to Zane and they both got one of Caleb's arms over their shoulder, then got him upright. The innkeeper came to the end of the wagon and said, 'Give him to me.'

They allowed Caleb to fall slowly over the large man's shoulder, and ignoring the blood that was soaking into his nightshirt, the landlord took the wounded man inside. 'Elizabeth!' he shouted as he entered the inn. 'Get up, woman!'

A few moments later a plump but still attractive older woman appeared on the stairs, as the landlord put Caleb on a table. 'It's Caleb,' said the man.

'Are you McGrudder?' asked Tad.

'That I am, and this is my inn, the Sleeping Rooster. And who might you two be, and how did my friend come to this sorry state?'

The woman quickly began examining the wounds and said, 'He's lost a lot of blood, Henry.'

'I can see that, woman. Do what you can.'

'Tad and I are from Stardock,' said Zane, and he quickly outlined the tale of their ambush.

'Damn road agents,' said McGrudder. 'Had a Keshian patrol from Yadom out looking for them a couple of weeks back.'

'Well, they're all dead now,' said Tad.

'All of them?'

'Five men,' said Zane. 'Tad and I killed two of them, Caleb the other three.'

'You killed two?' asked McGrudder, then he fell silent as the boys nodded.

When he said nothing for a few moments, Tad offered, 'We were lucky.'

'Indeed,' said McGrudder.

The woman called Elizabeth said, 'Henry, I

don't think I can do anything to save him. He's too far gone.'

'Damn,' said the innkeeper. 'Margaret!' he roared.

Within a minute a young girl, about the same age as the boys, appeared from a door in the rear of the common room. 'Get dressed and hurry down to the witch's hut.'

The girl's eyes grew wide. 'The witch!'

'Do it!' the landlord shouted. 'We've got a dying man here.'

The girl's face went pale, and she vanished back through the door. A few minutes later she re-appeared wearing a simple grey homespun dress and a pair of leather shoes. Turning to Zane, McGrudder said, 'Take the lantern and go with her. The old witch won't talk to strangers, but she knows Margaret.' To Margaret, he said, 'She'll not want to come, but when she tells you to be away, say this and no more, "McGrudder says it's time to repay a debt." She'll come then.'

Zane followed the obviously agitated girl out the door and across the small village square. This side of the village was upslope from a small stream and devoid of farms. The few huts bordering on the square were quickly left behind and they plunged into a thick copse of trees.

Zane hurried to keep up with the girl who seemed determined to get this over as quickly as possible. After a couple of minutes of silence, he said, 'My name is Zane.'

'Shut up!' said the girl.

Zane felt his cheeks burn but said nothing. He had no idea why she was being rude to him, but decided that was something best explored when things weren't so confused.

They came to a small game path and followed it, until they came near the edge of the stream. A flat clearing jutted into the stream, forming a small bend in the stream. The surface was rock covered by recently dried mud. Zane wondered why the hut that sat snug in the middle of the clearing hadn't been washed away by the recent flooding.

The hut was constructed of sticks covered with mud, with a thatch roof and a rude stone chimney at the back. It looked barely large enough to contain one person. A leather curtain served as a door and what looked to be a small opening high up on the left appeared to be the only window.

The girl stopped a few yards from the hut and shouted, 'Hello, old woman!'

Instantly a voice answered, 'What do you want, girl?'

'I'm Margaret, from McGrudder's,' she answered.

In a cross tone, Zane heard the reply: 'I know who you are, you stupid girl. Why do you trouble my sleep?'

'McGrudder says you have to come. There's a man in need of aid at the tavern.'

'In need of aid,' said the voice from within. 'And why should I give aid to any who pass through this village?'

'McGrudder says it's time to repay a debt.'

There was a moment of silence, then the leather curtain was pushed away as the old woman stepped through. Zane had never seen a smaller person in his life. She looked barely more than four and a half feet tall. He had met a dwarf once, travelling through Stardock on his way to the dwarven stronghold near Dorgin, and even he had been a good four or five inches taller than this old woman.

Her hair was white and her skin so sun-browned, like ancient leather, he couldn't tell if she had once been fair or dark as a girl. Her stoop made her even shorter.

But even in the dark Zane could see her eyes, alight as if glowing from within. In the dim moonlight he could see they were a startling and vivid blue.

Toothless, she slurred her words slightly as she spoke. 'Then come to McGrudder's I shall, for I let no man hold debt over me.'

She didn't wait for either Margaret or Zane, but marched past them purposefully, muttering to herself.

Zane and the girl easily kept pace, and when they reached the inn and went inside, Zane was amazed that the little woman looked even more frail and tiny than before.

She marched up to McGrudder and said, 'So, what debt do I owe you, McGrudder, that you'd call in?'

'Not me, old woman,' said the innkeeper. 'Him.'

The woman looked at the prone figure on the table and said, 'Caleb!' She hurried to his side and said, 'Get this tunic off so I may look at his wounds.'

McGrudder began to pull Caleb upright to attempt to pull his jacket and tunic off, and the woman nearly screeched as she said, 'Cut them off, you fool. Do you want to kill him?'

Tad had been keeping Caleb's hunting knife; he pulled out and reversed it, handing the hilt first to the innkeeper. McGrudder set to with practiced efficiency and cut away the jacket, then the tunic.

The old woman looked at the wounds and said, 'He's near to death. Boil bandages, and fetch me a cup of wine. Hurry.'

The woman carried a small leather pouch on a strap she wore over one shoulder. She moved to stand next to the table and rummaged around in the pouch, finding what she sought. She removed a folded parchment and when the wine was produced, she unfolded it, letting a fine powder fall into the wine. To Zane, she said, 'You, boy, hold his head up and don't let him choke as I give him the wine to drink.'

Zane did as she instructed and Caleb's lips moved slightly as she administered the potion. Then she went to the fire to check the cauldron. When the water began to roil, she put the bandages that had been cut from some spare bedding into it, and said, 'You, girl, fetch me soap and cold water.'

Margaret brought a bucket of cold water and the soap. The tiny woman ladled some hot water out of the cauldron into the bucket to warm the water then told Tad to put the bandages into the water.

She set to with surprising vigour and washed Caleb's wounds. She instructed McGrudder to use the metal ladle to fish out the bandages and let them drip on the floor, holding them before the fire so they would dry. When she was satisfied they were dry enough, she bound Caleb's wounds and said, 'Now, carry him up to a room and let him sleep.'

McGrudder picked up Caleb as a man might a child and lugged him up the stairs. Zane asked, 'Will he live?'

The old woman fixed him with a sceptical eye and said, 'Probably not. But he'll linger, and that's important.'

'Why?' asked Tad.

The old woman gave him a faint smile and said, 'Wait.'

McGrudder returned and asked, 'What more can we do?'

'You know what you must do,' and she turned to leave.

'Wait!' said Zane. 'That's all? A cup of wine and bandages?'

'My potion is more than a cup of wine, boy. It'll keep him alive long enough for McGrudder to fetch more help, and that help will save Caleb, son of Pug.'

'What help?' asked McGrudder.

'Don't dissemble with me, you old fraud,' said the woman. 'I know who your true master is, and I know if an emergency warrants you can send word in haste.' She hiked a thumb towards the stairs and said, 'His son lies dying, and if that's not an emergency, I don't know what is.'

McGrudder looked hard at the old woman and said, 'For a simple woman who claims to practice only herbs and root lore, you know a great deal more.'

'Live a long time and you learn things,' she said as she reached the door. 'But Caleb did me a favour, and his father did one years ago, and there was another, a friend of his father's who did me a great service as well, so that in the end, there is a great debt still. But to you and your masters I owe nothing; let us not be confused on that matter, McGrudder. The next time you disturb my sleep, you do so at risk.'

Saying nothing more, she left the inn and Tad and Zane exchanged glances. McGrudder saw the look and said, 'You boys can sleep in the room with Caleb, the second door on the left at the top of the stairs. He's in the only bed, but there's a large mat rolled up under the bed you can share.' He glanced at the girl and said, 'Get yourself back to bed, girl, we have a long day tomorrow.' He then motioned to his wife who had been quietly washing the blood off the table and floor and said, 'I'll help you in a moment, Elizabeth.'

She nodded. 'I know. You need to send that message.'

He returned the nod and left the common room through the door in the rear. The innkeeper's wife looked at the boys and said, 'Go up and get what rest you may. It is only three hours until sunrise, and there will be work for all tomorrow.' She indicated a candle on the bar.

Zane picked up the candleholder and the boys mounted the stairs without a word and paused a moment before the door, then entered. Caleb lay in his bed, a heavy down comforter pulled up to his chin, his face pale and drawn.

Tad knelt and pulled the rolled-up mat, and the boys lay on it.

'What do we do now?' whispered Zane after a while.

# CHAPTER 4

# DARK GODDESS

Tad came awake suddenly.

Someone was opening the door and he nudged Zane awake as it swung aside. It was near sunrise; the sky outside the window displayed a slightly rose-tinged grey light, but it was still too dark in the room to make out the features of the man who stood there.

'Huh?' said the half-asleep Zane as Tad fumbled to where he put the candle.

'You won't need that,' said the figure in the doorway as he held up his hand. Suddenly light filled the room, an unnatural white glow that held a hint of blue. Zane blinked and Tad stood up as the figure entered the room.

He matched Caleb in height and resembled the hunter, but his skin was fair and his hair was white. He had eyes of the palest blue, but their set and expression were exactly like Caleb's. As he entered the room, another figure, McGrudder, stepped into the doorway.

Zane scrambled to get out of the way as the stranger knelt to examine Caleb. After only a moment, the man said, 'You did well to contact

101

me. His breathing is shallow, his heartbeat is weak, and he burns with fever. If nothing is done, he'll be dead by noon.'

The man looked at Tad and said, 'Who are you?'

'Tad,' he answered. 'That's Zane. We were travelling with Caleb.'

'What are you to my brother?'

Zane exchanged glances with Tad, then he said, 'I suppose you would say Caleb was taking us to be apprentices.'

The pale man frowned and said, 'I wouldn't say. What you are to him will be sorted out later, now I must take him with me to save him. You stay here.'

'Wait a minute, Magnus,' said McGrudder coming into the room. 'You know they can't stay here.'

'Why not?' asked Magnus, standing up. 'You know I can't take them with me.'

'But you must,' said McGrudder. 'They've seen you, and even a chance remark to the wrong person . . .' He inclined his head towards the boys. 'You know.'

'Put them to work,' suggested Magnus.

'I can't. You know your father will move all of us out of here in a day or two. Those men might have been bandits, as the boys told me, or they may have been more than that. Either way, Pug will move us, just in case, and there will be another innkeeper and his family. They'll say that they're distant relatives, or that this place was purchased, or some story.' He glanced around, as if already regretting the need to leave this cosy little inn.

'The villagers know better than to say anything to strangers, but the old witch already knows too much and no one can keep her from doing whatever she wishes to; these boys just add two more potential problems if you leave them here. If they were followed, and if they were known to have travelled with Caleb . . . it's best if all of us were gone from here as soon as possible.

'Besides, if Caleb was apprenticing them as they say, you know what that means.'

Magnus glanced at the two boys and said, 'He sees something in them. Very well.' To the boys he said, 'Stand close to me after I pick up my brother.'

He reached down and even though Caleb was equal in size and weight, Magnus picked him up as effortlessly as if he were a child. 'Now, stay very close,' he said.

Tad and Zane did as instructed and were suddenly swept into darkness for an instant. The next second, they stood in a hall.

Zane almost fell over, so sudden was the change and following disorientation. Tad looked around, blinking like a barn owl blinded by a lantern.

The man McGrudder had called Magnus started walking down the hall, leaving the boys standing alone. They glanced at one another, each seeing a reflection of his own shocked, pale expression. Then Zane nodded and they were off, following after the man, for they had no desire to be left alone in this alien place.

Even carrying his brother, Magnus moved

rapidly, and the boys had to hurry to catch up. Their surroundings were lost on them until they realized that they were in some sort of massive building, for all the hallways they passed through had granite or marble walls and floors, illuminated by torches bolted by iron fittings to the walls on either side of a series of heavy wooden doors. Each door had a small covered window, barely more than a peephole, in its centre.

'This looks like a dungeon,' muttered Zane.

'And how would you know?' asked Tad in a whisper. 'You ever see one?'

'No, but you know what I mean. This is what dungeons are supposed to look like – from stories.'

'I know what you mean,' said Zane as they turned a corner around which Magnus had just vanished.

The boys came to an abrupt halt. Before them a large corridor emptied into a vast hall. The vaulted ceiling could barely be seen, its surfaces darkened by the rising soot from at least a hundred torches ringing the expanse. Against the far wall rose a heroic statue of a woman, her arms outstretched as if bidding those standing below to come into her embrace. Behind her, on either side, smaller bas-relief figures had been carved into the wall.

'Is that who I think it is?' whispered Tad.

'Must be, look at the net over her right arm,' said Zane.

Both boys made every ward of protection sign they had ever seen a gambler, teamster, or porter make and then slowly followed the rapidly hurrying

Magnus. They were in the temple of Lims-Kragma: the Drawer of Nets, the Death Goddess.

Several black-robed figures were emerging from a couple of doors to the left of the statue, and suddenly two men appeared behind the boys. One hurried past them, but the other paused and asked quietly, 'What is your business here, boys?'

Tad pointed to Magnus, who was now laying his brother at the feet of the statute, and said, 'We're with him.'

'Then come along,' said the man.

They nodded and hurried after him.

Zane studied the man out of the corner of his eye, afraid to look directly at him. He had plain features and was almost bald, save for stubble around the back of his head to his ears. He was otherwise unremarkable. Except for one thing; he wore the robe of a priest of the Goddess of Death.

An elderly man entered the hall from a door to the right, walking slowly with the aid of a white staff taller than himself. His white hair flowed to his shoulders and it wasn't until he was almost at Magnus' side that the boys saw that his eyes were filmed over; he was blind.

'Why do you disturb our slumber, Magnus?'

'My brother lies dying,' Magnus replied, standing to face the old man as the boys reached them. 'You know my father, and you know what we do. We need my brother's life spared.'

The old man stared into space, looking frail, but his voice was deep and strong. 'Our mistress gathers us all to her when it is our time. I may do nothing to alter that.'

'You can heal him!' said Magnus. 'I know what arts you are capable of, Bethanial.'

'Why didn't you take him to the temple of Killian or Sung? Healing is their domain.'

'Because my family made a pact with your mistress years ago, and she can choose not to take my brother. He is needed. It is not time yet.'

'When is it ever the time for those left behind?' asked the old High Priest.

Magnus stepped closer to him and said, 'It is not his time *yet!*'

'*When is his time?*' echoed a voice through the hall, and the boys instinctively clung to one another, for there was a cold note of hopelessness in it. Yet it also held a faint echo of reassurance, that left a feeling of certainty that all would be well in the end.

Magnus turned to look at the gigantic statue. 'When this world is safe,' he answered.

For a moment, all the torches flickered and dimmed.

Magnus found himself within a vast hall, with a ceiling so high it was lost in darkness above, while the walls were so distant he could only see the one to his right; the other boundaries had vanished in the distance.

He stood amidst a chessboard of stone biers. Men, women, and children rested upon them, though many were empty. As he watched, he saw a woman sit up and dismount her bier in the distance, and then start to weave her way through the maze of stone.

An empty bier next to Magnus was suddenly occupied by a baby, no more than a few hours old. Magnus paused to wonder how this infant, who obviously had not survived for long after its birth, would manage the feat of climbing down and walking to meet the Goddess. Then he reminded himself that none of this was real. Magnus knew that he was seeing an illusion of the gods – an image made so he could apply some reference and logic when dealing with a power far beyond his own. Magnus' patience was thin at the best of times, now it was slighter than parchment. He waved his hand and said, 'Enough!'

The hall vanished and he stood on top of a mountain, in another vast hall. It appeared to be fashioned from ivory and white marble. Columns supported a vast ceiling high above, but now Magnus could see the walls.

The hall opened on a vista of the distant mountain peaks, and the air was bitterly cold and thin. Magnus adjusted the air around his body so that he felt warm and could breathe easily. Outside, a sea of white clouds lingered just below the lower edge of the floor and he knew he stood in the Pavilion of the Gods, a place his parents had told him of. He smiled, for it was here they had first spoken together, and it seemed a reasonable choice for his meeting with the Goddess.

A figure in black robes sat alone on a simple marble bench. It was a young woman, and as Magnus approached, she pulled back her hood. Her skin was as white as the finest porcelain, yet her hair and eyes were black as onyx. Her lips were the colour of blood, and her voice was like an icy wind as she said, 'Your powers are prodigious for a mortal's, Magnus. You may someday eclipse your father and mother in your mastery of magic. You also have far more arrogance than either of them.'

'I lack my father's gift for patience and my mother's acceptance of expediency,' said Magnus, with a defiant note in his voice. 'My brother is needed. You know that.'

'I know no such thing,' answered the woman. 'Your father once came to me with his friend, the human who became Valheru,' she said, standing.

Magnus was surprised to discover that she was taller than him. For some reason that annoyed him. With one thought, he stood taller than the Goddess.

The woman laughed. 'Vanity, too?' She nodded. 'Your father then came to me a second time.'

'I know,' said Magnus. 'He told us of your bargain.'

'Did he?' She turned her back and walked away, as if studying the mountain peaks below. 'I remember no bargain. I do, however, remember giving him a choice.'

'I don't understand,' said Magnus.

'I know you don't. I do not know what your

father has told you about what is coming, but I have no debt to you or your family, just an understanding which I struck with Pug years ago. Your brother stands with no exemption from fate; he lies at the entrance to my realm and I am under no obligation to refuse him. It is his time.'

'No,' said a voice from behind Magnus.

He turned and saw a thin, frail old woman with skin like translucent bleached parchment stretched over ancient bones. Her hair was white and she wore a robe the colour of the snow on the distant peaks. Her robe and hair were arranged with ivory clasps and rings, and her feet were hidden by the hem of her robes. 'You may do as you wish, daughter, for you are ruler of your domain, but that is just the point: you may do as you wish.'

'I have an obligation to keep order, and don't call me "daughter", old woman. You do not belong here.'

'I belong nowhere, it seems.' She glanced at Magnus and smiled.

Magnus studied the old woman and said, 'You're the witch from the village.'

'No,' said the old woman. 'But I know her, as I know many others.'

Magnus revealed confusion, for the two women were identical, save that the witch had iron-grey hair and her skin was like leather. 'Then who are you?'

'I am one who once was and one who will be, but now . . .'

'She is no one,' said Lims-Kragma.

'Yes,' said the old woman, and suddenly she was gone. But her next words hung in the air. 'You may do as you wish.'

For a moment, neither Magnus or the Goddess spoke, then the Goddess of Death said, 'Very well. I refuse your brother entrance to my realm. His judgment shall await another time; take him to your island.'

'Who was that?' asked Magnus.

'One who was,' said the Goddess, then with a flicker of expression that suggested turbulent emotions, she added, 'and perhaps, as she says, one who will be again one day,' and with a wave of her hand she took the two of them back to the temple. Everyone stood frozen in time, likes flies caught in amber, and the Goddess said, 'Ask Nakor or your father about echoes.' Then suddenly she was gone, and everyone around Magnus began moving.

With a groan, Caleb opened his eyes. He blinked, then said weakly, 'Brother?'

'The Goddess answered your prayer,' said the high priest, bowing his head. The other priests followed his example and also bowed.

'Come,' said Magnus to the boys as he picked his brother up from the floor. Caleb's eyes closed and he fell unconscious again, his head resting against his brother's shoulder. The boys stood close to Magnus and again felt a sensation of darkness followed by a moment of disorientation.

They stood near the ocean. Tad and Zane could

smell the tang of sea salt in the night air. Tad pointed to the two moons in the sky and the boys knew that they were some miles northwest of McGrudder's inn. Magnus said nothing as he walked towards a large, square building.

The structure ran in a straight line across a grassy field. Paving stone marred its lush texture and led to a large open door, lit by torches set in sconces on either side. To the left of the path, by the house another building rested, from which smoke and the smell of baking bread issued. Magnus stepped inside the building and turned left. The boys followed, pausing a moment to stare through the opposite door which revealed a large inner court-yard that had been turned into a garden.

They hurried after Magnus who now turned right and moved rapidly down another corridor to a suite of private rooms. A short man with a dark beard, a woman in a royal blue dress of simple cut and a man in a faded orange robe tattered at the hem, were waiting for him.

The group ignored the two boys as Magnus entered a generously-sized, but sparsely appointed bedroom. He laid his brother down on the low bed and stepped away. The man in the tattered orange robe inspected Caleb and after a minute said, 'He needs rest, and when he awakes, some light food and drink.' He turned to Magnus. 'Tell us what happened?'

Magnus said, 'You'll have to start with these two,' and he pointed to the boys.

The bearded man approached Tad and Zane and said, 'I am Caleb's father, Pug. What happened?'

Tad spoke first and told them of the ambush and Zane inserted a comment from time to time. When they reached the part about McGrudder at the Sleeping Rooster, Magnus said, 'Let me continue.' He turned to Pug and said, 'The old witch in the village slowed his death.'

The short man in orange interrupted. 'Old witch?'

'I'll get to that in a minute,' said Magnus. He described his journey into the Hall of Lims-Kragma, and as he spoke Tad noticed Zane take a step closer to him, as if seeking comfort.

When Magnus had finished the story, he said, 'The white-haired woman looked exactly as I remembered the village witch. She said you two—' he gestured at his father and the other man, '—would know who she was. Lims-Kragma said she was an echo.'

Pug turned to the other and said, 'Nakor?'

Nakor shrugged. 'Do you remember Zaltais, whom we battled when the Emerald Queen invaded the Kingdom? I told you he was a dream.'

Magnus said, 'I have not heard of this.'

'There are many things you have not heard of.' Pug frowned as he looked at his son. 'What were you thinking, risking a visit to the Death Goddess's Hall?'

'I knew Caleb had no more than minutes, Father. And I knew you had been to see the Goddess twice, and had lived.'

'The second time was not of my choosing,'

reminded Pug. Magnus knew the story; his father had been almost killed by the demon who led the Emerald Queen's army during the Serpentwar.

'But the first time you went seeking Grandfather and returned,' countered Magnus.

'Tomas and I were nearly dead when we revived from our first visit to Lims-Kragma's Hall. You could have been trapped there.'

'Her hall is an illusion, Father.'

Nakor shook his head. 'The gods' illusions can kill as easily as steel or stone, Magnus. They are real enough when they need to be.'

Miranda said, 'It was madness! I could have lost both sons.'

Magnus' blue eyes narrowed. 'You've taught me well. I did not become ensnarled in the illusion; in fact I forced a change and met her in the Pavilion of the Gods.' Pug and Miranda exchanged glances at that.

'I would risk my own life for my brother's,' Magnus continued. When his mother said nothing, but let her expression show her displeasure, he added, 'Mother, I know you fear for us both, but you lost neither.'

'That is something for us to discuss in a moment,' said Pug. 'Nakor?'

'I will tell you what I know, Pug,' he said with a grin. 'But first,' he pointed one finger at the boys.

Pug turned and despite having just spoken to them moments before, it was as if he was noticing the boys for the first time. 'Who are you?'

Tad pointed at himself and inclined his head, as if asking if he was whom he meant. Pug's scowl made it clear. 'I'm Tad. He's Zane. We're from Stardock.'

'Why were you with my son?' asked Miranda.

Tad launched into the story of the festival and how they woke up in the wagon, and while it was a disjointed and somewhat rambling version, they got the story in one telling. At the end, Magnus said, 'You mean to say that you're not Caleb's apprentices?'

Tad and Zane exchanged guilty looks, and then Zane said, 'No. But we never said we were.'

'McGrudder said you were.'

Tad shrugged. 'Caleb was taking us to Yar-Rin and then down into Kesh to find us crafts that we could apprentice. If he couldn't place us together, there, he was going to take us up to Krondor. He was doing it for our mother.'

Pug stepped forward and said, 'You already know more than you should, just through what you've seen and heard in the last day.' He glanced at his wife and son then added, 'I think we'll give some thought about what to do with you. But in the meantime, why don't you get some rest.' He glanced at Nakor. 'We'll talk in a while, but would you please find them a room, now?'

Nakor nodded and moved quickly to the door, motioning for the boys to follow. Tad and Zane fell in behind.

'I'm Nakor,' said their guide. 'I'm a gambler. Do

either of you know how to play card games?' Both boys said no, and Nakor shook his head. 'I'm getting out of practice. No one on this island plays cards. What do you do?' He glanced over his shoulder as he asked the last question.

Both boys were silent as each waited for the other to speak first. Finally Tad said, 'Things.'

'What things?' asked Nakor as they reached a hallway lined with doors.

'Loading and unloading cargo,' said Zane.

'So you're young stevedores?'

'Not really,' said Zane. 'And we can drive wagons!'

'Teamsters, then?'

'No, not really. But I can sail a boat,' said Tad. 'And we've both done some fishing.'

'I can hunt a little,' said Zane. 'Caleb took me once and showed me how to shoot a bow. He said I had the makings, and I took down a deer by myself!' His pride shone clearly as he walked next to his foster brother.

'I help Fowler Kensey mend nets sometimes,' offered Tad. 'and he showed me how to catch ducks on the lake.'

'And I've helped Ingvar the Smith mend pots,' added Zane. 'He doesn't like to tinker so he showed me. And I know how to bank a forge so the fire's there the next morning, and how to temper steel –' Tad shot him a dubious look '– I've watched him do it often enough!'

Nakor led them into the room, which was empty save for four beds with rolled-up mattresses. 'Well,' he said, 'that's quite an impressive list of skills, far more than most boys your age have.' He waved to them to unroll the mattresses. As they did so, he pointed to a chest near the door and said, 'Blankets are in there. A candle and flint and steel, too, though you'll not need it. I expect you'll be asleep as soon as I close the door. It's three hours to sunrise here, so rest for a while. Someone will come and get you and take you to get something to eat when you wake. I expect you'll be hungry.'

'I'm hungry now,' said Zane with a slight note of complaint.

Tad shook his head slightly.

'But I can wait to eat,' he quickly amended as he went to fetch blankets out of the wicker chest.

As Nakor turned to leave, Tad said, 'Sir, a question.'

'Call me Nakor, not sir. What's the question?'

'Where are we?'

Nakor was silent a moment, then grinned. 'I can't tell you yet. You will know what you may after Pug decides what to do with you.'

'What do you mean, sir – Nakor?' asked Tad.

Nakor lost his smile. 'You boys have seen things and heard things that could get someone else killed.' Tad's face drained of colour and Zane's eyes widened. 'Pug has to decide what we can do with you. Magnus thought you were Caleb's apprentices, which meant certain things. You are not, which means certain other things. I can't be more specific, but soon you will know what Pug wishes.

116

Until then, you are guests, but don't wander off without a guide. Understood?'

Both said, 'Yes,' and Nakor departed.

They went to bed and as they lay down, Tad said, 'Killed?'

'He said someone else, not us.'

'But why?'

'I don't know,' said Zane. 'Caleb's father is powerful, he's a magician like his other son.' Both boys had the usual fear of things magic widespread among the common folk of the region, but it was tempered by the fact they were talking about Caleb's father. In the boys' minds Caleb was like a generous and kind uncle, which would almost make Pug something akin to a grandfather. At least they hoped so.

Zane continued. 'Everyone says that he owns Stardock Island. That would make him a noble of some kind. They have enemies. Nobles fight wars and things.'

Tad laid his head down on his arm. 'I'm tired, but I don't feel sleepy.'

'Well, you heard him; we can't go anywhere. Maybe we should try.'

Tad rolled over on his back and stared upwards in the darkness. 'I wish we were back at Stardock.'

Zane sighed deeply. 'Me, too.'

# CHAPTER 5

# SORCERER'S ISLE

All eyes were on Nakor.

He pulled an orange from his seemingly-bottomless rucksack and offered it first to Miranda, then to Pug, and then to Magnus. All declined. He stuck his thumb into the peel and began to remove it, a process all of them had witnessed a thousand times before.

'Nakor,' said Pug, 'what are you not telling us?'

'Nothing,' said Nakor. 'At least nothing I knew until Magnus arrived.'

'What do you mean?' asked Miranda, sitting on the side of the bed where Caleb lay sleeping.

Pug stood at his younger son's feet and Magnus occupied the other chair in the room.

'You know who the old witch in the village was, yes?' asked Nakor.

'Not really,' said Magnus. 'I've encountered her twice before and all I sense is that she's more than a common purveyor of charms and herbal remedies. There's power there, but it's muted.'

'You said the Goddess called her an echo,' said Miranda. To Nakor she said, 'What does that mean?'

Nakor glanced at Pug who said, 'I think I

understand, or at least, I have a partial under-standing. Tell us what you know.'

Nakor shrugged and his usual happy demeanour vanished. Instead, Pug saw the darkest expression Nakor had ever revealed to him. 'The Gods are beings of vast power,' Nakor began. 'Our under-standing of them is filtered through the limits of our perceptions.' He looked at the other three. 'All of you have been to the Pavilion of the Gods, so you know that it is both a physical place and a metaphor for something much less objective. It is a place of the mind as well as a place of the body.

'When I have encountered beings of a certain type in the past—' He stopped and was silent for a moment as if considering his choice of words, then he resumed. 'I mentioned Zaltais of the Eternal Despair,' he said to Pug, who nodded. 'Do you remember him being cast into a pit – I said he was a dream, remember?'

Pug nodded. 'You've said that each time he's been mentioned, yet you have offered no explanation.'

With a slight smile, Nakor said, 'I assumed, perhaps in error, that you would have gleaned the truth without my having told you since we discussed this all down in Krondor, before the Serpentwar destroyed that city.'

Magnus said, 'This is all new to me, so why not explain it now?'

'The Nameless One sleeps,' Nakor said.

All three knew of Nalar, the Greater God of Evil, who had been cast out by the other Controller

119

Gods, as the Greater Gods were sometimes called. 'That is the legend, anyway,' continued Nakor. 'When the Chaos Wars raged, the Nameless One seduced the Valheru and caused them to rise up and challenge the Lesser Gods, just as he had seduced the Lesser Gods to rise up and challenge the Controllers.'

Magnus said, 'I've studied the lore as much as any outside the priesthood, Nakor. But nowhere have I read about the Nameless One bidding the Lesser Gods to attack the Greater Gods. He was a Greater God. Why would he invite such an attack upon himself as well as the other Greater Gods?'

'To skew the balance,' answered Pug. 'To change the dynamics between the seven Controller Gods.' He looked at Nakor, who nodded, and Pug said, 'Before the Chaos Wars, when the old order died and the new order arose, there were seven Controllers.' He started to count on his fingers, as if emphasizing each in turn. 'The Nameless One, who is the Darkness; Arch-Indar, the Light; Ev-den, the Worker from Within; Abrem-Sev, the Builder; Graff, the Weaver of Desire; Helbinor, the Abstainer, and at the centre, The Balance.'

'Ishap,' supplied Magnus.

Pug nodded, and Nakor resumed. He finished his orange and put the peel into his bag, licked his fingers, and held them up as he counted on them. 'After the Chaos Wars, the balance changed.' He held up one hand, displaying four fingers and a folded thumb. 'Left behind were the Nameless One

120

and the four dynamic gods: Abrem-sev, Ev-den, Graff, and Helbinor.'

He then unfolded his thumb. 'Ishap, in the middle, is the balancer. He is, in a way, the most powerful, for he will add to any side that is disadvantaged, and he will oppose any side that seeks to gain supremacy, always striving to restore the balance.

'All of them are vital to the very existence of our world. One is action, one is reaction, one is higher purpose and mind, and the other is all things unseen and unknowable, but vital to our very being. And the last maintains the balance.'

He put his hands together, his fingertips and thumb forming a circle. 'They are a unity. They form the very fabric of our reality. But they are but expressions of forces. Those forces are vital, dynamic, and they are the expression of even more basic beings.

'The Selfless One, She Who is Light, and the Nameless One, He Who is Darkness, are the sources of those two basic powers. The Good Goddess died in the Chaos Wars, and the other five Controllers were forced to imprison the Dark One in another realm, under a mountain so vast that this entire world could rest upon a ledge on its peak.

'There he slumbers.' Nakor looked around. 'Zaltais was one of his dreams.'

Pug said, 'I thought I understood, but I didn't.'

'If one lies in a prison, might one not dream of a surrogate, a ruler who sits on a throne in a distant place and who can command armies to free the prisoner?'

Miranda said, 'Zaltais was trying to raise an army to storm a prison on another plane of reality?'

'No, it's just a metaphor,' said Pug.

'Everything is a metaphor,' said Nakor. 'The witch is but an echo of the Good Goddess.'

Magnus said, 'Wait. The old woman I encountered in the Pavilion may have been such, but the village witch is a real person.'

'Undoubtedly,' agreed Nakor. 'The gods will often place a tiny fragment of themselves within a mortal. It is how they learn to manifest their roles in this world, to understand fully their obligation to their worshippers. When the mortal dies, the spark returns to the god.

'The relationship between gods and humanity is complex. The gods are also manifestations of how humanity sees them. Ban-ath here in Midkemia and Kalkin in Novindus are essentially the same, yet they manifest differently, with slightly different charges and natures.'

'So the old witch has a divine spark within her?' asked Magnus.

'Just so,' said Nakor. 'Arch-Indar is dead as we understand such things, but her power was so vast, so profound and fundamental, that even ages after her death the echoes of her being still influence us.'

'Is that why you started that religion down in Krondor?' asked Miranda.

'I didn't start it,' answered Nakor. 'I only resurrected it. When the avatar appeared, I knew that eventually goodness will return. When that young girl, Aleta, started manifesting all those abilities, I knew that it was the right choice.

'When it does, the other Controllers will release the Nameless One from his prison and return the order of our world to its proper place. Without Arch-Indar to offset his evil, the Nameless One must stay imprisoned.

'Remember that Ishap is also "dead", but his followers have retained considerable power, some from the other Controllers, but some simply from the memory of the Balancer. He'll return before the Good Goddess because his temple has been restored for a longer time, and the one I reinstituted is still very young. But, when Ishap's back, and Arch-Indar eventually returns, then the other Controllers can release the Nameless One from his prison, and return the order of our world to its proper place. Without her to offset his evil, the Nameless One must stay imprisoned.'

'And having worshippers will cause that?' asked Magnus.

'Eventually,' said Nakor with a shrug. 'How long is anyone's guess.'

'Centuries,' said Miranda.

'If we're lucky,' said Nakor. 'It could be longer. Certainly it's unlikely that any of us will live long enough to see it – and we're all going to live a lot longer than most!' he added with a grin.

Magnus sighed loudly. 'You speak of centuries into the future, longer perhaps; what has this to do with our current situation?'

Nakor put both palms out and gave a dramatic shrug. 'I have no idea.' He looked at Pug. 'Do you?'

Pug nodded. 'A little. One of our problems is that the Nameless One still impacts on our world, even if it is over a vast distance and only indirectly. The Good Goddess may have left her echoes and memories, but she has no direct impact on this world, even on the level that her opponent does. So, in a way, we are her agents, attempting to counteract those who are being influenced by the Nameless One.

'I doubt that our old nemesis, Leso Varen, has even the most remote idea when he became a thing of evil. Perhaps it was something that he chose – striking a deal for power in exchange for service.'

'He may not even realise who he serves,' suggested Nakor. 'Remember that situation with the Tear of the Gods?'

Pug's expression darkened. 'I had a long and heated discussion with Arutha about not letting me know about that until after the matter was decided.'

Nakor nodded. He knew the story, but hadn't been directly involved. And he also knew it was a painful subject because William, Pug's eldest child, and Jezhara, one of his better students, had been at the centre of the confrontation.

They, along with the man who would later become Duke James of Krondor, had managed to thwart Varen and his agents in their attempt to steal the Tear of the Gods – the artefact that allowed the temples to communicate with their deity.

Nakor continued. 'We will never fully know some aspects of that story. From what we do know, the man called The Bear was acting on his own. He had ceased taking instructions from Varen, and that's one hallmark of those serving the Nameless One; they are often mad and go off at . . . whim and wreak havoc even among their own allies.

'That's one of our few advantages; the Conclave are united and even those who view us with some suspicion – such as the temples or the magicians at Stardock – don't interfere with what we're doing.'

'They don't know what we are doing,' offered Magnus.

Pug laughed indulgently. 'Do not underestimate them, son, nor attach too great an importance to ourselves. The temples and monarchs have a very good idea what we are about, else they might be less cooperative than they have been.'

Nakor laughed as well. 'When the day comes that we must confront the agents of the Nameless One, we may have great need of these people you disdain.'

Magnus had the good grace to look crestfallen.

Nakor continued. 'What troubles me is that these manifestations of godpower, these dreams and echoes and memories, are now appearing with more frequency. At least a dozen strange incidents that our agents have reported since the Serpentwar lead me to believe this is so.'

'What do you think it means?' asked Miranda.

'That something is coming. Something that is tied to the slumbering enemy.'

Pug looked at Nakor. 'The Dasati?'

'It was the Nameless One who influenced the Pantathians to bring the Saaur through the rift to our world. We know it was a ruse to loose demons here.

'Destruction and chaos are the Nameless One's allies. He has no cares for the short-term effects on this world, so long as horrors and evil are visited on people and his powers rise. I can only guess,' said Nakor, 'but I think he dreams of supremacy, else why try to establish Zaltais on a throne, instead of the Emerald Queen? He needed his surrogate, his dream being, in control, so he could hasten his return to this reality. He seeks to put himself above the other Controller Gods before they can return the balance.'

'Madness,' said Magnus.

'By its nature, evil is madness,' replied Nakor. 'Hence the Days of the Mad Gods' Rage.'

'The Chaos Wars,' said Pug.

Magnus said, 'So we must struggle and die and our children are to struggle and die after us?'

'Perhaps,' said Nakor. 'We may never know a moment of transcendent triumph, a time when we can say, "the day is ours!" and know the struggle has passed forever.

'Think of us as ants, if you will. We must topple a mighty citadel, a monstrous thing of stone and mortar, and we have only our naked bodies to spend in the effort.

'So we labour for years, centuries, millennia, even epochs; scraping away at stone with our tiny jaws. Thousands, tens of thousands, millions of us die, and slowly the stones begin to crumble.

'But, if we have a design, and possess knowledge, we can choose where to bite. We will not trouble all the stones, merely the keystone upon which all the others rest. And then we may wear away at the mortar around that stone, so that at last, the stone can be pushed aside, and once that is accomplished the massive stones above begin to move, and over time, fall.

'No, *we* may never see an end to this struggle, but in time the Good Goddess and the Nameless One may return, and the balance would be restored.'

'What sort of world would that be?' wondered Magnus.

'One with less strife, I hope,' said Miranda.

'Perhaps,' said Nakor. 'But even if it is not, the strife will be far more prosaic. What we do now is contest with worlds hanging in the balance.'

Magnus looked down at his younger brother. 'And the price of defeat is too grim to contemplate.'

Pug looked at his two sons and his wife, then said, 'As well I know.'

No one needed to say more, they all knew that Pug's first two children had died during the Serpentwar and that the loss was still bitter to him.

Nakor stood and said, 'We should go. I'll send messages to our agents in the region to see if the attack on Caleb was part of a greater design or merely an unhappy accident.'

'Wait a moment, Nakor,' asked Pug, as Miranda and Magnus left. 'McGrudder was right we should move him?'

'No,' said Pug. 'I think we leave him in place. If these are bandits alone, then no harm has been done. If those who attacked Caleb are Varen's agents, let them believe they gulled us into thinking the attack was by mere bandits. If McGrudder comes under scrutiny, it should not be hard to discern in so small a place; we can always dispatch a watcher to watch the watchers.'

Nakor nodded with a grin. This was the sort of underhanded plotting that appealed to him.

'There is another matter,' said Pug.

'What is it?'

'I received a message yesterday and I am greatly concerned about it. Will you give me your thoughts?'

'Always.'

Pug produced a scroll from inside the folds of his robe and Nakor glanced at it.

Pug said. 'It's not the first. They have been appearing on my desk from time to time for years now.'

'How long?'

'Since before we met. The first one gave me the instruction to tell Jimmy to say to you—'

'There is no magic,' finished Nakor. 'I know. When I heard that, and from a magician no less, I knew I had to come to Stardock.' He looked at the scroll again. 'Where are they coming from?'

'Not where, but when. These are from our future.'

Nakor nodded, then his eyes widened as he read it again. 'This is . . . from you!' he said, and for the first time since Pug had met him, the small Isalani was speechless.

Tad lay on the bed with his arm behind his head as Zane paced the floor. 'You're going to wear a groove in the stone if you keep that up,' he said.

'I can't help it. Someone brings us our food this morning, and we're told to wait. Then lunch. Then someone comes to fetch the chamber pot and bring us a clean one, and now it's almost suppertime and still no one has come to tell us what we're doing here.'

'It's obvious what we're doing here,' said Tad. 'We're waiting. What we don't know is what we're waiting for.'

Zane's expression darkened, and Tad sat up on the bed. He knew that look. Zane was a thin excuse away from taking out his bad mood on his foster brother.

Just as Tad sat up, anticipating Zane's pre-emptive attack, Nakor appeared at the door and said, 'You two, come with me.'

He left so abruptly that Tad almost unbalanced

129

himself trying to hurry after him. He caught up with Zane and the Isalani halfway down the hall and thought it odd how fast the little man walked.

'Don't stare,' Nakor said.

A moment later, Tad hit a doorjamb. He had just walked past a large open door that led into a courtyard dominated by a huge pool. At the edge of the pool and in the water was a group of young women. Tad's attention was diverted in equal measure by the fact that all the girls were remarkably beautiful, completely naked, and their skin was a pale green and their hair the colour of bronze wire.

Tad suffered another injury as he stepped backwards only to be knocked down as Zane turned around and came flying back to the doorway to verify if he had indeed witnessed the same scene.

The girls turned to stare at them and both boys realized that they had no irises and their eyes were pearl-white in colour.

Nakor helped Tad to his feet with one hand, and waved to the girls with the other. 'I told you not to stare,' he said, as Tad touched his nose to see if it was bleeding. 'Come along.'

Tad said, 'Ah . . .'

Nakor said, 'They are six sisters of the Pithirendar. They don't care for clothing much and they spend a great deal of time in water. They are not entirely human. Though they are human enough to get you boys into trouble, so stay away from them or I'll give you even more to think about.'

'Not human . . .' Zane muttered, trying to convince himself that his eyes hadn't betrayed him. Tad reached out and half-dragged him away from the door as they both followed Nakor.

They turned a corner and Nakor motioned them to stand to one side. A thing – for lack of a better word – came lumbering down the corridor towards them. It was half the height of the boys and twice as wide. It looked like a table with a black cloth hanging over it and it moved on legs that resembled a crab's. It also made an odd murmuring sound as it approached.

As it passed, Nakor said, 'Good morning,' and the thing answered in a surprisingly normal-sounding female voice.

After she had moved around the corner, Tad whispered, 'What was that?'

'A visitor,' Nakor replied. He led them to a room where Pug sat waiting behind a desk.

The short magician rose and motioned for them to sit in a pair of chairs that were opposite his own.

They did so and Pug returned to his seat. Nakor stood by a window to Pug's left. Looking at the two young men, Pug said, 'We're at something of a loss about what to do with you.'

Tad's face drained of colour and Zane flushed. He said, 'What do you mean, "do with you", sir?'

Pug smiled. 'No harm will come to you, if that's what concerns you.' He sat back and regarded the pair. 'You may have already concluded that this community is unlike any others.'

Zane just nodded, while Tad said, 'Yes, sir.'

Nakor laughed. 'You seem to be handling it well.'

Zane shrugged. 'I'm not exactly sure what to think, but Caleb has always been good to our mother and to Tad and me, so if you're his family, then I suppose . . . well, I think we're safe here.'

Pug sat back. 'I don't pry in the lives of my children, but tell me something about your mother.'

Tad spoke up as Marie was his real mother, though she treated Zane as his equal. He started off with the usual praise – that she was a good cook and kept the poor hut that served as home as clean as could be – but after a moment it was clear to everyone that the boy not only loved his mother, but respected her too. 'It was hard after Papa died.' He glanced at Zane. 'But she took Zane in because he was my best friend and had no one else, when others in town looked the other way. She made do, and kept us both out of trouble.'

Zane added, 'I've known her longer than I knew my real ma, so I suppose that makes her my real ma, if you understand, sir. She never took sides with Tad against me and she held me when I was a little boy. She loved me like I was her own.'

Pug sighed. 'Even without meeting her, I can understand why my son cares for your mother, boys, and I can see why he cares about you. You acted bravely going back to the wagon.'

Nakor said, 'Foolishly, from what you told me. Didn't Caleb tell you to make your way to the village if you eluded the bandits?'

'Yes,' said Tad. 'That's true, but we had killed two of them already, and thought maybe Caleb could use some help. We had gained two swords by then.'

Pug shook his head. 'And I for one am glad you disobeyed, and admire your resolve, for had you not done so, I'd have lost my youngest child.' His eyes grew unfocused for a minute as he looked away, seeing something in the distance, and he said, 'It's something I dread more than you can ever imagine.' He then turned to face the boys again and asked, 'So, then, what shall we do with you?'

'Caleb was taking us to Kesh to become apprentices, or on to Krondor, for there's no work at home,' said Zane. 'If you need any apprentices, we're willing.'

'Are you willing, Tad?' asked Pug.

'Yes, sir,' he said, nodding his head.

'We do have need for apprentices,' said Pug. 'But first we shall see if you're up to such a calling.'

Pug stood and so the boys did as well. He pointed to his friend and said, 'Nakor shall see to your instruction for a few days while my son heals, then I have other work for him, and then we shall have others test you. Now, I have work to do, so be off with you.'

They left, and Tad grinned at his friend. Their fears were now replaced with hope, for they had taken Nakor's intimation that they might be killed for what they knew seriously.

As they walked down the hallway, Tad asked, 'Nakor, what trade are we going to apprentice to?'

'That remains to be seen, my young friend,' said Nakor. 'I'm not sure we have a name for what you might do. Let's say that you'll be apprentice workers.'

'What sort of work?' asked Zane.

'All manner and type. Things you cannot even imagine. For if you are to become workers for the Conclave of Shadows, it is more than just a trade.' With a suddenly serious expression he said, 'It's a lifelong commitment.'

Both boys were unsure what that meant, but Nakor's expression told them they were not going to be happy about finding out.

# CHAPTER 6

# APPRENTICES

Zane's face was flushed with anger.

'I won't do it!' he said, defiance reverberating in his voice.

Tad said, 'You have to. If you don't, you'll get into more trouble than you can imagine.'

'It's stupid,' Zane insisted. 'If I haven't learnt by now, I never will.'

'You've lived on the shore of a lake for your entire life and you've never learnt to swim,' said Tad, his voice rising in frustration. 'That's stupid!' he shouted. 'Now, Nakor says you have to learn how to swim.'

The boys were standing near a tree at the edge of the courtyard lake. Other students were splashing in the shallows, and a few were swimming in the deeper water. Tad had always been a decent swimmer, but Zane had never learned. It took this recalcitrance to remind Tad that he had never seen his foster brother swim.

Just then the six sisters of the Pithirendar came over the hill, speaking softly in their alien language. Both boys had become accustomed to the strange nature of many of those residing on what they now

135

knew to be Sorcerer's Island. While the inhabitants included a number of very strange aliens, the majority were human, including a few human girls with whom the boys had become friendly. But for some reason the six sisters caused a reaction in most of the young males on the island, Tad and Zane being no exception.

Four of the girls were nude – as was their preference – while the other two wore simple white shifts, which they discarded when they reached the shore. The six of them slipped effortlessly into the water, as Tad said, 'All right, then. Stay here if you want, but I'm going swimming!'

Zane was on his feet saying, 'Maybe you're right. Maybe it's time to learn.' He hurried after his foster brother and splashed into the water.

Nakor and Caleb watched them from a short distance away. Caleb asked, 'How are they doing?'

Nakor shrugged. 'They're good lads, but if it hadn't been for your unfortunate accident with the bandits, they never would have come here. They possess no special abilities, gifts, or talents that we can see.'

'Except they are good lads,' said Caleb.

'We have good lads in abundance,' said Nakor. 'What we need are some ruthless bastards who will happily cut the heart out of their own mothers if need be.' He started walking away from the lake shore as the boys splashed and were splashed in return by the Pithirendari girls. Caleb fell into step beside him. They began the long trek from the lakeshore to the villa.

Caleb's wounds had almost healed completely and he was now moving around with the only the minimum of discomfort. 'You know, if my father wasn't who he is, I would also be merely a 'good lad'.

'You have a great deal of special ability,' said Nakor.

'Such as?'

'You're a remarkable hunter, have uncommon tracking and woodcraft abilities, close to those of the elves.'

'As would any youngster with a little talent who had been sent to live with the elves, Nakor.' He looked around the island and said, 'Do you see many skilled hunters here?'

Nakor remained silent.

'We both know that one of the reasons I was sent to stay with Tomas in Elvandar was my unhappiness here. Father thought a change would do me good, and he was right. There's a difference between being the only human boy among elves and being treated with respect, to being the only youngster without magical abilities among magic users and being treated with contempt.'

'Contempt is too harsh a word, Caleb.'

Caleb looked at Nakor. 'You weren't always there, nor was Father. Mother saw, and she tried to shield me, as did Magnus, but children can be cruel, Nakor. You want your heartless bastards, get them when they are children and don't let them learn compassion.'

'You sound bitter,' said Nakor as they approached the cookhouse.

'Do I?' Caleb shrugged. 'I don't feel bitter, but I guess some wounds, even childish wounds, never heal. They just grow faint.'

'What is truly troubling you, Caleb?'

They passed the cookhouse and continued on to the main building of Villa Beata. 'I feel useless, and in the wrong place.' Caleb stopped as they reached the open doorway into the connecting hall. 'I'm a messenger for the most part, carrying missives that aren't important enough for Magnus or yourself or any magic-user transport.

'I know that I can blend in where Magnus can't, but other than that, what use am I?'

Nakor began to say something, but Caleb held up his hand. His brown eyes were set in a serious expression and his voice held a tinge of anger. 'Do you think if Tal Hawkins or Kaspar of Olasko had been in that wagon they'd have borne a scratch after dispatching those bandits?'

Nakor remained silent.

'I'm an adequate swordsman, Nakor. Better than average, but not remarkable. I am a good hunter – perhaps even a great one – but how useful is that in dealing with our enemies? So, I can scout. So can a lot of other men.

'My point is, there is nothing special for me to do, nothing that lets me pull my own weight.'

Nakor shook his head and put his hand on Caleb's shoulder 'My young friend, how wrong you are. The day will come when you will understand your true potential, Caleb, and finally realize just how special you are. Until then, if you want to feel sorry for yourself, feel free. I just don't have time to stand around and listen.' With that, he turned and walked off.

Caleb stood for a minute locked in inner conflict. Then, he started to chuckle, and that became a full-blown laugh. Talking to Nakor always lifted his dark moods. Caleb decided to return to his quarters to rest and give some thought to what he was going to do with Tad and Zane.

Zane lay on the shore, coughing and trying hard not to look ridiculous. Tad helped him to sit up and said, 'If you're going to wade out over your head, you should at least learn how to paddle.'

Zane spat water and coughed some more. Then he said, 'I got distracted.'

'He is all right?' asked one of the sisters from behind Tad. The six of them were gathered as were other students, all looking on with a mixture of concern and amusement.

'He'll live,' said Tad, pulling his friend to his feet. The sisters whispered and giggled, then fled back to the water. 'What were you trying to do?' asked Tad.

Zane spoke while his eyes followed the retreating backs of the sisters. 'One of them . . . Zadrina, I think, pulled me out and kissed me.'

'I can't tell them apart,' said Tad. 'And they'll all kiss you if you let them.'

'But this was a kiss! She really kissed me.'

'And then you opened your eyes and discovered you were under water?'

Nodding his head, Zane echoed, 'I opened my eyes and discovered I was under water.'

'Which is when the drowning started.'

'Which is when the drowning started,' agreed Zane.

'I am going to have to teach you to swim.'

'Soon,' said Zane, watching the girls splashing with some of the other boys. 'But not today. I drank enough of the lake so I may never be thirsty again.'

'Well, let's head back.' Tad looked in the direction of the villa. 'Caleb and Nakor were talking just before we went swimming. I wonder if they've decided what to do with us?'

'Well,' said Zane. 'Whatever they decide I hope they wait until tomorrow, because I'm supposed to meet Zadrina after evening meal in the pool garden.'

Slapping his foster brother on the shoulder, he said, 'Just don't drown yourself.'

'I won't.' As they walked towards the villa, Zane said, 'Do you know they come from a world that's mostly water? That's why they're in it most of the day.'

'I'm still having trouble imagining another world,' conceded Tad.

'Worlds,' said Zane. 'I would too, but everyone here takes it as a matter of course, so I'm getting used to the idea.' He looked around as they walked. 'When we were boys, it was easy to think of Kesh and the Kingdom, because people from both nations passed through the town all the time, but other nations were hard for me to imagine. This is like that, I think, only more so.' He glanced at Tad. 'If that makes sense?'

Tad nodded he understood.

They hadn't quite reached the main building when a slender man wearing a pair of tights and a billowing shirt appeared from out of a doorway and said, 'Ah! There you are. You are the two boys from Stardock?' He didn't wait for an answer but motioned them to follow. He moved like a dancer or acrobat, fluidly and with an economy of motion, and on his feet were ankle-high boots of odd design, cross-gartered at the top and tied above the anklebone, but with soft soles of what looked to be doubly reinforced leather. His hair was the palest blond, and flowed to his shoulders.

They went to the side of the village opposite the small lake, and he looked over his shoulder, once, regarded them for a moment with pale blue eyes, then said, 'Don't fall behind.'

The boys found themselves climbing a path up a ridge, and by the time they reached the crest, they were almost breathless. The man who led them didn't pause, simply saying, 'No time to rest now, boys.'

Tad and Zane as one took a deep breath and followed after, heading down a steep path that led to the seashore. Off to the left they could see a black edifice rising from a promontory. 'What's that?' wondered Zane.

'The castle of the Black Sorcerer,' answered the man.

'Who's the Black Sorcerer?' asked Tad.

The man looked over his shoulder, grinning. His face looked young, perhaps only a few years older than the boys, but his blond hair was shot through with grey. 'Pug's the Black Sorcerer when he's here. If he's not, then sometimes Nakor, or Magnus, or Miranda, or someone else. It's whoever's handy.'

Tad said, 'I don't understand,' and he stopped, to catch his breath. 'Can you wait a minute?'

The man stopped and said, 'Winded? At your age?'

Zane also stopped. 'That was a long climb.'

'That was nothing,' said the man. 'Wait until I get done with you; you'll be running up and down those paths without thought.'

'The Black Sorcerer,' said Tad between breaths, pointing at the castle.

'Well, you boys know about the Black Sorcerer, of course . . .'

'No,' interrupted Zane. 'We don't. That's why we're asking.'

'I thought everyone on the Bitter Sea knew about the Black Sorcerer,' said the man.

'We're not from the Bitter Sea,' said Tad. 'We're from Stardock.'

'Ah,' said the man, nodding as if he understood. 'Stardock.' He turned. 'Come along; rest is over.'

The boys took deep breaths and hurried after the rapidly walking man. 'There used to be a man who lived up there,' he said, 'by name Macros. He started the legend of the Black Sorcerer so people would leave him alone. He left this island to Pug, who continues the legend, so that ships are not likely to put in here. It keeps things relatively quiet.'

As they headed down towards the beach, they came to a path leading from the castle that intercepted their own. 'If you go that way,' said the man, 'you'll go straight to the castle. It's empty. It's a pretty drab and uninviting place, though we brighten up the windows with some interesting lights if we think someone's spying on us.' He looked back grinning. 'Good show.' Turning his attention downhill, he said, 'Now, here's what I want you two to do,' as they reached the sand. He pointed to a distant point on the beach where large rocks hid the curving shoreline. 'Run that way, very fast. Go to that rock. Then run back here.'

Tad could barely stand. 'Who are you?'

The man put his hands on his hips. 'Tilenbrook, Farsez Tilenbrook. I am to be your tutor in all things physical for a while. You two have grown lazy and are unfit for the rigours you may face as Caleb's apprentices.'

The boys exchanged glances. 'We're to be his apprentices?' asked Zane.

'Perhaps you are. Now run!'

The boys set off at a slow run, still fatigued by the hike over the ridge. Farsez stood patiently waiting as they half-ran, half-stumbled down to the distant rock, then turned and started running back. When they reached his position, both boys fell to their knees on the sand, Zane then half-rolling, falling onto his back as they panted for breath. 'My,' said Tilenbrook, 'you two are in the most deplorable condition for boys. Comes from lazing about all day with nothing to do, I wager.

'Now, get up!'

The boys staggered to their feet. 'A quick march back to the villa!'

He set off at a brisk pace, not looking backward, and the boys groaned as they moved after him.

Nearly an hour later two very tired boys, drenched with perspiration, stumbled down the hill to the village, where sat Tilenbrook waiting on the low stone garden wall, a large mug of something in his hand. He sipped at it as they came to stand before him. He glanced at the angle of the sun and said, 'Very well. We are done for today. We shall do this again tomorrow, and every day after until I think you've achieved a speed to and from the rock that I deem appropriate.'

Tad and Zane looked at one another, then Zane closed his eyes as he leaned forward, hands above his knees. Tad tried to ease his aching body by just walking in circles.

As Tilenbrook dismounted the wall, he said, 'I will see you two as soon as you've finished your morning meal, right here.' He then left without another word.

Zane looked over at Tad and said, 'I think I'll just kill myself now.'

Tad nodded and started slowly walking back

towards their room. When they reached their room, Tad made a show of sniffing and said, 'If you're meeting one of the sisters after the meal, I suggest you bathe.'

Zane groaned. 'I forgot.' He stood while Tad threw himself across his bed. 'Let's go to the lake, now.'

'What about supper?'

'Are you hungry?'

'Not really,' said Tad.

'Good. Then teach me to swim and let me wash the stink off.'

With an audible protest, Tad forced himself upwards and said, 'Get clean clothes, at least.'

Both boys did and headed out the door of the room, Tad saying, 'Grab a bar of soap at the bathhouse.'

They reached the bathhouse and found it empty as they expected this close to the evening meal. It was a three-chambered structure with a room of very hot, warm, and cold water. There was some ritual of bathing Nakor had explained to them, but both boys just washed off in a bucket and then soaked in the hot tub when they cleaned themselves off.

Looking at one another, Zane said, 'The lake can wait until tomorrow.'

They quickly stripped off their clothing, filled buckets with warm water, and washed off the grime of the day. When done, they both stepped into the hot water and with audible sighs of relief let the heat sink into their tired muscles. The water was kept hot, as the centre room – the *tepidarium* – was kept warm by running water pipes through the kitchen, where fires burned day and night as cooking was a constant undertaking for the population of Sorcerer's Isle.

Within minutes both boys dozed off.

Abruptly Zane came awake to see a beautiful face inches from his own. Eyes that looked white in the distance, but this close revealed pale green flecks, set in a darker green face lit up with delight as an exotic voice whispered, 'There you are. I was looking for you.'

Zane ran his hand over his face and said, 'I must have fallen asleep.' His eyes widened as the girl's hand ran down his chest and stomach and she leaned in to kiss him.

Over her shoulder he could see one of her sisters – he had no idea which one – and saw she was likewise giving Tad what could only be called loving attention. Closing his eyes as he started enjoying sensations that were new and wonderful to him, he silently thought, *I hope this is Zadrina and not one of her sisters.*

For weeks their training followed no pattern that was clear to them, save it often seemed arbitrary, pointless, and exhausting. After two weeks of making the daily run to the rock and finally doing it without slowing the entire way, Tilenbrook sent them back a second time, and then demanded they run up the ridge and back to the villa.

Zane was forced to admit it was getting easier to do and also found he was sleeping better at night. Tad complained he had to find someone to take in the waist of his trousers.

The only happy aspect of their lives were the sisters – Zane with Zadrina and Tad with the one named Kalinda. After the night in the bathhouse, Tad now claimed he had no trouble telling them apart.

Still most of their day was taken up with running, and while they were getting better at it, they saw little purpose to the constant exercise.

Three weeks after the daily running began, they were returning from a run that had to be more than five miles each way, to an outcropping of rocks Tilenbrook had described to them, and found their instructor waiting for them, along with another man. As the now only slightly out-of-breath youths slowed and walked the last few yards, Tilenbrook opened a bundle and threw two swords to them. 'Defend yourselves!' he shouted.

Tad grabbed his sword out of the air but Zane missed his. The second man came at him like an on-rushing bull, holding a wicked looking curved sword. Before he could react, Tad was knocked over by the man's shoulder, while Zane was slapped across the side of the head with the flat of the blade, a blow that sent him to his knees.

'Your enemy will not care if you are tired,' said the bearded man as he grabbed Zane by the tunic, jerked him upright, and put his sword to his throat. With a flick of his wrist, he slapped Tad on the shoulder, hard, with the blade's flat, and said, 'You both are now dead.'

Tilenbrook said, 'This is Bolden. He will be your instructor for a while. My work is done now that you two are no longer a pair of slugs.'

'Get to your feet!'

The boys did so as Tilenbrook walked back towards the path to the village. 'Do you know what separates the living and the dead most times in battle?' asked Bolden.

Zane put a hand to the side of his head, where his sore ear was still ringing from the blow. 'No,' he said, rubbing his cheek.

'Purpose,' said the heavy-shouldered man. His dark eyes regarded the boys. 'A warrior is little more than a man with a sword and a purpose. And no hesitation. You both are dead because you hesitated. If I had attacked two experienced warriors, I would now be the one with the sore head – or I'd be dead.'

He motioned to the two swords that lay on the sand. 'Pick them up.'

They did and suddenly he was attacking again. Once more they were quickly disarmed. 'You are both dead, again!'

He motioned for the boys to once again pick up their weapons and said, 'Do you know why a few armed men can control much larger groups?'

Tad said, 'Purpose?'

Bolden nodded. 'The frightened man runs, tries to hide, or just surrenders. Most men are frightened.' He motioned for them to follow as he turned and started walking back to the village. 'Other men attempt to reason and are dead before they can make their argument. A half-dozen bandits can destroy a village of two score people, or more, because they have purpose and the villagers are frightened or try to reason.

'If the villagers had purpose, if they acted without thought, the six bandits would be dead men.'

Reaching the base of the trail up the ridge, he said, 'Hold your sword and keep it with you, no matter what else. If I see either one of you anywhere in the village without that sword, I will beat you. Understood?'

'Yes,' said the boys.

They walked back to the village in silence.

Bolden, a man of his word, had thrashed Zane once and Tad twice in the following weeks. The last had been the most humiliating, as he had been found swimming in the lake with Kalinda, the sword lying on the shore next to their clothing.

The weapons study proved difficult, due more to Bolden's demands on how they act and think than on any physical requirements. Any hesitation, any lack of certainty in responding to his orders brought punishment, from sitting alone all night on a rock overlooking the sea, to being beaten with a stick.

And for days on end they saw nothing of Caleb.

The other tasks set to them seemed a little more reasonable, but not much. Both boys learned to handle the bow with some skill and were taught the rudiments of tracking game and recognizing signs in the woods, learning from a man named Lear. They used their prior experience to good effect helping with the gardening, farming crops on the far side of the island, and tending to the animals.

But some of the things they did made no sense to them. When they helped in the kitchen, they were forced to endure long lectures on how dishes were prepared, and when they were given household duty, they were expected to master every aspect of tasks from bed making to cleaning out bedpans. Both boys thought of these things as 'woman's work' and grumbled, until Zane said something to one of the girl students, a fetching redhead named Brunella, who promptly smacked him across the back of the head and walked off.

Today the boys were wondering aloud what gods they had offended lately, as they hauled stones up the path from the beach to a place designated by a dour man named Nasur. He was squat, had powerful shoulders, and a mass of thick, black hair and a beard to match. He had appeared that morning after the first meal and informed them he would be overseeing their training for a while.

He had taken them over the ridge and pointed to a crumbling rock wall that flanked the path leading to the castle, then to where piles of them rested at the bottom of the hill. 'They've been washing down the slope for years and Pug thinks we ought to dress up the wall. So be a couple of good lads and hie yourselves down there and fetch the stones back up here. Find a way to place them back so the thing doesn't fall down again come the next rain. Any idiot can use mortar; it takes a good eye to place them so they hold together because of weight and size. I'll be back with something for you to eat come midday. So, get yourself about it.

'Better strip off your tunics so you don't tear them,' he said. They did so, then started with the smaller, more manageable rocks and were now forced to lug larger stones up the hill. The sun was high in the sky and they were certain Nasur had forgotten about them, but as they set the rock gently into place with the others they had lugged upward, he hove to over the ridge.

He carried a large sack and a covered pail. The boys sat down, drenched in their own perspiration, and waited until he reached them. He handed the pail to Tad, who lifted the lid and said, 'Ale!' He took a long pull while Zane opened the bag.

'Food!' said the dark-haired boy. He reached in and pulled out something wrapped in a cloth.

'Called a fist meal,' said Nasur. 'Put some cheese and meat or whatever else you got between two slabs of bread and you can eat without a plate or knife.'

Zane handed one to Tad, pulled out a second and saw there was a third, which he handed to

Nasur. 'These are some chicken and cheese with little slices of cucumber and tomato on 'em,' he said before he took a large bite. 'I put some mustard grain paste on it for spice.' He looked thoroughly pleased with himself. Then he reached for the beer pail, which Tad handed him.

After he drank, he handed the pail to Zane who took a long pull. 'Go easy, boys,' he said, 'wouldn't do for you to get too light-headed. You've still got the best part of a day's work ahead of you.'

Zane rolled his shoulders as if he could ease the ache by stretching them. 'Why the sudden desire to restore this wall, Nasur?'

The bearded man shrugged as he gulped down a mouthful of his meal. 'I don't know. Just something to do, I expect. Keep you two busy and build some muscle on you. Bolden says you're as good as you're going to get with the sword, so no more point in banging you two about. But he said you could be stronger, so I guess that is why you're doing this.'

Tad said nothing while Zane was thoughtful for a moment, then he said, 'Does anyone know what they're going to do with us?'

Nasur said, 'Pug, for certain. Probably Caleb, Miranda, Nakor, and Magnus, too. They're the ones who make decisions around here. Me, I'm just a ward maker. I fashion little trinkets to keep little bad things away. They're used to dealing with big bad things.' He stood up. 'Listen, around here it's wise not to ask questions, in case you don't like the answers. And, you can't tell what you don't know. They'll tell you what's what in time. But know this much: everything they teach you, even if you don't quite know why now, will help some day to keep you alive.' He pointed to the rocks. 'Now, you've got a bit of work to do and you'll do it until the sun vanishes below the western sea, then come back to the villa, clean up and get ready for supper. Right?'

They said right and he vanished over the hill. They finished their meal and looked at the stones at the bottom of the hill and finally Tad said, 'Well, they won't roll up here by themselves, will they?'

'Not unless you've suddenly become a magician,' said Zane as he stood and began to walk down the path.

After they finished the wall, they spent a week clearing a cove of storm debris, and then they were put to the task of painting the villa itself. That took nearly a month, and when they were done, they were sent to the opposite side of the island, where an isolated hut rested on a bluff overlooking the ocean and told to clean it out and repaint it. Zane managed to come crashing through the weather-weakened roof of sticks and thatch, earning himself a new scar in the process, a cut down his left upper arm. Tad dabbed at it and said, 'Get someone to look at it when we get back. It's not bleeding much.'

Zane nodded. Both boys were now sunburned brown and sporting a variety of small scars from scrapes well earned over the last few months. But both had also put on a good deal of muscle – Tad was no longer the whipcord-thin boy from Stardock, and Zane was no longer the stocky lad. They were now both fit and broad of shoulder, with flat stomachs and possessing more arm-strength than they had ever known. They could run far and fast and still arrive ready to fight, and if it came to that, they knew they would act with purpose.

When they were done with the hut, they were turned back over to the care of Tilenbrook, who had recently returned from whatever mysterious mission he had been on.

Their first morning with the slender man, he bid them meet him in an open stretch of grass near the lake, and said, 'It's time for you to learn a bit about fighting.'

Seeing no weapons, Tad said, 'You mean like brawling?'

'A bit more than that, but basically, yes.' He looked at the two boys and said, 'Which one of you lads wishes to be first?'

Tad and Zane glanced at one another, then Tad said, 'You're always the first one to throw a punch. Go ahead.'

Zane smiled and raised his fists, circling to his left, his left fist up beside his head. 'Very good,' said Tilenbrook, moving forward like a dancer. 'The position of your left hand protects your head.' Then suddenly he was driving his left fist under Zane's elbow, knocking the wind out of him and making his knees wobble.

'Of course,' said Tilenbrook, 'you need to learn how to protect your side when you do that.'

He stepped forward to Zane and steadied him, saying, 'Watch me.' He showed the boys how to draw their elbow into their side and bend slightly to take the blow on the arm or hipbone. 'Make your opponent tire himself out flailing at your arms, shoulders and hips. You'll be sore and covered with bruises the next day, but you'll be alive. Your opponent, however, will be heavy of arm and huffing for breath. Because of all your running, you will still have your wind and even if he's a better fighter than you by nature, you should be able to win the brawl.'

He spent the morning showing the boys how to use their fists, then in the afternoon he showed them the true art of brawling: fists, feet, knees, elbows and the forehead butt. 'The eye gouge is especially effective if you can manage to quickly get both thumbs in there, for it leaves your opponent sightless just long enough to effect some serious damage to other parts of his body.' He glanced at the setting sun and said, 'I think we're done now.'

Both boys were exhausted when he was done and as he dismissed them he announced, 'Tomorrow we'll move on to common weapons.'

Tad and Zane looked at one another but each boy was too tired to speak.

The next morning they finished their early meal and reported to the lawn where Tilenbrook was supposed to be waiting for them. Instead they found Caleb, now fully restored from his wounds, who stood with two travel packs at his feet and a third over his shoulder.

'Where's Tilenbrook?' asked Tad.

'About other business,' Caleb answered. 'Your training is going to be cut short, because we have to leave, and this very morning. Grab a pack. Each has shirts, trousers, extra boots, and other items you'll need. We'll get you weapons once we get to the ship.'

'Ship?' asked Tad.

Caleb smiled. 'Sometimes it does well not to arrive by uncommon means.'

As he picked up his pack, Zane asked, 'Where are we bound, Caleb?'

'Kesh.'

'To Yar-Rin?' asked Tad.

'Jonril?' asked Zane.

'No, to the great city itself,' said Caleb as he started walking. 'I'll tell you more once we're under way, but we are heading to Port Vykor, then onward past Stardock – we'll drop in to see your mum – then down into the heart of the Empire.'

'What are we going to do there?' asked Tad.

With no smile, Caleb said, 'That's a long tale to tell and we'll have time on the ship.' Saying nothing more, they marched on.

# CHAPTER 7

# RALAN BEK

Magnus watched thoughtfully.

Three Tsurani magicians gathered around the Talnoy he had brought to Kelewan more than a year before. They all stood in a large chamber set deep in the bowels of the Assembly of Magicians on the Tsurani home-world. Light was provided by a series of magical devices fastened to the walls, as torches tended to fill the air with a haze of smoke.

'We believe we have come to understand the nature of this . . . thing, Magnus,' said a magician named Illianda. 'We have consulted with priests of several orders on the possibility of this crea-ture housing a . . . soul, as you called it.'

Illianda, like his brother magicians, was dressed in a simple black robe. Unlike his brothers he was a tall, thin man. His height approached that of a citizen of the Kingdom, making him very tall for a Tsurani. Since the Riftwar, many Tsurani children had been exhibiting this uncharacteristic height. Illianda's face was smooth shaven, like most Tsurani magicians, and he also shaved his head. His eyes were dark as sable and they were fixed on Magnus as he spoke. 'Our main concern, however, is the problem of this thing acting like a beacon for this other world.'

Fomoine, a stout magician of a more traditional Tsurani stature, said, 'We received a report yesterday of a wild rift located in an isolated valley to the north of the city of Barak in Coltari Province.' Magnus' interest was quickly piqued. 'A herder saw a black rift appear in the sky and a flock of ill-omened birds flew through it. Vile creatures from his description.'

The third magician, Savdari, added, 'One of our brothers transported himself to the valley and found a measure of residual energy from the rift formation. It is certainly not of this level of existence, and must be from this Dasati homeworld of which you have spoken.'

Fomoine said, 'He also found the birds and destroyed them, but not until they had killed several of the herder's needra. Our brother returned with three specimens and the remains are being examined now. These birds from the Dasati homeworld are analogous to the carrion birds of your world – crows I believe you call them – or the janifs here on Kelewan. They are, to say the least, far more aggressive and dangerous than our birds; the herder was forced to hide in a nearby thicket to save his life.'

'This is troubling, indeed,' said Magnus. 'What luck have you had in duplicating the wards against these occurrences?'

158

'Little. We feel humbled, once again, by the work of your legendary grandfather.'

Magnus' eyebrow lifted slightly but otherwise he kept his face expressionless. He always found it nettling to have Macros the Black referred to as his grandfather. Macros had died before Magnus was born, and all he and Caleb knew about the man was what their mother had told them – most of which was hardly flattering. That he was a prodigious practitioner of the magical arts was undoubted, but in many ways he had proved a bigger confidence trickster than Nakor, and was a man who often pushed compassion and ethical considerations aside. By conservative estimates, tens of thousands had died as a result of his manipulations. The debate lay in whether they were necessary sacrifices, or if there could have been other means available to him to achieve the ends he sought? It was the sort of conversation Magnus and his father had enjoyed many times over the years: discussing the consequences of choices made by those with great power.

Magnus knew the official histories of the Kingdom well, and had studied various chronicles from historians in the Free Cities and a few personal journals that had come into Pug's possession, but nothing rivalled the tales about the trials of the Riftwar, told to him and Caleb as boys by his father and Tomas when the boys visited Elvandar.

From time to time, Magnus felt the odd premonition that like his father and grandfather before him, he too would be tested. He feared failing that test, for he knew that like his progenitors, he would not bear the consequences of his choices alone.

Only Magnus' mother seemed able to distance herself from such concerns. Miranda's position had long been that without the Conclave's participation in the conflict between the forces of good and evil, evil stood a far greater chance of reigning unchecked. Magnus tried not to visit that debate too often; he felt that his mother was more like her own father than she cared to admit.

Magnus said, 'It's unfortunate that those who found the Talnoy destroyed most of the warding spells when they removed the thing from its crypt.' He again wondered how the Tsurani Great Ones would feel if they knew that there were an additional ten thousand of the creatures concealed in a vast vault in Novidus. Fortunately, the ward around that chamber was intact. Nakor, Magnus, Pug, and Miranda had all taken turns to study and try to learn Macros' secrets.

Magnus saw the three Great Ones staring at him, as if they expected him to continue, so he said, 'Perhaps my father has gained some insight since last I spoke to him.'

They nodded and Magnus felt frustrated. He had spoken to his father only an hour before coming back to Kelewan, so he doubted that Pug had come to any grand revelation since then. He had seemed more distracted by news coming from Great Kesh, that the Nighthawks were once more manifesting. He sighed. 'I shall consult with him and return here in two days. I know he would want to be informed at once about the new rift you mentioned.'

Illianda stepped forward. 'Please tell him that we think we have made one breakthrough. As I was saying, with the consultation of some of the more powerful priests of a number of temples, we think we can safely say that it is not a soul that empowers these things, but a spirit.'

'I fail to see the difference,' said Magnus.

'For the sake of brevity, we'll avoid most of the lengthy discussion we had with the priests. The soul is a specific quality of mind unique to the individual, and it is the part which flees to the realm of the gods upon the death of the body. The spirit, on the other hand, is a form of life energy and that is what drives the Talnoy.'

Magnus' eyebrows raised and he looked genuinely surprised. 'In other words, they're haunted?'

'The energy that once served the soul is now trapped within the creature. In our own experience, the soul and spirit are inexorably linked, but within these creatures, or rather the creatures who provided the life energy, they appear not to be. In other words, it is, at the heart of things, just another form of energy.'

'And what can we infer from that?'

'Two things,' said Fomoine. 'First, that most priestly arts will avail us little or nothing because we are not truly dealing with a soul—'

Savdari interjected. 'Assuming that creatures of the lower circles have souls as we understand them.'

161

Fomoine threw his companion a dark look. '—therefore, all exorcisms, spiritual banishments and the like, will have no effect on them. It also means that they are mindless objects, and the spell of control used to fashion the ring you provided is truly a marvel of design, for it interprets intent and then translates it into commands for the Talnoy.' His voice dropped, and he added, 'Which means they have magicians of prodigious arts.' Then he smiled. 'But if there is any good to be found in all of this, it is this: because it's a life force, it's limited.'

'Limited?' said Magnus. 'How can that be? The Talnoy has been resting under the hill on my world for thousands of years and is still active.'

Fomoine said, 'It is our considered opinion that as long as none of the life force within the Talnoy is being utilized, it remains in reserve. But as it acts, moves, fights and does whatever it is instructed to do, the life energy runs out, and eventually . . .' He shrugged. '. . . it will stop functioning.'

'How long?' asked Magnus. 'This could be very important.'

'Days, a few weeks at the most,' said Illianda. 'From what you told us, it walked and fought for what must be less than a few hours before you brought it here. Yet we can see a slight weakening in its strength as we have experimented on it. We have used the control ring to test its strengths and abilities and our entire use of it has amounted to less than half a day.'

Magnus was quiet for a moment, then said, 'That would explain Kaspar's report about why the Dasati seem to use their own soldiers in most of their conflicts. These Talnoy must be special assault troops.'

'Their strength is in numbers, they would be nearly invincible for a short while. After that, however, I think they could be easily neutralized.'

Magnus nodded. 'I can think of several ways to do that.' He turned towards the doorway and said, 'I will speak to my parents about the ward and in a day or two one of us will return with more information on the problem. Even if these things are few in number and short in endurance, the Dasati themselves are still a danger that should not be underestimated. We need to discover how Macros hid this thing from detection. Please keep us informed of any new rifts, if you would be so kind. Good day.'

The three magicians bowed as Magnus left, heading for the rift room where he would power up the gateway between Kelewan and Midkemia. Then they returned their attention to the Talnoy. All felt the same thing, there was something about this creature that Magnus was not telling them.

Nakor climbed through the narrow passageway between the outer cave and the vast inner chamber housing the ten thousand Talnoy. A solitary figure stood before him. 'Greetings, Nakor,' said the warrior decked out in white and gold armour.

'Hello, Tomas. I hope your stay hasn't been too tedious.'

The tall warrior nodded and said, 'It brings back old memories. I spent months at a time in deep tunnels with the dwarves of the Grey Towers during the early years of the Riftwar.' He glanced behind him at the row upon row of Talnoy standing motionless, like soldiers at attention, and said, 'Still, there has been a noticeable lack of good conversation for the last few days.'

'Pug appreciates your help,' said Nakor with a grin.

Tomas stiffened and his head came up. 'Do you hear horses?'

Nakor turned and looked towards the light streaming in through the small tunnel. After a moment, he said, 'I do now.' He glanced at the human-turned-Dragon Lord and said, 'Your hearing is excellent.' Tomas moved to investigate the noise, but Nakor said, 'I'll look. You stay here unless there's trouble. It's probably just a few ragged bandits. I'll chase them away.'

Tomas laughed quietly as Nakor departed. Like many others before him, he had discounted Nakor when they had first met. The spindly-legged little man in the tattered robe, with the ever-present leather rucksack, seemed about as menacing as a day-old kitten, but over the years Tomas had discerned something of Nakor's true nature. Now, he was inclined to agree with Pug – that Nakor might be the most dangerous man either of them had ever met.

Still, Tomas was not one to sit idly by if there was trouble approaching, and he was also bored, so he waited for a moment before climbing through the narrow tunnel to the smaller cave where the original Talnoy had been discovered, and waited near the back.

He could see Nakor standing before the cave's entrance as a band of horsemen reined in.

'Hello,' said Nakor with a wide grin, one hand on the rucksack at his left hip, the other waving in greeting. Tomas edged closer so he could see past his friend.

There were five riders, young men with the look of a rag-tag bunch of wild adventurers rather than hardened bandits. They hardly seemed the type to offer real danger, but they were all armed and looked prepared for trouble should they find it.

One rode forward a few feet and laughed. 'You are the most amusing thing I have seen in years, old man. We heard from a wagoner down in Jakalbra that there was a cave up here with treasure in it. So we thought we'd ride up and see for ourselves.'

He was a youngster, only twenty years of age or a bit older, but very broad of shoulders and tall, perhaps nearly as tall as Tomas' six feet, six inches, and he had thickly-muscled arms and neck. He wore leather chest armour and leather riding breeches tucked into leather boots. His arms were bare, except for heavy leather bracelets circling his wrists. Raven hair hung past his shoulders and his ears were bedecked with golden rings. He had eyes the colour of night, set in a handsome face of sun-bronzed skin. And there was something about him that made Tomas draw his sword slowly.

Nakor shrugged. 'If there was any treasure here, do you think I'd be wasting time sheltering myself from the hot sun? No, I'd be living like a raj down in Maharta!' He laughed. 'Treasure? Think on it, my young friend: if that had ever been true, by the time word of it reached you, someone would have already looted this cave.' He turned and indicated with a gesture that the cave was empty.

'Oh, sometimes people miss things,' said the young man. 'I think I'll have a look for myself.'

Nakor stepped nimbly in front of him. 'I don't think you wish to do that.'

'Why not?' asked the young man, drawing his sword.

Tomas stepped into their view and stood barring the entrance. 'Because I would be very annoyed if you tried.'

Nakor stepped to one side, his eyes scanning the area, making certain that he knew where the other four riders were. The young man's companions took one look at the towering presence that was Tomas and suddenly an afternoon's lark became a potentially deadly confrontation. One of the young men nodded to the other three, and they all turned and began riding away.

The young man glanced over his shoulder and laughed. 'Cowards,' he said. He eyed Tomas as he started circling to his left. 'You're a big one, that's for sure.'

During Tomas' boyhood, chance had placed him in a deep cavern where a Valheru, a Dragon Lord, one of the ancient rulers of Triagia world, once resided.

By donning the Valheru's armour – the very suit he wore this day – Tomas' mind and body had been changed, until he had become a living embodiment of that ancient race. The role of consort to the Elf Queen, being a father, and protecting of his adopted people had shaped him far more than the ancient legacy he carried, but it made him no less dangerous. There were perhaps only a dozen men who could face Tomas in combat and survive, and all of them were magic users. Even the finest swordsmen around, such as Talwin Hawkins, might only delay being cut down a few extra minutes.

Nakor turned his attention from the fleeing riders back to the lone youngster approaching Tomas. There was something about him that made Nakor feel uncomfortable. The little Isalani gambler walked over to the young man's horse and took the creature's reins. He led him a short distance away, giving the two combatants more room.

With a slightly mad glint in his eye the young man said, 'You're really going to try to keep me from going in there?'

'I'm not going to try, boy,' said Tomas. 'You will not set foot in that cave.'

'That makes it more difficult for me to believe

there's nothing of value in there worth seeing,' he replied.

'What you choose to believe is of no concern to me,' said Tomas, as he stopped moving and made ready to receive the attack.

With a fluid motion and a speed which Nakor would not have thought possible, the black-haired youth stepped forwards and threw a wicked combination attack that actually caused Tomas to step back. Tomas blocked his blows, but they were fast and hard and he couldn't take his eyes off his opponent.

Nakor felt around and found a short bush to tie off the horse as he kept his eyes fixed on the combat. The young warrior was more than merely a boy. There was an efficiency of strength and motion in his swordplay that outshone even the greatest swordsmen on Midkemia. And more, the ferocity of his blows was actually forcing Tomas to retreat.

The ring of steel on steel was as loud as hammer on anvil, and Nakor knew that this was far more than an ordinary youth they faced. As each second passed, the pitch and intensity of the battle increased, and soon the flow of the combat seemed like nothing but a frenzied assault.

As the youth continued his attack, Nakor suddenly realized what he had been sensing. 'Don't kill him, Tomas. I want to question him!'

Tomas was now hard pressed not to try for a kill, but he shouted, 'I'll try to keep that in mind,

Nakor.' The human-turned-Valheru had greater weapons than the strength of his arms, and he now decided that the contest had gone on long enough.

Tomas had attempted to tire his opponent out at first, having no desire to harm a young man whose only crime appeared to be recklessness. Yet now he was hard pressed to keep an advantage, and the youth seemed to be growing stronger with each passing minute.

Tomas said, 'Enough!' He began to disengage his blade when his opponent followed through. Tomas pushed forwards with all his strength, sliding his own golden blade along the boy's steel so that they stood face to face. Suddenly, Tomas reached out with his left hand and seized the man's right wrist.

Instantly he felt his own right wrist being seized in return, for it was the only move the youngster could make without being defeated quickly. Tomas was surprised by his strength, as it was far greater than that of any human he had faced. But it was still no match for the strength of a Dragon Lord reborn and Tomas used that strength to force the lad backwards.

Then came the instant that Tomas sought: his opponent was off balance In a move so swift that Nakor could hardly credit his senses, Tomas pushed, yanked and twisted his own blade, sending the youth sliding backwards on the seat of his trousers across the ground. His sword tumbled through the air to be caught in Tomas' free hand.

The youngster was halfway to his feet before he

felt two crossed blades pressed against either side of his neck. 'I wouldn't move,' suggested Nakor.

Motionless, the young man looked at each blade, knowing that with one quick slice, Tomas could remove his head from his shoulders as easily as slicing a turnip. His eyes darted from the warrior, to Nakor, and back, and he said, 'I wouldn't dream of it.'

Tomas said, 'Now, if I let you get up are you going to show some manners?'

'Assuredly,' agreed the dark-haired youth.

Nakor came over and as Tomas stood away, the little man asked, 'What is your name?'

The youth, towering over Nakor, looked down and grinned. 'I'm Ralan Bek, little man. Who are you?'

'I am Nakor. I'm a gambler. That is Tomas. He's a Dragon Lord.'

Bek looked at Tomas and laughed. 'As no man has ever bested me with a sword, I'll accede to being bested by a legend. A Dragon Lord? I thought you were beings of myth.'

Tomas raised an eyebrow. 'Only a few know about the myths. Where have you heard of the Valheru?'

Bek shrugged. 'Here and there. From this tale and that. You know, stories around the campfire.'

Nakor said, 'I would like to know more about you and your life.'

Bek laughed again. 'I stand here without a weapon, so I'm inclined to tell you anything you wish to know, little man. Shall we have peace?'

'Peace?' echoed Nakor, looking at Tomas.

Tomas nodded. He reversed Bek's sword and handed it to him. 'Peace.'

The young man re-sheathed it and said, 'So, there is some treasure in there, then?'

Nakor shook his head. 'Gold and gems, no. But there is something of special interest to us and it would bring nothing but ill to anyone else. It is important, but it is also very dangerous.'

'I'll not dispute him again,' said Bek, indicating Tomas, 'just to see if you are lying or not. But what could be more valuable than riches?'

'Knowledge is always valuable,' said Tomas.

'And dangerous, I have found,' said Bek. He motioned to his horse. 'If you have no objection, I should catch up with my companions. They are an unruly and troublesome bunch without me to tell them what to do. Besides, they'll have drunk the inn at Dankino half dry by the time I get there.'

'Actually,' said Nakor, putting his hand on Bek's arm – a soft gesture, but one which stopped the larger man immediately, 'I was wondering if you would care to earn some gold in a more honest fashion than brawling?'

'What do you mean?'

Nakor pointed to Tomas and said, 'He guards the stuff I need to study. If we had another pair of sharp eyes and keen ears here, Tomas could return home and spend some time with his family.'

'Dragon Lords have families?' said Bek, a look of surprise on his face.

Nakor grinned and almost giggled when he said, 'Where do you think little Dragon Lords come from?'

Tomas shook his head, but a warning glance from Nakor kept him silent. He didn't know the Isalani gambler as well as Pug did, but over the years he had developed a respect for his instincts. If the little man wanted Bek to remain, there had to be a good reason.

Bek laughed at Nakor's joke. 'What does it pay?'

'Straight to the point,' said Nakor. 'I like that. We're pretty out-of-the-way here, but as you've just demonstrated, sometimes things happen that you don't anticipate. We'll pay you handsomely.'

'How handsomely?'

'Two gold coins a day, plus food.'

'For how long?'

'For as long as it takes,' responded Nakor.

Bek lost his smile. 'A few coins for a few days work guarding a cave from wild dogs and the occasional bandit is one thing, little man. But I wouldn't welcome camping out here for longer than a week or so, even if I was paid three gold coins a day.'

'You have somewhere else to be?' asked Tomas.

Bek threw back his head and laughed. 'Not particularly, but I always find it difficult to stay in one place for very long. My father used to hunt me down and beat me when he found me.'

Nakor's eyes narrowed at the description. 'You left home when you were, what? Thirteen, fourteen?'

'Thirteen,' said Bek, examining Nakor's face. 'How did you know that?'

'I'm familiar with the story,' said Nakor. 'Would three gold coins a day make you a more patient man?'

Beck shrugged. 'For three, I'll give you a month, but after that I'll want to go somewhere with beautiful whores and good ale to spend it!'

Nakor grinned. 'Done.'

Tomas said, 'Nakor, a word if you please,' and directed the little man to join him on the other side of the cave. Softly, Tomas asked, 'Are you certain you wish to do this?'

Nakor's sunny expression vanished. 'Not wish, must. This lad is . . . not ordinary.'

'I cannot argue with that, Nakor. Of all the mortal swordsmen I have faced, he is easily the most dangerous. There is something supernatural about him.'

'Exactly. His story sounded familiar because it is very similar to my own. I was that boy in a way. I had the same problems staying at home, and my father used to beat me too. I ran away when I was very young. It's – it's all the same!'

Glancing at the young swordsman, then back at the little gambler, he said, 'Not entirely the same.'

'Granted, I became a card cheat and he became a bandit, but the point is we have much in common. And it's the same story that Macros told of his youth. It's too much to be a simple coincidence. I wish to explore that further.'

'There's more, isn't there?'

'You remember the old saying: "*keep your friends close and your enemies closer*", Tomas?'

Tomas said, 'I remember.'

'I think we want this lad to stay very close indeed. If my instincts are not playing me false and there's an advantage to be had from this encounter, I'll find it.'

'No doubt you will. Now, what do you want me to do?'

'Go home for a while. I'll keep an eye on Bek and I'll keep a watch on the cave until Magnus gets back from Kelewan. I have some ideas about how to control those things in there that I want to discuss with him.'

Tomas said, 'Very well. I am pleased to be returning to my queen so soon.'

'Do you need an orb?' Nakor asked as he pulled a shiny metal object from his rucksack and offered it to Tomas.

'Thank you. I could call a dragon to take me, but it does attract notice. And anyway, this is faster,' he said, pressing a button with his thumb before disappearing.

Nakor turned to Bek and said, 'Do you have any food in that saddlebag?'

'Not really.'

Nakor approached the young man and drew a round object out of his sack. Tossing it to Bek, who caught it in the air, he said, 'Want an orange?'

Bek smiled. 'Love one.' He began to peel it with his thumb. 'What do we do now?'

'We wait for some friends. You out here; me in there.' He pointed at the cave mouth.

'One thing,' said Bek.

'What?'

'The three gold. It starts today.'

Nakor shrugged. 'OK, then make yourself useful and get some wood for a fire.'

Bek laughed and turned to hunt firewood.

Bek rose slowly in the darkness and moved without making a sound. He tiptoed around the fire, picking up a small brand of buring wood as he gave Nakor's slumbering form a wide berth. He entered the cave and quickly saw there was nothing inside, save the narrow tunnel.

He entered and quickly found his way to the ledge overhanging the pathway down to the floor of the cavern. Even in the flickering light he could see the motionless Talnoy standing in their ranks.

His eyes widened like a child's as he looked over each black metal warrior in glee. He grinned and whistled softly. 'What have we here?'

Outside the cave, Nakor lay motionless. He had heard Bek enter the cave and knew that the young man would now be looking at the army of Talnoy.

After a few more minutes, he heard Bek return. Nakor was ready to move the instant he felt threatened, and after having seen Bek battle Tomas, he knew there might only be a moment for him to employ his most deadly 'tricks' to protect himself.

But Ralan Bek simply lay down on the other side of the campfire and quickly fell sound asleep. Nakor continued to lie motionless, but he was still awake when the sun rose the next morning.

# CHAPTER 8

# HOMECOMING

The road stretched to the horizon.

Once again, Tad and Zane rode in a cart, as they had almost half a year before. This time however, they were approaching the village of Stardock.

Reaching Shamata, Caleb and the boys had found a shipment of goods that were being sent along the shore of the Sea of Dreams down to the Great Star Lake and the Academy. Caleb had volunteered to take the shipment and arrange for someone to return the wagon to the trading concern when they arrived. As the company was owned by his father, Caleb encountered no objection.

He had told the boys that they would pass through Stardock on their way south, but that they would only stay for one night. Tad rode next to Caleb on the driver's seat, while Zane sat in the back, behind the cargo with his feet hanging over the back of the wagon.

It was late afternoon by the time they reached the outer boundary of Stardock Town. The first of its buildings heaved into sight along the shore of the lake to their left. They had been passing farms for a day now, so they had guessed that they would reach the trading warehouse before sundown.

As they rolled into the outskirts of the township, Tad and Zane waved to a few familiar faces, most of whom stared back vacantly before they recognized the boys. Tad said, 'People are looking at us strangely, Caleb.'

'You've changed, Tad,' answered the tall hunter, now dressed like a driver. The boys wore the same old tunics and trousers they had worn when they left the town half a year before. Both complained frequently that the clothes were too tight, so Caleb had promised to buy them new garments when they reached Kesh.

The boys were off the wagon before it came to a complete halt, and as they started to move away, Caleb halted them. 'Where do you think you're going?'

'To see Mother,' answered Tad.

'Not until you've unloaded,' he said, hiking his thumb at the cargo.

'Grooms and his boys will unload,' said Zane.

'Not this lot,' said Caleb. 'I want you to take the wagon over there—' he pointed to an empty cargo pallet at the edge of the stabling yard, '—and unload everything onto that.'

Both boys knew that meant the cargo was destined for the island. They also remembered loading the wagon, and Tad asked, 'Can we get some help at least?'

Caleb nodded. 'Tell Grooms I'll settle with him later.'

'Where are you going?' asked Tad, as Caleb started to walk away.

Turning to walk backwards, he said, 'To see your mother. I'll tell her you'll be along shortly.'

Tad jumped back up to the driver's seat and moved the team over to the indicated area, while Zane sought out Grooms – the manager of the shipping warehouse – to secure some help in the unloading.

Caleb hurried to Marie's house and found her in the back, tending her garden. Seeing Caleb, she sprang to her feet and embraced him. 'I have missed you,' she said between two passionate kisses. 'It has been so lonely here since you took the boys away.' She hugged him tightly for a moment, then said, 'You said you'd have the boys write,' with a slightly accusatory tone.

'I did,' he answered, pulling a folded sheet of parchment from out of his tunic. With a grin he said, 'But I thought I'd bring it myself rather than send it by courier.'

She kissed him and said, 'Come inside and have some tea and tell me what you did with them.'

He followed her inside and saw that she had a kettle simmering next to the fire. 'I find I do little cooking now that it's just me. I bake just one loaf of bread a week instead of three or four.' She poured tea and said, 'What of the boys?'

'They are well,' he said. 'Much has changed in the six months since we left.'

She sat after she had served them at the tiny table which still managed to occupy nearly a third of the room. 'Tell me.'

'Things didn't turn out quite as I had wished,' he said. 'The apprenticing I had hoped for . . .'

'At least tell me that you've found them honest labour, Caleb. They could become layabouts and wastrels here as easily as anywhere else.'

He smiled. 'Nothing like that.' Then he sighed. 'Currently, they are working as wagoner's lads.'

'Teamsters?' she said, her eyes widening slightly. 'That's strange, neither of them cared much for horses and mules.'

'They still don't, but it's necessary,' said Caleb. He smiled broadly. 'They're over at the warehouse unloading a wagon with some of Grooms' lads. They should be here soon.'

'You wicked man!' Marie cried, hitting him on the arm. 'Why did you wait to tell me?'

'Because I wanted a few minutes alone with you, and once the boys are here I won't be spared more than a few seconds of your time.'

She kissed him. 'They are old enough to understand that their mother needs more than to cook and sew for—'

Her words halted as Tad came in through the door with Zane behind him. When they'd left they had been boys, but in less than half a year, Marie hardly recognized her sons. Both were sunburned, their shoulders had broadened and their faces had lost whatever echoes of childhood she remembered.

Their cheeks were hollow, and the baby fat had been replaced by stubble along their jaws. Below the short sleeves of their tunics, their arms were muscled and their hands hard with calluses.

Marie stood and both boys rushed to embrace her. 'I thought I might never see you two again,' she said, her eyes glowing with moisture. She hugged them tightly, then stepped back. 'You've . . . changed. Both of you.'

'Hard work, Mama,' said Tad. 'I've never worked so hard in my life.'

'What have you been doing?' she asked.

The boys exchanged a quick glance with Caleb, then Tad said, 'Stone work, mostly. A lot of wall-building. Some hunting and fishing.'

'A lot of wagon-driving too, and loading and unloading,' said Zane. 'And I learned how to swim!'

Marie's mouth opened and closed before she said, 'You finally got over your fear of the water?'

Zane blushed. 'I wasn't afraid. I just didn't like it very much.'

Tad sniggered. 'He had a good teacher.'

Zane blushed even more.

Puzzled, Marie looked at Caleb, who said, 'Let's go to the inn and eat.'

'Might as well,' she offered. 'I haven't got enough here to feed you three.' To the boys she said, 'You two hurry ahead and wash up. We'll be along in a minute.'

After they left, she kissed Caleb again, passionately. Then she whispered, 'Thank you.'

'For what?' he replied in a soft voice.

'For looking after them. And for turning them into men.'

'They've a way to go yet,' he said.

'But it's a start,' she said. 'When Tad's father died . . .' She began to weep.

'What is it?'

'Just me being foolish,' she said, forcing back her tears. 'It's just so wonderful to see you all, and so much has changed in so little time.' She waved away the moment and took a deep breath. She preceded him out of the door and he fell into step by her side as they slowly walked to the inn.

He looked at her in the failing afternoon light. 'We'll have a little time tonight, Marie, just the two of us.'

She smiled. 'That is most certain.'

'How have you been getting by?' he asked, noticing that she had lost weight since he had last seen her.

'As always: I sell what I grow, and buy what I need. I take on a little sewing now and again when someone needs help and I am planning to buy some chickens soon so that I can have eggs to eat and perhaps a few to sell.' She hugged his arm. 'I get by.'

He said nothing, but his heart almost broke as he realised what little thought he had given to her needs before he had taken her boys away. He slipped his arm around her slender waist and hugged her as they walked. After a moment of silence, he said,

'Perhaps we can come up with something better than just getting by.'

'What do you mean?'

'Later,' he said as they reached the inn.

Dinner was almost festive. Even though it had only been six months, many of the local towns-people stopped the boys – after a second glance – to welcome them back and remark on how much they had changed. Several girls had also stopped them to let them know that they would be in the square after sundown should the boys happen by.

At supper Marie gently informed the boys that Ellie was due to have a baby in a few months' time. But the pair simply exchanged looks, and burst out laughing.

'What's so funny?' asked their mother.

The boys said nothing. Their feelings for the girl seemed distant now compared to the vivid memories of parting with the sisters. Over a three-day period all six girls had expressed individual regret at the boys' departure in ways that until then, had been beyond either of their imaginations a year earlier.

They hurried through supper, anxious to visit their friends. After they left, Marie looked around the otherwise deserted tap room of the inn and asked, 'Are you staying here tonight?'

Caleb rose and offered his hand. '*We* are staying here. I told the boys to sleep in their old beds tonight.'

Marie said, 'I expect they're old enough to know what's going on.'

'They've known for a long time, Marie. But let's just say that now they have a much fuller understanding.'

'Oh!' she said, as he led her up the stairs to his room. 'You mean—?'

'Yes.'

'They *are* becoming men, aren't they?'

'That's more than any mother should know,' said Caleb as he led her into his room.

The next morning, Caleb and Marie found Tad and Zane asleep in the small hut where they had been raised. Caleb roused them from the pallets with a couple of playful taps from his boot. 'Get up, you two.'

The boys arose with pallid complexions, blood-shot eyes and groans of protest. 'Someone found a bottle of something, it seems,' said Caleb.

'Matthew Conoher and his brother James,' said Zane. 'It was . . . brandy, he said. Tasted more like wood varnish.'

'But you drank it anyway?' said Marie.

'That we did,' said Tad. He stood, stretched and yawned, wearing only his trousers.

His mother looked at her son's chest, stomach, shoulders and arms. 'Where did you get all those scars?' she asked, her voice revealing alarm and her eyes narrowing as she crossed the hut to trace a particularly nasty-looking scar on his right shoulder with her finger.

Tad flinched as her touch tickled him. 'I was

carrying a pretty big stone up the path from the beach and it just got away from me. If I'd have let it go, I would have had to walk all the way back down the path and pick it up again, so I tried to hang on to it and it ripped right though my shirt.'

She glanced at Caleb, then at her son. 'I thought for a minute—'

Tad grinned. 'What? That Caleb had been beating us?'

'Only a little,' said Caleb. 'And only when they needed it.'

'No,' said Marie, her expression slightly petulant as she became annoyed by their teasing. 'I thought that perhaps it was from a weapon.'

Tad brightened. 'Not that one.' He pointed to another faint scar along his rib cage. 'Now, this one was from a sword!'

'A sword!' exclaimed his mother.

'I've got one, too,' Zane said, pointing to a long mark across his forearm. 'Tad gave me that when I didn't get my blade around fast enough on a parry.'

'You two,' she said firmly, pointing to the boys. 'Get dressed.' Turning she said, 'Caleb, outside.'

She led him out of the hut and said, 'What have you done to my boys?'

Caleb shook his head slightly and said, 'Exactly what you thanked me for last night, Marie. I'm turning them into men. Things didn't happen exactly the way I wanted . . .' He paused for a moment. 'Let me tell you about the ambush.'

Caleb told her about the ambush, without glossing

over how injured he had been nor overstating how resourceful the boys had proved. He told it as calmly as he could. 'So, when it became clear that my father thought they were my apprentices anyway . . . well, let's say we were too far down a particular road for me to drop them at some fuller's or baker's door and say, 'Turn these lads into journeymen, will you, please?' They are now my responsibility and I'm going to take the best care of them that I can.'

'But teaching them to fight, Caleb? Are they to be soldiers, then?'

'No, but they will need to know how to take care of themselves. If they're with me and working for my father, they will be in danger occasionally. I want to make sure that they are able to survive those dangers.'

Marie seemed unconvinced, but said nothing for a moment.

Tad stuck his head out of the door of the hut and said, 'Can we come out now?'

Caleb waved the boys out and Marie said, 'I'm their mother and they will always be my babies.'

'This baby would like something to eat, now,' said Tad.

Marie slapped him on the shoulder. 'Then we must go to the market and get—'

'We'll eat again at the inn,' interrupted Caleb, 'but there is something I need to discuss with all of you first.'

They stood in the early morning chill, the boys still half-asleep and squinting against the glare of the low-hanging sun. Caleb said, 'There are perhaps, better times and places for these things, but this is where I am, so now is the time.'

'Caleb,' asked Marie, 'what are you talking about?'

'Your boys have been cast by fate into my care, their lot decided by the unselfish act of returning to see to my welfare, and in so doing, saving my life.'

He looked at the boys and said, 'You know I love your mother more than any other woman I know, and I have been true to her for years.' He looked at Marie and said, 'I can not promise to be here any more than I have in the past, so I want you to leave Stardock and come and live with my family.'

'But this is the only home I've known,' said Marie.

'We'll make another home, the four of us.'

'What are you asking, Caleb?'

'Let us wed, and I will name the boys as my adopted sons. If all of you will have me.'

The boys grinned at one another and Tad said, 'Does this mean we get to call you "Papa"?'

'Only if you wish to be beaten,' said Caleb with a smile. But his eyes were fixed on Marie.

She leaned into him and said softly, 'Yes, Caleb. I will go with you.'

He kissed her, then said, 'Zane, go to the inn and tell Jakesh to break out his best ale and wine. Tell him to prepare roast oxen, and trot out his best foods, for tonight we shall treat the town to a feast.

'Tad, find Father DeMonte and tell him that he has a wedding to perform at sundown.'

'Today?' asked Marie.

'Why wait?' asked Caleb. 'I love you and want to know that no matter what happens in the future, you and the boys will be cared for. I want to know you are waiting for me.'

With a wry smile she said, 'I'm always waiting for you, Caleb. You know that.'

'As my wife?' he said. 'That's what I want.'

She buried her face in his shoulder and hugged him tightly. Then she said, 'Yes, I'll marry you.'

The boys whooped and ran off on their errands. After a moment, Marie said, 'Are you certain?'

'Never been so certain about anything in my life.' He kissed her. 'I nearly died out there, and the thought of never seeing you again . . .' His eyes shone with moisture and emotion as his voice wavered. 'Then those boys, those two wonderful boys that you raised, Marie—' He stopped, then said, 'I didn't know whether to throttle them for disobeying me . . . but had they not, they would now be somewhere in northern Kesh, seeking a man who they only knew by name, without means, while I would be rotting by some roadside. It's as if the gods have planned this, my love, and I'll not wait another day.'

'When will we move to your home, Caleb?'

'Tonight, after the festival, for that's what it will be – a festival!'

'I have so much to do—' she began.

'All you must do is be beautiful, and that is already done.'

'Still, if we are to travel this night, I must pack.'

'Pack what? What do you need to bring with you? You have the boys, and nothing in the hut is necessary where we are going. You'll see. What else is there? A few keepsakes?'

'Some.'

'Then gather those and then spend the rest of this day preparing for your wedding. Find the dressmaker and spare no expense, and find the women you wish to stand with you.'

She nodded, tears forming. She put her hands over her nose and mouth and said, 'Here I am crying like a foolish girl.'

He kissed her and said, 'Nothing foolish about you, Marie. Nothing foolish at all.'

She kissed him again, then said, 'I need to go to the dressmaker now. If I know Bethel Roachman she will kick up a real fuss about having to make something for me between now and sundown.'

'Let her. Just see that it's done to your liking.'

She smiled, nodded, and hurried off, holding her hem above the mud, and Caleb watched her go.

Standing alone he wondered at his sudden need to formalize what had been unspoken between them. He felt a moment of worry, then pushed it aside. He knew his reason: he wanted the world to know that he loved this woman, and cared for her boys as if they were his own. He wanted a priest of a temple to bless their union and he wanted to go to his father with this ready-made family certain in his own mind that he could take no other course of action.

After a moment, he muttered under his breath, 'Sun's hardly up and I need a drink already.' With doubt gnawing at his stomach, he forced himself to turn and walk back to the warehouse. He had to send a message to his parents and brother, and he needed to do it now.

Pug and Miranda stood to one side, and watched their youngest son and the woman he loved exchange their vows before Father DeMonte, the local Priest of Killian whose tiny church served the Stardock region.

Magnus stood a few feet behind his parents, studying his younger brother with a mixture of pleasure and envy. That Caleb could find a little joy in the dark world they inhabited pleased Magnus enormously.

Pug was impressed by how much had been done in so short a time. Garlands of blooms hung from a lattice of grape-stakes constructed by some local boys under Tad's direction. Zane had organized the food and drink, and the tables around the town square were loaded. Once word of the wedding had passed through the town, the local women had pitched in with freshly-baked goods and preserves, and by sundown it was – as Caleb had predicted – a full-blown festival.

Tad and Zane stood on Marie's side of the square, behind the three women who were standing with her. They glanced at Ellie and Grame Hodover who stood watching silently. Ellie smiled back at the boys who noted her swelling stomach and silently agreed that fate had put them on a better path than they had anticipated.

Spending a few minutes with Ellie during the course of the afternoon had restored the balance of their lives, and she was once again like their sister. Grame, as always, was a self- important bore, and neither Tad nor Zane could understand what Ellie saw in him, but as she loved him they decided that was a good enough reason to put up with the pompous fool.

When the priest had finished and the crowd had cheered, Pug motioned for the boys to come over and join them. He whispered something to his wife and she nodded. Miranda turned her attention to Marie, and as Pug led the boys off to the side of the crowd, Pug felt a faint pang. Marie looked older than Miranda. She would grow to be an old woman while Pug, Miranda and probably Magnus would remain unchanged. What would become of Caleb wasn't clear. There were aspects to his son's nature that no one else understood, or even suspected, save perhaps Nakor. Pug had realized years ago that it was futile to try and keep anything the Isalani found interesting a secret.

Reaching a quiet corner of the town square, Pug said, 'Boys, I suppose it's a good thing that I decided not to have you drowned when you first came to my island.'

Both boys looked startled for a moment, then grinned.

'From this moment you are grandsons to me, and with that comes privilege and responsibility. We'll talk more in the morning, but for the moment, go to the festival and share your mother's joy.'

They hesitated, then with a spontaneity that surprised Pug, hugged him fiercely. 'Thank you, Pug,' said Zane. 'We'll make you proud of us.'

Pug suddenly found himself flushed with emotion. 'I know you will,' he whispered hoarsely.

They hurried off to the party while Magnus and his mother moved to where Pug stood. Miranda said, 'You look nonplussed.'

'Just taken by surprise, that's all.'

'What were you surprised by, Father?'

'That two boys I hardly know could suddenly become important to me.'

Miranda smiled. 'You have always allowed people to become important to you, Pug.' She slipped her arm around his waist. 'It's one of the things I love about you, yet which causes me no end of annoyance.'

Softly, Pug said, 'They remind me of William.'

Neither Miranda nor Magnus said anything for a moment. William, Pug's first-born child, had died years before, but his father still grieved. Magnus rested his hand on his father's shoulder and the three stood motionless for a long time before they moved back to rejoin Caleb and his wife in the festival.

As the festival came to a close, Pug joined his younger son for a short walk. When they were out of earshot, Pug said, 'I've just gotten word from home.'

'And?'

'There has been another murder in Kesh.'

Caleb didn't need to hear any more. He knew that since Nakor had returned from his visit to Knight-Marshal Erik von Darkmoor, Pug had alerted every agent the Conclave had in Kesh to be on the lookout for evidence of a Nighthawk resurgence. For this murder to have come to their attention so swiftly, the victim had to have been someone significant. 'Who was it?'

'Just a minor noble, but one linked directly to an important faction in the Gallery of Lords and Masters. I don't have a completely clear picture of what's taking place down there, but I think we could be seeing the beginning of a major power-shift in the Empire.'

'A little murder has always been part of politics in Kesh, Father.'

Pug nodded and said, 'Yes, but many murders remind me too well of the last time someone tried to seize power down there.' He grinned. 'Although that odd set of events also led Nakor to me.'

'I've heard the story,' said Caleb, following his father's news with a sigh. 'I had hoped that Marie and I could spend a little more time together to celebrate our nuptials.'

'I'm sorry to say you only have a few days, as I need you down in Great Kesh within a week. Marie and the boys will have to get used to the idea that although you often travel by common means – horse or wagon – you're just as likely to be whisked from here to there by magic.' Pug glanced over his shoulder and seeing no need to be cautious continued, 'I've already sent Tal, Kaspar, Pasko and Amafi to the capital. Kaspar looks so different no one will recognize the newly named Comté du Bassillon from the court of Bas-Tyra until he reaches the palace.'

'With all the correct papers, no doubt.'

Pug nodded. 'Tal is a well-known former Champion of the Masters' Court, and his notoriety will help him gain invitations to various functions and places where we need eyes and ears. But there are also places a teamster and his two apprentices can go—'

'Wait a minute, Father! I want you to take the boys back home with you.'

Pug turned on Caleb and seized his arm. 'I have treated you like a man since you first showed me that you could accept a man's responsibilities. Do you remember how old you were?'

'Seventeen,' said Caleb. 'I remember asking you to send me on a mission.' He hung his head, knowing where this conversation was headed.

'How old are Tad and Zane?'

'Seventeen this Midsummer's Day.'

Pug was silent for a minute, then said, 'You had no choice but to bring the boys back to our island. But that decision made them a concern of the Conclave, even though there were limits to their obligation and what we might ask of them once we were certain that they could be trusted. You asked for neither my nor your mother's counsel when you chose to wed Marie and bring the boys into our family.'

Caleb nodded. 'I realize as much.'

'I could never tell you where to find your happiness, Caleb. No man can. I realize that your life has been harder in many ways than Magnus'. You were always the odd boy out, the one who couldn't do magic. I do understand that. But your choice has put those two boys in a situation they hardly understand. It is your duty as their stepfather to teach them what it means to be part of this family.'

Pug looked into the darkness for a moment. 'I had been a prisoner in a Tsurani work camp for two years, and Tomas fought alongside the dwarves in Grey Towers when we were Tad and Zane's age.

'Maybe it's fate,' said Pug, as he looked into his son's eyes. 'But be it fate, chance or whim, they are now part of this and you must teach them what that means.'

'Marie will not be happy.'

'I know, but we will do everything we can to bring her into our family.' Pug then smiled. 'Do you think she's ready for what she'll find on Sorcerer's Isle?'

Caleb said, 'She's pretty level-headed, I think she'll manage.' Then as they turned back to the festival, he added, 'But it might be wise to prevent her becoming too friendly with the Pithirendar sisters until she's had a chance to adjust. There are some things a mother doesn't need to discover about her sons.'

Pug nodded. 'You mean like that time your mother popped into that brothel in Salador because she was looking for you?'

Caleb laughed. 'That's exactly what I mean. I don't know who was more upset, me, Mother, or the whore.'

Pug patted his son's shoulder. 'My money would be on your mother.'

Caleb said, 'You're probably right.'

They returned to the festival and Caleb sought out his bride. A heavy sadness descended upon him as he considered just how he would tell her that he and *their* sons would be leaving without her at first light.

# CHAPTER 9

# KESH

Tal feigned patience.

Petro Amafi stood at his master's right arm, once again playing the role of dutiful manservant to Tal's bored Kingdom noble. Far in the distance he could make out Kaspar, now using the name André Comté du Bassillon, from the Duke's court in Bas-Tyra.

Like all visiting nobility, he was honour bound to present himself to the Imperial court upon arrival in Great Kesh. Emperor Diigai was too busy, of course, to see them: Kaspar, now a low-level functionary, despite carrying marques from the King of the Isles naming him trade envoy plenipotentiary, and Talwin Hawkins, minor noble and Champion of the Masters' Court in Roldem, were simply not of sufficient rank to warrant taking up any part of the old Emperor's time.

They would be greeted in turn by a minor functionary of the court, one of sufficient rank to not slight visitors, but not of high enough rank to give them too high an opinion of their status. As Kaspar had explained to Talwin before they had left Roldem together, while Roldem considered itself the cultural centre of the Sea of Kingdoms, Kesh viewed itself as the virtual centre of the known world, with some justification.

It was historically the most powerful nation on the entire world of Midkemia, and only the constant issue of keeping the southern vassal states, the so-called 'Keshian Confederacy', under control prevented the Empire from extending its borders further. Two hundred years earlier a revolt in the south had allowed the northern province of Bosania, now split into the Duchy of Crydee and the Free Cities of Natal, and the island province of Queg, to break free of the Empire.

Currently Roldem's navy was combined with the Kingdom of the Isles' great Eastern Fleet, supported by a loose agreement among the small eastern Kingdoms to come to one another's aid against any Keshian incursion, which kept the Empire contained in the east.

In the west, it was the Kingdom's Western Fleet and the navy of the Empire of Queg, plus the economic strength of the Free Cities of Natal that had kept Kesh in check. So for the time being the political landscape over the entire continent of Triagia was stable for the first time in centuries. Which meant that the fighting now ran along economic and political lines, a great deal less overt, but no less nasty and dangerous than a military confrontation.

Talwin was doing his part to ensure that the stability presently being enjoyed by the citizens of all nations continued: it was clearly to their enemy's advantage to see chaos descend in the region.

Tal noticed Kaspar trying to catch his eye and whispered to Amafi, 'Go and see what Lord André needs.'

Petro Amafi, one-time assassin and betrayer of both men, quickly moved forwards past the others who were waiting quietly in the anteroom to the presentation hall.

There was a rough pattern to where people chose to stand, for everyone coming to be presented to the Emperor's court had some sense of where they were likely to be in the order of those called. Near the door waited those of sufficient rank to be almost worthy enough to be presented directly to the Emperor: minor princes from distant lands, nobles who were related by blood to royalty, and envoys of lower than the rank of ambassador.

Kaspar had once enjoyed higher status, since he had been the ruler of the Duchy of Olasko. It was more than five years since he had last visited Kesh on a state visit, and he doubted many would recognize him – though he was occasionally given a second glance by one functionary or another who seemed to think that Kaspar was someone who they should know but didn't quite remember. He was by his own estimate at least thirty pounds lighter than he had been when ruler of Olasko. A year of hard living and less than bountiful food, followed by a strict regimen of strenuous training and light eating had kept him slim. Instead of the closely cut beard he had once sported, he was now clean shaven, and he had let his hair grow to his shoulders. With clothing bought from the most fashionable tailor in Bas-Tyra, he looked entirely like a gentleman of that court.

'Master Talwin asks what it is you need, Magnificence?' said Amafi when he reached Kaspar's side.

With a slight nod of his head, Kaspar said, 'Tell the Squire I may be indisposed. I believe I may have been recognized.'

Amafi turned around inconspicuously, as if to talk to Pasko, the old agent who had served as one of Talon's early teachers. Speaking of nothing of note, Amafi let his eyes sweep the room, not lingering long enough to establish eye contact with anyone, but still managing to identify every potential threat. Smiling, he turned back to Kaspar and said, 'I assume my lord is referring to the minor functionary standing near that small door on the right?'

'Actually, it was the man who spoke to him a moment ago before disappearing through that door,' said Kaspar. 'The other fellow is merely keeping an eye on me, I suspect.'

'I will convey to my master your concerns,' said Amafi. 'If we do not see you at the rendezvous this evening, we shall assume the worst.'

With a bland expression and a forced smile, Kaspar said, 'You do that, Amafi.'

Pasko said, 'Convey word to those who might care about such things.'

Amafi nodded. Pasko, a dour man of middle years, had been dispatched by the Conclave to keep a close watch on Kaspar. The former Duke of Olasko had earned a great deal of good will by carrying word to the Conclave of the threat from the Dasati the year before, but he was still not entirely trusted. So, Pasko kept an eye on Kaspar, while Talwin watched Amafi.

The plan was straightforward: the Conclave had sent three groups of agents – Kaspar and Pasko, Tal and Amafi, and Caleb and the boys – to the City of Kesh. Kaspar, as a minor envoy, would have access to many key government ministers and functionaries; Tal would be able to move easily through the social circles of the minor Keshian nobility: as a past Champion of the Masters' Court and with his reputation as a womanizer and gambler he would have no shortage of social invitations. Caleb and the boys would be able to negotiate their way through the common citizenry of the Empire, from honest labourers to criminals. It was hoped that by using three different sets of agents some clue could be uncovered as to the whereabouts of the leader of the Nighthawks. And Pug hoped through one of these channels that he would learn the whereabouts of his old enemy, Leso Varen.

Amafi relayed Kaspar's message to Tal, who said, 'If we are separated and questioned, you know what to say.'

'Yes, Magnificence,' replied the grey-haired assassin. 'You have met the Comté on a number of occasions in Bas-Tyra and elsewhere. You have even played cards with him, and you were pleased to discover yourselves travelling on the same boat from Caralién to Kesh. We travelled by land from Pointer's Head to Ishlana, then by river boat. The Comté said he had come from Rillanon, so I assume he came by land from Deep Taunton to Jonril then by boat to Caralién. It was a most fortuitous happenstance as the Comté is convivial company.' With an evil smile, he added, 'And an indifferent card player.'

'Don't overdo it,' said Tal. 'But if they assume I'm staying close to him to cheat him at cards, they will perhaps not suspect that we are plotting together.'

'A small bad intention is often far more easily believed than a big one, Magnificence,' whispered Amafi. 'Once I avoided the gallows by merely claiming to have entered a certain house to have a dalliance with the man's wife instead of attempting to kill him. The woman vigorously denied it, but the odd thing was, the louder she claimed it wasn't so, the more the authorities believed it was. I was put in a cell, from which I escaped a few days later; the man beat his wife, causing her brother to kill him in a duel, and I collected my fee for the man's death, despite the fact I had not placed one finger upon him. I did, however, revisit the wife to console her, and found her behaviour clearly demonstrated why the constables were inclined to believe me and not her.' With a half-wistful look, he added, 'Grief made her ardent.'

Tal chuckled. There had been several times in their relationship when he would have happily murdered Amafi, and he was certain there had been more than one occasion when the former assassin would have killed him for the right price, but at some odd point along the way he had become fond of the rogue.

His feelings for Kaspar were a great deal more complex. The man had been responsible for the wholesale destruction of his entire people, and but for a freak act of fate Tal Hawkins, once Talon of the Silver Hawk, would have been dead along with the majority of the Orosini.

Yet Kaspar was now an ally, another agent working for the Conclave of Shadows. And Tal understood how many of Kaspar's murderous decisions had been made under the influence of the Conclave's most dangerous enemy, the magician named Leso Varen. Yet even without Varen's influence, Kaspar could be a cold-hearted, unforgiving bastard. Yet even when he had served Kaspar with the intent of betraying him to revenge his people, there was something about Kaspar Tal admired. He found himself in the confusing situation of knowing he would give his life to save Kaspar against their common enemies, but that in other circumstances, he would happily kill the man.

'You look lost in thought, Magnificence. Is something troubling you?'

'Nothing more than the usual, Amafi. I find the gods have an evil sense of humour, sometimes.'

'That is true, Magnificence. My father, an occasionally wise man, once said that we were blessed only when the gods remained ignorant of us.'

Tal's gaze returned to Kaspar. 'Something's happening.'

Amafi turned to see a minor court official speaking to Kaspar, and after a moment, Kaspar and Pasko followed him through the small side door Kaspar had mentioned to Amafi. Tal sighed. 'Well, now we shall see if our plans fall apart before they begin.'

'Let us hope the gods are ignoring us today, Magnificence.'

Kaspar was led by a very polite functionary through a long series of corridors. He was taken by side passages around the smaller reception hall used for greeting visiting dignitaries towards the suite of offices reserved for the higher ranking government officials.

The palace of the Emperor occupied the entire upper half of a great plateau that overlooked the Overn Deep and the lower city at the foot of the tableland. Ages before, Keshian rulers had constructed a massive fortress on top of this prominence, a highly defensible position to protect their small city below. Over the centuries the original fortress had been added to, reconstructed and expanded, until the entire top of the plateau was covered. Tunnels extended down into the soil, some leading into the lower city. It was like nothing so much as a hive, Kaspar thought. And as a result he rarely knew where he was. Of course, before this particular journey he never had to worry about getting lost, because as a visiting ruler, he had always had an attentive Keshian noble or bureaucrat to see to his needs.

Kaspar understood the organization of the Keshian government as well as any foreigner could, and he knew that this nation, more than any other on Midkemia, was controlled by bureaucracy, a system that had endured longer than any ruling dynasty. Kings might give edicts and princes command armies, but if the edicts were not handed down to the populace no one obeyed them, and if orders to move food and supplies around weren't forthcoming, the prince's army quickly starved to death in the field, or mutinied.

On more than one occasion, Kaspar had been thankful his duchy was relatively small and tidy by comparison. He could name every functionary in the citadel that had served as his home for most of his life. Here he doubted the Emperor could name even those servants who worked in his personal apartment.

They reached a large office, and Pasko was instructed to wait on a stone bench outside. Kaspar was motioned through a door into an even larger room, one that was an odd mix of opulence and functionality. In the middle of the room sat a large table, behind which rested a man on a chair. Once powerful, he had gone to fat, though there was still ample muscle under that fat. Kaspar knew that there was a shrewd and dangerous mind in that old man's head. He wore the traditional garb of a Trueblood: a linen kilt around his hips bound by a woven silk belt, cross-gartered sandals on his feet, and a bare chest. He also wore an impressive array of jewellery, mostly gold and gems, though there were some interesting polished stones among the dozen or so chains he had around his neck. These stood in stark contrast against his night-black skin. He regarded Kaspar with eyes so dark brown they looked sable, and then he smiled, his white teeth dramatic in contrast to his face.

'Kaspar,' he said in a friendly tone. 'You look different, my friend. I'd say better, if you think that not overstepping the mark.' He waved the escort outside, then with a motion of his hand ordered the two guards by the door to go as well, leaving Kaspar alone with him.

Kaspar nodded slightly. 'Turgan Bey, Lord of the Keep, why am I not surprised?'

'You seriously didn't think the former Duke of Olasko could sneak into the Empire without our notice, did you?'

'One can hope,' said Kaspar.

Lord Turgan indicated that Kaspar should take a seat. 'Comté Andre?' He looked at something written on a piece of parchment. 'I must confess it took a great deal of self-control not to have you picked up at the border, but I was interested in seeing just what you were up to. Had you sneaked into the city or met with known insurgents or smugglers this would all make sense. But instead you submit a petition to present yourself as a trade envoy plenipotentiary from the Duke of Bas-Tyra's court? And then you walk in here and stand around like . . . like I don't know what.'

The still-powerful-looking old man drummed his fingers on the desk for a moment, then added, 'So, if you have a reason why I shouldn't throw you and that servant of yours into the Overn to feed the crocodiles I'd love to hear it. Maybe I'll toss in your friend Hawkins as well.'

Kaspar sat back. 'Hawkins and I play cards, and I think he cheats. Nothing more. I thought perhaps arriving with a famous squire of the Kingdom might give me a little more credibility.'

'Or get the youngster killed before his time.' Turgan Bey chuckled. 'You think for a minute I don't know that Talwin Hawkins was in your service for over two years? Or that I don't know he was key to your over-throw? But here you are, in my own keep acting as if you're casual travellers idling the time away with meaningless card games.' He shook his head. 'I can't say that I hold you in any affection, Kaspar. You've always been someone we watched because of all the mischief you caused, but as long as you confined yourself to your own little corner of the world, we didn't much care. And, to be fair, you've always honoured your treaties with Kesh.

'But as you are no longer ruler of Olasko, certain political niceties need no longer be observed. And since you're attempting to enter the palace under

207

a false identity, can we safely assume you're a spy?'

'You may,' said Kaspar with a smile. 'And I have something for you.' He reached into his tunic and pulled out the black Nighthawk amulet. He slid it across the table to Turgan and waited while the old minister picked it up and examined it.

'Where did you get this?'

'From a friend of a friend, who got it from Lord Erik von Darkmoor.'

'That's a name to make a Keshian general lose sleep. He's cost us dearly a couple of times at the border.'

'Well, if your frontier commanders didn't get the urge to conquer in the name of their Emperor without instruction from your central authority, you'd have less problems with von Darkmoor.'

'We don't necessarily send our brightest officers to the western frontier,' Turgan Bey sighed. 'We save those to build up our own factions here in the capital. Politics will be the death of me yet.' He tapped his finger on the amulet. 'What do you make of this?'

'Keshian nobles are dying.'

'That happens a lot,' said Turgan Bey with a smile. 'We have a lot of nobles. You can't toss a barley cake from a vendor's cart in the lower city without hitting a noble. Comes from having a vigorous breeding population for several thousand years.'

'Truebloods are dying, too.'

Turgan Bey lost his smile. 'That should not have

been apparent to von Darkmoor. He must have better spies than I gave him credit for. Now, this still leads me to wonder why the former Duke of Olasko has wandered into my city, into my very palace, to hand me this. Who sent you? Duke Rodoski?'

'Hardly,' said Kaspar. 'My brother-in-law would just as soon see my head adorn the drawbridge leading into his citadel as he would see it across the dinner table. Only his love for my sister keeps it on my shoulders; that and staying far away from Olasko.'

'Then von Darkmoor sent you?' said Bey, his brow furrowing.

'I've only met the esteemed Knight-Marshal of Krondor once, some years ago, and then we spoke only for a moment.'

Bey's gaze narrowed. 'Who sent you, Kaspar?'

'One who reminds you that not only enemies hide in shadows,' said Kaspar.

Turgan Bey stood up and said, 'Come with me.'

He led Kaspar though a chamber that appeared to be a more comfortable working area with a pair of writing desks for scribes, as well as a large divan chair which could comfortably accommodate him. He motioned Kaspar to step out onto a balcony overlooking a lush garden three storeys below and at last said, 'Now I can be certain no one is listening.'

'You don't trust your own guards?'

'I do, but when members of the Imperial family,

no matter how distantly related they may be, start turning up dead, I don't trust anyone.' He glanced at Kaspar. 'Nakor sent you?'

'Indirectly,' said Kaspar.

'My father told me the story of the first time that crazy Isalani showed up in the palace. He and the Princes Borric and Erland, as well as Lord James – he was a baronet or baron back then I believe – kept the Empress alive and arranged it so that Diigai would sit upon the throne after her by marrying her granddaughter to him. They defended her in the very Imperial throne room! Against murderers who wished to put that fool Awari on the throne. From that day forward my father had a different attitude towards the Kingdom. And he told the story of how Nakor pulled that hawk from his bag and restored the mews here in the palace.' Leaning back, he added, 'It was a remarkable day. So you can imagine my surprise the first time Nakor turned up at my father's estate up in Geansharna – I must have been about fifteen years old.' His eyes narrowed. 'That crazy Isalani has been surprising me ever since. I won't ask how you came to work with him, but if he's sent you, there must be good reason.'

'There is. I had in my employ, or so I thought, a magician by the name of Leso Varen. It turns out he was partially to blame for some of my excesses over the last few years before I was exiled.'

Bey began to speak, thought better of it, and

210

Kaspar continued. 'If at some point you'd care to listen to a detailed appraisal of what I did and why, I'll burden you with it, but for now suffice it to say that Varen may be at the centre of your current troubles, and if that is true, then there is more at risk than merely a bloodier-than-usual game of Keshian politics.

'If what Nakor thinks is true, then the entire region may become destabilized and we might see a lot of needless warfare.'

Bey stood motionless for a moment, then said, 'Who else knows you are here?'

'Hawkins, of course,' said Kaspar. 'Nakor, the men with us, and a few other agents of the Conclave up in the north, but no one here in Kesh besides yourself.' He thought better of revealing Caleb's role in this; it was always better to have a few things held back against the risk of being compromised.

'This is going to be a problem,' said Turgan Bey. 'Several of my agents know, and while I like to think they are all above suspicion, history teaches otherwise. So, how do we take this situation and turn it to our advantage?'

'Political asylum?'

Bey was silent for a while, then he said, 'That may serve. Then we could not only not worry about your forged documents – I assume they're the best?'

'Impeccable.'

'No one will bother examining them. We can say this all was a ruse to get you safely away from . . .

well, make up a list, Kaspar. There are a lot of people who would love to see you dead.'

'As much as it pains me,' said Kaspar, 'I'm forced to concede that is true.'

'So, we need a few details to embellish the tale, but let's say this: despite your brother-in-law's promises to your sister to spare you, his agents are out and about, seeking to bring you to a quick demise. Fleeing Olasko, you have come to the one place left to you where you might find safe harbour, Great Kesh. Is that about right?'

'It will bear scrutiny,' Kaspar conceded. 'Rodoski is a man of his word, but few will bother to remember that, and I did promise to leave Olasko.'

'I'll find someone to sponsor you, Kaspar. It can't be me. The Master of the Keep is the last vestige of protection the throne has, and if what I suspect is true, that throne is soon to be under attack.

'The Emperor uses magic to prolong his life, and is now over one hundred years of age. A number of those in the Gallery of Lords and Masters long to see a change. The Emperor's sons are dead and his daughters are long past bearing new heirs.'

'Who stands to inherit?'

'Sezioti, the eldest son of the Emperor's eldest son, but he's not a charismatic leader. His younger brother, Dangai, is very popular. He's a brilliant hunter – and you know as well as any how important that is to the Trueblood – and has been a warrior, and he now oversees the Inner Legion, which is a very powerful position in the Empire.

'Sezioti is a scholar, and while he's well liked, he's not seen as a natural leader. But he has the support of the Master of Horses, Lord Semalcar, and the Leader of the Royal Charioteers, Lord Rawa, which is more than a match in influence for the Inner Legion.'

'In short, you once more have a divided Gallery of Lords and Masters and a wholesale civil war is not out of the question.'

'I'm sorry to say that is a possibility,' said Turgan Bey.

'I think we have common cause,' said Kaspar.

'Apparently we do,' said Bey. 'I'll have quarters made up for you and see about finding someone who can sponsor you to see the Emperor. Trust me, it will be pro forma by the time you appear before His Majesty.' He paused. 'But what do we do about Hawkins?'

'Leave him about his business for the time being. Just do what you would have done had he arrived without me.'

'Well enough,' said Bey. 'I'll have your servant sent for, and in a day or two we'll start to see what good you can be to us.'

'More than the safety of the Empire rests on this, I should remind you,' said Kaspar. 'I may not be welcome in Olasko, but I love my nation and my sister, whom I cherish beyond anyone on this world, and her family are there. A war down here that spills over the borders brings threat to them. Civil war in Kesh can easily breed regional instability.'

Kaspar thought it best not to mention the Talnoy and the risk from the Dasati. Bey had enough on his mind already.

Bey nodded. 'I long for simpler times, Kaspar, when all I had to worry about were fractious rebels in the south or ambitious Kingdom generals to the north.' He waved Kaspar away and added, 'Border wars are so much less complex than all this magic, intrigue, and secret alliances. Rest well. We'll speak again soon.'

Kaspar followed a servant to his new quarters and was pleased to see they were fit for royalty. Seven rooms comprised his apartment, complete with servants – some of whom were astonishingly lovely young women, all wearing the traditional Trueblood garb, the same linen kilt and bare chest affected by the men, with a torque of rank around their throat.

When Pasko arrived, he found Kaspar sitting on a divan, nibbling at a platter of fruit while two beautiful young women stood by awaiting his instructions. The former teacher of Talon of the Silver Hawk and long-time agent for the Conclave said, 'Did all go as planned?'

'As we expected,' said Kaspar. 'Lord Bey is everything we were told he would be.'

Both men looked around at their opulent surroundings. Kaspar glanced at one of the girls, who smiled back at him warmly. He then looked at Pasko and said, 'Had I thought it would turn out like this, I would have asked for political asylum long ago.'

# CHAPTER 10

## THREAT

Ralan Bek was gone.

Nakor sat up, looked around and saw no sign of the young man. Then something moved just over the top of a small rise to the east of the cave. As he stood, Bek hove into view carrying a large bundle of sticks.

'You're up,' said the young man with a grin, adding, 'obviously.'

'Yes,' said Nakor with a smile. 'I am.'

'I noticed the fire burning low and thought I'd get more wood.' Again he added, 'Obviously.'

Nakor nodded. 'You hungry?'

'Always,' said the young man, putting the firewood down and sitting close to where Nakor fumbled through his rucksack. 'No more oranges, I hope. I'm getting the flux.'

Nakor shook his head. 'Travel food.' He took out a packet wrapped in oiled paper and said, 'Here.'

Bek opened the paper and found half a loaf of bread, some hard cheese and dried beef. 'Not the worst I've eaten,' he said, shovelling the first bite into his mouth.

As they ate, Nakor studied the young man. There was something about him that Nakor almost understood, but he had to look hard, as if somehow it would just take a bit more will to perceive it.

'What?'

'What?'

'You're staring at me. It's . . . odd.'

Nakor grinned. 'You and I have had similar beginnings. My father used to beat me when I wandered off as a boy.' Nakor went on to tell Bek about his own youth, being a gambler, and running into Pug and the other magicians.

'So that explains why the big man in white and gold was here.'

'Why do you say that?'

'Because I don't understand half of what you're saying, Nakor, but I do understand that these are very important people you're talking about, and important people have powerful allies. And I suppose those things in the cave are important and powerful, too.'

'You snuck in there?'

Grinning, Bek said, 'You know I did. You were awake, I know you were.'

'Why do you think that?'

'Because I wouldn't have slept if I had thought that someone might try to take advantage of me.'

'Why didn't you?' asked Nakor, then he took another bite of food.

'Because I'm not stupid, even though sometimes things don't make sense to me.'

'So that's why you didn't try to attack me or flee on the first night?'

Bek shrugged. 'I have nowhere else to be, and those things in there are as interesting as anything I've seen in a while. And I know not to take stupid chances.'

'And leaving or attacking me would have been stupid?'

Bek nodded. 'I've met your type before, Nakor. You act silly and harmless, but you know what you're doing. You wouldn't have stayed here alone with me unless you were confident that you could keep me from hurting you, or you knew you could hurt me.'

Nakor shrugged, and Bek pointed an accusing figure at him. 'You're some kind of magic user, right?'

Nakor shrugged again. 'I know some tricks.'

Nodding as he chewed, Bek said, 'I thought so.'

'What are your plans, Ralan?'

Bek shrugged. 'I don't think like that. I just go out and find some lads, find a fight, find a woman, whatever. I don't see the point in making plans. It's not as if I have anything anyone wants; I mean, I can't mill or plough, or do anything that people want to pay you to do. All I can do is fight and ride.'

'There are many places where a man who can fight like you can earn a living.'

'Soldiering!' He spat. 'Wear a uniform and take orders – yes sir, no m'lord – and all that? Never. I tried being a mercenary once, but that was boring. I just need –' He stared off into space for a moment, then his dark eyes regarded Nakor. 'I'm not sure what I need, but something drives me.'

Nakor nodded. 'I think I understand.'

'If you do, then you're the first.' Then he stood up and drew his sword from his scabbard. Nakor's eyes widened slightly but he didn't move. 'Trouble's coming,' said Bek.

Then Nakor heard horses on the trail. He stood as Bek crested the rise and started down the track. Nakor hurried to the top of the rise so he could see the vista below.

A hundred yards down the trail he saw two riders approaching Bek. Both reined in and stood their ground when the armed man approached them on foot. As one of them began to speak, Bek leapt an amazing distance, covering the ground between himself and the first rider. Before either horseman could react, Bek swung as hard as he could, and removed the first man's arm at his shoulder.

The other man was momentarily stunned, and then started to turn his horse to flee. Bek reached back and hurled his sword, launching it like a javelin, and the blade speared the man through the back. He fell from his horse and hit the ground before Nakor could take two steps.

By the time Nakor reached the scene of the carnage, Bek had retrieved his sword and was cleaning the blade on the tunic of one of the two men. 'What happened?' asked Nakor.

'You wanted to keep this place a secret.' Bek

reached down and took a hat from one of the dead men: a broad-brimmed, black felt thing with a low crown wrapped with a leather hat-band and decorated with glass beadwork. 'I like this hat,' he said, putting on his head to see if it fitted. He adjusted it, and said, 'Nice hat.'

'But—'

Bek shrugged. 'Got any more to eat?'

Nakor watched as Ralan Bek calmly marched over the rise. He followed him and found the young man sitting exactly where he had been moments before, and eating what was left on the oiled paper. 'Got one of those oranges left?'

Nakor reached in and got one and tossed it to him. 'Why did you kill those men? Why not just send them away?'

'Because they would only assume that there was something here and inevitably come back, and maybe bring more men with them. I thought I'd save a lot of needless talking and took care of the problem swiftly. It was either kill two men now, or many more later.' His eyes narrowed as he asked, 'Is there something wrong with that?'

Nakor shook his head. 'It's murder.'

Bek shrugged. 'If they could have killed me, they would have.'

Nakor's voice rose, 'In self defence! I've seen you fight. You tested Tomas, and the only mortal man who could come close to doing that was Talwin Hawkins, and he was a Champion of the Masters' Court! They never stood a chance!'

'Never heard of him.'

'You wouldn't have, down here.' Nakor studied Bek while the young man finished his food. Bek leaned back, looked at Nakor and said, 'Now what are we going to do?'

Nakor said, 'We wait.'

'Wait for what?'

'For another to come and study those things, so that I can go about some other business.'

'Perhaps I may go with you?' said Bek, flashing a grin.

'Perhaps you should,' said Nakor. 'You have an impulsive nature and a complete lack of concern for any consequences.'

'Why should I worry about consequences?' asked Bek. 'Someday I'll die; but before that I want to have things, and anyone who stands in my way will suffer for it.' He smiled. 'And I enjoy making them suffer if it comes to that. If someone is strong enough to kill me, then it will be over.'

'You don't worry about what will happen when you arise in Lims-Kragma's Hall, to face your judgment?'

Bek shrugged. 'Why should I? I am as the gods made me, aren't I? If one of them has a problem with my behaviour, then let them act. I can't stand against a god, so if I'm wrong why hasn't one of them . . . turned me into a bug yet?' he asked with a laugh. 'Because, I don't think the gods care what I do. I don't think the gods care what anyone does.' He nodded, as if he had given this a lot of thought. 'I guess you could get into trouble if you sacked a temple, or killed a priest for no reason, but if you leave the gods alone, then they leave you alone. That's how I see it.'

Nakor said, 'What about friends? Family?'

Bek looked at Nakor. 'Do you have friends and family?'

Nakor said, 'Family, no. I had a wife once, but that was a very long time ago. But friends? Yes, I have many friends, the most and best I've ever had, right now. People whom I trust and who trust me.'

'Then you're lucky, I suppose.' Bek looked off into the distance as if he was seeing something in the air.

'Sometimes I think that there's something about me that scares people. I never find I have much in common with most of them.' He looked at Nakor. 'Mostly I find young bravos to ride with, looking for a good time, trouble or quick gold. From time to time I meet a few I like; usually lads who really enjoy a brawl. There was this one lad, Casamir, he liked to drink and fight. It didn't matter if there was no reason for it; he just would find somebody, hit them and start one. He really enjoyed pain.' Bek's eyes shone as he talked. 'I enjoyed watching him beat up people, until a guardsman down in Kiptak broke his head with the butt of a sword. I finished off the guardsman but had to flee Kiptak. So now I travel with whoever I find who's looking for fun, but there's nobody I'd call a true friend.'

★   ★   ★

221

Nakor was silent as he considered what he knew about this young man, which was very little, and what he suspected, which was a great deal. Finally he said, 'When did you start hearing voices?'

Bek stared at Nakor for a long minute then said, 'When I was about eight or nine years old. How do you know about the voices?'

'Because I heard them when I was that age, too.'

'What did they say to you?' asked Bek, looking eagerly at Nakor as he waited for an answer.

'That I . . . needed to be somewhere else.'

Bek's face lit up as he smiled. 'That's what I hear, too.' Then he lost the smile. 'That and other things.'

'What other things?' asked Nakor.

'I don't know.' Bek shrugged and looked down. 'Sometimes they're not really voices, but . . . feelings that I need to do something. Hurt someone. Take something. Go somewhere.' He looked back at the cave. 'That's how I felt when I heard about this cave. Some of the boys with me didn't want to bother, but I knew I had to come here.'

Nakor nodded. 'When did the dreams start?'

Bek closed his eyes, as if something suddenly pained him. 'I don't remember not having them.' He opened his eyes and again stared into space. 'They're—'

After a moment of silence, Nakor said gently, 'They're what?'

Bek looked at Nakor. 'It's like I'm looking through a window or standing on a tower looking down. I see things . . . places . . . people doing things.' He looked away again. 'Violent things, Nakor. I see battles, rapes, burning cities . . . Sometimes it can be too much for me. It's like when you meet a girl who likes to be slapped when you're coupling, and so you slap her. And then you reach the point where she wants you to stop . . . and you're there, with your hand held back and you know that she's not enjoying it any more, but you also know that hitting her just one more time will feel so good. She gets frightened and starts crying, but that only makes you feel even better. But if you hit her now, she'll stop being afraid because she'll be unconscious—'

'Or dead,' said Nakor softly.

Bek shrugged. 'Or dead. It's that place in the middle, it's being on the edge of it, knowing that in an instant everything could change. It's like jumping your horse over something that may just be a little too high, or the feeling of running through a door, knowing that just inside the room someone's waiting to kill you.' His eyes were wide now and he stared at Nakor with a manic expression. 'I always wake with a sense of dread and, as if I'm waiting for something to happen?'

'Constant anticipation?'

'Yes! Anticipation, as if those scenes are . . . just out of reach . . . you know?' He lost his frenzied expression and his face resolved into a mask of thoughtfulness.

'Yes,' said Nakor softly. 'I know.'

Bek's features distorted once again. 'But if I do

the things—' He held his hand open and looked at his palm. 'If I hit the girl. Hard. Really hard. Or if I ride the horse over the jump – even if it guts itself on the fence or breaks a leg landing – or if I run through the door and kill whoever's there—'

'The dreams stop for a while,' finished Nakor.

'Yes!' said Bek, standing up. 'You do understand! How do you know?'

'Because many years ago I had dreams, too.'

'Did they make you do things?'

Nakor shrugged. 'If I acted on them they did stop for a while, yes. I became a gambler and if I cheated someone out of a lot of money, then the dreams would stop for a few days. I became a confidence trickster, and if I swindled someone, they would stop for a week or so. The greater the harm I did by cheating, lying and stealing, the longer I went without the dreams.'

Bek shook his head. 'If I start a fight, or get someone to do something—'

'Bad?'

Bek shrugged. 'I don't understand bad or good, just know what I want to do. If I force someone to do something they don't want to do—'

'Such as?'

Bek said, 'About two years ago Drago and me were in a town near Lanada. Drago was this man I met at a whorehouse down there. We were both drunk and we took these two girls upstairs – I don't know whose idea that was, his or mine.'

Bek's eyes grew distant once more, as if he was seeing what he remembered. 'One of the whores liked being slapped around – I always ask for those. This one was a tiger. She'd whoop and holler and scratch and bite.' He fell silent for a moment, then shrugged. 'Anyway, somewhere along the way it got rougher than she liked, I suppose, because she went from whooping and hollering to crying and screaming. Drago grabbed my arm and told me to stop, so I killed him. Then both girls were screaming, so I killed them, too.' Bek looked at Nakor. 'I really don't know how things got so out of hand, but they did.'

'Yes, they did.'

Bek smiled, then said, 'But it feels good when things get out of control, you know?'

Nakor stood. 'I do.' He stepped over to stand next to Bek, who looked up at him with no change in his mad expression.

'You're going to hurt me now, aren't you?'

'Yes, I am,' said Nakor, putting out his hand over Bek's head. As Bek began to move to defend himself, a light sprang from Nakor's palm, freezing the large young warrior where he sat. His teeth clenched and his eyes started to roll in his head, and he began to make an odd sound. It began deep in his chest, a low grunting noise that rose in pitch as it made its way up to his throat where it became a raspy exhalation. The noise became louder, a higher-pitched shout of pain, which rose into agony.

It continued until Bek had no air left in his lungs to exhale, and could only shake uncontrollably. His teeth were still clenched and his face turned red. His eyes had now completely rolled backwards in their sockets, showing only the whites. Then he started turning a darker colour – from red to purple – and when his complexion approached blue, Nakor removed his hand.

A ragged gasp cut through the quiet as Bek shuddered and fell over backwards. He lay on the ground quivering and twitching, his eyes finally closed.

Nakor remained motionless, watching the huge youth shake like a man in a seizure. After a full five minutes, the frenzy subsided. Then Bek's breathing slowed and he became still. He lay as if asleep for another five minutes, then groaned and opened his eyes.

He blinked twice, then settled his gaze on Nakor. Sitting up slowly, he said, 'That was . . . amazing.' He took a deep breath, let it out slowly, then he grinned. 'I liked it!'

Nakor extended his hand and helped Bek to his feet. 'You enjoy pain?'

Bek patted his body to ensure that nothing was damaged as he said, 'Sometimes I do. Pain . . . wakes things up. It makes you alert, aware. At first there's that desire to pull away, to make it stop, but when it doesn't stop, you can . . . go deeper into it, I suppose you could say. You break through the pain and on the other side there's . . .' He looked at Nakor as if fighting for the concept or word.

'Clarity.'

Bek's eyes widened and he nodded. 'Yes! Clarity. Then you see things differently! It's like nothing else. The pain turns into a feeling like nothing I can describe. But you know what I mean!'

Nakor nodded. 'Sadly, I do.'

'What did you do to me?'

'It's just a trick I know,' said Nakor. 'There's something inside of you, the thing that makes you the way you are. I had to find it, then I had to . . . confine it.'

Bek stood with his hands on his chest as if feeling for something. 'Confined? I don't feel any different.'

Nakor turned, looking over the horizon. 'I know. But for a while you'll find yourself less inclined to cause trouble. And you won't dream either.' He turned back towards Bek. 'The day is still young and I need to do some work. I'm going to leave you here for a few minutes. I'll be back shortly.' He reached into his rucksack and took out a golden-coloured orb. He pushed a preset button and vanished.

Pug looked up as Nakor appeared in his study. 'What is it?'

'Remember that youth I mentioned in my message yesterday?'

'The one who tested Tomas? Of course.'

'I've had suspicions about him since the moment he arrived at the cave, and now I'm certain.'

'Certain of what, Nakor?'

'I told you about the gods' dreams and memories. But what have I told you of . . . fragments?'

Pug said, 'That occasionally a god will manifest his power directly in a mortal. A tiny piece of the god is placed within the soul of a person. Why?'

'I don't believe it any longer. I know it. Bek is such a person.'

'You're certain?'

'Yes, and he is both a great opportunity and a great danger.'

Pug's eyes narrowed as he stared at Nakor. 'Go on.'

'I used a trick that I have to . . . touch something inside a person. It's handy when you want to know if someone has something unusual inside them, like being possessed by a demon.'

'I can see where that would be handy.'

Nakor said, 'It also helps you know when someone's lying to you. But that's not what's important. When I searched Bek, I found the tiniest fragment of a god. The smallest possible manifestation of divine consciousness, and with it the powers that make Bek so dangerous and unpredictable.

'Pug, Bek possesses a fraction of the Nameless One.'

Pug sat back, his face an expression of pure

astonishment, followed an instant later by alarm. 'You're sure?'

'Absolutely. I am certain.'

Pug sat back. 'What does this mean?'

'It means that forces are at play on a larger scale than we suspected, for if the Nameless One can manifest even the tiniest part of his being here—'

'Eventually he will be able to manifest his full being.'

'Yes, Pug.' Nakor looked at his friend of many years. 'He has found his way back into Midkemia. And we must find a way to prevent his return.'

# CHAPTER 11

## CONSPIRACY

The riders came to a halt.

The three dust-covered figures stood on the crest of a rise on the road from Khallara to the city of Kesh. Caleb pointed to the lights playing against the underside of clouds in the distance and said, 'That's Kesh.'

Zane asked, 'How big is it?'

Caleb dismounted. 'Very big. It's the biggest city in the world.'

They had been riding for four days – long enough for the boys to gain more experience on horseback and cover themselves in enough road grime and sweat to convince the guards at the city gates that they had ridden all the way from the Vale of Dreams. Even if they had traded for fresh mounts along the way, the journey should have taken three months or more. But the boys were quickly learning that their stepfather had resources they could not have possibly imagined a year before.

They had all left Stardock the day after the wedding, ostensibly returning north to some vague destination where Caleb's family lived. Instead, once they were clear of the town, Caleb had used one of those spheres that the boys had come to think of as 'travel orbs', to transport himself, Marie and the boys to Sorcerer's Isle.

Caleb had taken a full day to acquaint his new wife with his family and the decidedly unexpected inhabitants of the island. Most of the concepts behind the place – great magic, alien words and travel to them, races not of Midkemia – were understandably lost on her, though he knew that she'd come to understand in time. But her poise when confronting the many unexpected sights, pleased Caleb, as did her attempts to be at ease with his parents. He was even more pleased by her obvious joy at their living quarters, which were palatial compared to what she had known in Stardock, and that she gained the affection of his parents easily.

The one tense moment had arrived with the appearance of the six sisters of the Pithirendar, bedecked in garlands of white oleanders and little else, to welcome the boys back to the island. Their overt displays of affection were more than Marie could bear to watch.

Caleb had steered her away from the reunion and had said, 'Much of what you see here will be strange, but keep one thing in mind above all others: there is no one on this island who wishes you or the boys aught but good.'

Glancing over her shoulder at the girls who had thrown their arms around her son's necks, she had frowned. 'That appears to be a little more than good, Caleb.'

'You're from Stardock, Marie. You've seen different people from the Kingdom and the Empire. Each nation has different customs and beliefs. You've already seen everything one can imagine about people.'

'I've not seen green-skinned girls trying to undress my boys in broad daylight!'

Caleb had laughed at that. 'They only want the boys to go swimming with them.' He pointed. 'My father built a lake down there before I was born—'

'He built a lake?'

'—because my mother hated walking all the way to the beach to go swimming. Anyway, the youth of the Pithirendar need to spend a great deal of time in or near water. It's vital for their health.'

Marie hadn't looked convinced, but Caleb had understood that for mothers, sons never truly grow up. He knew that from personal experience.

They had spent one more night together, and the next morning, Caleb and the boys had left Sorcerer's Isle. They had used an orb to reach a stable in Landreth owned by the Conclave and then used it again to transport themselves to the road upon which they now travelled.

Caleb unsaddled his horse and the boys did the same. 'Why aren't we pushing on now?' asked Tad. 'The lights look close.'

'Because they're not. It's a half a day's ride to

the foul borough – outside the ancient wall – and then another two hours of riding to reach the gates. We'll be there by late afternoon tomorrow.'

Zane put his saddle down and tied off his horse where he could crop grass by the road. Kneeling he said, 'It must be big. I've never seen so many lights in the sky.'

'Thousands of lanterns and torches, Zane,' said Caleb.

Tad joined his foster brother and they both watched the city in the distance which appeared brighter in contrast to the darkening sky.

Caleb made a fire and after they had eaten their rations, he sat back and said, 'Again.'

The boys looked at one another, and Tad gestured that Zane should begin.

'You're a trader from the Vale, by the name of Caleb.'

Tad added, 'I think we can remember that much.'

Caleb picked up a pebble and tossed it at him. Tad grinned as he dodged it easily. 'We are your two very talented, very bright and able, handsome, and very brave apprentices, Tad and Zane.'

Zane nodded. 'Also easy enough to remember.'

'What do we trade?'

Tad said, 'Anything and everything. We are always looking for rare items of great worth to sell in the Kingdom. Gems, jewellery, fine craftsman-ship, anything that is easy to transport and renders a large profit.'

'But we don't carry large amounts of gold,' Zane added. 'We deal in letters of credit, and know money lenders from here up to Krondor.'

'Why are you not with your master?'

Zane said, 'He has sent us out into the bazaar to seek out items that nobles and wealthy commoners in the north might wish to purchase. If we see something noteworthy, we report it to our master who returns to judge if the item is worth purchasing.'

Tad added, 'We are not permitted to bind our master to any transaction and if we give the impression of committing to a sale we shall be severely beaten.'

Caleb kept drilling the boys in their story and provided them with enough basic questions and things to look out for to allow them to pass as traders' apprentices. Then he started running them through the other things they needed to know: who to contact if something happened to him, places they could find a safe haven, and finally, what to do if they knew he was dead.

He saved that point for last, for he wanted to impress on the boys just how dangerous the way before them might prove. It had taken several conversations to convince them that he was not overstating the danger of belonging to his family and working on behalf of those on Sorcerer's Isle.

The boys turned in and Caleb took the first watch. He noticed how quickly Tad and Zane fell asleep. In the flickering light of the campfire, they looked like the boys they had been, rather than like the men they were becoming. For not the first time he silently prayed he had not overestimated their potential, or underestimated his own ability to keep them safe.

The three rode slowly through the crowds, trying to navigate while the boys gawked at the exotic sights of Kesh. It was just as Caleb had promised – a city unlike any other on the world of Midkemia.

They had come to appreciate the incredible scale of the place about midmorning, after they had seen the upper city and the citadel on top of the plateau overlooking the lower city and the shores of the Overn Deep. From a distance it had looked like the top of a faraway mountain, but as they approached, the view resolved itself into what it was – a massive palace surrounded by a fortress-city, built high above every approach from land or by water: the heart of the Empire of Great Kesh.

The day had been clear and their view of the great citadel was unencumbered by fog, haze, or clouds. The boys remarked at least a half a dozen times on how large the building was. Caleb explained that the vast structure had been erected over generations, and that it housed a virtual city itself. He told them of the cavernous halls and many apartments occupied by the Imperial family, the administrators of the empire, the entire household staff – under the watchful eye of the Master of the

Keep, the overseer of the building – and how it still had enough space for apartments and suites of rooms for the Lords and Masters of Kesh, as well as the great Gallery of Lords and Masters itself. Gardens were also scattered throughout the building, some encompassing fountains and pools.

At one time, only the Trueblood – the original Keshian tribe that had occupied this region around the great Overn Deep – had been permitted within the building after sundown. The only exception had been visiting royalty, ruling nobles and am-bassadors, and they had been confined to a specific corner of the Imperial palace from sundown to sunrise.

Now, Caleb said, things were a little less formal, for certain non-Trueblood nobles were now permitted to stay within the upper city, but it was rare and counted as an enormous privilege. Caleb had never visited the upper city, but knew many who had.

As they made their way through the crowded streets, the boys turned this way and that trying to make sense of the confusion of images, smells and sounds around them. Caleb had pointed out a few major landmarks for them to remember, so that they would learn the layout of the city and be able to navigate it quickly, but the boys were overwhelmed by the newness of everything and Caleb knew they had no idea where they were.

Tad and Zane were in awe. Everywhere they looked they encountered novelty: the Keshian garb, the cacophony of languages, the smells, the sights. Citizens from every corner of the Empire and travellers from all over the world flocked to Great Kesh. Proud Ashunta horsemen with their broad-brimmed felt hats bedecked with feathers, Cosodi traders with their bright robes of orange, red, yellow and lime patches, and Jajormir mystics dancing in circles with their beggar bowls at their feet all slowed the three riders to a crawl. A slave coffle made its way through one of the smaller markets, and both boys stared in horror at the abject misery of the unfortunates on their way to the slave block.

Each corner they turned brought them new sights, and they were constantly besieged by beggars, hawkers and thieves. The boys often batted away curious hands that were reaching to see if a purse might be tucked away behind a saddle or at the girth.

Charioteers of the Trueblood forced their way through the streets by cracking their whips above the heads of the commoners, who ducked out of the way to let the nobles pass. The heavy thud of boot-heels hitting cobblestones caused the boys to turn in their saddles. They saw a full company of black-armoured soldiers heading their way.

Caleb motioned for them to move their horses to the side of the road, and by the time they had reached the street's verge, the soldiers were passing them. Even the charioteers moved out of the way of the hundred men who marched towards them. They were armoured from head to foot – black pointed helms with nose bars and chain neck guards, black chest plates over black leather jackets, decorated with a single Keshian royal hawk, grieves and leggings – all fashioned from black steel. Their shields were square and slightly curved, so that they could form an interlocking shield wall, and each soldier carried a short spear over one shoulder and a shortsword at his side.

The sergeants' helms had short ridges across them and were topped with a horsehair bristle. The officers rode behind them in matching uniforms save that their crests sat fore to aft, and their horsehair bristles were a hand's span taller than the sergeants'.

'That's the Inner Legion,' said Caleb as the boys watched in awe. 'Kesh's dog soldiers are stationed from here to the Vale, but these lads are given the protection of the capital and the imperial palace. They'll not budge from this city, which is a good thing for their neighbours, as they tend to pick the toughest bastards in the army for that legion.' He pointed up towards the citadel on top of the plateau.

When the soldiers had passed, he motioned for them to start moving again and after another half an hour they reached an inn. Its sign showed three willow trees in a row. Caleb led Tad and Zane through the gate into the stabling yard and a boy hurried to meet them.

Once the horses were turned over to the lackey,

they entered the inn. It had a spacious, clean, and quiet common room, and they headed straight for the bar, where they were greeted by a tall, thin man with iron-grey hair and a full beard. 'Caleb! he cried out in greeting. 'It's good to see you again. Who are the lads behind you?'

'This is Tad,' Caleb said putting a hand on Tad's shoulder, 'and this is Zane,' he added putting his other hand on Zane's shoulder. 'They are my sons.'

'Sons!' said the barman, coming around to extend his hand in greeting. 'All these years I've known you and never one word about being married, let alone having sons.'

'It's a recent thing. I've adopted them.' He gave their shoulders a playful squeeze and slapped them on the back, then said, 'Boys, this is Pablo Maguire, owner of the Three Willows.'

The boys exchanged glances at the names – for they were as alien to Kesh as Tsurani names would have been – and the old innkeeper noticed. Smiling he said, 'My mother is from Rodez, – hence *Pablo*, after my grandfather – and my father came from Kinnochaide,' he said, using the Kinnochman's name for Kinnoch Province. 'Which is why I'm a Maguire, and as for how I came to be running a tavern in the heart of Great Kesh is another story for another time.' He spoke with the lilting rhythm the people of Kinnoch gave to their speech, and apparently to any language, as he spoke Keshian.

'I'll need two rooms,' said Caleb. 'Or the one big one at the end of the hall if it's free.'

'It's not, sad to say, for it's already occupied by a great lady and her daughters.' He glanced at the boys and said, 'Better steer a wide course away from them, lads, for they are Truebloods.'

Caleb's eyebrows went up in silent question, and Maguire feigned offence. 'What? A fine lady can't heave to at my inn?'

Caleb laughed. 'Obviously one can and has.'

Pablo's eyes were merry as he said, 'I know what you're thinking: with all the great residence houses in the city, why here? Well, truth to tell, they're not all wealthy or high-born, though—' he directed his remark to the boys '—they all act as if they're related to the Emperor and even the lowest Trueblood is still higher-born than the highest of the rest of us!' Looking at Caleb, he continued, 'This lady's in for the Midsummer's Festival.'

'It's a month away,' said Caleb.

'Well, she and the girls are buying things right now. I believe her husband is some governor or an important man in one of the southern provinces, and he's coming up to pay his respects to the Imperial family, or something like that. She tells me nothing, so I've had to piece that information together over the last week. They'll be here a while, so—' again he looked at the boys '—if you want to keep your heads on your shoulders give the girls room. The Trueblood have no sense of humour when it comes to their daughters' association with common boys.'

Tad and Zane glanced at one another and Tad shrugged. 'We'll behave ourselves,' he said.

Caleb gripped them both by the shoulders again and said, 'I'll make sure they do. Now, let's get cleaned up and have something to eat. I have a quick errand I must run, and then we can see some of the city in the evening. Tomorrow, we start working.'

Tad and Zane nodded, they knew that working had two meanings, and they were very nervous about the one that wouldn't be obvious.

Zane pointed. 'Look at those.'

Tad nodded and they approached the vendor whose booth was set up against the southernmost boundary wall of the main bazaar in the Hajana District of the lower city. The boys had been in Kesh a week now and were still hard pressed not to get lost.

They had carried out the same mission each day while Caleb was off on his own business. They wandered the merchant districts of the city, paying attention to everything they saw, and then at the end of the day they told Caleb what they had witnessed. Their cover-story was that they were scouting for possible items of interest to sell in the north – Krondor specifically, and that they were from the Vale of Dreams, hence their odd accents.

The newness of the Keshian city was beginning to wear off, though they were still easily distracted by some of its younger female inhabitants who passed by. Dress customs ranged from head-to-toe tribal dress that left only the eyes exposed, to the near-nudity of the Oshani lion hunters, Dingazi cattle herders and the Truebloods themselves. The boys would often stand in mute amazement as a dark-skinned girl of alien beauty walked by, ignoring the gawking northern youths. But even that distraction was beginning to wear off as they grew accustomed to it. And from a couple of ill-timed overtures made to passing girls in the city, they had learned that outlanders were seen as barely worthy of civility, let alone friendliness. Caleb had warned them that Kesh was an empire of many nations, some of whom were bitter enemies of others, and only the iron rule of the Emperor kept them from open warfare. Civility was a function of the rule of law, not a social concern.

Zane motioned for Tad to follow him to the vendor's table, passing a hawker offering lemon-flavoured cool water from an earthenware jar strapped to his back. The boys were dressed in their lightest clothes and were still not used to the heat, though they had been told that the city would get even hotter over the next few months.

The items that had caught Zane's eye were an unusual bunch of religious icons. Some of them were familiar to the boys, but others weren't. They examined them under the wary gaze of the merchant, who appeared ready in case they attempted to dash off with an item without paying for it. After a few minutes, he demanded, 'Buy now or move along. I have no time for such as you.'

Tad's eyes widened. He had been repeatedly

scolded to buy or move on by merchants all week, for penniless boys held no interest for them. He said, 'My master bids us find saleable items to take north and sell in the Kingdom of the Isles.'

'And who might your master be, O host to a thousand fleas?'

Zane tried not to laugh. He found the usual insults of the market extremely amusing. Tad just got irritated. 'Caleb, a merchant of wealth and standing in the Vale of Dreams. He trades from one end of the Bitter Sea to the other. Do you have sources that can supply curiosities such as these in quantity?'

Still appearing dubious, the merchant nevertheless modified his tone and said, 'If that is true, it would be a matter of what constitutes "quantity". Some of these items are of great craftsmanship and took many days to fashion.'

Zane stood examining the various icons and amulets. He held one up and stared at it even more intently. Slowly he put it back. Tad said, 'Say, perhaps a dozen of each of the more common gods worshipped in the north?'

'A week, two perhaps,' said the man, smelling a possible windfall.

Zane grabbed Tad's wrist and squeezed, saying, 'We will speak to our master and if he's interested, we will return tomorrow.'

Zane didn't wait for Tad to add anything more, and half-steered, half-pushed him away from the booth. When they were lost in the crowd and far from the merchant's view, Tad said, 'What?'

'One of those icons looked like the one Caleb told us to watch for. The thing that looked like a hawk.'

Tad glanced over his shoulder and then said, 'We should get back to the Three Willows and tell him.'

The boys hurried off and took the shortest route back to the inn they could remember, though it still took them almost an hour to find it.

Caleb sat at a table in the corner with another man; a stocky fellow wearing a red turban, a heavy brocade vest – despite the summer's heat – over the finest linen shirt. His face was dark, like sun-tanned leather, and his darker eyes regarded the boys as they approached the table.

Zane halted while Tad said, 'Caleb, may we speak to you for a moment, please?'

Caleb turned to look at the boys and said, 'You're back early.'

'We found something we think you might be interested in,' said Zane.

Caleb nodded as the other man stood. 'Boys, this is Chezarul, a trader from the west of the Empire. He's as stingy in a bargain as he is generous with his friends.' To the man, he said, 'These are my adopted sons.'

'Then I bid you welcome to the greatest city in the world. You are welcome guests in my home from now until the end of your days.' He bowed, and then shook hands with each of the boys.

Chezarul took his chair again and Tad said, 'Caleb, if we could have a moment, in private . . . ?'

Both men rose and Caleb said, 'If you will excuse me?'

Chezarul bowed and said, 'Bring the boys to my shop tomorrow, Caleb.'

He departed and they moved upstairs to the privacy of their room. 'What is it?'

Zane quickly described what they had seen and said, 'I don't know if it's the same amulet you told us to watch out for, but it could be.'

'I wish I had thought to show you the one in my father's possession,' said Caleb. 'There were just too many things going on when we left.' He paused, then nodded. 'I'll go with you tomorrow and if the vendor is there, we'll purchase some of his trinkets, with a promise to buy more. That should move him to contact his supplier and we can have him followed.' He put his hand on Zane's shoulder. 'You did well.'

Zane looked pleased with himself.

'I've got some errands to attend to for the next two hours. Go and do whatever you wish, but try not to find too much trouble. Be back here in two hours and we'll have supper together.'

'Yes, Caleb,' said Tad as their stepfather left the room.

'What now?' asked Tad.

'I don't know,' answered Zane. 'We could just rest here for a while?'

'Too hot,' he said. 'I'd just as soon keep exploring and see if there's anywhere we might be welcome – someplace to have some fun.'

Zane grinned. 'You mean someplace where the girls won't spit on us just because we have an odd accent.'

'That, too,' said Tad, returning the grin. 'I hear there's a small plaza over by the eastern caravanserai gate where foreigners gather. Maybe there . . . ?'

As Zane pulled the door wide open, he was confronted by a momentarily confusing sight. A slightly portly older woman, dressed in the fashion of the Trueblood, moved down the hall to his right, followed by two beautiful girls. Both were dressed like their mother, in linen skirts fastened with brooches at the hip and wearing decorative torques around their necks. A great deal of beadwork adorned their hair, and rings and bracelets made a racket as they moved. One of the girls caught his eye and smiled at him, while the other seemed intent upon something her mother was saying.

Zane halted suddenly and Tad bumped into him, forcing Zane to step into the hall. The girl who had turned to see who was at the door giggled and moved aside, causing her sister to also look in the boy's direction. Zane was on the verge of uttering an apology for startling them, when their mother turned to see the two somewhat dishevelled boys, still covered in grime from their day in the city under the sweltering sun.

'Mamanaud!' she said, her voice rising to an angry tone and she pointed at the boys.

Zane turned to look at Tad and said, 'Mamanaud?'

Just then, two fists the size of hams gripped the

boys' shoulders and the largest man they had ever seen shoved them hard, back into their room. Both lads collapsed in a heap, while in the hall, the older woman screamed what sounded vaguely like insults at them. The large man entered the room and pulled a very long, very sharp curved dagger from his belt.

Everything had taken place so quickly, the boys were not quite sure what had happened. The huge man took a menacing step towards them but suddenly a sword blade rested on his shoulder at the crook of his neck, and a voice from behind him said, 'Try not to move, my friend, unless you wish to bleed profusely.'

The huge man frowned and froze in mid-step, his face looking like a dark brown pumpkin with eyes and a tiny nose above his broad mouth. The woman shouted something unintelligible from the hall and a man's voice answered her. 'I'm sure it was all just a misunderstanding, madam, and the boys meant no harm or insult.'

Still prevented from seeing anything through the door by the motionless behemoth who occupied their entire field of vision, the boys then heard the voice of Pablo Maguire saying, 'What is going on here?'

A three-voiced conversation then ensued; the woman shouting in an almost hysterical pitch, while two male voices appeared to be trying to assuage her concerns.

The big man in the doorway put his dagger away

slowly and backed out the door, so now the boys could see a swordsman standing behind him, his blade resting on the man's neck. 'Now, I'm going to remove my sword from your neck,' he said, 'and you'll go see to your mistress without any more fuss.'

The bodyguard moved forward a step and turned. Just before he could face the wielder of the blade, he found the point of the weapon at his neck once more. 'Ah ah ah!' said the young man holding the sword. 'That wouldn't be very wise.'

The big man stepped away, threw a nasty glance at the two boys and turned and vanished into the room at the end of the hall.

The man with the sword walked over to the door and said, 'You boys all right?'

Tad and Zane both nodded. Tad said, 'We are in your debt.'

'Not really,' said the man, putting his sword into its scabbard. He had dark hair and blue eyes, and his movements were cat-quick. He smiled and looked younger than he had a moment before. 'I followed them up the stairs, and when I saw the confusion ahead of me, I thought it best to keep that mountain of a man – assuming he is human and not some troll they've shaved – from gutting you two.' He glanced around. 'Actually, I was looking for a man named Caleb.'

'That's our step-father,' said Zane. 'He's going to be gone for a while.'

'Ah,' said the swordsman. 'Well, I guess I need to come back later. How long might he be?'

'He said two hours,' answered Tad. 'We were going to do some more exploring over by the eastern caravanserai.'

He nodded. 'I think I shall wait here for a few more minutes.' He indicated the end of the hall with a lift of his chin. 'Just to make sure you're not followed. I don't think Caleb would appreciate me letting you get turned into chopped meat any time soon.'

'I'm Tad, and this is Zane.'

The man bowed, and the boys could see he was finely dressed. 'I'm Talwin Hawkins, an old friend of Caleb.' He winked at the boys. 'Go on, then; see if you can find some fun that doesn't involve bloodshed.'

He stood aside as the boys left the room and then followed them into the hall and down the stairs. Reaching the common room, Tal said, 'I have a message for Caleb, when you see him.'

'Sir?' asked Tad.

'Tell him the usual time, same place, tomorrow night. Got it?'

Tad repeated the message back to him.

'I need to be off, just in case.'

'Just in case, sir?' asked Zane.

'Yes, exactly,' said Tal, moving towards the door. 'If I were you, I would head outside and keep yourselves busy until Caleb returns. That bodyguard up there could eat you both for lunch and still have room for an ox.' He disappeared out the door.

Tad looked at Zane. 'Well, we still have some daylight. Let's wander around the bazaar.'

Seeing no reasonable alternative, the boys returned outside and decided to use the last hours of sunlight for something more enjoyable than being thrashed by Mamanaud.

# CHAPTER 12

# DISCOVERY

Nakor looked around.

'What exactly are we looking for?'

Pug motioned around himself, swinging his arm in a wide arc ahead of them. 'Since Leso Varen fled Olasko, we've been trying to find the range of his "death rifts", for lack of a better term.'

'That much I know,' said Nakor, walking through knee-high grass.

They were standing with Ralan Bek in the middle of a wide grassland that swept down from the mountains to the east, approximately three days' ride from the border between the Kingdom of the Isles and the Duchy of Maladon and Semrick. Had they travelled by horseback from the nearest city, Maladon, it would have taken another four days.

Bek stood watching the two men wandering through the grass in front of him and laughed. 'Are we going to be walking around in circles all day?'

Pug glanced at the troubling young man and nodded. 'If needs be. Over a year ago we found evidence of some very powerful, very dark magic, and without boring you further, let's just say that there is a relationship between that magic and a great deal of trouble yet to come.

'It would help us if we could find . . . the track, if you will, between the place this magic originated – in Olakso's capital, Opardum – and somewhere else. Our best calculations indicate that we should find a place where we can pick up that trail somewhere near here, if that makes sense.'

Bek shook his head and laughed. 'You name places I've never heard of. One moment it's midwinter, and the next it's summer. You speak with a strange tongue, yet I can still understand most of what you say.

'Besides,' he added with another laugh, 'I was not given the choice about being here or not. So, here I am.' He narrowed his gaze at Pug. 'And none of it makes sense.'

Pointing to a stand of trees a hundred yards to the north, he added, 'But I think you'll find what you're looking for over there.'

Pug raised his eyebrows as he looked at Nakor, who shrugged. The two men turned towards the trees and Nakor said, 'I don't sense anything.'

'Varen worked hard to disguise his work. Look how long it took us to trace the link this far.'

Turning to Bek, Nakor said, 'Stay here so we can mark this spot if we find nothing in the trees.'

Bek took off the black hat he had taken from the man he had killed at the Talnoy's cave and feigned a courtly bow. 'Your wish is my command, Nakor.'

The two old friends walked towards the trees and Pug said, 'Have you thought about what we should do with him?'

Nakor said, 'The simple solution is to kill him.'

'We've murdered for our cause, but only when we judged that there was no other way.' Pug glanced back at Bek who stood quietly where they had told him to wait. 'And had you thought that there was no other way, I am certain you would never have brought him to Sorcerer's Isle.'

'True. Potentially, he may be the most dangerous man we have ever encountered.' Nakor reached into his bag, pulled out an orange and offered it to Pug who shook his head. The little gambler started to peel it. 'As powerful as he is at twenty summers old, can you imagine what he might become in a hundred years, two hundred?'

'Will he survive that long?' asked Pug as they reached the edge of the trees.

'Look at you, me and Miranda,' said Nakor as they stepped between the boles. The white and brown peeling bark confused their vision for a moment, as did the sudden shadow after standing out in the midday sun. 'You and Miranda have powerful magic to keep you young, but me, I only have my tricks.'

Pug nodded, smiling indulgently. 'Call it what you will, Nakor. I'll concede that your talent has no logic or system to it, but you may still be the most adept practitioner of magic on this world.'

Nakor shrugged. 'I don't think so, but that's not

the point.' He lowered his voice, as if there was a remote chance Bek could overhear them. 'I have something inside me, Pug. I don't know what it is, but I know it's been here,' he tapped his chest, 'since I was a boy.

'I am like Bek in some ways. But I think that whatever it is inside of me, it is not a piece of the Nameless One. But it is similar. I think that's why I can do all my tricks.'

Pug nodded. 'We've drunk many a cup of wine before the fire whilst discussing this sort of thing, Nakor.'

'But this is not a theory anymore, Pug. He is real.' He pointed in Bek's direction. 'And when I touched that thing within him, there was no doubt about what I found. No doubt at all.'

Pug nodded, saying nothing.

'One of our favourite discussions is about the nature of the gods.'

'Many times,' said Pug.

'I once told you that I suspected that there is an ultimate god. A being that is connected to everything – I mean everything, Pug. And everything below him, her or it, is also connected.'

'I remember. It's as good an explanation for how the universe hangs together as any I've heard. Your theory is that the Greater Gods, the Lesser Gods, and all other beings, were this ultimate god's attempt to understand himself.'

'I've said that he's like a baby before – pushing things off a table to watch them fall, over and over and over. Watching and trying to understand what is happening. But we are talking about a time scale of millions of years; billions, perhaps. This supreme being has all the time in the world, more – it has all the time there ever was or will be.

'Would it then not make sense that the gods beneath this one might also somehow reach down and touch lesser beings, so they too might come to understand their place in the universe?'

'So the Nameless One placed a tiny piece of himself inside Bek in order to learn about his place in the universe?'

'No,' said Nakor. 'It's possible, but I don't think that is his intention.

'I think the Nameless One has had many agents like Varen working on his behalf over the years.' Nakor looked at Pug. 'Tell me about him.'

'You've heard all I know already.'

'Tell me about the time you first encountered him.'

'When I first got word of him, he was already an accomplished practitioner of the dark arts. Arutha was the prince in Krondor then, and Duke James his principal agent, a young Baron at the time; he, my son, and one of my most able students confronted a magician named Sidi, who I now believe was Varen in a different body.'

'I remember that story about the amulet,' said Nakor. 'No one's ever found it, have they?'

Pug shook his head. 'It's still out there somewhere. Until the assault on Elvandar and our island last year, seizing the Tear of the Gods was Varen's last overt attempt at bringing chaos to our world.

'Between those events he was content to work in quiet, out-of-the-way, places.'

'Like Kaspar of Olasko's Citadel?' asked Nakor with a grin.

'Hardly an out-of-the way place, I'll grant you, but how many people knew he was there? It was a very well-kept secret outside Kaspar's household,' Pug said. 'His necromancy has given him the power to move from body to body. My research indicates that somewhere there is a vessel in which his true *soul* – for lack of a better term – resides. This allows his mind to capture bodies and use them at will.

'He will not stop until he destroys the Conclave or any other opposition to his mission, which is simply to propagate evil at every hand. So, he is a problem.' Pug pointed in Bek's direction. 'And now, from what you say, we have another one right over there.'

'But I don't think he's like Varen,' said Nakor, tossing aside the orange peel. 'Varen was recruited, or seduced, or trapped, conned, or whatever term you like, either with the promise of power or eternal life or something. No sane man gives himself over willingly to evil.'

'There is nothing sane about Leso Varen.'

'But he may have been at one time,' said Nakor, 'merely a luckless man who blundered into the wrong place at the wrong time. That amulet you spoke of can take over a weak-willed man and drive him mad. And sanity is all that stands between good and evil.

'There is no possibility that this young man will be remotely sane in a few more years. He's already lost any sense of morality; he is driven by impulse and little else.'

'What possible use can we have for a man with no morality, no moral compunctions against doing evil?'

'We found a use for Kaspar, didn't we?' asked Nakor.

Pug was silent for a moment, then said, 'Point taken, but he was under Varen's influence. This lad is directly touched by the Nameless One. Isn't that a difference?'

'I don't know, Pug, but I know we either have to kill him soon, before he becomes too dangerous, or try to change him somehow.'

'I can understand your reluctance to kill him outright, Nakor, but why the desire to change him?'

'Because what if my surmise is correct, that the gods put tiny pieces of themselves in us to learn?'

'Fair enough, but you said you doubted the Nameless One was motivated by such.'

'Yes,' said Nakor with another grin. 'But there are often unintended consequences of our acts. What if we can send back this tiny message that without a balance, and without good, evil can not exist?'

'From what you've surmised, would it make any difference?'

'It must, for it is the nature of reality. Consider the ancient symbol of the Yin and Yang, the circle contains both black and white, but within the white is a spot of black, and within the black a spot of white! Opposing forces, but each with a touch of the other within. While he may be mad, the Nameless One must recognize it as a fundamental truth.'

Pug laughed ruefully. 'We may never know, and that is fine, for the gods have given us limited scope in our powers and knowledge. I'm content with that. But I must put those things I can understand and control ahead of your theories, no matter how wondrous they may be.

'In the end, should Bek prove a threat to the Conclave, I will destroy him as I would step on a cockroach. Without hesitation. Are we clear on this?'

'Very,' said Nakor, losing his grin. 'But I think we need to study this youngster for a while longer before destroying him.'

'Agreed, but I want you to consult with others back at the Island. And before that, I want you back in Novindus with the Talnoy. They are a real and immediate threat. We need to find a way to control them without using that ring.'

Nakor nodded in agreement. The ring that controlled the Talnoy had the unfortunate side effect of driving the wearer mad.

Pug looked around. 'Now, let's see if we can find that trail.'

'It's over there,' said Nakor, pointing to a tiny shimmering fragment hanging about five feet in the air, among some brush. 'I noticed it while we were talking.'

Pug hurried over to the tiny fragment of energy, less than eight inches long, floating in the air, between two branches of a bush. 'We could have been out here for years,' said Pug. 'How do you think the boy knew?'

Nakor shrugged. 'This is a very evil thing, and given his nature . . . ?'

'You think he's somehow attuned?'

'Apparently,' replied Nakor. He studied the tiny energy fragment. 'Do you have any idea how this thing works?'

'When I fought against the magic of Murmandamus, under the city of Sethanon, I encountered something like this, but far less subtle. It was the brute force approach to the problem. This is delicate, almost . . . artistic.'

'Given the carnage we found in that abattoir Varen lived in at Kaspar's citadel, this is un-expected,' Nakor observed.

'Varen might be a murderous madman, but he's not stupid. In fact, were he sane, he might have been a valuable asset to us.'

'Were he sane, there might not be any "us", Pug.'

'Not the Conclave, perhaps, but there would have been some group of us or another working together.'

Nakor studied it and said, 'Where does this

259

go?' He pointed to the tiny thread of energy, a shimmering silver-green light that was no more than a foot long.

Pug pointed to the end that was closer to himself. 'This comes from the last place it manifested. There's a quality about it that is the same.' He pointed to the east. 'About a hundred or so miles that way.'

'Did it look like this?'

'No,' said Pug softly. 'There it was a sphere, about the size of a grape. And it was somehow anchored in place by energy that tethered it to the ground. It was invisible to the eye and without substance, so you could walk through it and never notice. It took a particularly adept spell to reveal it to us. This appears to be . . .' He looked back along the line of the energy, as if seeing something. 'I don't know how he did this. It looks as if . . .' Then his eyes widened. 'He's found a way to make this energy jump, Nakor!'

'What do you mean by *jump*?'

'This end here,' Pug said, pointing, 'is not a hundred miles from the sphere. It's connected to it.' He stood silent a moment, then said, 'It's akin to the Tsurani spheres we use to transport ourselves from place to place.'

'But those are devices,' said Nakor.

'Miranda doesn't need a sphere,' said Pug softly. 'She can will herself from place to place if she knows where she's going.'

'But no one else can.'

Pug smiled. 'So I thought, but you forgot to use one when you left the cave on the island the last time we met.'

Nakor shrugged. 'It's a trick.'

Pug nodded. 'She's been trying to teach Magnus and me the trick, then; we still haven't got it, but then we've only been working on it twenty years or so.'

'If that end attaches to the sphere,' said Nakor, 'where does the other end attach?'

Pug squinted at it, as if he might see where it led. After a few minutes of almost motionless study, his eyes grew round. 'Nakor,' he whispered, as if afraid to raise his voice.

'What?'

'It's a rift!'

'Where?' said Nakor.

'At the end of that energy thread. It's tiny beyond imagining, but it's there. Varen made his rift work. At first I thought he was storing vast energy to create a rift of normal size, but I was wrong. He just wanted a tiny rift, but one left open . . . for years.'

Nakor took a deep breath. 'You know more about rifts than any man living, Pug, so I'll not doubt you, but how can one exist that's so tiny?'

'The level of control to fashion one like this, and to keep it stable, in place, for the year or more we've been seeking this . . . it's unbelievable.' Pug stood upright and said, 'Someone out there knows more about rifts than I do, Nakor. I could never fashion something this delicate, this precise.'

261

'We better get back to Bek,' said Nakor, 'before he sets fire to the grass just to have something to watch. What do you want to do about this?'

'I'm going to send a few of our better scholars and ask Magnus to see if we can entice a pair of Tsurani Great Ones to come and examine this thing. We will not have unravelled the mystery of what Leso Varen was doing in Kaspar's citadel until we find the other end of this energy thread, and that means the other side of the rift.'

Nakor put his hand on Pug's shoulder and squeezed slightly, as if reassuring him. 'The other side of the rift could be a very bad place.'

'It almost certainly is,' said Pug.

Nakor said, 'And we still need to talk about those messages you've shown me.'

'I don't know what more to say, Nakor.' Pug's expression grew thoughtful. 'I may have erred in showing them to you. I haven't even told Miranda.'

Nakor lost his smile. Pug rarely saw the little man look this thoughtful, so he knew whatever was said next would be something serious. Suddenly the grin was back, and Nakor said, 'Then you are in very serious trouble when she finds out.'

Pug laughed. 'I know, but she's got the worst temper of anyone in the family, and if she read those messages . . . we both know that time travel is possible. I journeyed to the dawn of time with Macros and Tomas, but I don't know how to do it.'

'Apparently, in the future, you do.'

'But you know what the big question is, don't you?'

Nakor nodded as they turned away from the tiny glowing thread of magic. 'Are you sending messages to yourself to ensure a thing happens, or are you sending a message to prevent a thing that has happened to you from coming to be?'

'I thought about the very first message that appeared to me, the morning before Earl James and the boy Princes left for Kesh.'

'Tell James if he meets a strange man to say, "There is no magic."' Nakor nodded. 'How do you think you knew that would be me?'

'My theory is that we met much later in life, perhaps sometime yet in the future, and when things were much more dire than they are now. Perhaps it was my way of ensuring we had years to work together.'

'I wondered much the same thing,' said Nakor. 'But we'll never know, will we?'

'If the future is fluid, then whatever I did changed things . . .' He laughed. 'Macros.'

'What about him?'

'His hand is in this, I know,' said Pug. 'Like everything else in my life . . .' He shrugged. 'If you get the chance, next time you see Tomas, ask him about the armour he wears and his dreams from the past, and . . . well, let him tell you. But that was Macros, and it also involved time travel.'

'I will.'

They walked out of the woods, and neither man spoke a word until they reached Bek. The young man grinned. 'Find it?'

'Yes,' said Pug. 'How did you know it was there?'

Bek shrugged. 'I don't know. I just felt it was there.'

Pug and Nakor exchanged a look, then Nakor said, 'Let's go.'

'Can we get something to eat?' asked Bek. 'I'm starving.'

'Yes,' said Pug. 'We'll feed you.' Silently, he added to himself, *And we'll care for you as long as you don't become a threat. Then we'll kill you.*

Pug took out a Tsurani orb and the three of them vanished from the grassy plain.

# CHAPTER 13

## ICONS

Kaspar strode into the room.
Talwin Hawkins and Caleb both nodded greeting.

'It's done,' said Kaspar.

'Political asylum?' asked Caleb.

'Of a sort. But it will do for our purposes.'

'It's good to have friends in high places,' said Tal.

They were in a small room in the back of an inn, located in a different district of the city from where Caleb and the boys were staying, one frequented by foreigners and those from distant corners of the Empire. The coming and going of three obviously non-Keshians would not draw attention here. It was late and the city was quieting down, though this area was replete with revellers, as the plaza outside was frequented by the youth of this district. Against his better judgment, Caleb had left the boys outside near a fountain where a dozen or so young boys and girls had gathered. Still, he suspected they would find less trouble out in the open than if he left them in their room next to the two Trueblood girls, their excitable mother, and their personal bodyguard.

When he had finally seen the man, he wondered, like Tal had said, if he was really human.

'Turgan Bey has told me what his agents have discovered, so far,' said Kaspar. A pewter pitcher rested on the table and he poured himself a cup of wine. Drinking it, he made a face. 'We should chuck this business and set up a wine importer from Ravensburg and some of the districts in the Eastern Kingdoms. We'd make a fortune if this is the best they have.'

'This is not the River House,' said Tal with a smile, referring to the restaurant he had established in Roldem. 'And this is not the best wine that can be had in Kesh, as you know.'

Caleb took a sip. 'It is, however, the best that can be had here.'

Kaspar leaned forward. 'There is no pattern in the deaths, save one. Every murdered noble, Trueblood or not, is part of a loose alliance of Lords and Masters who are favourable to the ascension of Prince Sezioti to the throne when Diigai finally dies.'

Caleb said, 'And is that supposed to happen any time soon?'

'You tell me,' said Kaspar. 'Your father and brother are more likely to understand the information on the Emperor's use of magic to extend his life than anyone.

'But it's clear from what Bey told me that many of the Lords and Masters are unhappy with him being the first Emperor to do so. His predecessor, Empress Leikesha, made it to over ninety on sheer spite – according to what I've been told she may have been the toughest old boot to ever sit on that throne – so the extra ten years or so for Diigai isn't a problem yet, but it's his use of magic that is. Seems the opinion of a majority of the rules of Great Kesh is the old boy is losing his political edge. He spends most of his time with his courtesans – which at his age, I think is heroic – and many of his edicts seem capricious. But none of them alter significant policy, so the level of distress over his current rule hasn't reached a critical juncture, but the Gallery of Lords and Masters' collective patience is wearing thin, and eventually the Emperor will be pressured to name an heir.'

'Sezioti is a scholar who is respected, but not admired.' Kaspar went on to tell them the rest of what Turgan Bey had shared about the politics of the Empire.

'So,' said Tal, 'we can assume someone is trying very carefully to reduce Sezioti's chances to rise to the throne, in favour of Dangai. Why?'

'If the Nighthawks were not involved,' said Caleb, 'I would assume it's the usual bloody Keshian politics. But with the Guild of Death working here, we must assume Leso Varen's hand is in there somewhere, which means whatever he wants, we want the opposite.'

Kaspar stood. 'I can't stay. I am no doubt being followed, and while they know Tal and I are in contact, they don't know about you. I suggest you leave last.' Caleb nodded. 'There's a reception at the townhouse of Lord Gresh in a week,' Kaspar said to Tal. 'See if you can get yourself invited. It's just your sort of crew: a lot of libertines, bored noble wives, curious daughters, degenerate gamblers, and hot-blooded boys looking to make a name for themselves by killing someone famous. You should be able to make half a dozen enemies in one night with some luck.'

Tal regarded Kaspar with a dour expression. 'I'll try my best.'

'I'll send Pasko with word as soon as I know anything worth reporting to you,' said Kaspar, and he left.

Tal said, 'He's almost certainly right about being followed. I'll leave next, and then you should wait a bit. Do you think you can get through the commons without being spotted?'

'If no one saw me enter, yes,' said Caleb. 'And I was here for a full half-hour before either of you arrived, so I think I'm safe.

'Still, now that we know Kaspar and you are being watched, I should undertake to be more cautious in the future. I'll make arrangements so our next meeting is more secure.'

Tal glanced around the room. 'What about being observed by . . . other means?'

Caleb reached into his belt purse and pulled out a small item. He handed it to Tal who looked at it. It appeared nothing more than a carved bone icon, some obscure household god, perhaps. 'Nasur, a magician of the Lesser Path on my father's island, made this. It prevents scrying or other magical eavesdropping. As long as I have it, no one can see or hear us by magical arts.'

Tal said, 'A good thing to have. You wouldn't have an extra one, would you?'

'Even if I did, I wouldn't give it to you. If you are being marked by Varen's agents, they might be using arts to see or hear you. If you vanish from their ability to detect you here, why it's simply a case of something not working right, or perhaps you or Kaspar ensuring this room was safe. If you vanish from sight all the time, they'll know you're more than what you appear to be.'

'And what do I appear to be?'

'Right now both you and Kaspar are agents of the Crown of Roldem, and not very good ones at that. It took some very aggressive rumour mongering to get that one spread in the right quarters.

'Kesh is always nervous about Roldem, because of their navy. Give them something obvious and reasonable to worry about, and they won't spend a lot of time concerning themselves with the subtle. No one who isn't working for Varen even suspects the Conclave exists here in Kesh.'

'Except for those agents in the government who work for the Conclave.'

Caleb nodded. 'It's taken my father years to get to the place he is right now. We have friends in very high positions in courts all over the world, without the entanglements of being obliged to any one government.

'Now, it's time for you to go and should I need to see you, I'll send one of the boys with a message.'

Tal rose, shook hands with Caleb, then left. As he reached the door he turned and said, 'When this is all over, would you like to head up to Kendrick's and do some hunting for a few days?'

Caleb grinned. 'After we see the wives for a bit, yes. That would be welcomed.'

Tal returned the smile and left.

Caleb sat back, content to wait for another hour before leaving, to ensure he wasn't being followed. He idly wondered how the boys were doing.

Zane struck the ground, sliding backwards on his rump. He hit the edge of the fountain hard enough to knock the air out of his lungs. Tad shouted, 'What was that for?' as he leaped between Zane and the young man who had just pushed him hard enough to knock him over.

The fellow stopped and said, 'What's it to you?'

'That's my brother you just shoved.'

The fellow was large, and brutish looking, with massive shoulders and a thick brow. His chin receded slightly, which gave him an almost malevolent expression when he grinned. 'And that's my girl he was talking to.'

The girl in question, a plump but very pretty blonde who had moments before been flirting with both boys, shouted, 'I am not your girl, Arkmet. Stop telling people I am.'

'You're my girl if I say you are,' he said with a sound that came close to an animal growl.

Tad smiled. 'She says she's not your girl.'

Arkmet pushed at Tad, but unlike Zane he was ready. He bent his right knee, while extending his left leg, grabbed Arkmet's outstretched left hand at the wrist and gave it a tug before releasing it. Meeting no resistance, the heavier boy went crashing face down on the cobbles.

Zane was back on his feet and standing next to Tad when the larger youngster rolled over. His face was flushed and he said, 'You shouldn't have done that!'

Standing side by side, both boys were ready for a fight, and Zane said, 'We're not starting anything, fellow, but if you want to take us on alone, we're ready.'

With another evil grin, the young man on the ground slowly rose and said, 'Who said I was alone?'

The boys looked behind themselves and saw that a group of large boys gathered. 'And who are you?' asked Tad.

A blond lad said, 'We're the apprentices of the Bakers' Guild.' He hiked his thumb over his shoulder to the four boys who stood behind him. 'Arkmet is an apprentice baker.'

Tad looked at Zane and rolled his eyes. 'So he's a friend of yours?'

The blond lad said, 'No, pretty much none of us can abide the slug, but we have a rule. You hit one Bakers' Boy, you hit all of us.'

Zane said, 'Wish someone had told us that before we got here.'

Until a moment ago, Tad and Zane had been lazing around the fountain, flirting with some approachable local girls. The plaza seemed to be frequented by young men and women from other parts of the Empire, youngsters who were far more amenable to speaking with two boys from the distant Vale of Dreams.

'I don't suppose there's a Guild of Boys From Other Parts of the Empire around here,' said Zane, glancing first one way, then the other. Several young men were giving the coming battle a wide berth, but one boy of roughly the same age as Tad and Zane came and stood beside them.

'Six to two's no kind of fair dust-up.' He was large, with powerful shoulders, a red-headed boy with a preposterous amount of freckles across his face, green eyes, and hands the size of a smith's hammer. With an almost demonic grin he said, 'But six to three seems a little better.'

One of the Bakers' Boys said, 'Ah, Jommy, not again?'

The red-headed boy cocked his right fist next to his ear, and with his left hand beckoned the bakers' apprentices to approach. 'Always, mate. I love a chance to put your flour-dusted butts in a sling. Com'on!'

The resolve seemed to leach out of the five apprentices, just as a bellowing shout came from behind. Zane and Tad turned, but nothing as fast as the redhead, who turned with stunning speed and with a straight punch caught Arkmet right in the face. The bully's eyes rolled up in his head and he collapsed to the ground, blood fountaining from his broken nose.

Jommy turned and said, 'Five to three; even better!'

'You're a madman,' said the blond baker's apprentice.

Jommy held up his hands palms out. 'I realize you boys have your sense of honour and duty, but come on. Do you really want to bleed for that lout?'

The blond lad looked at the four who stood behind him and just from the way they exchanged glances told Tad and Zane the fight wasn't going to start. 'Not really,' said the blond boy. 'The last time you hit me I couldn't hear out of my left ear for three days.'

'Well, you bully boys of the Bakers' Guild should realize that you're not bloody damn cocks-of-the-walk around here and start treating others with respect, mate. Now take your idiot friend here home and leave well-meaning strangers alone.'

The five bakers' apprentices helped the still groggy Arkmet to his feet and led him away. Zane turned to see the blonde girl had somehow vanished during all the trouble, while Tad stuck out his hand and said, 'Thank you, my friend.'

'No worries,' said the affable redhead. 'Name's Jommy Kiliroo.'

'You're not from around here, are you?' asked Zane.

'Ha!' said the boy. 'Far from home.'

Caleb walked up. 'If I recognize that accent, very far,' he said. 'I saw what happened.' To Tad and Zane, he said, 'You boys managed to avoid a fair beating it seems.'

'Probably would have taken one, if it hadn't been for Jommy here,' said Zane.

'Ah, most of the bakers' lads aren't really too bad a lot, but that Arkmet is a real canted bastard, if you take my meaning. He's going to end up hung for murder, mark my words.'

'You're from around Serpent River?'

The young man's face went alight. 'You've been down there, have you?'

'A couple of times. Where are you from?'

'Mooree, little town a couple of days upriver from Shingazi's Landing.'

'How'd you come to Kesh?'

'That's a long story in the telling. The short of it is my mate Rolie and I got tossed out of our homes by our fathers, who told us to be on our way and start our own lives. We worked our way downriver to the City of the Serpent River and tried to get jobs, but if you've been there, you know everything is controlled by the clans. Not ashamed to say I took up a little thievery to get by. Ol' Rolie and me got a berth on a Keshian ship, bound for Elarial. We had no better prospects, so we signed on and became sailors. Only one voyage for me to tell it wasn't my kind of life, so when we berthed, we took our pay and left. Got jobs as teamsters and, well, one thing leads to another. Ol' Rolie got himself killed in a brawl up in the town of Chigatha, and I just kept working the caravans, and here I am. Been stranded here for almost a year now.'

'Where do you live?' asked Tad.

'Here and there. Weather's warm most of the time so sleeping in an alley or by a fountain's not a problem. Once in a while I find a girl who takes me home.' He inclined his head to the fountain. 'Most of the youngsters from other places come around here, so there's less trouble, unless a bunch like those bakers' lads show up. I've mixed with them before, and they remember.' He grinned. 'Now, how'd you find your way to Novindus?'

'That's a long story, too,' said Caleb. 'How'd you like me to stand you to a meal and a warm bed?'

'Find by me, but I'd rather find steady work. Truth to tell, this city may be the greatest in the world, but it's a fair bastard on a lad without family or guild, and that's the truth.'

'Walk with us,' said Caleb, 'and I'll tell you about my trips to your homeland.'

Tad and Zane exchanged questioning looks, but said nothing. But they had an odd feeling that somehow they had let a stray dog follow them home and fed it. What they didn't know is if the dog would bite.

★   ★   ★

Zane stood quietly next to Caleb as he examined the religious icons. Tad had been sent on a pointless errand with Jommy, who it seemed had attached himself to Caleb and the boys with no apparent effort. They had sat around the table at the inn the night before and exchanged stories, and Tad and Zane both had found the new boy likeable, amusing, and a reasonable companion. Caleb hadn't told either of his stepsons why he had decided to keep Jommy close, but given how difficult this city could be, and how handy the large redhead was in a brawl, they were glad of the addition.

Caleb examined and ordered a full half-dozen pieces before picking up the hawk. It was not the same icon as the one on the amulet worn by the Nighthawks, but it was close. 'I don't recognize this,' said Caleb.

The merchant, named Mudara, said, 'It is strange to me, as well. I purchased it from a boy, a beggar or thief perhaps, but before that, its provenance is unknown. I have seen similar icons from time to time, but not one quite like this.' He was a thin, nervous man, with a beak of a nose and a receding chin. His eyes, however, showed a man of shrewd judgment, an experienced businessman who should not be underestimated.

Caleb shrugged, as if it was of little importance, and he looked at two others before returning to the hawk. 'You say you've seen others almost like this?'

'Yes. There's a sect of worshippers of Lims-Kragma, far to the south. They come to the city from time to time, and they can be identified by an amulet they wear. I do not know what they are called.'

Caleb ordered two more items, and said, 'I will not need the hawk amulet. If, as you say, it is worn by a minor sect far to the south, none of their faithful will be found in Krondor.' The merchant looked slightly disappointed and immediately began showing other pieces. After a moment, Caleb returned to the hawk. He shrugged. 'Perhaps I am being hasty.' Hope spread across the merchant's face. He had already realized more profit from this one transaction than he earned in a month, but like all of his class, he was anxious for even more. 'As a curio, perhaps. You say you haven't seen one exactly like this, but others that are close?'

'Yes, my friend,' said Mudara. 'They are heavier, iron or a metal blend I think, and worn with a stout chain. Under the tunic, as a rule.'

'Do you think you can find some of those?'

Instantly the man's face became expressionless. 'Not of those, I fear. But I have a source for these, if you can wait a week. There are many fine craftsmen in the city who can duplicate anything you give them to copy.'

Caleb shrugged. 'For my buyers, authenticity is required. They are . . . collectors, and have no interest in cheap imitations. If you can get some of those medallions you speak of, contact me at the Three Willows. I will be here another two weeks. Send a message to Caleb.'

They finished their transaction and shook, and Caleb departed. As they walked, Caleb said, 'I want you to hang around this plaza for the rest of the day and watch that merchant. Try not to be seen, but if he does catch a glimpse of you, smile and wave like you're just about my business. Look at some merchandise, but keep your eyes on him. If he talks to anyone, mark them. If he leaves, follow him, but under no circumstances let him see you following him. If it comes to it, I'd rather have you give up the chase and return to the Three Willows than get spied out. We can always follow him another time. Do you understand?'

Zane nodded, and moved at once to another part of the plaza, so he might circle around and come back to the merchant unseen. Caleb walked purposefully towards Chezarul's shop, for he needed an experienced agent to track the merchant. He wanted Zane off the man's trail as soon as possible, but in case the merchant left before one of Chezarul's men could replace him, he needed eyes on the man. Caleb cursed himself for not thinking of this before he went to see the merchant. He knew his mind wasn't on the tasks his father had set before him, and now he understood the risks his father had spoken of before he had met Marie. Having people around you about whom you worry is a distraction and makes you vulnerable. He never should have brought the boys with him, he thought.

★   ★   ★

Zane watched as the market began to build up with people seeking to buy goods on their way home from their own work. Zane knew from experience that this flurry of shopping would end quickly and then the market would soon become deserted as the merchants and their helpers rapidly broke down stalls and tables then carted goods away. He had watched in amazement the first time when the entire market square went from so crowded it was almost impossible to move without jostling someone to deserted in less than an hour. He was almost certain Mudara had not noticed him, but he knew that as soon as the stalls began to break down, hiding would be more difficult.

Zane started looking for a vantage point and spied a deep doorway in which he could hide. He slipped into it and watched. As he anticipated, Mudara was anxious to be on his way to place his order with his suppliers for the items Caleb had purchased. He was among the first to close down his stall and put his amulets and icons into a deep bag. He hefted the bag over his shoulder and quickly moved away.

Zane fell in behind him. He knew that no one was likely to find him now, and was determined not to let Caleb down. He tried his hardest not to skulk and draw attention to himself, but he felt obvious and self-conscious. He kept people between himself and Mudara, and was pleased that the merchant never paused or looked over his shoulder.

They left the crowded streets of the prosperous

merchants' quarters and entered what looked to be a less populated section of the city, dominated by warehouses and the other businesses Zane associated with commerce, leather workers, stables, cartwrights, wheelwrights, an office for porters, and an office that appeared to provide mercenary guards.

Mudara entered a business establishment that had copious amounts of smoke coming from a stone chimney in the rear, and the sounds of hammers ringing out on metal filled the air, despite the late hour. Zane assumed this was the where he had his icons and amulets cast.

Zane couldn't tell how much time passed while Mudara conducted business inside, but it seemed like hours. It was dark when the man finally came out, and Zane watched him from a vantage point behind some large crates sitting outside a currently unoccupied warehouse.

He decided to follow the man. Either the merchant would go home or lead him to another supplier. The merchant again paid no heed to his surroundings nor appeared to be concerned about being followed, and hurried along.

Zane dodged the occasional passerby, and kept the merchant in his sights. Soon, Mudara's manner changed, and Zane almost was spotted as the merchant suddenly turned to see if he was being followed. It was only by chance that Zane had been deep in a shadow at that moment, else he would have been found out.

Zane realized at that moment that this was exactly

the sort of behaviour Caleb had warned him to be cautious of. The merchant was going somewhere he did not wish to be observed, and without understanding why, Zane knew it was dangerous.

Caleb had impressed on both boys the risks they would face with the life that had been thrust upon them, and for the first time Zane fully understood what Caleb had meant. His mouth was dry and his heart pounded, but Zane mustered his courage and stalked the merchant.

Zane kept track of turns and occasional landmarks, for he was now deep into a district of the city alien to him. He had a sense that this was not the place to be found alone after dark. There was a foreboding aspect to this quarter, streets lacking lanterns and distant, hushed voices. A woman laughed in the night, a harsh shrill sound and Zane knew there was no joy in that sound.

Mudara turned a corner and Zane hurried, then peeked around. On the opposite side of the street, the merchant stood before an unmarked door, knocking loudly, in an odd pattern. One strike, then a pause, then two, then one again, then three.

The door opened and the hair on the back of Zane's neck rose and a shiver passed through his body. In the doorway stood a man clad in black, his features unseen in the shadows. But the tunic, trousers, and head-covering were exactly as had been described to him before leaving Sorcerer's Isle. The man was an Izmali assassin, a Keshian Nighthawk.

Mudara spoke rapidly to him and handed him the amulet. The assassin was not pleased to see him and looked out past him, glancing first one way up the street then the other. Zane prayed the man had no special powers, for he knew should he be discovered his life would be forfeit.

Zane watched the two men argue, for it was clear from Mudara's gestures that he was attempting to convince the assassin of something. Mudara raised his voice, and Zane could hear him say, '. . . worth the risk. If these are the ones we were warned of, we may use them to lead us to . . .' the assassin gestured with his hand to lower his voice, and Mudara complied. Zane could not hear what was said after. The assassin spoke softly for a moment longer, and then stepped back into the building, closing the door in Mudara's face. The merchant turned his back towards Zane and started moving down the street.

Zane began to follow after him, when two powerful hands grabbed him from behind and spun him. Before he could say a word a powerful hand clamped down over his mouth and a voice in his ear said, 'If you want to stay alive, say nothing.'

Zane's heart felt as if it would explode out of his chest, but he managed to keep his wits and nod.

The hand released him and a man with a heavy dark beard whispered, 'Follow me and say nothing until I tell you it is safe.'

He hurried away and Zane followed. They spent the better part of a half-hour ducking in and out of shadowed doors and passing through alleys. After they reached a more populated and better lit section of the city the man turned and said, 'You are Zane?'

'I am,' said the young man, out of breath and his knees trembling from exhaustion and fear.

'Chezarul sent me to find you in the plaza, but you were leaving behind the merchant when I got there. You followed him, and I followed you, for I feared that should I overtake you, the merchant might have seen us.'

Zane nodded. 'Why did you grab me, then?'

'If you had followed after the merchant from where I found you, you would have been killed. It is their practice to leave their meetings by a false path, and any who follow are slain. We lost four good men until we discovered their practice.'

'Who are they?'

'The Guild of Death. The Nighthawks,' said the bearded man. 'I am Choyoba.' He looked around. 'Come. I will take you back to the Three Willows.' Zane nodded and followed the man.

'You did well,' said Chezarul to Zane.

Caleb nodded agreement. 'Yes, you did.'

Zane was too drained by the experience to even smile. He just nodded.

'So now you know where to find the Nighthawks?' asked Tad.

Chezarul shook his head and said, 'No, my young friend. The Nighthawks have found us.'

When Tad's expression showed he didn't understand, Caleb said, 'It's a trap.'

'A trap?' asked Zane.

Caleb said, 'The mock amulet was put there so that I, or someone else from the Conclave, would find it. Anyone else would have ignored it or even purchased it as a charm, but for me to inquire about one that was similar, that signalled to the Nighthawks that I was seeking them. It may have been out there for months. It's the sort of thing that would be of no interest to anyone but us.

'And we are "taking the bait".'

'I don't see . . .' began Tad.

'The Nighthawks are setting traps. They know that with the killings in the city it would only be a matter of time before we investigate,' said Caleb. 'So they put out a false amulet, one that looks enough like their own society's mark that anyone looking for the Guild of Death would be curious as to its origin.

'We did as they expected us to do. We inquired, and they deliver what we ask. The argument you observed was probably over telling us no to the true amulets, and then trying to follow us from the market, or agreeing to give us copies, then setting a trap: when we come to pick up the goods, they will either take us or, more likely, follow us back here to see where we are based. Then comes the killing.'

Chezarul said, 'These murderous dogs are a plague on the peace of our city. More, they're bad

284

for business. We shall see an end to them one day, and I hope that day is near.' He turned to Caleb. 'Avoid the market tomorrow. I need to make preparations for our coming encounter, and some of my men are out of the city. Give me two days to muster my forces, then go see this merchant. In three days they will come here, and we shall be ready for them.'

'Pablo will not be pleased we're going to turn his inn into a battlefield,' said Caleb.

'Nothing so bad happens that Pablo's humour can not be improved by gold,' said Chezarul. 'Besides, in his way he's as steadfast as any of us.'

Caleb nodded and said, 'Very well. I shall take the boys riding tomorrow, out of the city towards the shores of the Overn. We will be looking at something or another out there, perhaps exotic fish caught in the lake.'

Chezarul grinned. 'Crocodiles, perhaps?'

'Something. We shall return in two days and see Mudara.

'Good,' said the trader. 'Until then, I bid you good night.'

He left and Caleb said, 'Tad, go to the common room and tell Jommy he can come up now.'

Tad left, and Zane said, 'Are you planning on keeping Jommy around?'

'I think so, for a time. He's a rough and tumble sort of lad, and moreover, being from Novindus means he's unlikely to have any ties to the Nighthawks. And there's something about him I like.'

Zane nodded. 'He stood with Tad and me without cause.'

'He had cause,' said Caleb. 'A sense of fairness most people lack.'

Tad and Jommy came into the room and Caleb said, 'Jommy, can you ride?'

'Well enough to not fall off if we're not in too great a hurry,' answered the red-headed boy.

Caleb said, 'Good, because we're riding out to the lakeshore tomorrow and I'd like you to come along.'

'A job?'

'Of sorts,' said Caleb. 'I'll tell you about it as we ride. For now, get some sleep.'

The three boys left Caleb's room and crossed the hall to their own. Pablo Maguire had brought up a straw-stuffed pallet the previous evening at Caleb's request and Zane now unrolled it and put it between the two beds. Jommy flopped on it, and Tad said, 'I hope that's not proving to be too hard for you.'

Jommy laughed. 'I've been sleeping on stone and dirt for most of the last year, and my last bed was a hammock in a ship at sea. I haven't seen a proper bed to call my own since my dad threw me out. This'll suit me just fine.'

Tad blew out the lantern and the room was plunged into darkness. Tad and Jommy were both quickly asleep, but Zane lay there, the image of a black-clad killer barely seen in the doorway lingering in his mind.

# CHAPTER 14

# BREAKTHROUGH

Magnus watched carefully.

Nakor hovered over the Talnoy. Three Tsurani Great Ones also watched. 'It's nothing obvious,' said Nakor. 'And I may be wrong, but . . .' He moved his hand over the thing's helmet, and added, '. . . if my idea works –'

The Talnoy sat up. Magnus' eyes went wide and then he smiled. 'You did it.'

Magnus was holding the ring which had previously been required to control the creature.

Nakor said, 'I think I can now devise a way to control the Talnoy without using the ring. That would be a good thing since using the ring eventually drives you mad.'

Illianda said, 'Very impressive, Nakor.'

Of the Great Ones who had met the wily Isalani, Illianda was the least bothered by the fact that Nakor didn't fit into the Tsurani magical hierarchy of the Greater and Lesser Paths. Most of the time, Nakor even denied that he was a practitioner of magic. Illianda didn't seem to care what he was, as long as there were results.

'But we still need to concern ourselves with the

rogue rifts that are attracted to our world by this thing,' said Fomoine. 'If we can't establish protective wards we must return this thing to Midkemia, to divert the risk from our world. We have had another possible occurrence of a rift since you were last here. Nothing definite, but two of our brother magicians are visiting the site now to determine if such a thing did occur.'

Nakor nodded. 'I will tell Pug. He's also attempting to understand the wards which shielded this thing from magical detection for so long.'

Magnus said, 'Perhaps we can divert whatever magical forces follow it, by removing it to Midkemia, but what if it's already too late?'

The three Tsurani magicians exchanged questioning looks before Savdari said, 'If it is too late, then we shall have to look to our own resources to preclude an incursion into our world. If not, at least we can buy both of our worlds some time by switching the Talnoy between them? A few weeks there, then back here, then back to Midkemia?'

'It's possible,' said Magnus. 'I'll speak to my father tonight. I hope, however, that shuttling the Talnoy between our worlds will not prove necessary and that an effective ward will be provided soon.'

Nakor said, 'If we have to, we can move the Talnoy through the rift quickly, to Stardock and then perhaps somewhere else.'

The three Tsurani magicians bowed. 'As always,

convey our respects to Milamber,' Illianda said, using Pug's Tsurani name.

Magnus and Nakor returned the courtesy. 'I will, and as always he sends his respects to the Great Ones of Tsuranuanni.' They left the room containing the Talnoy and walked through several halls to the rift room.

Unlike in the past, the rift between the Assembly of Magicians on Kelewan and the Academy at Stardock was not left open continuously anymore. With the current concern over rifts from the Dasati world, Pug and the Great Ones of Tsuranuanni had thought it best to only open a rift when they most needed to.

Magnus stood before the rift device and held out his arms, incanting the appropriate spell. Nakor watched him without comment and the younger magician went through the ritual necessary to attune the energies that would bridge the gulf between the two worlds.

An odd buzzing filled the room for a moment, and the hairs on Nakor's and Magnus' arms and neck stood up, as if a lightning strike had occurred nearby. Then, a shimmering grey void appeared before the two men. They both stepped through without hesitation and suddenly they found themselves upon the island of Stardock.

A few magicians had gathered when the rift had appeared, but upon seeing Magnus and Nakor they nodded their greetings and departed. Magnus turned and with a wave of his hand he willed the rift out of existence. With a wry smile, he said, 'My father told me he almost died trying to close the first Tsurani rift.'

Nakor said, 'I've heard the story. Before you become too full of yourself, just remember he had to shut down a machine created by a dozen Great Ones, and he had to have your grandfather's help to do it.'

Magnus shrugged. 'I wasn't comparing myself to my father, or grandfather, Nakor.' He started walking towards the beach. 'I was merely remarking on . . . oh, never mind. It's just an idle thought.'

When they reached the edge of the lake, Magnus drew out an orb, and an instant later the two men stood at the door of Pug's study. Magnus knocked and Pug's voice answered: 'Come in.'

Nakor paused and said, 'You tell your father what we've done and found. I'm going to go and look for Bek.'

Magnus nodded, and Nakor took his leave.

A few minutes later he found Bek sitting under a tree watching some students listen to Rosenvar lecture. When he saw Nakor approach, he jumped to his feet and said, 'Are we leaving?'

'Why, are you bored?'

'Very. I have no idea what that old man is talking about. And the students here are not very friendly.' He looked at Nakor and said accusingly, 'And that thing you did in my head . . .' His expression was one of frustration verging on tears. 'One of the boys insulted me and normally I would have just hit him very hard, probably in the face. And if he had gotten up, I'd have hit him again. I'd have kept on hitting him until he didn't get up.' With an almost pained expression, Bek said, 'But I couldn't, Nakor. I couldn't even ball my fist. He just stood there looking at me like there was something wrong with me, and there was! And then there was this pretty girl I wanted, but when she wouldn't stop to talk to me and I tried to grab her, the same damn thing happened! I couldn't bring my hand up to—' Bek looked as if he were on the verge of tears. 'What did you do to me, Nakor?'

Nakor put his hand on the large youngster's shoulder and said, 'Something I would rather not do to anyone, Bek. At least for a while, you can't do harm to someone else except if you're defending yourself.'

Bek sighed. 'Am I always going to be this way?'

'No,' said Nakor. 'Not if you learn to control your own impulses and anger.'

Bek laughed. 'I never get angry, Nakor. Not really.'

Nakor motioned for Bek to sit and sat next to him. 'What do you mean?'

Bek shrugged. 'Sometimes I get annoyed, and if I'm in pain I can really break things up, but I find most things either funny or not funny. People talk about love, hate, envy and the rest of it, and I think I know what they're talking about, but I'm not certain.

'I mean, I've seen how people act around each

other and I sort of remember feeling things when I was really little, like the way it felt when my mother held me. But mostly I don't care about the same things that other people care about.' He looked at Nakor and there was almost a pleading quality to his expression, 'I often thought that I was different, Nakor. Many people have told me I am.

'And I've never cared about that.' He lowered his head, looking at the ground. 'But this thing you've done to me, it makes me feel—'

'Frustrated?'

Bek nodded. 'I can't . . . do things like I used to. I wanted that girl, Nakor. I don't like not being able to have what I want!' He looked Nakor in the face and the little gambler could see tears of frustration forming in Bek's eyes.

'You've never had anyone say no to you, have you?'

'Sometimes, but if they do I kill them and take what I want, anyway.'

Nakor was silent, then he thought of something. 'Someone once told me a story about a man travelling in a wagon which was being chased by wolves. When the man reached the safety of a city, he found the gates closed and while he shouted for help, the wolves overtook him and tore him to pieces. How do you feel about that tale, Ralan?'

Bek laughed. 'I'd say that it is a pretty funny story! I wager he had a really amazing look on his face when those beasts caught up with him!'

Nakor was silent, then he stood. 'You wait here.

I'll be back shortly.' The Isalani walked straight to Pug's study. He knocked, then opened the door before Pug told him to enter.

'I need to speak with you, now,' Nakor said.

Pug looked up from where he sat before an open window, enjoying the summer's breeze. Magnus sat opposite him and both men studied the excited looking Isalani. 'What is it?' Pug asked.

'That man, Ralan Bek, he is important.'

'So you have said,' Magnus replied.

'No, even more important than we suspected. He understands the Dasati.'

Pug and Magnus exchanged startled expressions before Magnus asked, 'Didn't we agree not to speak of them to anyone outside our group?'

Nakor shook his head. 'I've told him nothing. He knows them because he is like them. I now understand how they came to be the way they are.'

Pug sat back and said, 'This sounds fascinating.'

Nakor said, 'I don't mean I understand every detail or even exactly how it is so, but I know what has happened.'

Pug motioned for Nakor to sit and continue.

'When Kaspar described what Kalkin had shown him of the Dasati world, we all had the same re-action. After our concern over the threat they pose, we asked ourselves how such a race came to be. How could a people rise, grow and prosper without compassion, generosity and some sense of common interest?

'I suspect they had them once, but evil became

ascendant in that world, and this man is an example of what we will all become if the same evil gains pre-eminence here.' Nakor paused, then stood and began to pace as if struggling to form his thoughts.

'Bek is as the gods have made him.' He looked at the young man, who nodded. 'That is what he said to me, and he is correct. And he knows that he is not as the gods made other men. But he doesn't yet begin to understand what that means.'

Nakor glanced around and continued, 'No one in this room was made as other men are made. Each of us has been touched in one fashion or another, and because of that we are condemned to lead lives that are both uniquely wonderful and terrible.' He grinned. 'Sometimes both at the same time.'

His face resumed a thoughtful expression. 'During our struggles with the agents of evil, we have pondered what purpose such evil serves, many times, and the best answer we have reached is an abstract hypothesis: that without evil, there could be no good, and that our ultimate goal, for the greater benefit of all, is to achieve a balance where the evil is offset by good, thus leaving the universe in harmony.

'But what if the harmony we seek is an illusion? What if the natural state is actually a flux, the constant struggle? Sometimes evil will predominate, and at other times good. We are caught up in the endless ebb and flow of tides that wash back and forth over our world?'

'You paint an even bleaker picture than usual, Nakor,' Pug interrupted.

Magnus agreed. 'Your ant-seige on the castle sounds more promising than being swept away on endless tides.'

Nakor shook his head. 'No, don't you see? This shows that sometimes the balance is destroyed! Sometimes the tide sweeps away all before it.' He pointed to Bek. 'He is touched by something that he doesn't understand, but his understanding is not necessary for that thing to work its will upon him! The Dasati are not evil because they wanted to be that way. In ages past, I'd wager that they were not unlike us. Yes, their world is alien and they live on a plane of existence that would be impossible for us to endure, but Dasati mothers loved their children once, and husbands loved their wives, and friendship and loyalty flourished ages ago. The thing we call the Nameless One is but a manifestation of something far greater, a thing not limited to this world, this universe, or even this reality. It spans—' he was lost for words. 'Evil is everywhere, Pug.' Then he grinned. 'But that means, so is good.'

Nakor struck his left palm with his right fist. 'We delude ourselves that we understand the scope of our decisions, but when we speak of ages, we do not understand them. The thing we fight has been preparing for this conflict since men were little more than beasts, and it is winning. The Dasati became what they are because evil won on their world, Pug. In that universe, what we call

295

the Nameless One overturned the balance and it won. They are what we will become if we fail.'

Pug sat back, his face drawn and pale. 'You paint a grim picture, my friend.'

Nakor shook his head. 'No, don't you see? All is not lost – if evil can win there—' He looked at Pug, then at Magnus and his grin returned '—then good can win here!'

Later, Pug and Nakor walked along the sea shore, letting the warm breeze and salt spray invigorate them. 'Do you remember Fantus?' Pug asked.

'Kulgan's pet firedrake that used to hang around the kitchen from time to time?'

'I miss him,' said Pug. 'It's been five years since I last saw him, and he was very old, dying I think. He wasn't really a pet, more of a house-guest.' Pug looked out at the endlessly churning surf, the waves building up and rolling in to break upon the beach. 'He was with Kulgan the night I first came to his hut in the woods near Crydee Castle. He was always around back then.

'When I brought my son William from Kelewan, he and Fantus became thick as thieves. When William died, Fantus visited us less and less.'

'Drakes are reputed to be very intelligent, perhaps he grieved?'

'No doubt,' said Pug.

'Why think of him now?' asked Nakor.

Pug stopped and sat on a large rock nestled into the cliff face where the beach curved into an outcropping. To continue their walk, they would have had to wade through the shallows around a headland. 'I don't know. He was charming, in a roguish sort of way. He reminded me of simpler times.'

Nakor laughed. 'During our years of friendship, Pug, I've heard you talk of your simpler times but I would hardly count the Riftwar, your imprisonment in Kelewan, becoming the first barbarian Great One and then ending the war,' he laughed, 'and the Great Uprising, and all those other things you, Tomas and Macros accomplished as being anything close to *simple*!'

'Maybe I was just a simpler man,' said Pug, fatigue evident in his voice.

'Hardly, I'll accept you had a simpler understanding of things years ago. We all did, in our youth.'

'Fantus had a capricious nature, he could be as unpredictable as a cat or as steadfast as a dog. But I think the reason that I dwell on him today is because he and William were inseparable.'

'And you think of William?'

'Often. And my adopted daughter, Gamina.'

'Why this reflection now, Pug?'

'Because my children are in harm's way again.'

Nakor laughed. 'I know they are your sons, Pug, but the term *children* hardly applies to Magnus and Caleb any longer. They are not only men, but men of great resolve and strong character – men whom any father would be proud of.'

'I know, and I do feel proud,' said Pug. 'But I

am fated to watch all those I love die before I do.'

'How do you know this, Pug?'

'When I fought the demon Jakan as his fleet sailed into the Bitter Sea, I attempted to destroy his armada single-handed – one of my more arrogant moments. As a result, I was almost killed by a powerful magical ward.'

'I remember that,' said Nakor.

'In the Hall of Lims-Kragma, I was given a choice by the Goddess. Only my family know of the decision I made, and then only part of it. In short, I was allowed to return and continue my work, but in exchange I must watch everyone I love die before me.'

Nakor sat on the rock next to Pug and was silent. After a long minute, he said, 'I don't know what to say, Pug. But perhaps there is one other thing to consider.'

'What would that be?'

'I am older than you, and everyone I knew as a young man is also dead. Everyone. Sometimes, I remember faces yet cannot put names to them. It is the curse of being long-lived. But, you might have been cursed even before you spoke to the Goddess.'

'How so?'

'As I said, I have also outlived everyone I knew in my youth. My family was never much of one; my mother died before my father, but he died soon after her. It didn't matter, for I hadn't seen them for more than thirty years, and I didn't have any brothers or sisters either.' He shrugged. 'But that doesn't mean I haven't come to love people, Pug. And losing them is always painful.

'There is an ancient Isalani blessing intoned at the birth of a baby: "Grandfather dies, father dies, son dies". It is a blessing because it expresses the natural order. I have never been a father so I can't imagine what it was like to lose William and Gamina. But I remember how it affected you. I saw that. I saw what it meant for you to lose them.'

Nakor shook his head as if struggling to find the words he sought. 'But I have lost a wife, twice. The first time I lost her when she left me to seek more power. And the second time . . . I killed her, Pug. I killed Jorma. The body I knew her to possess had died decades before, and she occupied a man's body when I ended her life,' said Nakor with a slightly rueful laugh. 'But that didn't change the fact that she was someone whom I had loved, in whose arms I had lain, and whose presence made me more than I was without her.' He looked at Pug and his eyes were shining with moisture as he continued. 'You, I and Tomas, have been chosen for something by the gods, and that honour has its price.

'But I have to think it is because it must be done. Maybe it's vanity, but only we three. Not Miranda, not Magnus, not anyone else. Just we three.'

'Why?'

'Only the gods know that,' said Nakor with an evil chuckle. 'And they're not telling us the truth.'

Pug stood up, motioning to Nakor that it was time to return to the villa. 'They're lying to us?'

'Well, they're certainly not telling us everything. Consider who Kaspar met on the peaks of the Ratn'garies.'

'Kalkin.'

'Yes, Ban-ath, the god of thieves . . . and tricksters, and liars . . .'

'So you think the Dasati may not be as big a menace as Kalkin portrayed?'

'Oh, I still think they are all that and more, but I think Kalkin showed Kaspar only what he wanted Kaspar to see. The gods have their reasons, I'm sure, but I'm a cynical bastard at times and I'd like to know what Kaspar didn't see in that vision.'

Pug stopped and put a restraining hand on Nakor's shoulder. 'You're not suggesting what I think you're suggesting, are you?'

Nakor grinned. 'Not yet, but in days to come, we may have to visit the Dasati world.'

Pug stood motionless for a moment, then started walking again. 'Intentionally opening a rift to the Dasati home world? Could there possibly be a more reckless act?'

'I'm sure there is. We just haven't thought of it at the moment,' said Nakor with a laugh.

Pug laughed with him. 'I'm not convinced, Nakor. That could be the worst idea in the history of really bad ideas.'

Nakor continued laughing. 'Perhaps, but what

if travelling there prevents the Dasati from coming here?'

Pug's laughter stopped abruptly. 'What if—?' He walked with his eyes down as if he was lost in thought, then he said, 'Perhaps it is something we need to discuss.'

'Good. And while we're at it, when are you going to tell me more about these messages from your future self?'

'Soon, my friend,' said Pug. 'Soon.' He looked up at the afternoon sun sparkling across the waves. 'I wonder how Caleb and the others are doing down in Kesh? We've not had word from them in days.'

'Oh, I'm sure we'd have heard if there was anything of importance going on.'

Caleb lunged to his left as the assassin drove the point of his sword through the air, barely missing his chest. Caleb ignored the burning pain in his left shoulder as it slammed into the moss-covered stones of the sewer, and drove his own sword point into the Nighthawk's stomach.

The trap had been diabolical in its planning and execution. Caleb cursed himself for being a smug fool. Not only had he and Chezarul's men failed to stay one step ahead of the Nighthawks, they were now clearly at a disadvantage.

The only reason they were still alive was blind luck.

Chezarul had agents following the merchant and other men watching the house where Zane had spied Mudara speaking with the Nighthawk. The night before, one of Chezarul's agents had reported uncovering the Nighthawks' base. It had taken days, but now it seemed that their patience was paying off.

Chezarul had identified a basement of an abandoned warehouse as the Nighthawks' headquarters, and had planned a double-pronged assault on them, with men emerging from the sewers, while others attacked the building from the street.

As the Nighthawks were most active during the night, it was decided that a mid-afternoon attack would catch the majority of the assassins as they slept.

Guided by one of Chezarul's men, Caleb had taken his group through the sewers, taking an entire morning to work their way to positions surrounding the Nighthawks' suspected lair.

What they had found instead of the nest was a trap, which had only been revealed because a company of rats had been disturbed and one of the men felt a stray gust of breeze which had carried a faint hint of smoke. Caleb barely had time to call out a warning before the sewer swarmed with black-clad Nighthawks. Three of Caleb's men had died before they realized what was occurring and the rest fell back in a disordered manner.

The attack had been turned into a rout, and now Caleb's only concern was getting the surviving men out of the sewers alive. He urged them past him while battling the Nighthawks at a slower pace, so

302

that eventually only he and four others held the mouth of the tunnel at the entrance to a large junction.

Caleb knew that he needed to keep the inter-section clear for at least another couple of minutes so that the rest of the Conclave's agents could flee into the city above.

He had no doubt that other Nighthawks would be waiting in the vicinity, but he doubted that any of them would assault Caleb's men in broad daylight. The City Watch was usually dis-interested, but proved aggressive and brutal when it came to public unrest. Armed conflict in the streets of Kesh was close enough to rebellion to provoke a swift reaction, and if the fighting got out of hand the Inner Legion would answer their call. If that happened, the only options would be run, or die.

The man next to Caleb gurgled as his lungs filled with blood from a puncture wound to his chest. Caleb slashed down hard and removed the offending Nighthawk's arm at his elbow and he fell back into the foul water screaming. Caleb stood his ground with two of Chezarul's men at his side, and for a brief moment the Nighthawks gave them respite as they regrouped.

A scream from further down the tunnel told Caleb that another of the Conclave's men had been slain. Caleb could only hope that the end had come swiftly, for the Nighthawks would think nothing of peeling the skin from a man inch by inch to extract whatever information he might have before finally killing him.

Caleb had lost his lantern when they had retreated. Some light filtered through a distant grating in the ceiling twenty yards to his left, otherwise the tunnel was shrouded in murk.

The three men at the junction stood fast as the Nighthawks rushed at them. The lack of light and their black clothing made it difficult for Caleb to judge how many there were until they were almost upon him.

He slashed at a man who dodged back, then thrust past the man's retreating form to take another Nighthawk in the thigh. The assassin crumpled with a groan of pain as the man on Caleb's right sliced at another Nighthawk who also fell down.

Then, without any verbal communication, three remaining Nighthawks stepped back. The one nearest to the wounded assassin skewered the man with the point of his sword, sinking his corpse beneath the sewage that swirled around their legs.

The Nighthawks retreated slowly, until they vanished into the gloom. After a moment, Caleb said, 'Follow me,' and led his men towards the sunlight streaming from the grate above.

Upon reaching the pool of light, he found the iron rungs fixed to the wall and indicated the two men with him should climb out of the sewer. When they were safely up the ladder, Caleb climbed out.

It was quiet as the three filthy, blood-splattered

men emerged from the sewer in the centre of a backstreet in the warehouse district.

Caleb said, 'Go to your appointed safe havens. If Chezarul has survived, he'll know where to find me. If not, then whoever takes his place will know how to reach me. For now, trust no one and say nothing to anyone. Go!'

The men hurried away, and when they were safely out of sight, Caleb took off in the opposite direction.

He paused at a public fountain and leaned over, ducking his entire head under the water. He came up sputtering and shook the water from his long hair – he had lost his hat somewhere in the sewer.

Caleb glanced around and knew that he couldn't be sure if he was being watched. He could only hope to lose whoever might be following him on his route to his safe house.

As he set off, he wondered about the boys. He had given them strict instructions to follow if he were not back by sundown. They were to walk out of the Three Willows by the route he had taught them until they came to a particular home. There, they should knock on the back door and say a particular phrase. He prayed they would do as they were told.

Caleb dodged around some crates stacked on the corner of two alleys, and a slashing blade cut deep into his left shoulder. He staggered backwards and made ready to receive the attack that would follow.

Two Nighthawks blocked his escape route. Caleb knew the men would have to die in as short a time as possible else he would lose consciousness and bleed to death from his wounds.

The Nighthawk who had caught him by surprise charged first, the other man moved to Caleb's left, so Caleb took the one opportunity presented to him. He ducked, thrust upwards, and then with an explosive leap, yanked his sword from the stomach of the first Nighthawk, twisting himself completely around and swinging his sword in an arc. The second Nighthawk saw Caleb duck and instinctively moved his blade to his own left, assuming that Caleb would now swing at him from that side, but with the sword turned in a complete circle, the attack came from his right, and before the Nighthawk could bring his sword around to block, Caleb's blade bit deep into his neck.

The second man fell and Caleb stumbled past him, clumsily putting his sword into his scabbard as he moved in what looked like a drunken stumble. He pushed his hand against his twice-wounded shoulder, to stanch the flow of blood and turned his mind to one thing: reaching the safe house before he lost consciousness.

'Three treys,' said Jommy, laughing as he scooped up the copper pieces. Zane groaned and threw his cards down on the table.

Tad laughed. 'I told you not to bet.'

Jommy was about to say something when the

smile suddenly faded from his face. His eyes darted around the room and he lowered his voice. 'Heads up. It's about to get nasty in here.'

Tad and Zane glanced around the taproom and saw that four men in matching grey cloaks had entered and now stood around the room, effectively sealing off each exit.

'What is this?' asked Tad.

'Don't know, but it's not good,' answered Jommy. 'Stay close to me, lads.' He stood up and waited until Tad and Zane did likewise. He said, 'Get ready.'

'For what?' asked Zane, just as Jommy walked towards the nearest man.

The direct approach of the large red-headed boy must have confused the man, for he didn't attempt to draw his sword until Jommy had picked up a chair and sent it crashing towards him, foiling his attempt to pull out his weapon.

While the man ducked under the first chair, Jommy picked up another and smashed it down on the man's head, at about the same time Pablo Maguire came hurrying out of the kitchen to see what the problem was. Before he made two steps, one of the grey-cloaked men had pulled a small crossbow out from under his cloak and fired at the old man. Pablo ducked behind the bar and avoided being killed, and rose up with a sailor's cutlass in his hand.

Jommy and Pablo both shouted, 'Run!' at the same time, and Tad and Zane ran out the door. Jommy paused only long enough to kick the downed man in the face, before he leaped through the doorway, with the two closest men following after him.

The boys had reached the boulevard and were heading into the plaza by the time the men began to overtake them. Jommy glanced over his shoulder to make sure Tad and Zane were still behind him and shouted, 'Follow me!'

He hurried to the fountain where the usual gang of apprentices and girls were gathering and came to a grinding halt in front of Arkmet and the other Bakers' Boys. He said, 'You feel like hitting someone?'

'You?' asked Arkmet, taking a step back.

'No,' said Jommy as Tad and Zane caught up.

'Them?' said Arkmet with a grin.

'No,' said Jommy, pointing past the brothers at the two grey-cloaked assassins who had pursued them into the plaza. 'Them.'

Arkmet shrugged. 'Sure.'

Jommy, Tad, and Zane took off, and the two assassins moved forwards, their cloaks hiding their weapons from the city watch. The Bakers' Boys moved to intercept the two men and Arkmet said, 'What's the hurry?'

One assassin, a grey-bearded man with a bald pate, threw back his cloak, revealing a sword and dagger in either hand, and said, 'You don't wish to know, boy.'

Seeing weapons, the Bakers' Boys stepped away but continued to block the route Tad, Zane, and Jommy had escaped by. Putting up his hands,

Arkmet also backed away, and said, 'No one said anything about blades.'

'No one said anything about stupid boys getting in the way, either,' said the assassin. He made a menacing gesture with the dagger in his left hand, while his companion slipped around him to the right, and tried to see which way the three boys had fled.

'Stupid?' said Arkmet as the man tried to shoulder past him. 'Stupid?' With stunning fury, the broad-shouldered boy lashed out, catching the assassin on the left side of his face, right at the point of his jaw. The man's eyes rolled in his head and his knees buckled. His companion turned to see what the noise was and was greeted by a brick, thrown with precision by another Bakers' Boy. The brick caught the man on the bridge of his nose and his head snapped backwards.

Someone pushed him over and the Bakers' Boys gathered around the two fallen men and proceeded to stomp and kick them, continuing long after they had fallen unconscious.

Tad, Zane, and Jommy hugged the wall in the darkness. They had been on the move for hours and at last were fairly sure they were not being followed. Perspiration dripped off all three of them, for the night was hot and they had not had the chance to rest for ages.

'What now?' asked Zane.

'We go where Caleb told us to go if something

309

went wrong,' Tad replied. 'Four men trying to kill us is most certainly something *wrong*, don't you think?'

'You'll get no argument from me, mate,' said Jommy. 'Where did he say we were supposed to go?'

Tad said, 'Follow me.'

He led his two companions through the streets of the city, getting lost twice but eventually finding his way to the appropriate home. As instructed, he did not approach the house directly, but from a narrow alleyway, and through a broken board in the back fence, which let the three boys into a small garden behind a modest building. At the kitchen door, he knocked and waited.

'Who's there?' demanded a man's voice.

'Those who seek shelter in the shadows,' Tad replied.

The door opened quickly and a broad-shouldered man in a simple tunic and trousers urged them inside. 'Come in, quickly!'

He said nothing but moved towards the centre of the room and rolled back a carpet. Under it lay a trap door and he motioned for Zane and Jommy to pull it open. A narrow flight of stairs led down into the gloom. The man lit a lantern from a taper thrust into the fire in the kitchen, then led the boys down. 'I'll close that when I come back up,' he said at the bottom of the stairs.

The stairs gave way to a narrow tunnel which headed away from the house in the direction they had come. A deserted shed had stood on the opposite side of the alley, and Tad judged they were now somewhere beneath it.

The man paused at a door and knocked twice, paused again, and then repeated the knock. Then he opened the door.

They entered a small chamber with barely enough space to hold them. Within the room sat a single bed, a chair and a tiny table. Obviously this hideout had been meant for one person. The man turned and said, 'You'll wait here until tomorrow night, then we shall move you.'

As he moved past the three boys, Zane and the others finally realised that a figure already lay on the bed, unconscious. At the door, the man turned and said, 'We've done all we can. He had lost a lot of blood before he got here.' He closed the door.

The boys looked down. 'Caleb,' Tad whispered, regarding the still form on the bed. His bandages were soaked in blood.

Zane slowly sat on the one chair, and Jommy and Tad settled on the floor to wait.

# CHAPTER 15

# DECEPTION

Tal considered his cards.

He sat back slightly and glanced to his right, where Amafi stood motionless against the opposite wall. The former assassin-turned-servant had his right hand folded over his left. His eyes scanned the huge hall, which was unlike any gambling establishment in the north. Most gaming up in Roldem and the Kingdom of the Isles was done in well appointed salons or common taverns and inns. The Mistress of Luck was Kesh's finest gambling establishment, without rival in any other nation.

Here, the normal venue appeared to be palaces, or as close to a palace as a commoner could find. This particular building had once belonged to a wealthy merchant, but in years past had become a haven for card players and gamblers of every stripe. It was located at the end of a long boulevard, on top of a hill, with a view straight up to the plateau and Imperial Citadel, and a rear vista of the lower city and the Overn Deep.

Tal sat in the middle of what must have been the grand hall where the merchant had entertained his guests, for instead of a wall, behind Tal stood columns of carved marble forming a colonnade that provided a panorama of the beautifully maintained gardens and the city below. The weather in Kesh was either hot or really hot, so the night air rarely invited a chill. Tal's immediate concern however, was not for the décor, but for his safety, as his back was exposed to the garden, and lately people had been dying at inopportune times.

Tal had used his celebrity to gain admission to several galas, receptions and parties, as well as gambling establishments, and since arriving in Kesh he had wasted hours listening to idle gossip. But he had finally heard something that had led him to this place, and now he waited.

If what he had overheard two nights earlier was true, an imperial prince would be present in the hall tonight – incognito – ostensibly to relax and enjoy a night on the town. From what Chezarul's agents had heard, there was a fair chance there would be an attempt on this Prince's life soon. Tal was there to ensure that it did not happen tonight.

Earlier, Amafi had noticed that a pair of young nobles had been using a fairly obvious set of signals to communicate their respective hands, and that whoever was the weaker bid upped the pot and helped the other win more money.

It wasn't a foolproof system, because the better hand still needed to beat everyone else at the table, but they won more often than not, and the pots here were much higher than average, so by the end of the evening, they usually found themselves ahead. Tal would have liked to teach them a lesson, but he had other concerns this night.

The son of a tribal leader, thrown into the intrigues of the Conclave of Shadows at a young age, one of the many useful things Tal had learned whilst growing up was how to cheat at cards. His skills had been both tested and sharpened playing four-handed poker with Nakor, Kaspar and Amafi – all skilled cheaters. One game had disintegrated into a cheating contest, with each hand becoming more outrageous than the last as large quantities of wine had been consumed, and ending only when three extra kings and two extra sevens appeared in the deck.

Tal played indifferently tonight, winning just enough to break even, but losing enough to keep attention away from himself. He excused himself from the table, saying, 'I need a bit of air,' and motioned for his servant to join him.

They went to the gardens, ostensibly to stretch their legs, but Tal wanted another quick inspection of their surroundings. When they were alone, Amafi said, 'Something troubles you, Magnificence?' He spoke Roldemish, to lessen the likelihood of being overheard.

'Many things trouble me, Amafi.'

'Not those two boys, certainly?'

'No. Someone will teach them a lesson, but I'm afraid it won't be me.' Tal looked around the garden. 'So far we've learned that our enemies are taking

314

great care in deciding who they kill and where. But why are we now seeing them—' he looked around the garden, and with a wave of his hand included the building behind them '—here, in this palace?' He stared at the city below them, and said, 'There must be twenty or more private rooms upstairs, so we don't even know where the prince is going to be.' He looked at Amafi. 'This used to be your stock-in-trade. Would you attempt to kill a royal here?'

Amafi said, 'No, but then I always preferred shadows to confusion.'

'I'm not sure I follow,' said Tal.

The former assassin took his master by the elbow and slowly turned him around to face the building. Tal saw a tableau that looked like a theatre stage, for from the garden, the ground floor of the house could be seen. Save for the entrances to kitchens and garderobes, it was simply one vast enclosure.

Amafi said, 'Everyone is in plain sight, and that is good. Should someone wish to go upstairs, they must enter there.' He pointed to the main entrance. 'There is but one access to the upper rooms, that stairway against the right wall. I have not surveyed this monument to conspicuous greed completely, Magnificence, but I see no other exits. There may be a bolt hole to the street from a basement, but that's immaterial, for anyone wishing to use it would first have to go through this room.'

'So it is a good choice?'

Amafi shrugged. 'When you kill, you must leave immediately. There can be no hesitation or you will stand a good chance of being caught. I prefer shadows. I prefer to be far from my victims before they are cold, let alone found. Others prefer chaos to cover their tracks.' Amafi looked around the garden. 'Were I forced to kill a man in there, I would be hiding somewhere . . . here, in the garden. In the confusion that followed upon the death of someone in there, I would be leaving from out here.'

Tal tried not to look obvious as he again turned to take in their surroundings. The garden was rectangular in shape, with a single rectangular pool at its centre. Low hedges lined the sides of the garden, and narrow paths took amblers to where they could look out over the city and down to the shores of the Overn Deep. A few benches and torch holders were also scattered around.

'Crossbow?'

'Too inaccurate,' said Amafi. 'But if no other alternative presented itself, perhaps. You, of course, could use a bow with great efficiency. I, on the other hand, would choose a dart.'

'Dart?'

'Tipped with poison.' Caught up in the plan, Amafi glanced around. 'I would conceal a blowpipe under my cloak. Or, if the night was warm, secrete it beneath my tunic, or up a sleeve. It needn't be a long one, no more than thus,' he held his hands about a foot apart – 'and the dart would be hidden in a tiny pouch, strong enough to prevent me from being pricked and killed by my own weapon.

'I would stalk my quarry until he made his intentions clear to me – he might sit at a gaming table here, go upstairs, or come into the garden. The skill lies in being ready in a moment; to have the blowpipe out and the dart inserted in seconds, then to strike the target and run before you see them fall to the floor.'

'How can you be certain?'

'There are several lethal venoms and plant extracts, Magnificence, that merely have to prick the skin to cause quick and certain death. They are very dangerous to handle, but if you are trained—' He shrugged. 'Not my first choice, but I know the art.

'I would have already planned a way out of this garden,' said Amafi, pointing to the rear wall, 'I would have tied a rope to a statue hidden in a hedge, and I would climb down into the rear garden of the house below this one while the women up here began to scream and call for the guards, in short, I would be hidden by chaos.'

'What would you use if not a blowpipe and poison?'

'An expertly-thrown dagger could suffice, but that would increase the risk of being seen.'

'I should think so.'

'You would be amazed at what people do not see, Magnificence. They watch the body fall, they see the blood, they hear the women scream and the men curse, then they glance around to see if they are in danger, and they do not notice the unremarkable man in unremarkable garb no longer standing at the edge of the crowd. It is better if there's a lot of running and screaming.

'No, killing a man is fairly easy. It is killing him and not getting caught that makes it difficult.'

'So, assuming the prince appears tonight, how would you kill him?'

'Magnificence, I would never undertake such a contract. Killing rich merchants and even the minor nobility is one thing – there is a chance of retribution, but not a large one. Sooner or later the sons inherit their father's estates and whatever is being paid to the local constabulary to hunt down the murderer is seen as an unnecessary expense; after all, it will not bring back their departed, no matter how beloved and missed.'

'You are a cynical bastard, Amafi. Did anyone ever tell you that?'

'More than once, Magnificence, but then, consider my trade.' He smiled and shrugged. 'No, to kill royals you'd have to employ fanatics. Those willing to give up their lives to see a son of the imperial house dead. A professional would never undertake such a contract.'

'What about the Nighthawks?'

Amafi took Tal by the elbow and steered him to the farthest corner of the garden. 'Among my calling, they are legendary. Being legends, there are equal measures of truth and myth to their story.'

'Go on.'

'It is believed that they were once a family, a large family of men and women who took the occupation of killing to a higher level, making it an art form. For generations they plied their trade quietly and without notice, save by those in need of such skills. Then, a hundred years ago something happened to them, they became a cult and their numbers multiplied. Then they were nearly obliterated by the soldiers of the Kingdom.

'Since then, there have been rumours of their return.'

'More than rumours,' said Tal. He glanced around. 'Find us a fast way out of here.'

Amafi nodded and Tal returned to the game. He played indifferently for another hour, waiting for some sign that royalty had arrived. He estimated it was roughly three hours past sunset and that by now anyone setting out for a night in the city would be arriving at their destination. Tal picked up his winnings and went looking for his servant.

Amafi stood quietly by a column on the left side of the room, just in front of the broad steps which led down into the garden. When Tal reached him, Amafi said, 'It is done. I have discovered two possible exits that do not require using the front door.

'The first is a rope ladder used by the gardeners to assist in the trimming of the border-hedges surrounding the garden. It is long enough to reach the rooftop of the villa directly below; on the other side of the garden lies a rocky path – it is steep, but it can be used to descend the hillside to a place where one may jump to a road below without fear of injury. Either would suffice as a quick departure.'

'You did well.'

'I serve at your whim, Magnificence.'

Tal resisted the temptation to point out that Amafi had also tried to kill him on at least two previous occasions when it had suited him, and said, 'Now, tell me, again. If you were to ambush a prince of the royal house of Kesh, how would you do it from here?'

'I would not,' said Amafi. 'I would pick my spot and ensure someone brought him to me.'

'That would require an agent inside the royal party.'

Amafi shrugged. 'And that is not possible?'

Tal considered. 'Very possible.' He stood lost in thought for a while. Then he said, 'But if a royal prince doesn't appear tonight, it's our information that's at fault, and this has been a pointless exercise.

'We wait for another hour, and if no one has arrived, we shall return to our quarters.'

'Yes, Magnificence,' Amafi replied with an inclination of his head. 'You will return to the cards?'

'No,' said Tal. 'I'm not in the mood. I think I'll stroll the floor for a while and see who's come in since I left the table.'

Amafi took up an unobtrusive position near the closest escape route, and Tal walked the floor.

As gambling halls went, this was the largest and most opulent he had encountered, but it was also odd by his standards. Every gambling house in the Kingdom of the Isles, Roldem, Olasko and elsewhere in the north was choked with gaming tables to maximize the earnings of the entrepreneur, but here large stretches of the hall had been given over to piles of cushions strewn around low tables where the wealthy and noble relaxed, held conversations, or indulged in other vices. In one darker corner several young Trueblood men lounged, passing around a long pipe, and from the sickly-sweet aroma, Tal knew it wasn't an exotic cut of tabac they were smoking.

Some extraordinarily attractive young women had appeared, and several smiled invitingly at Tal as they strolled by. Gambling, drugs, whores and drink, Tal thought. One would never have to leave this place, it could satisfy any appetite.

An hour passed, while Tal played a few more hands. Then he rose, pocketed his modest winnings and found Amafi. 'No one is coming,' he said to the former assassin.

Amafi said, 'That is strange, Magnificence. But it is not unusual for nobility – especially royalty – to change their mind.'

'I don't think so. I think we had bad information,' said Tal.

'To what end?'

'I don't know, but tell me – what has changed in the room since we last spoke?'

Amafi may have been advancing in years, but his skill was not dulled. 'A man sits alone near the foot of the stairs as if he is lost in thought while he drinks, but he has not refilled his cup in the past hour.

'Two courtesans meander through the hall, yet twice I've seen them rebuff men of means who have sought their companionship.' He looked at the second exit on the other side of the room. 'And someone also bars the way should anyone choose to leave by the narrow path at the back.'

'And if anyone suspected you had deployed the gardeners' rope ladder, there would be someone guarding that, I think.'

'It's a trap?'

'I think so,' said Tal.

'For us?'

'It would be foolish not to assume so.'

'So the rumour of the prince's attendance and the possible attempt on his life was just bait?'

Tal nodded. 'So, if I'm the target, and not the prince, what would you do?'

Amafi looked around, assessing the room with new eyes. 'A direct attack in public is out of the question, Magnificence. Also, no one would be foolish enough to challenge a Champion of the Masters' Court in Roldem with a blade. Should I sent three swordsmen, you would likely prevail, unless they were very, very good.

'But I would not want three others knowing who I intended to kill . . . unless those three others were family.'

'Nighthawks.'

Amafi nodded. He watched the two young women and said, 'I suspect those two are not Nighthawks. I would simply employ them to lure you upstairs to a quiet room where a dagger waited for you behind a curtain. Or I would persuade them to keep you here until someone else arrived.' He shrugged. 'As to the manner of your demise, my preferred approach would be to wait outside the front door, concealed in shadow, and take my chance at striking from behind before you can draw your fabled sword.'

Tal smiled. 'If memory serves, that's how we met.'

'I was not attempting to kill you, Magnificence, only to join your service. Had I wanted you dead, I think I might have been able to be more circumspect.'

'Well enough, but what about tonight? Chaos or shadows?'

Amafi looked around again, laughing like Tal had said something funny. 'I do not know. If there were more people here tonight, chaos. But there are still too many for shadows.'

'So, you think I'm safe until we depart?'

'I suspect so, Magnificence, but I would keep your wits about you and be especially cautious if you must visit the garderobe.'

'Having one's throat cut while relieving oneself would be a most undignified death.'

'It has been done.'

'The man guarding the back path, is he a Nighthawk or hired help?'

Amafi said, 'It is difficult to say, Magnificence. They would not place someone to confront you there, rather someone to signal others that you have left by another route . . . I would wager hired help.'

'Signal who?'

Amafi said, 'Certainly not those two girls.' He said, 'Return to the tables and I will attempt to find out who his confederate might be.'

Tal nodded and returned to a different table from the last one, tired of watching the cheating brothers and pretending not to be annoyed by them. At this new table he found two merchants from the south and a minor palace-functionary losing modest amounts of gold to two travellers from the Kingdom.

Even so, the gentlemen at the table were affable. When introductions had been made, the two travellers expressed some interest in Tal's relationship to people that they might know in Yabon.

Tal deflected their questions by stating although he was a court baron in Yabon, he had spent most of his time travelling and living in the east, especially in the city of Roldem. This led to one of the men realizing that he was a past Champion of the Masters' Court, which while no less tedious a conversation for Tal, did at least free him from further scrutiny regarding his fictional Yabonese background.

The hours dragged by, then roughly two hours after midnight, a party of drunken young men entered the gambling hall. Two of them quickly found girls and headed upstairs, while three others found seats at a large table where a game of knucklebones was in progress. One sat down and seemed to doze off quickly.

Amafi came to Tal's side and said, 'Magnificence, a word, please?'

Tal excused himself and they moved to a deserted corner of the room. 'Someone has grown impatient. You see the man who appears to doze in the corner?'

'I see him.'

'He entered with the drunken youths, but he was not with them. He is older and he feigns intoxication. Even now I think he watches from under hooded lids.'

'Is he a Nighthawk?'

'Almost certainly, for they would not send a mere underling to drive you into their arms.'

'How dangerous?'

'Very, for he will willingly die for his clan, which means that his task may be to allow you to kill him, then as you flee, others will take you outside.'

'Fanatics,' Tal said as if it were a curse word.

'What would you have me do?'

'Wait,' said Tal. He approached the two girls who had been circling the floor for hours, trying to look as if they were having a good time. They brightened up noticeably as Tal closed in on them. Both were dressed in a various Trueblood fashion, though it was clear from their fair skin and light eyes that they were not Trueblood. In addition to their linen kilts and torques, they wore gauzy wraps which covered their breasts, if only slightly. Their jewellery was cheap and obvious and it was clear to Tal that both girls were not in their usual habitat. He would probably find them in a moderate brothel or haunting the modest inns of the city on most nights. In a few years when their looks faded, they would be walking the streets in the poorer section of the city.

The taller of the two with reddish-brown hair said, 'I was just telling my friend that if one man in the room were to come talk to us, I wished it would be you, handsome!'

They both giggled. Tal smiled and leaning forward said, 'How would you two like to make even more gold than you've been promised?'

The girls' expressions turned to shock. Tal put his arms around their waists and pulled them slightly towards him as if getting familiar, but his grip was firm as he said, 'Smile, girls; you're being watched, and those men who promised you gold after you have lured me upstairs are going to cut your throats instead. Now, what will it be? Life and gold, or do you want to see some fairly spectacular bloodshed right here, right now?'

The shorter girl with raven-dark hair looked as if she were on the verge of fainting, but the taller one said, 'They promised us that no one would get hurt. They said it was a prank.'

'It's not a prank. Now, what do you have?'

'What do you mean?'

'What did they give you to poison me with?'

'Not poison,' said the shorter girl, her voice wavering with fear. 'Just some drops to make you sleep. They said they were going to drag you out of here and put you on a caravan to the south. They said you had caused some trouble with a man's wife and they were going to teach you a lesson.'

Tal shook his head and laughed loudly. Then he whispered, 'And you, of course, believed that.'

The redheaded girl said, 'For ten gold coins, I'd believe you were Sung the Pure for the night.'

'Good, here's what I want you to do. Come upstairs with me and give me the drops.'

He motioned for Amafi to come over and said, 'I'm going to spend some time with my friends, here, before playing again. Settle it with the landlord.'

Amafi bowed and went to find the owner of the establishment, while Tal stood with his arms around both girls. They ran their hands up and down his arms in a display of affection, but their eyes darted anxiously around the room. 'Don't look for anyone,' whispered Tal. 'Keep your eyes on me.'

Amafi returned in a moment and said, 'Top of the stairs on the next floor, Magnificence, the room at the end of the hall.'

Tal took the key, knowing that the man by the garden or the one feigning sleep in the cushioned seat would have a duplicate. Tal whispered to Amafi, 'Follow the sleeping man when he rises. When he reaches the door, help him enter the room.'

Tal took the girls upstairs, and once they were in the room, motioned for them to stand in the farthest corner from the door. He was grateful that it was a large room. One immense window overlooked the garden, directly above the corner where Amafi had secreted the rope ladder. Like in most Keshian homes, there was no glass in the window, just wooden shutters which could be closed to provide shade, or warmth on those rare days when the temperature fell below a comfortable level.

Tal said, 'Give me the potion.'

The redhead gave him a small vial and Tal took out his own purse. 'There are about three hundred gold coins in here,' he said, tossing it to the dark-haired girl. 'When I tell you to, leave quickly, but do not appear to be fleeing. If you want to live to spend that gold, do not go back to your brothel or where you live – they will have someone waiting for you. Wait until the market opens at dawn and buy robes like those worn by the desert women of the Jal-Pur. Cover yourself so only your eyes can be seen. Then, hire a guardsman from the mercenaries' guild – he should cost you no more than ten pieces of gold.'

While he spoke, Tal measured every angle of the room: the large bed on the floor, the two tables, one on each side, the large tray of fruits and sweets at the foot of the bed, and an earthenware crock in which pitchers of wine or ale could be cooled.

'Take passage on the first caravan north. Then, if you can find your way to the Kingdom, Queg, Roldem or any place not in the Empire, you may live.'

The dark-haired girl looked on the verge of fainting. 'Leave Kesh? What will we do?'

Tal smiled, 'Exactly what you've been doing since your parents threw you out, girl. Sleep with men for money. If you're wise, you'll find a rich old husband before you lose your looks. Otherwise, save your gold.

'Now, that's all the advice I have to give and I think we're about to be joined by an unwelcome visitor. You two get over by the bed and talk as if you're still playing with a customer.'

Tal went to the door and cracked it open slightly, so he could see anyone coming down the hall. He waited patiently while the girls prattled, trying hard to sound festive while being frightened.

Nearly half an hour passed before a figure appeared at the top of the stairs. As Tal suspected, it was the man who had feigned sleep.

As the man neared the halfway point in the hall, Amafi appeared behind him. Although the old former assassin had lost his appetite for killing as a livelihood, he had not lost all his skills. He ducked behind a column an instant before the Nighthawk glanced behind to see if he was being followed, and Tal marvelled at the old killer's ability. He had watched him move into the shadow of that column but he couldn't see where he was now.

The Nighthawk was only a few feet from the door and Tal waved to the girls. The redhead forced a giggle and the dark-haired girl's laugh sounded, but the Nighthawk didn't appear to notice.

As he got close enough to notice that the door was slightly ajar, Amafi came out from his hiding place, and within two strides fell upon the Nighthawk.

The assassin must have sensed his approach for he turned at the last minute, a blade appearing in his hand as if by magic, and Amafi barely avoided being skewered.

Tal didn't hesitate. He reached through the door and struck the man with the hilt of his sword behind the ear, and the Nighthawk went down in a heap. Tal caught him under the arms as Amafi grabbed his feet and they carried him into the room. The man groaned as they tossed him onto the bed, and Tal quickly administered the draught.

'From what I've been told, these lads have a nasty habit of killing themselves,' said Tal. 'So, not only are we going to frustrate them tonight, let's see if we can get this one back to where we might get some answers out of him.'

'Doubtful,' said Amafi, 'but we can try. What of these?' he said, inclining his head towards the girls.

'Time to go, ladies,' said Tal. 'Now, if you wish to stay alive, do as I told you. You might increase your chances of survival if you invite some of those loud and annoying drunks to walk you back into the city.'

The girls nodded and left, saying nothing. 'What now?' said Amafi.

Tal reached up and pulled the window-sashes down. He ripped off the heavy cords that hemmed them and said, 'We'll tie him up and lower him to the ground below. If we can stay close to the side of the window the lookout at the other corner of the garden who is watching the stairs for his friend to come down, may not notice us.'

'We can but try.'

They tied up the man, and Tal was first to climb out of the window. He hung by his hands and then let go, landing on his feet with a soft thud. He looked across the large opening into the main room and saw the lookout with his eyes trained inside, on the stairs.

He motioned for Amafi to lower the Nighthawk, and almost had the man dropped on his head. A moment later, Amafi landed hard on his backside next to Tal. 'I'm not what I once was, Magnificence,' he whispered.

'Next time, you go first and I'll drop him on you.'

'As you say, Magnificence.' Amafi and Tal dragged the unconscious man around the corner and down the path to the outside hedge. Amafi lowered the rope ladder and quickly climbed down. Tal threw the man over his shoulder and carefully negotiated his way to the bottom of the ladder. Then with one arm, he lowered the man to where Amafi could guide his fall.

Tal leapt onto the roof of the house and said, 'Do we have a fast route away from this home, Amafi?'

Amafi pointed and helped Tal sling the Nighthawk over his shoulder, and they tiptoed across the roof of the house. Tal could hear tiles cracking under their boots and silently asked the owner of this fine home to forgive him when the next rains struck Kesh. He followed Amafi and prayed that they could reach the closest safe house without incident.

# CHAPTER 16

# WAITING

The door swung open.

Tad, Zane and Jommy all looked up from their dozing, fitful attempt at resting. A girl about the same age as the lads entered the room carrying a small kettle, a stack of bowls and under her arm, a wrapped bundle.

The three boys stood up and gave her access to the table. When she had put down her burdens, she unwrapped the bundle to display half a loaf of bread and a small wheel of cheese. 'My father told me to bring these to you,' she said in a low whisper. She was plump with a pretty smile, big brown eyes and long dark hair.

Jommy handed the utensils around. He shared out the soup and the girl went to look at Caleb. 'He's lost a lot of blood,' she observed, 'but his colour looks better than last night and he's breathing well. If he wakes up, give him something to eat.' She glanced into the kettle and said, 'Which means leaving some of this for him, all right?'

Tad nodded and tried to talk with a mouth full of cheese. Zane said, 'Thank you.'

Jommy said, 'Miss, do you know what we're supposed to do next?'

She glanced around the room and said, 'Wait,' then closed the door.

Kaspar hurried through the halls of the palace with Pasko at his heels. It was barely first light, yet the summons had come nearly a quarter hour earlier. He had dressed without the benefit of a bath or shave and had become very used to the Keshian practice of consuming large mugs of hot coffee in the morning with the meal and after.

He reached the office of Turgan Bey who waved him into a chair and motioned for Pasko to wait outside. The Conclave agent posing as a manservant, bowed and left the room, while Bey's clerk closed the doors.

'Coffee?' asked Bey, indicating a large earthenware carafe sitting on the table next to two mugs.

Kaspar poured himself some of the hot, bitter, habit-forming drink and said, 'Thank you. I've become accustomed to it in the mornings since I've been here.'

Bey smiled. 'It may be even more addictive than some of the drugs you buy in the market.' He motioned for Kaspar to follow him to the balcony overlooking the garden.

The night sky had given way to the soft grey light of dawn, with rose and silver hues foreshadowing the bright blue sky to come. It would be another hot day as the Empire approached the Midsummer festival of Banapis. Kaspar had come to expect the nights to be hot and the days to be hotter. If he didn't think that he'd look ridiculous in Keshian garb, he would have already sent Pasko out for a linen kilt and a set of sandals.

Softly, Bey said, 'There was some bloody work afoot last night, Kaspar.'

Kaspar said, 'I've heard nothing.'

'You're hearing it now,' said Bey.

'Who died?'

'For certain, Prince Nauka.'

Kaspar said, 'The Emperor's great-nephew?'

'The same, and a staunch supporter of Sezioti.' Bey shook his head and blew out a long breath as if he was trying to release his frustration. 'Here's the maddening part of it; I know that Dangai is behind this.'

'You're certain he's not being used by others?'

'When Leikesha was ruler, her son Awari was being used as a dupe by One Whose Name Is Forgotten.'

Kaspar nodded. He knew enough recent Keshian history to know that as part of his punishment for treason, Lord Niromi's name was removed from every historical reference, and all Keshian families were now forbidden from ever naming a child Niromi.

Bey continued. 'Dangai is no one's dupe. He has taken complete control of the Inner Legion and if things come to a bad pass, we may even see a repeat of the last attempt to seize the throne, when

Empress Leikesha's Guards battled the Inner Legion in this very palace.'

He looked out at the garden for a moment, then turned to face Kaspar again. 'Do you know that over one thousand officers of the Inner Legion were cast into the Overn? The crocodiles feasted for months.' He sighed. 'However, this time I do not know if the Palace Guard would stand against the Legion, for Sezioti is not a popular figure. Respected, yes, and even liked somewhat, but he's not popular.'

'Why all the bloodletting? Why not a straight appeal to the Gallery of Lords and Masters? From everything I've heard, it seems that Dangai would carry the day.'

'Because we are a nation of traditions, if not of laws.' He looked at Kaspar and said, 'We have no tradition like the Great Freedom as they do in the Kingdom of the Isles, and here there is no confirmation of the King by the Congress of Lords. If the Emperor, blessings upon him, names Sezioti as his heir, then Sezioti is the next Emperor, or at least he will sit upon the throne until Dangai seizes it by removing his brother's head from his shoulders.

'But I need proof, Kaspar. I need some evidence that not only is Dangai behind this, but that he is also in league with those enemies only a few of us know exist: Varen and his Nighthawks.'

'What can I do to help?'

'Much more than the death of Prince Nauka

occurred last night. The Mistress of Luck is a gambling hall located atop Summer Winds Hill – one of the better districts in the city – it's also a brothel, and last night several strange things occurred there. Talwin Hawkins disappeared. He went upstairs with two whores, and was followed soon after by two men, one of them Talwin's so-called servant, the old assassin Petro Amafi, and some time soon after that, the two girls came down alone, invited some drunken louts out and left. The room upstairs was empty, save that a cord from a curtain-sash hung from the window.

'We can surmise that Hawkins avoided a trap of some sort. But I want to know who the mysterious man who went up the stairs before Amafi was. And where has Talwin Hawkins and Petro Amafi taken him?'

Kaspar said, 'I have no idea.'

'Well, I suspect your man Pasko might have some means of getting word to him.'

'I'll have him go about it as soon as we're done here.'

'I have two masters, Kaspar. I serve those whom you serve, because I believe their cause is just and in the long term your objectives also aid my other master, the Emperor. I can best serve by bringing proof of a plot to him. Not guesses, not vague circumstances, but proof.

'The other matter is that last night word reached me of an assault at an inn called the Three Willows, owned by a former Kingdom citizen by name of

Pablo Maguire. A trader from the Vale of Dreams was in residence, a man of vague nationality, seeming both Keshian and Kingdom, and with him were three boys, apprentices apparently. The master was away on business, and the boys were eating their supper when an altercation broke out.

'Why these three lads were singled out is uncertain, but it is clear that there's more going on than meets the eye.' Bey looked at Kaspar. 'This Maguire isn't another of your agents, is he?'

'I'm like you, Turgan; I only get told what I need to know, and no more.'

The large old man let out a deep sigh. 'I understand why our masters act as they do, but I must confess that it annoys me no end to have other agents – potential allies – close at hand and be ignorant of them.'

'It's all to a purpose,' said Kaspar. 'You can't divulge what you don't know.'

'Then send your man to wherever he must be sent and start spreading the word: I need proof of Dangai's duplicity, and I need it soon, or Kesh may be plunged into a civil war.'

'What have your own agents found?'

Turgan Bey flexed his hands in frustration. 'I can not trust more than a handful of those who are purportedly in my service – too many alliances have been formed and reformed around the succession.

'The Banapis Celebration begins in less than two weeks, and the city will be thronging with

337

visitors. The Emperor is due to make what may be his last public appearance. He will address the Gallery of Lords and Masters and then stand on a balcony waving to the crowds below, though it is unlikely that they will be able to see him.

'In short, if there is to be a coup d'état it will most likely happen then. The Inner Legion will be in the city, but the Royal Charioteers and the Imperial Army will not be.'

'I'll see what I can come up with. Any idea where Tal might have gone to ground?'

'No. Talk to your man Pasko, or go to the Merry Juggler, the inn where he was staying. Track him down and see if he has found anything.

'Talk to our friends in the north, too, do whatever it takes, Kaspar. Help me keep this Empire intact, and if your brother-in-law won't have you back in Olasko, I'll see that Sezioti makes you a prince of the Empire.'

Kaspar smiled. 'Thanks, but my appetite for power seems to be a thing of the past. I find that working on behalf of our friends in the north gives me ample cause for rising each morning, and no man can ask more than that.' He bowed and left the room.

He signalled to Pasko who was waiting quietly on a bench outside the room, and the old servant fell into step with him. 'I'm going to an inn called the Merry Juggler. You go wherever you need to go if unexpected trouble occurs. Something went sour last night, and our friends have gone to ground . . . assuming they haven't got themselves killed.' Lowering his voice, he said, 'I need to speak to Tal and Caleb, and sooner is better than later.'

Pasko nodded and hurried off, turning down a corridor that would eventually take him to the lower city via the servants' entrance. Kaspar hurried to the office of the Keeper of the Imperial Household, to request that a mount be readied for him as soon as possible. He wondered if he could find another mug of coffee somewhere, and perhaps a bread roll or slice of ham to eat before he went riding out to confront chaos.

The warehouse was surrounded by guards loyal to the Conclave. Inside, Tal watched dispassionately as Amafi continued to question the assassin. It had taken a great deal of luck as well as skill to carry the unconscious man to a safe house, and they had barely reached this deserted warehouse before dawn.

But now they were secure, at least for a while, and the prisoner could make as much noise as he wished and no one would be the wiser. And despite his refusal to talk, he had been making a great deal of noise for over two hours.

Amafi turned away from the man, who had been bound by leather ties to a heavy wooden chair, which was in turn tied to a supporting-beam in the middle of the room. It had been necessary after he had tried to break his own skull against the dirt floor. Fortunately for Tal, all it had done was render the assassin unconscious for less than an hour.

Amafi said softly, 'We have reached a place where both he and I must rest, Magnificence.' With a jerk of his head, he indicated that Tal should walk with him to the far side of the warehouse.

When they were some distance from the prisoner, Amafi said, 'Torture is an art form, Magnificence. Anyone can beat a man into insensibility. Anyone can inflict enough pain so that the prisoner becomes nearly mindless.'

'Where are we with him?'

'This man has been trained, Magnificence, and he is a fanatic. He would rather die in agony than betray his clan. So the trick is to convince him that the agony will be endless. Then he will talk.

'But when he talks, he must also believe that the truth is his only escape from pain, from betrayal and from whatever drives his silence. For if he is too resilient, he will still speak lies. And if he is too damaged, he will just say whatever he thinks we wish to hear.'

Tal nodded. He took no enjoyment from watching Amafi inflict pain, but he had seen so much death and suffering since his childhood that it disturbed him only a little. He always remembered that those he opposed were at the heart of what had befallen his people – they had caused the near-obliteration of the Orosini. He also had a family in Opardum that would suffer, along with everyone else on Midkemia, should the Conclave fail.

'What do we need to do?'

'First, I need some of the men outside to cover

the windows, so it is always dark in here. We must confuse his sense of time, so that he thinks he's been here longer than he has. I should return to the inn and secure a change of clothing or two for us, so that we can confuse him about the passage of time that way too. Lastly, we need to bring in some food and wine – brandy would be better – so that we can soothe him when it becomes necessary.'

'Do what you must.'

Amafi hurried out of the warehouse, and Tal walked over to where the semiconscious prisoner sat, befouled by blood and his own body-waste. Tal and he exchanged a long look, and neither man spoke.

Caleb groaned as he sat up. The boys had been trying to stay calm all day, but without any way to judge the passing of time in the small room, the minutes dragged by.

Tad and Zane had already reached the point of confrontation due to their frayed nerves, but Jommy had broken up the scuffle before it could really start.

The girl had returned with another meal and said, 'It won't be long before they'll decide where to move you,' but she would not stay with them or answer any more questions.

Now Caleb had recovered, the boys told him of what had happened at the Three Willows. He said, 'So, we were not half as clever as we thought we were.'

'Are you all right?' asked Tad.

'Not as bad as I look,' said Caleb. 'I took two cuts in the shoulder, but neither was deep. I got a slice across the scalp and although such wounds bleed like mad, it looks far worse than it is – and we were safely away when I slipped and don't remember much, save some of the lads carrying—' He glanced around. 'Wherever are we?'

Tad told him and Caleb nodded. 'Now, how did you lads get here?'

The boys told him about the four assassins, and Caleb said, 'Had they meant you dead, you'd be dead. They were herding you so that you would lead them here.' His voice showed his concern.

'We lost them,' said Jommy, with a grin. 'I steered them into the Bakers' Boys and like the bullies they are, they decided to have some fun with those assassins. I glanced back as we cleared the other side of the square and the Bakers' Boys were doing a right job of stomping the two who chased us.'

I'm surprised the Bakers' Boys aren't all dead,' said Caleb.

'Surprise works wonders,' said Jommy.

'And stupidity. You could have got those boys killed, Jommy.'

Jommy lost his grin. 'Well, I wasn't expecting a "thank you," for saving these two lads, but I didn't except criticism. Would you rather it been us instead of them?'

Caleb put his hand up, signalling his surrender. 'You're right. I'm sorry. I wasn't there.'

'What do we do now, Caleb?' asked Tad.

'I need to rest for a few more days, but not here. We've put these people in enough danger already. So, we need to find ourselves a place to hide out.' He ran his hand through his long hair and found it matted with dried blood. 'And I need to clean up.'

He sat, trying to catch his breath for a few minutes, then said, 'I need to clean up.'

'You said that already,' said Zane.

Caleb nodded. 'If they know where were are—'

'They don't,' said Tad. 'If they knew where we were, they'd have been here by now.'

'Yes,' said Caleb. 'I . . . you're right.'

Jommy said, 'Why don't you lie down again, mate? I'll keep an eye on things.'

Caleb lay down, and within minutes he was asleep.

'Well, then,' said Jommy, 'I think this is as good a time as any to ask why so many people want to kill us?' He fixed Tad and Zane with a neutral expression and sat back in the single chair, waiting for an answer.

Two more meals came and went before Caleb roused again. The boys had judged the time to be mid-morning sometime when he sat up with a groan, and said, 'My head must be broken.'

'Not so's we could see,' answered Jommy. 'Wait here.' The older boy stood up and worked his way past Tad and Zane who were still sitting on the floor, and left the room.

'Where's he going?' Caleb asked.

'Don't know,' answered Zane. 'Maybe to piss?'

'You haven't been outside, have you?' asked Caleb as he stood up, using the back of the recently vacated chair as support.

'No,' said Tad. 'They've got a chamber pot outside the door.'

The door opened. Jommy entered and set a porcelain bowl on the table. He pulled a folded towel out of it, and handed it to Caleb. He poured water into the bowl from a matching pitcher. 'You said you needed to clean up,' he said to Caleb.

Caleb pulled off his blood-splattered shirt and began to wash. Jommy said, 'There's fresh clothing for you, too. I'll get 'em.'

Jommy left and returned moments later with a clean shirt and a new hat. 'You seemed to have lost your hat, Caleb, so I asked our host if he could find you a new one.'

'Thanks,' said Caleb. 'It'll help hide the mess.'

'Now,' said Zane. 'We were talking about what to do next when you passed out last time, Caleb.'

'I'm a little vague on what was said, but if I remember things correctly, you were almost taken by four men, right?'

'That's right,' said Jommy. 'And from what these two have told me, we're hip-deep in crocs, and the swamp's started to rise.'

'What did you tell him?' asked Caleb.

Tad and Zane exchanged glances, but it was

Jommy who answered. 'Enough to know that I'm either with you to the end or a dead man the second I try to leave the city, Caleb. I'm not sure I understand most of what they said, and I'll leave it to you to fill me in on what you think I should know, but understand something about me, mate: I won't let you down. You've treated me more than square, and you've fed me when all I did was keep these two from being treated like drums at a festival. Now, don't blame the lads too much for telling me; I convinced them that if I was going to get myself killed, then I deserved to know why.'

Tad said, 'It's only fair, Caleb.'

Caleb looked at Jommy. 'You've bought yourself a lot of danger.'

The boy from Novindus shrugged. 'I've been in and out of danger ever since Rollie and me left home. It could easily have been me who died. So, what's a little more danger? I figure you're good blokes and if I'm going to throw my lot in with someone, it might as well be good blokes.

'So, that's settled. Now, where do we go from here?'

'An inn not far away. I'll need you,' he pointed to Zane, 'to go ahead of us. It's not far and you shouldn't have any trouble getting there; if they're still out hunting, our enemies will be looking for three lads, not one. Your dark hair makes you the obvious choice to go – you look the most like a

345

Keshian here. I'll tell you what to say. We'll follow along in a while.'

Zane listened as Caleb gave him instructions. After he had left, Caleb told Jommy and Tad, 'I need to go somewhere before I join you. If I do not arrive at the inn by first light tomorrow, go to the innkeeper and tell him you must leave the city on the first caravan north. Go to the caravanserai, but do not travel with the caravan. It is a code, someone will be there who can take you home quickly. Understood?'

'Where are you going?' asked Tad.

'To see a man about what went wrong last night—'

'Two nights ago,' Tad corrected.

'Very, well, two nights ago,' said Caleb. 'Someone knew we were coming, Tad, and we were given a proper thrashing. I'm sorry to lose so many good men, but what I need to discover now is how they knew we were coming and how they knew that you boys would be at the Willows, and if any other mischief has been done while I've been unconscious.'

'Be careful, Caleb,' said Tad. 'I don't want to have to tell Mum you're dead.'

Caleb said, 'That makes two of us, son. Now, wait for a few minutes and then go where I told Zane to go. Jommy, you first and Tad, you leave shortly after. If anyone's looking for you, they'll be looking for three boys together, not a single one on some errand. May Ruthia smile on you,' he said, invoking the Goddess of Luck.

'You, too, Caleb,' said Jommy.

After Caleb left, Jommy said to Tad, 'You've got yourself a hell of a dad there, mate.'

Tad just nodded.

Caleb had gathered his hair on the top of his head and stuck it under his hat. He wore a cheap cloak which hid his leather vest and trousers. He didn't plan on being in public for long, but he didn't want to run the risk of being spotted. Without a corpse to prove he was dead, Varen's men would certainly be on the lookout for him.

He had left the safe house, surprised it was midday – he had lost all track of time since he had entered the sewers two days before. He worked his way through the city, just another outland-traveller not dressed for the Keshian heat, but hardly the first foreigner to insist on wearing such outlandish garb.

Caleb's first stop had been a modest money-lender with a shop on the edge of a minor plaza. After that he had visited a sword maker, where he purchased a new blade. Then he had headed to his present location – an alleyway leading into one of the more unsavoury parts of the city.

He had lurked in the shadows for nearly an hour, before what he'd been waiting for appeared: a young boy – but not too young; he had no use for urchins – he needed a youthful, inexperienced thief or beggar.

As the youth passed him, Caleb reached out and

grabbed his collar. Pulling him backwards, he almost lost the boy as he tried to wriggle out of his tunic. Caleb tripped him and then put his boot on the boy's chest.

He was scrawny, with black hair and dark eyes, and his skin could have been the colour of cocoa, but it was hard to tell under all the dirt on his face. He wore a simple grey tunic and shorts matching in filthiness, and his feet were bare.

'Mercy, master!' he cried. 'I have done you no harm!'

'No,' said Caleb, 'and I shall do you none, if you do me one service.'

'Name it, master, and I will serve.'

'How do I know you won't run off the moment I lift my boot?'

'I swear on all the gods, master, and by my grandmother, blessings upon her, and in the name of the Emperor, blessings be upon him!'

Caleb took a coin out of his purse and held it up. The boy's expression instantly turned from terror to overt greed. Caleb removed his foot and the boy was up in a bound. He reached for the coin, but Caleb pulled it away. 'After you have served me.'

'Master, but how shall I know that I will be rewarded when the task is done?'

'Shall I take an oath on my grandmother?' asked Caleb.

'No, of course, but –'

'No argument, Little Lord of Lice,' Caleb

answered in idiomatic Keshian. 'If you do not as I ask, then another shall see my gold.' He knew that a single gold piece was more than the boy could steal or beg in half a year.

'What must I do?'

'What is your name?'

'If it pleases you, master, I am called Shabeer.'

'Go hence, Shabeer, and carry a message for me, then return here with an answer.'

'And if the answer displeases you, master?'

'You shall still be rewarded.'

'Then what is the message, and to whom do I carry it?'

'I must meet with whoever speaks for the Ragged Brotherhood. I need to speak with he who may bind the thieves and beggars of Kesh to a bargain. Much gold may be had, though there is equal danger.'

'In matters of gold and danger, there is someone, master.'

'Then go at once and I will remain here, but know that I have powerful friends. Treachery will bring you death; faithful service will bring you gold.'

'I hear and obey, master,' said the boy and he scampered off.

Caleb faded back into the shadows and waited.

# CHAPTER 17

# INTELLIGENCE

Tal moved silently through the sewer.
He had no doubt about the authenticity of the message he had received earlier that day from Caleb and had been relieved to discover he was alive. Caleb had relayed messages between him and Kaspar, and now the three of them were to meet.

Tal's only concern was the location of the meeting. He was following a filthy beggar boy named Shabeer through a river of sewage in a huge culvert under the slaughterhouse district of the city of Kesh. 'My eyes are bleeding,' said Tal.

'In truth, master?' asked the boy, concerned that if anything went amiss on this journey it would be considered his fault. The other foreign master had been generous beyond imagining and the beggar boy was desperate to keep him happy.

'No, just a manner of speaking.'

'You get used to it, here, master,' said the boy.

'How long does that take?'

'A year, two maybe.'

Tal would have laughed, but he was trying hard not to breathe too deeply. He had been in several places over the years that he had judged to be unequalled in stench – Kaspar's prison, known as the Fortress of Despair being foremost among them – but nothing could have prepared him for the overwhelming smell of this Keshian sewer.

He appreciated the reason for holding the meeting here – the slaughterhouses, tanners and other malodorous enterprises had been sectioned off near the edge of the lake, so they were far from the residential areas of Kesh, and lay on the lee side of the city so that the prevailing breezes blew the stench away. But the entire area still reeked.

They reached an outflow and Shabeer stepped on an uneven stone which was a cleverly disguised toe-hold. He levered himself into the outflow, and disappeared into the darkness.

As he was holding the lantern, Tal said, 'Slow down, boy.'

He followed Shabeer and had to duck to stop his head from hitting the ceiling of the smaller outflow tunnel. The boy led him about two hundred yards, until they came to what appeared to be a large circular catchment area.

Several streams of malodorous fluids trickled down from above, and Shabeer motioned for Tal to stay close to the left hand wall as he inched around to a series of iron rungs set in the brickwork.

Tal followed the climbing boy, until he pushed upon a trapdoor overhead. They emerged into a well-lit room. Caleb and Kaspar were already there, and sat opposite a large table. Next to them was an empty chair.

As soon as Tal had cleared the trapdoor, he heard a voice from the other side of the room say, 'Be seated, if you will.'

The large table dominated the room. It was a rough thing of no artistry, but it was sturdy and Tal realized that its primary purpose would be to slow down those seeking to attack whoever was on the other side of it.

That person was a large man in a striped robe, similar in fashion to those worn by the desert men of the Jal-Pur, but the wearer was no desert man. He had the neck of a bull, and his head was completely shaved. His eyebrows were so fair that it looked like he had none. His age was unfathomable – he could have been as young as twenty-nine, or as old as sixty. The single candle didn't provide enough light for Tal to guess more closely. On either side of him stood a well-armed man: bodyguards.

Once Tal had taken his seat, the man said, 'You may call me Magistrate, an honorific given to me by those who dwell in the sewers and alleyways, and it will serve for now.

'Your friend, Caleb, has been most generous and has bought you some of my time, my friends. Time is money as I am sure you are all aware, so let us get directly to the question: what have you to ask of the Ragged Brotherhood?'

Caleb asked, 'Do you speak on their behalf?'

'As much as any man can,' came the answer. 'Which is to say, not at all.' He looked directly at Tal. 'We are not like your famous Mockers of Krondor, with strict oversight and iron rule, Talwin Hawkins of the Kingdom.'

Kaspar glanced at Caleb, and the Magistrate continued, 'Yes, we know who you are, Kaspar of Olasko.' He pointed at Caleb. 'You my friend, however, are known by name only, your provenance is a little murky. In any event, the Upright Man might command in Krondor –' he put his hand on his chest and gave a slight bow, '– but here, I merely suggest. If it is a good suggestion, it will almost certainly be heard.

'Now, what may I do for you?'

'We seek the Nighthawks,' answered Caleb.

'From what I hear you found them a week ago. There was an unusually high number of corpses floating towards the Overn to feed the crocodiles, and a fair number of them were wearing black.'

'We were led into a trap,' admitted Caleb.

'Likely,' came the answer.

Kaspar said, 'We need intelligence. We need to know where their real nest is.'

'As I said,' replied the fat man, 'this is not Krondor and we do not have any real organization. Kesh is divided into precincts, each has its own rules and rulers. Above ground, you'll find the street gangs, beggars, pickpockets and enforcers – I believe they are known as "bashers", in the north, and all answer to their own leaders. Those leaders answer to more powerful figures and each of them guards his authority jealously.

'The Slaughterhouse Gang controls the area we now occupy, and to the southwest of here are the Dockstreet Boys. There are over a hundred such gangs, all with equally colourful sobriquets: the Grab-And-Runs, the Big Plaza Gang, the Sweet Hounds, the Caravan Rangers, and many others. A thief may work with impunity in one quarter, but should he be caught in another he might be dealt with harshly; such is the order of things in Kesh.

'Below ground, the sewers are also divided into precincts, or small cantons, and each is home to those who exist at the sufferance of the gang above them. The rest is a no-man's-land and all are free to travel, but at some risk. There are no formal rules, but there are customs and conventions.'

'And you?' asked Tal.

'My place in all of this is of little importance; I broker understanding. I am something of a magistrate among the Ragged Brotherhood, hence the honorific. If conflict occurs, I am called upon to adjudicate. I also provide services, and . . . information.'

'At a price,' said Caleb.

The man smiled, showing two teeth capped in gold. 'Obviously. I am getting old and need to consider my future. I have a little farm on the other side of the Overn. Someday, I shall retire there and watch my servants grow crops. But I am in no hurry; I can not abide farming.

'So, you wish to know the whereabouts of the Nighthawks' base. That will cost a great deal of gold.'

'How much?' asked Caleb.

'A great deal.'

'And how much is a great deal?'

'Quite a lot actually,' said the man. 'I will need to bribe quite a few very frightened thieves. The more afraid they are, the higher their price, and few things in this city scare them more than the Nighthawks.

'There are several areas of the city, including the sewers below, where wise thieves do not trespass. Those who do, tend to disappear. There are the usual stories of monsters, Imperial thief-catchers and rogue gangs. But one of these areas will turn out to be the place your black-feathered birds have made their nest.

'If we can find it.'

'If?' asked Tal.

The fat man nodded. 'There are rumours of magic and evil spirits. While thieves are among the most superstitious fools in Kesh, I would not discount the rumours. If they are true, even the most stealthy of the Ragged Brotherhood might find the areas difficult to approach. There is no easy way past a ward that strikes you dead should you even gaze upon it.

'So, I make no guarantees. Now, to the bargain. I will need three hundred gold coins to begin with, for bribes and rewards, and for my fee I'll need another hundred. Once the information is secured,

I ask ten gold coins in blood money to the gangs for each of their men killed in the hunt, and another five hundred for myself.'

'Done!' said Caleb, standing up.

'Ah!' laughed the fat man. 'I knew I should have asked for more. But done is done.'

The others rose, and Tal said, 'Where shall we find you?'

'I will find you, Tal Hawkins. Kaspar guests at the palace and that is one place most difficult for us to reach, and Caleb must lie low, as he is a marked man.

'Now, while there's a question about an attempt upon a foreign noble at The Mistress of Luck some nights back, I think it safe to say that for at least a few days you can move about the city without fear of instant death.'

'Why do you say that?' asked Tal. 'They weren't afraid to try and kill me at The Mistress of Luck.'

'Had the Nighthawks wished you dead, young lord, you would now be dead. Your prowess with a sword is renowned, so you would have received a deadly dart or a splash of poison in your drink and no one would have noticed. No, they wanted to take you alive, because they wanted to question you. No doubt in the exact fashion in which you now question their man.'

'You know?'

'I make it my business to know,' said the large man, rising to his feet. 'Do not worry; the Nighthawks are a danger, but they are few in number and their attention cannot be everywhere at once. On the other hand, I have eyes and ears everywhere.

'Unlike the nobles and wealthy merchants in the city above, I do not walk through the day fearlessly, convinced that no harm can befall me because of my station or birth. I know there are hands in shadows and daggers in those hands. I will warn you if I learn of any trouble headed your way.'

'And why would you do that?' asked Caleb.

'Because if you are dead, you can't pay me.' He pointed to the trap. 'One at a time, and in this order: Kaspar of Olasko, then Caleb, then Talwin. Each of you will find a guide back to a safe exit from the sewers. I suggest you take a bath when you reach your quarters, the stench here seeps into your very skin. Now, good evening and safe journey.'

The three moved as instructed and were soon on their way back through the tunnels, each hoping that they were on their way to turning the tide of this struggle at last.

Turgan Bey stood motionless. He was wearing the ceremonial torque of his office, a magnificent creation of polished stones and enamelled metal set in gold.

He was presenting Kaspar to the Emperor, even though the question of his asylum had been decided weeks earlier. Kaspar would swear an oath of fealty to the Empire and in exchange they wouldn't hang him, flay him alive, or throw him to the crocodiles.

For the first time since losing his duchy, Kaspar

of Olasko looked upon Diigai, the ancient Emperor of Great Kesh.

A frail man, Diigai still held himself erect, but his movements barely hinted at his once formidable prowess as a hunter. Like his ancestors, he had hunted the great black-maned lion of the Keshian plains. His shrunken chest still carried scars from those hunting triumphs, pale though they might be.

The throne he sat on was made from ivory set into black marble, and behind the Emperor a bas-relief of a falcon with its wings outstretched was carved into the wall: the great seal of Kesh. Before it stood a wooden perch, upon which rested a live falcon, who preened and watched the inhabitants of the room from hooded eyes.

The Master of Ceremonies stood next to the foot of the dais – a thirteen-step ivory-inlaid mass of carved stone – his great headdress was resplendent with rare feathers and gold badges. Around his waist he wore the traditional golden belt of his office as well as the plain linen kilt, but rather than baring his chest, he was permitted to wear a leopardskin over one shoulder.

*Not that he needs any more indication of his status*, Kaspar thought; the headdress looked as if it might topple off his shiny pate at any second. Still, in typical Keshian fashion, the introduction and offering of the petition had been relatively expedited, taking only half an hour so far, and already the man was nearly done.

Kaspar had stopped listening after the first five minutes, turning his thoughts to the coming confrontation and the events that had led up to his own overthrow. While he harboured no love for the Empire, its ruler was a man without stain on his honour and he deserved better than to see his empire ripped away from the rightful heir.

Kaspar also knew that the hand behind all this trouble was not really an ambitious prince, but a mad sorcerer who had also played a large part in Kaspar's downfall. The paths of the two rulers might be different, but the end result would be the same: more chaos in the region and an advantage for those who served the forces of evil in this hemisphere.

He relived the events that had led to his downfall – the insinuation of Leso Varen into his household, his influence over Kaspar, which was subtle at first then overt later, and finally his ruination. Despite having reclaimed a portion of his misplaced humanity, and finding his moral compass at last, Kaspar still thirsted for Varen's blood.

Years of enduring court etiquette asserted their influence as he then realized he had just been introduced. He reverted his attention to the present and stepped forward to bow smoothly, as if he had been hanging on the Master of Ceremonies' every word.

He had been presented to the Emperor twice before, first as Crown Prince when he had first travelled to Kesh with his father while still a boy, and then later as the young Duke of Olasko.

But this time he was here as a suppliant, seeking haven from retribution, or at least that was the story Turgan Bey had devised to win over Lord Semalcar, the First Chancellor and Master of Horses – the title given to the head of the Imperial Cavalry. His petition for asylum had also been endorsed by Lord Rawa, who was the leader of the Royal Charioteers.

Kaspar noticed that the two princes, Sezioti and Dangai, were absent from the court.

Kaspar looked up and as custom dictated, he said, 'He who is Kesh, I crave the boon of your shelter, succour against injustice and a haven to call my own. I pledge to you my loyalty and swear to defend you with my life and honour, if it pleases the Empire.'

Diigai smiled and waved his hand. 'It is done. Is that you, Kaspar?' he whispered. 'We haven't seen you in, what? Twenty years!'

'Yes, Majesty,' said the former duke.

'Do you still play?'

Kaspar smiled, for while the Emperor was old, his memory seemed intact. They had played a chess match when he had been a boy and Kaspar had managed five good moves before being soundly defeated. 'Yes, Majesty, I do.'

'Good, then have Turgan Bey bring you to my apartments after the evening meal. We shall play a game. Just the two of us.'

'It would be my honour, Majesty,' said Kaspar, bowing as he backed away from the throne. When he had reached the appropriate distance, he turned and walked towards the main entrance, where Pasko waited patiently.

'After the evening meal, I'm to play chess with the Emperor,' Kaspar said as Pasko fell in beside him.

'A personal invitation to visit the Emperor in his quarters tonight?' the old servant asked, with eyebrows raised.

'Yes,' said Kaspar with an annoyed expression.

'You do not seemed pleased, m'lord.'

'I'm not,' said Kaspar, keeping his voice down. 'The old gentleman is a non-factor as long as he lives. It's only his death that is important.' They rounded the corner and headed back to the apartment they had been given in the guest quarters. 'And if anything is likely to get me marked for death, this visit would be it.'

'Why?'

As his boot heels rang out on the marble floor, Kaspar whispered, 'Because in Kesh, everyone belongs to a faction, and if I have the Emperor's ear but am not a member of your faction . . . ?' He shrugged.

'You must, then, be a member of the opposition.'

'Exactly. Expect at least two social calls this afternoon, and have my finest garments cleaned and ready for tonight.'

'You're already wearing your finest, m'lord.'

'You know, Pasko, there were times when ruling your own nation had its advantages, and a prodigious wardrobe was one of them. See if you can find a tailor in the city who can fashion me trousers, a shirt and a jacket in the Olaskan fashion by sundown. And find me a bootmaker, too. I can't have new boots made in one afternoon, but I can have these repaired and polished. And a hat, I suppose. You know what to do.'

Pasko bowed and said, 'I know what to do, m'lord,' and he departed.

Kaspar hoped Pasko did, because at the moment, he hadn't the remotest idea what to do. He trusted that something would come to him by that evening to guide him.

The prisoner slumped down on the chair. 'Revive him,' said Tal.

Amafi came to stand before him and said, 'Magnificence, I have been applying my arts for two days now. This man is conditioned to die rather than betray his clan.' He glanced over his shoulder at the unconscious man. 'I am a killer by trade, Magnificence. There are those who enjoy this sort of undertaking, but I do not. However, I find that torture, like everything else in life, can be done well or poorly, so while I do not enjoy this, I still take pride in my skills.

'He should be ready to speak if we let him rest for a while. We must find a cell in which to isolate him and let him awaken with no one around, to let him recover and restore himself a little. Uncertainty is our ally at this point.'

'We don't have time,' said Tal. 'Revive him now.'

'Magnificence, I shall do as you bid, but he will only tell us what he thinks we wish to hear, without regard for the truth.'

Tal was frustrated. He had no doubt that Varen's forces were on the offensive after the ambush that had killed half of Caleb's forces, and the attempt to take Tal prisoner. He agreed with Kaspar's assessment that if Varen's goal was to plunge Kesh into chaos, a major coup d'état attempt at the Festival of Banapis would present the perfect opportunity.

Tal considered what Amafi had said, then nodded. 'Do what you can, but if Leso Varen is in this city, I want to know where he is. I won't ask Pug or Magnus to come here unless I know for a fact that the sorcerer is in Kesh.'

'Magnificence,' said Amafi with a bow. He motioned for two of the guards who had been there since the warehouse had been secured and said, 'We must move him.'

Tal knew there was risk in taking the Nighthawk prisoner to another location, but if Amafi was correct, any hope of gaining information from him was now dependent upon withholding torture as much as on applying it.

*Damn* thought Tal. He turned his back on the proceedings and headed for the door. He would make his way to another inn, where another barman would take another message and see that it somehow got to Sorcerer's Isle the next day.

\* \* \*

363

Nakor hurried into the study.

Miranda and Pug sat at a small table speaking of the day while enjoying their midday meal. 'I have news,' announced the wiry little gambler.

'From Caleb?'

'No. From Talwin Hawkins. He suspects that Varen is in the city of Kesh.' Nakor looked at the message that had arrived in a special cylinder created to transport such missives quickly, and handed it to Pug. 'Caleb is well, if a little damaged from springing a trap.'

Miranda looked concerned. 'Damaged?'

'He got himself wounded, again,' said Nakor with a serious expression. He shook his head. 'He's amassing a fine collection of scars. Still, he is well and I will tell Marie only that, and leave out the part about the scars.'

'That would be wise,' said Pug as he scanned the report. 'Kaspar has made contact with Turgan Bey as we expected, and Caleb thought he had found the Nighthawks, but apparently, they had found him instead.'

'Should we go down there?' said Miranda. 'If Varen is in the city, those three have no protection against him.'

Pug shook his head. 'That's not entirely true. I have sent some people down there to keep an eye on our three agents, and we can be there in minutes if we must.'

'Well, why not just go now?' she asked, always the protective mother.

'Because if I appeared in Kesh and Varen got wind of it, he might eschew subtlety and try to blow up the city just to kill me. He also knows you, Nakor, and Magnus by reputation so it is just as dangerous for you to show.'

'What's keeping him from doing that now, then?' asked Miranda.

Nakor shrugged. 'If he wanted to plunge the Empire into chaos, that would work, but the effects would be short-lived; an external threat would bring them together and make them put aside their differences. If one side gains pre-eminence in the Gallery of Lords and Masters, especially if there's bloodshed, then that is another thing entirely, and would cause years of turmoil in Kesh.

'If there's enough bloodshed in the capital, the frontiers could become unstable. The governor of Durbin might feel confident enough to declare himself the ruler of a free city, or the tribes of the Jal-Pur might be encouraged to rise in rebellion. And it's almost guaranteed that some of the client states in the Confederacy would rebel.

'Varen wants evil to linger, not a quickly resolved conflict.'

Pug said, 'Our mandate is to ensure that Varen doesn't get what he wants.'

Miranda said, 'I want him dead.'

'It's keeping him dead that seems to be the problem,' said Nakor.

'What about that death rift in Opardum? Does that hold some answers?'

'I think so,' said Nakor. 'The problem with the way our universe works is that all the necromancers are working for the other side. If we could find one who would work on behalf of good –' He shrugged.

Pug said, 'The rapidity with which Varen has managed to jump from body to body leads me to believe that he must be using a vessel of some sort to house his soul.'

'I thought soul jars were only a myth,' said Miranda.

Pug shrugged, looking annoyed. 'I have seen too much in my life to assume anything a myth. It is usually just something I haven't seen yet.'

Miranda looked at her husband and frowned. 'I meant the ones in the stories.'

'Were based on fact, apparently,' said Nakor. 'There are many ways to possess another – your mother, for example, became very good at it. But she was vulnerable; if the body which she inhabited died, then she would die too.'

Nakor had never told Miranda that he had been the one to destroy the spirit of the woman who had been his wife and her mother. Miranda believed Jorma – also known as Lady Clovis – had died when the demon Jakar had taken over the Emerald Queen's army.

'But Varen survives the death of his host and is able to find another body. This must mean that his spirit, soul, mind, whatever you wish to call it, must rest somewhere else, and that part of it is tethered to something – perhaps a soul vessel, or another object. It could be a paperweight on his desk as easily as a true urn.' Nakor shrugged. 'It's somehow related to that death rift he was fashioning. That is why I think it's important that we keep trying to trace it back from that rift thing we discovered west of Maladon.'

'Our son?' asked Miranda impatiently.

'I will send Magnus,' said Pug. 'He's due to return from Kelewan shortly, and as soon as he does, I'll send him down to Kesh to confer directly with Caleb. Tal's report is certainly not comprehensive enough.'

Miranda looked only slightly mollified. 'I'd rather go myself.'

Pug laughed. 'First, Kesh is a culture where women of any rank whatsoever do not venture out after dark alone, and secondly, Magnus has a much more even temper than you, my love.'

She glared at him but said nothing.

'I'll go down with you if the time comes to do serious harm to Varen,' Pug added.

Miranda seemed satisfied with that. 'Very well, but I want to know as soon as we hear from Caleb.'

'Yes, dear,' said Pug as he looked at Nakor. The little gambler grinned.

Kaspar waited surrounded by Imperial Household Guards.

Each man was physically impressive – not one of them was shorter than six feet, and many were closer to seven. All were dark-skinned, suggesting their lineage, if not Trueblood, came from the closely-allied tribes around the Overn. They wore the Trueblood linen kilt, and belts of bronze-studded leather. Their sandals, Kaspar noticed, were closed-toed, and he suspected they were designed for combat, not comfort. Each carried a long, curved blade at his hip and they all wore battle torques of silver-decorated iron.

Servants led Kaspar and his escort through gallery after gallery, many adorned with fountains or exotic birds, until he found himself in a gigantic room, dominated by an enormous bed. The bed easily measured twelve square feet, and it sat on top of a dais in the centre of the room.

The room, however, looked more like a pavilion, hung with many curtains that could be moved as privacy dictated. Currently, they were all thrown back, affording the Emperor a stunning view of the palace below and the city beyond, in every direction.

Diigai sat on a curved chair a few feet in front of the bed. Upon a table before him rested the most splendid chess set Kaspar had ever beheld. The Emperor waved him closer and said, 'Sit, boy. Let us play.'

Kaspar sat and looked around. All around the chamber stood young women of stunning beauty, dressed in the scant Trueblood fashion. Not a man given to being swayed by a pretty face or ample bosom, even Kaspar was impressed by their exquisiteness and sheer number.

The Emperor waved his hand and said, 'I wish as much privacy as possible, my loves. Go away.'

The girls left with whispers and giggles, and servants drew gauzy curtains so that only one view of the city was left open.

'This is as much privacy as I'm allowed, Kaspar,' said the Emperor, dropping the formality of speech used in public. 'I'll give you white.'

Kaspar nodded and picked up a pawn.

The board appeared to be carved from rosewood and had been crafted with eye-catching precision. The squares appeared to be ebony and ivory and were framed with tiny bands of gold set so perfectly that the surface was completely smooth. The pieces were not only made from the finest black onyx and white chalcedony, the carvings were also works of art. Kaspar picked up the white queen and beheld a face of regal beauty. Each crown was made of gold, and as he inspected the other pieces more closely, he could seen the tiny gems set into the priest's sceptre and that the horseman's sword was fashioned from platinum.

'Move, boy,' urged the Emperor, and Kasper pushed his king's pawn forwards. He smiled. It had been many years since anyone had called him 'boy'.

The Emperor leaned forward and said, 'I wager you're wondering about all those pretty girls.'

Kaspar laughed. 'I must confess, Majesty, I was nearly overwhelmed by their beauty.'

The Emperor grinned, and Kaspar was struck

by how strong and white his teeth appeared against his aged, dusky skin. 'What is the saying? "I'm old, but I'm not dead yet"?' He chuckled. 'They are only here to spy on me. I think each of them works for some different minister, general, nobleman or guild in the city. They're all presents, you know?'

'Slaves?'

'Hardly. No slave would be permitted within a hundred paces of the imperial personage. And Truebloods can never be slaves. If you break the laws enough to deserve slavery, we toss you to the crocodiles instead.' He moved his own pawn. Then, lowering his voice even more, he said, 'One of the benefits of rank. I bed one now and again and even if . . . nothing significant occurs, I do hear things.'

Diigai motioned for Kaspar to lean closer and whispered, 'They think I'm senile.' He chuckled, and Kaspar saw a light in his eyes for the first time since he had been a boy. 'And I let them think so.'

Kaspar said nothing, wondering why he, a renegade outlander was being admitted . . . no, not admitted – dragooned – into the Emperor's inner circle. Kaspar moved again.

The game continued slowly, until Diigai said, 'Kaspar, I suspect that at this time next year I will not be alive.' He surveyed the board, and added, 'Perhaps not even this time next month.'

'Someone plots against you, Majesty?'

'Always. It's the Keshian way. My sons all died young, and only one had a son of his own. If I had a reasonably intelligent granddaughter, I'd marry her off and make her husband emperor, just as I was named when Leikesha married Sharana to me.' He smiled as he moved a piece. 'Now, there was a woman. Did you ever sleep with her?'

Kaspar chuckled. 'I never had that honour.'

'You may have been the only ruling noble to visit Kesh who didn't.'

'I believe I was only fifteen years old at the time, Majesty.'

'That wouldn't have stopped her. She was probably too busy bedding your father, then.' Before Kaspar could respond, the Emperor continued, 'I have it on good authority that she took both the princes of the Isles to bed. But it was before we wed. Ah, Trueblood women of power; there are none like them in the world.'

'I can easily believe that,' said Kaspar.

'Sharana was a strong-willed, opinionated woman with an unforgiving nature. There were times she wouldn't speak to me for weeks if she was mad. I must confess I grew to love her after a fashion.' He sighed. 'I still miss her after forty years.

'If I had a granddaughter like her, I'd marry her off to you, Kaspar.'

'Me, sire?' said Kaspar, genuinely surprised.

The Emperor took one of Kaspar's pieces and said, 'Four moves to checkmate if you don't pay attention. Yes, you, and it's not because I like you particularly, because I don't. You're a murderous bastard with no remorse in your soul, but that's exactly what it takes to run this empire.'

'Thank you, Majesty. I think.'

The Emperor laughed. 'At least you'd hang on to what was given to you, with every trick you have. I fear that my grandson will see the Empire broken up into many smaller nations before he's done.'

'Sezioti?'

The Emperor shook his head. 'No, Dangai. Sezioti is a scholar, so our hunters and warriors underestimate him, but he would find a way to keep the peace. But he is unlikely to inherit the throne, Dangai is too powerful. Even though Lord Rawa endorses the elder prince, many of his Royal Charioteers are friends of Dangai. The same is true of the Imperial Cavalry; Lord Semalcar is close to Sezioti, but many of his riders are not.

'You must remember that these men are not common soldiers. Each soldier in the Cavalry and Charioteers is a noble of the Trueblood.' The Emperor took a sip of wine. 'We have too many damn nobles in Kesh, Kaspar.'

'Lord Bey says you can't toss a barley cake from a vendor's cart in the lower city without hitting one.'

The Emperor laughed. 'He did, did he? That's funny, and true.' Lowering his voice again, the Emperor said, 'You're working with Bey, aren't you?'

'I don't know what you mean, Majesty,' said Kaspar, moving a pawn to blunt the Emperor's attack.

'Bey's a good man, one of the best, but like the

rest, he thinks I'm a doddering old fool, and like the rest of them, I let him.

'I'll get to the point. I don't know what you are doing here, that pathetic attempt to sneak into the Empire disguised as a Kingdom noble was so transparent that even a "doddering old fool" like me didn't take it at face value. You obviously expected to be caught, and you expected to end up in Turgan Bey's tender care. I must admit the asylum request was unexpected, but a nice touch. Who thought that up?'

'I did, Majesty.'

'Well, I don't expect you'll stay in Kesh one minute longer than it takes you to deal with whatever brought you here in the first place – I expect you to ignore that oath you made—'

'I will never violate that oath, Majesty.'

'Then you are a fool, Kaspar. Oaths are made to be broken, if you can get away with it. If Dangai comes to the throne, Kesh may be pitted against your masters, whoever they may be, and you will take arms against us.'

'Masters?'

'Your nation did not rise against you without help, Kaspar.' He pointed his finger at the former duke. 'Have you forgotten that those were Keshian soldiers assaulting your citadel while the Kingdom was taking its merry time wandering around Opardum? And don't think I'm not aware of how you were banished to the backside of the world, but here you are less than three years later, and you didn't arrive in rags. You had resources, Kaspar, and some of the most skilfully forged documents I've ever seen – yes, I had them filched from Bey's office and studied them closely. I wouldn't be surprised if the Prince of Krondor and Duke Erik didn't draw them up for you.

'I know you're here for a reason, and what I wish to hear is whether that reason makes things in Kesh better, or worse?'

Kaspar sat back. 'I hope to make things better, Majesty.' He leaned forward. 'You are right, I serve men who wish to see a dangerous situation put right.'

'That crazy magician, Varen?'

'Now I am impressed.'

The Emperor leaned forward as well. 'With all the spies running around Kesh these days, didn't you think that a few of them might work for me?' He sat back. 'We've had suspicions for some time now, but your arrival convinced me. The reports from Opardum said he died at the hands of Talwin Hawkins – by the way, that was the one thing that did genuinely surprise me, the two of you arriving together, alive.'

'We've come to an accommodation.'

'Anyway, I've received reports that didn't make sense, so I took them to some of my magicians who can interpret things – a few up in Stardock. The consensus was that either a crazy sorcerer named Sidi whom we tried to kill about a hundred years ago has returned to haunt us, or that your Varen had escaped and was here in Kesh, or that a third monster had risen from nowhere who just happened to be a powerful necromancer as well. The second choice seemed the most likely.'

Kaspar saw no harm in telling the Emperor what he had learned from Pug. 'It appears that Varen *is* Sidi.'

'Ah, that explains a lot. I prefer simple answers and that is the most elegant answer to the problem. And why are you here?'

'I've come to settle accounts.'

'Good, and while you're at it, see if you can keep my empire intact for a while longer.'

'I'll do what I can, Majesty.'

'I have a plan, if I can live long enough to see it to fruition. If Dangai can resist his worst usurping impulses a little longer, I may have a solution that will bring about another hundred years of peace. If not, I fear that we face civil war.'

Kaspar said, 'Our goals are much the same, for a great deal of the Empire's current problems can be traced back to Varen. He wishes rebellion.'

'Why?'

'Because he serves evil, Majesty. The rebellion wouldn't even have to succeed; the repercussions of the sedition would be felt throughout the Empire for a decade or longer. Guilt by association would be an acceptable standard and even the innocent would suffer.

'And if the coup was successful, other powerful families would be fair game for jackals and the other carrion-eaters.'

The Emperor said, 'Why?'

'Varen's goal isn't to obtain power for himself, he seeks to undermine everyone else's power. He thrives on chaos and has a larger agenda, he wants nations at war, crowns toppled and armies on the march.'

'I've lived too long,' said the Emperor. 'By the way, you're in check,' he said moving a piece.

Kaspar considered his situation while he looked at the board. The more chaos there was in the land, the more room there was for evil. After spending nearly two years with Pug and his colleagues on Sorcerer's Isle, and after what the god Kalkin had shown him about the Dasati, Kasper knew that Varen was but the first of many worries facing the Conclave.

But for all his power, Varen was still mortal and he could be taken.

Kaspar laid down his king, conceding the match. 'Your game, Majesty.'

'It always is, Kaspar,' said the Emperor with a keen eye. 'I'm not dead yet.'

Presuming much, Kaspar reached over the table and took his imperial hand, 'Not for some time to come if I have any say in it.'

They shook and Diigai said, 'It is time for you to return to your quarters, and time for me to resume the part of a lecherous old fool.' Raising his voice, he shouted, 'Where are my pretties?'

Instantly, the curtains began to be moved aside and the young women returned. The Emperor said, 'There are worse roles to play.'

Kaspar nodded. 'Indeed.'

A servant showed him out of the royal complex, and as he returned to his own quarters, Kaspar wondered about the Emperor's role in the performance that was unfolding. *Am I a true ally?* he wondered. *Or is he merely playing another game with me?*

Kaspar returned to his room, but found it difficult to sleep that night.

# CHAPTER 18

# PLANS

The prisoner slowly opened his eyes.

A pretty girl hovered over him. Her dark hair was tied up and her dress marked her as a daughter of the Mejun people – plains nomads who followed the great antelope herds of the grasslands to the south of the Overn Deep.

She dabbed at his face with a cool cloth, and whispered, 'Quiet. You're safe for the moment.'

The man could barely speak, his face was swollen from the repeated beatings he had taken at Amafi's hands. He had been tied to a chair for days, he'd been beaten, forced to relieve himself where he sat, denied food and had been given the minimum amount of water needed to keep him alive.

But he had not betrayed his family.

'Can you sit up?' the girl asked, her accent further betraying her nomadic origins.

He groaned quietly as he let her pull him upright. She put a cup of liquid to his lips and said, 'Drink slowly. This will revive you.'

He did and found that the bitter liquid did indeed make him feel more alert and also dulled his pain. 'Who are you?' he whispered hoarsely.

'Someone who is being paid to free you. My name is Iesha.'

'Free me?'

'All I know is that I'm to get you out of this room and into the sewers below. Someone will be waiting there to take you away; I do not know who he is or where he is taking you, and I do not want to know. The men who've held you prisoner frighten me, I am leaving as soon as I get my gold.' She pulled on his arm. 'Can you stand up?'

He did so and groaned, but kept his balance. 'Come, we only have a few minutes,' Iesha said.

'Where are the guards?'

'They think you're dying, so they are lax. A message called one away, and the other is sleeping at his post. It is only a short way, but we must be quiet.'

'Let us go.'

They were in a small room in what appeared to be an abandoned house. Iesha slipped her arm around the Nighthawk's waist so that he could lean on her. They moved to an empty kitchen with a single table, on which rested a lantern. A man lay across the table, snoring quietly. The girl helped the prisoner move around the table and into another room, then out of a door into the street.

He looked around; it was the dead of night and only the faint noises of the city in the distance interrupted the silence. 'Where are we?' he asked in a near whisper.

'The Kumhar district. We have less than half a block to travel.'

Iesha helped him to an iron grate set in the middle of the street. She leaned down and tugged at it, but it only moved slightly. 'Let me help you,' said the weakened prisoner and he almost cried out in pain as he leaned over to grab the rungs. Together they moved it out of the way and in the light from a distant lantern they could just about see the iron rungs set into the stones. 'Can you climb down?' she whispered.

'I will,' he said and with great difficulty, as he sat down in the hole and let his feet dangle. Then he turned and slowly worked his way down the iron rungs. By force of will alone he managed to make it to the bottom where two strong hands reached out to steady him.

A man dressed in rags waited for them, and when the girl reached the bottom, he said to the prisoner, 'I am to take you from here.'

'I do not know you,' said the Nighthawk.

'And I do not know you, but I have been paid to take you to a place where we will meet another. Now, we must hurry before you are discovered missing.'

'Wait,' said the girl. 'What about my gold?'

The ragged man said, 'I have this for you.' With a sudden move he pulled a dagger from his sleeve and drove it into the girl's stomach. Her eyes widened and her mouth moved, but she made no noise. Then her eyes rolled into the back of her head and she fell backwards into the filthy water running through the sewer.

'Come,' said the ragged man.

The prisoner glanced at the dead girl and said, 'That was wise. She can't tell anyone where she led me now.'

'I am being paid handsomely to ensure there are no loose ends. As soon as I hand you over to your friends, I will return here and replace the grating. Now, hurry.'

The prisoner was weak, but he was revitalized by the prospect of escaping his torturers. He slogged through the sewage as the ragged man led him towards a major intersection where a further two men waited, both dressed in black. Their faces were covered so only their eyes could be seen.

The prisoner hurried, overtaking the ragged man and reaching the two black-clad assassins. 'Kill him,' he said softly.

One of the Nighthawks nodded. His sword slid from his scabbard with a metallic hiss, and with a quick thrust, he brought the ragged man down. One of the two Nighthawks put his arm around the waist of the injured man and whispered, 'Come, brother.'

They moved into the large tunnel and turned right. After a step, the former prisoner said, 'Wait! Why are we—' His words fell away.

Suddenly he reached up and pulled away the face covering of the man who held him. 'You!' he hissed and he stepped back.

Amafi lashed out quickly and cut the prisoner's throat with his dagger. The man fell back with blood fountaining from his neck, and he landed in the sewage.

Tal undid his own mask and said, 'Now we know.'

'Yes, Magnificence,' said Amafi. 'Now we know for certain.'

They moved back to the ragged man and Tal said, 'You can get up now.'

Chezarul sat up in the slop and shook his head, 'The things we do for our cause,' he said.

Tal laughed. 'I completely understand.'

The three men then went over to where the girl lay sprawled, and Tal said, 'Lela, has anyone ever told you that you die beautifully?'

The girl sat up and said, 'Thank you, Tal.'

He extended his hand and helped her to her feet. 'You both did very well.'

Chezarul said, 'So are you certain of your information, now?'

'As much as I will ever be,' said Tal. 'There were but two places left that could serve as the Nighthawks' nest, and when our friend objected to going north, it meant that their hiding place is most likely to be in the south. He would die before he spoke, so this was the only way.'

Amafi said, 'Magnificence, when do we strike?'

'Tomorrow, at noon,' said Tal. 'They are creatures of the night, so we shall catch them at their weakest. Tell Caleb to gather everyone,' he instructed Chezarul, 'and I'll take care of the rest.'

Chezarul nodded and set off upstream through

the sewer. Amafi said, 'I shall go and see to those who are still at the safe house, Magnificence, and I shall carry word to Pasko at the palace, so that Kaspar is aware of what we will do.'

'Be careful,' said Tal. 'They are still looking for us.'

'I was hiding in the shadows before these curs were born, Magnificence.' He climbed up the ladder.

'What next for you?' Tal asked Lela. He smiled warmly at her, although his features were masked in the dim light from the street above. Lela had been his first lover, years before, when he had still been Talon of the Silver Hawk, the Orosini boy just beginning his education with the Conclave.

'I am going back to Krondor and my position as tavern wench, where I listen to a great deal of nonsense. I catch a nugget of useful information from time to time.' She stepped closer to him and put her hand on his cheek. 'I wish I could stay a little longer, it's going to get exciting, and I must say I have thought of you from time to time over the last few years.'

Tal laughed. 'I'm married, Lela.'

She laughed with him. 'That makes little difference to many men, Tal, and truth to tell, I don't care either.'

He hugged her. 'Would that it were possible, but now you must be on your way. The further away you are from this city the better it will be for you. When next we meet, let's hope it's under happier circumstances.'

Looking at her filthy dress and hands, she said, 'Cleaner, too. Very well.' She kissed him on the cheek and started to climb the rungs. He waited for a while, and then followed her.

Once above ground, Lela scampered off into the darkness, while Tal replaced the grating into the street. He looked around, ensuring they were unobserved, knowing that in a few minutes he would be back to the safe house for a bath, a change of clothes and then some rest, for tomorrow would bring bloody work and he knew that many good men were likely to die.

Tal couldn't rid himself of the hollow feeling in the pit of his stomach that made him wonder if they were missing something. As he continued to scan the area, to see if he was being observed, he took a small orb out of his black tunic and held it to his lips. 'Noon, tomorrow,' he spoke into it, then he depressed a button on top of the device. Tal held out his hand so that it rested upon his open palm; he had no desire to discover what would happen if he clutched it in his fist. After a few seconds, the orb began to vibrate, and then suddenly it vanished.

Putting aside his never-ending wonder over the devices created by the magicians on Sorcerer's Isle, he pulled off his black tunic and headdress and stuffed them between the rungs of the grating, letting them fall into the sewer below. Then without hesitation he turned away from the grate. He had a great deal to do before noon tomorrow.

★   ★   ★

Caleb asked, 'Are you certain?'

'No,' answered Tal, 'but I'm as sure as I can be. The Magistrate of the Ragged Brotherhood told us that the Nighthawks had to be secreted away in one of two locations. We took the prisoner to a major sewer tunnel that led directly to both of these possible sites. I knew that if we went in the right direction, he'd say nothing, but if we went in the wrong direction, he'd make some objection. He did, and that was as much as we were ever going to get out of him.'

Pasko and Amafi were in Tal's room at the fourth inn he frequented since the attack at The Mistress of Luck. Kaspar was currently dining with the two royal princes, Sezioti and Dangai.

'And you have sent word of the attack to Father?'

'Yes,' said Tal.

Caleb said, 'One thing still troubles me.'

'What?'

'If the Nighthawks are secreted in the area of the sewers to the south of the city, what is killing the thieves who venture near that other location in the north?'

'You're thinking there may be two nests?'

Caleb shrugged. 'It isn't likely, but would Varen have his quarters near the Nighthawks? I understand that they work for him, but not as servants.'

'You think Varen also has a hide-out in the sewers?'

'You saw his quarters in Opardum, I didn't. Would there be a better place to hide the sort of thing he does than under the slaughterhouses?'

Tal said nothing for a moment. 'That location is not that far from where we held our meeting with the Magistrate.'

'What if the prisoner wasn't concerned that you were leading him away from his family's roost? What if he was fearful that you were taking him somewhere else to be punished?'

'So,' said Tal, 'I could easily rush off in the wrong direction and get everyone killed.'

Caleb shrugged.

Tal said, 'I liked it better when I was a student and you were my teacher, Caleb. Then you had to make all the tough decisions.'

Caleb shrugged again, but this time with a smile. 'It is sort of like deciding to venture into a cave to hunt a bear, isn't it?'

Tal nodded. 'It's far safer to get him to come out, than going in after him.'

At the same moment, both men got a wide-eyed expression. Caleb nodded as Tal asked, 'Are you thinking what I'm thinking?'

'We don't go in after them; we flush them out.'

Turning to Pasko and Amafi, Tal said, 'Pass the word. Everyone is to stay where they are until further notice. We've got some more planning to do.'

Amafi said, 'Magnificence,' and moved to the door.

Pasko spoke in the low rumbling tones that signalled the importance of his words. 'You'd better hurry, Banapis is only one week away, and the first round of minor festivities begins tomorrow. By this time next week there will be chaos on every corner, at every hour.'

Caleb nodded, and stood. 'I need to find that beggar boy and get word to the Magistrate. We need to know just how close we can get to those two areas of the sewers.'

'Let's hope his information is good. I'd hate to be the one to find out that he was just a little off,' Tal said, holding his forefinger and thumb close together.

'We'll find a safe way to lure them out,' said Caleb. 'Father arrives early tomorrow in preparation for the attack, and I think he'll be able to come up with a trick or two.'

'Speaking of tricks,' asked Tal. 'We could probably use Nakor down here, too. There's no sneakier bastard in this world.'

'I'll ask Father,' said Caleb. 'Now, find Shabeer and I'll start making plans for tomorrow.'

As he reached the door, Tal said, 'What about Kaspar?'

'I'll send Pasko back to him before he retires for the night.' Tal left and Caleb turned his mind to the task at hand: how to get the Nighthawks to swarm out of their nest without getting killed in the process.

Kaspar had discovered that in Kesh, even an informal dinner with the two claimants to the throne involved a dozen other luminaries of the Empire, a score of table servants, another two dozen servants to fetch and carry from the kitchen, musicians, jugglers, a high number of very attractive women, fine food and plenty of good wine.

Kaspar had been ceded a spot of honour on the left of Prince Dangai, who sat at one end of the long table across from his elder brother, Prince Sezioti. The seat at the end of the table was purposely left empty, indicating that no one of higher rank was present, and preventing any conflict should either brother presume.

Kaspar had received the 'informal' invitation – a handwritten note perfectly scribed by a royal secretary held on a velvet cushion carried by one servant – earlier that day. His plans to meet with Caleb and Tal had to be put off, for no one could say no to the royal princes. Kaspar assumed the abrupt invitation was a direct result of his dining with the Emperor the night before. He suspected his surmise to Amafi had been correct, and now both princes wished to see if Kaspar was in the other's faction.

The meal had been perfectly prepared but Kaspar had eaten sparingly. He expected to be in a fight for his life in less than fifteen hours.

Prince Dangai said, 'Is the food and wine not to your liking, m'lord Kaspar?'

'On the contrary, Highness. It is beyond compare.'

'It's just that you seem to be eating very little and drinking less.'

Kaspar regarded the younger claimant to the throne. He was a man of middle years, perhaps only a few years older than Kaspar, but he was still battlefield-fit. His shoulders and arms were heavily muscled, and there seemed to be little fat on him. His head was clean-shaven, but he wore a moustache and a beard. Like his father and brother, his skin was the colour of dark walnut and in the heat of the evening his face shone. Kaspar wished he had the temperament to take off the traditional Olaskan garb and don a Keshian kilt, for they had to be far more comfortable.

'My stomach is a little off tonight, Highness, and I wish to ensure that I am well enough to enjoy all the festivities of the coming week.'

'It's quite a show,' said Prince Sezioti, from across the table. 'Every year the Master of Ceremonies attempts to put on a festival grander than the year before.'

Dangai snorted. 'How many elephants on parade or monkeys riding zebras do you need?' He laughed. 'A few of them are entertaining, but after the first half an hour they're . . .' He shrugged. 'Still, the populace seems to love it.'

Sezioti laughed. 'As did you, little brother, when you were six. 'You'd shout "hold me higher, Sezi!" until I thought my arms were about to fall off.'

Dangai nodded. 'I remember, brother. I remember.'

Kaspar compared the two men. The family resemblance was obvious, but Sezioti was less muscled than his brother. He had killed his lion, like all of the Trueblood, but that incident may have been the last hunting he had done, and that probably occurred thirty-five years earlier. He looked more like a man given to study, and he had a thinner face than Dangai.

One thing still troubled Kaspar: the two brothers genuinely seemed to enjoy one another's company. There was a filial ease between them, a familiar banter that came from decades of being together. Kaspar had been an only child, as was his daughter, but even a blind man couldn't miss that these brothers were close.

Kaspar tried to imagine what would make them enemies, and failed. He could imagine them disagreeing; all brothers argued at times. He could even see them turning passionate over how the Empire should be run, but to him the answer seemed obvious: Sezioti should remain heir and the command of the army should be given to Dangai – all of the army. They could make the Master of Horses, Leader of the Imperial Charioteers and the commanders of the Inner Legion all answer to him. Give Dangai the care of the Empire, and he would not see his brother harmed.

*What am I missing?* Kaspar thought. *What is here that I am not seeing?*

Deciding to explore, he asked, 'Prince Dangai, before my departure from Olasko, we were considering some minor trade disputes between Olasko and Kesh. Have they been resolved yet?'

Dangai broke the small bone of a game hen in two and sucked out the marrow. He pointed the bone at his brother and said, 'That's more Sezi's area, I'm sorry to say. Military matters tend to occupy most of my time. Sezi?'

'Olasko was never the problem,' said Prince Sezioti. 'It was Roldem's insistence that all the goods from Kesh which sailed from Mallow Haven or Pointer's Head had to tranship through Roldem on their way back to the Eastern Kingdoms.

'We could dispatch the goods to the Kingdom ports of Deep Taunton or Timons by land, but then we'd have to pay Kingdom duties. Or we could ship out of Queral and Hansulé and sail around the Peaks of the Quor, but those pirates in Roldem claimed dominion over all the shipping in The Sea of Kingdoms.'

'Except for the ships of the Isles,' said Kaspar.

Sezioti nodded and smiled ruefully. 'Indeed, which is because the Kingdom has a navy which even Roldem respects. Kesh, however, is a land animal, and our navy are little better than pirates themselves.'

Dangai said, 'Now you're talking about a matter I feel strongly about, brother.' He looked at Kaspar. 'We have both urged our father to build a squadron of modern ships out of Pointer's Head. Dock a dozen large warships up there, and Roldem might reconsider their demands.'

Sezioti agreed, and the conversation continued at length, covering trade and military needs, and their relationships with neighbouring countries.

When the dinner was over, Kaspar left with the thought that these two men were ideally suited to ruling in partnership, whichever of them sat upon the throne. Where was the rivalry that he had heard so much about?

He pondered the question until he reached his quarters, where Pasko waited for him.

'What news?' Kaspar asked.

Pasko beckoned him to step on to the balcony and when they were outside he said, 'Caleb has convinced Talwin that we need more intelligence before we strike. He argues that there could be two nests of Nighthawks or that perhaps one of the forbidden areas under the city conceals the sorcerer's lair. Pug arrives tomorrow and will decide what we'll do next.'

'Damn,' said Kaspar.

Pasko smiled. 'Were you anxious for a fight, m'lord?'

'No,' said Kaspar. 'But had I known that we weren't going to have one tomorrow, I'd have had more to eat, and a hell of a lot more to drink.'

# CHAPTER 19

## TRAPS

Caleb moved cautiously through the darkness. Hours before, he had left the safe house and entered the large sewer with Tal Hawkins. They had split up, one going north, the other south, and both were being shadowed by other members of the Conclave. Knowing that their backs were covered gave both men the freedom to concentrate properly.

Caleb advanced only a few feet at a time, as he waded through knee-deep water thick with sewage. He and Tal had volunteered to scout the two unknown areas because they had both been trained at Sorcerer's Isle in the magical arts. Even though they were not magic users, their sensitivity to the presence of magic gave them a better chance to survive. If experienced thieves were dying, then there was more than vigilant sentries involved.

Caleb knew that Tal was being equally cautious in his approach and that neither man would push beyond a safe limit. Still, there were no guarantees and both of them knew they took a great risk.

Pug and Magnus had arrived that morning, against the possibility of Varen taking direct action.

The risk of detection was outweighed by Pug's decision they needed to be close at hand. It was not Varen's usual mode of attack, but he had shocked Pug when he had personally led the assault on Sorcerer's Isle two years before. Caleb considered his father's likening of Varen to a cockroach to be very appropriate, as both Talwin Hawkins and Kaspar of Olasko had killed the magician in the last three years. He just wouldn't stay dead.

Tal and Caleb had been given the scouting assignments against the possibility Varen might have wards in place specifically attuned to magic or magicians. Both men had been trained as much as any non-magic user could be to detect the presence of magic, and Pug judged the two stealthy men best able to reconnoitre and return unharmed.

Something bumped against Caleb's leg and he looked down. A dead cat floated on the water, its body stiff with rigor mortis, but then Caleb sensed something. He reached forward with his left hand and as his fingers ventured closer to the animal he felt a faint tingling sensation. Caleb paused. It hadn't died a natural death, something had killed the cat.

Caleb closed his eyes. He tried to relax and shut out the soft noise of the sewers: the lapping water, the faint echoes of distant mill wheels, water falling and the rumble from the street above as heavy wagons passed over it. He let his senses wander, seeking nothing . . . until he found something!

He opened his eyes and searched the murk,

knowing that it was almost impossible to see anything, even if there was decent light. The only illumination came from where the sunlight filtered through oddly-spaced gratings in the road above him. Caleb's eyes were used to the shadows, but he knew that the wards he detected were probably invisible.

He took two steps forwards and the hair on the back of his neck stood up. He knew he was close, but also knew he could go no further in safety.

Caleb waited for almost an hour. According to the map which Nakor had provided, if there were any Nighthawks in this area of the city, he should be able to hear something: a faint whisper, a footfall on stone, or the movement of a chair or the clink of a cup.

He continued to wait.

After the second hour had passed, Caleb was convinced that there was no one there.

He stepped backwards and took out his dagger, then he quietly made a mark in a stone on the right hand wall of the sewer tunnel. Then Caleb turned and hurried back to where his father waited for him.

Pug considered what he had been told. Talwin had returned with an almost identical report. He hadn't encountered any dead cats, but he had felt the same discomfort and had reached the point where the hair on his neck and arms had stood up. Then he had also retreated to watch and wait.

And again there had been nothing.

Tal had realized that unlike every other area of the sewers, there were no signs of rats around this place. He found no indication of their presence. At last he had come to the same conclusion as Caleb, and had marked the tunnel wall and returned.

Pug asked, 'What do we know of the city above those locations?'

Chezarul said, 'The area Caleb visited is far to the south, near the tanneries, slaughterhouses, dyers and other businesses that require large amounts of water and smell bad.'

'So, a it is place people only go when they must,' said Pug.

'The other is a very poor part of the city in the north, containing hundreds of shacks, tiny inns and businesses of all stripe, all crowded closely together.'

'A place where few people will notice the comings and goings of strangers.'

'Just so,' said the Keshian. 'Like many poor quarters of the city the area is a hotbed of crime. You'll find anything you desire, for a price, no matter how illicit.'

Pug weighed his options. 'Both appear well-suited as places to hide, albeit for different reasons. Both have quick access to the streets above and the surrounding sewers.'

Magnus said, 'Do we send agents to those locations and try to reach them from above?'

'Those wards will certainly guard against that,'

said Pug. He sighed. 'I think there's no way around this, I must go down and examine the wards personally.' He looked down at the hem of the long robe he wore – the same type of black robe that he had worn since returning from Kelewan a lifetime ago – and said, 'This is one time I would prefer to be wearing trousers and boots rather than a robe and sandals.'

Magnus said softly, 'We can always find a change of clothing at home, Father.'

'You know what we must do?'

'You take the north and I the south.'

Pug nodded. 'Caleb, you will come with me. Magnus will accompany Talwin.'

Chezarul said, 'What of the others? We've had men in place for over two hours now. The longer we wait, the more chance there is of someone stumbling across them.' His frustration was evident. He had arrived that morning ready for a full assault on the Nighthawks, but instead he was being told to keep the men on a short leash.

'Wait a while longer,' said Pug. 'If all this comes to naught, they can return home in ones and twos. If we attack Varen prematurely, many of them might lose their lives needlessly.'

The trader nodded, but his expression didn't change.

The two magicians followed Tal and Caleb, then split up at the large tunnel. Pug waved a silent farewell to Talwin and his elder son as he followed Caleb into the darkness.

They moved as quietly as possible, stopping many times to ensure that they were not being followed or walking into a trap set after Caleb's last visit.

When they reached the place where Caleb had marked the tunnel wall, Pug whispered, 'I can feel it.'

He patted his son on the shoulder and said, 'Move back to the last corner and make sure no one surprises me. This may take some time.'

Caleb moved where he had been told to and waited, watching his father from a distance. In all the years since he had started working for his father, this was the first opportunity Caleb had had to observe him utilize his powers properly, rather than performing demonstrations to students on the island. He could be confronting a dangerous enemy, an enemy perhaps more treacherous than any he had ever known, and Caleb was visited by a feeling he had never known before: concern for his father's safety.

Magnus said, 'Move back.'

'How far?' asked Tal as he began backing down the tunnel.

'If you can see me, there may still be some risk,' said the white-haired magician.

Tal said, 'Very well. I'll wait around the corner.'

Tal retreated around a corner and waited. He kept his eyes moving, trying to apprehend any hint of approaching danger in the gloom, keeping his ears tuned to the rhythms and ambient sounds of the sewer. His training as a hunter served him well as a sentry, for there were few men alive stealthy enough to sneak up on the Orosini.

His mind turned to how his improbable journey had begun, back to his youth in the mountains the Orosini called home, and how Kaspar's mad ambitions had led to the utter destruction of his people.

Kaspar. He could still kill him with his bare hands if he needed to, yet his contact with Kaspar, the former Duke of Olasko, had influenced and shaped his life more than anything else. Yes, Pasko, Caleb, and others had been his teachers, but they had used his desire for revenge against Kaspar to force him to change into something far beyond what he had dreamed possible as a boy.

Yet during his time with Kaspar – when he had infiltrated the Duke's household, then later as Kaspar carried the warning of the Talnoy and Dasati to the Conclave – he had discovered several things that he found troubling. Foremost among these was that he had genuinely come to like the man. He had discovered that Kaspar was a charming, educated and witty companion. He was also an accomplished hunter, only surpassed by Talwin and Caleb's skill. And he as a swordsman, was second only to Tal among the Conclave. Away from Leso Varen's influence, he seemed like a remorseful man who sought to atone for his actions by serving the very people who had brought him to ruin.

Yes, it could be argued that Kaspar had brought

it upon himself, and that the Conclave had been more interested in removing Leso Varen from the picture than Kaspar of Olasko's petty ambitions, but it had been Talwin, aided by the Conclave, Great Kesh and the Kingdom of the Isles who had crushed Kaspar's nation in one blindingly swift attack and it was he who had exiled the former ruler to a year of misery on the other side of the world.

Tal smiled. If the stories that Kaspar had related over the last two years were accurate, he had faced some pretty humbling tasks during that time, but the one that always caused Tal to chuckle was the image of Kaspar hauling the Talnoy halfway up the Pavilion of the Gods on his back without knowing that all he needed to do was slip on the ring in his pocket and order the thing to carry him!

Tal chuckled, trying to keep silent.

Then the tunnel exploded.

Pug felt the spasm in the magic he was confronting before the sound and shock reached him. He automatically erected a barrier across the tunnel inches away from the energy wall he was exploring.

It was, as he had suspected, a death trap for anyone who walked through the passage without the proper key. He knew the artificers on Sorcerer's Island could duplicate the spells needed to pass through unharmed, but he didn't have time for that, and was attempting to counter the magic with

400

his own when the sewers rocked from the distant boom.

He had barely raised his shield before the defensive spell across the tunnel erupted with a brilliant white light. Pug instantly knew what had happened; his older son had grown impatient and had decided to destroy the guardian spell rather than neutralize it.

It was the sound of lightning striking close at hand. Then, an actinic smell overpowered the sewer's usual stench for a few moments, followed a moment later by a sudden compression of the air in the tunnels which heralded a huge thunderclap.

Caleb covered his eyes and then with his ears ringing, turned to see what his father was doing.

Pug motioned for his youngest son to join him and Caleb asked, 'What was that, Father?'

'Your brother.' Pug looked over his shoulder and said, 'The two barriers were linked, and when Magnus got impatient . . . well, I expect they're both down now.'

Pug closed his eyes for a moment, then said, 'Come.'

He had signalled for the rest of the men to leave their places of concealment and follow both magicians into the supposed Nighthawks' lairs.

Pug started walking towards their destination shielded by deadly magic only a moment before. 'What did Magnus do?' asked Caleb.

'Lord James, the former Duke of Krondor, was

a thief in his youth known as Jimmy the Hand,' said Pug.

'I know, Father. You've told me enough stories about him.'

'Well, Jimmy once observed that there were two ways to get past a tricky lock without a key.' He looked at his son as they reached a long dark passageway and held up his hand and a light sprang up around it. As he walked, he held his glowing hand aloft as if it were a torch. 'One way was to pick it.'

'What was the other?' asked Caleb.

Pug smiled ruefully and said, 'Get a *really* big hammer.'

'Patience was never Magnus' strong suit, Father.'

'Subtlety, as well. Much like your mother, I'm sorry to admit.'

'Don't blame Mother,' said Caleb. 'Personally, I blame Nakor for being such a bad influence on him.'

Pug chuckled. 'Those years you spent with the elves have given you dark humour in the face of danger.'

They saw a light at the far end of the tunnel and Pug extinguished his light. When they reached the end, they felt the floor steepening, as if was a ramp. At the far end of this long tunnel, a large grate admitted a fair amount of light from above. Before them lay a large wooden door.

Pug said, 'I think the time for subtlety has passed.' Caleb nodded, and Pug said, 'Shield your eyes.'

Caleb turned away. A sizzling sound filled the air and he felt a momentary flash of heat.

'You can look now,' said Pug.

Caleb looked at the door that was now a smouldering bit of charcoal, as he heard voices approaching from behind. A company of thirty men, all loyal to the Conclave and under the direction of Chezarul were catching them up. Pug looked through the smoke now rising through the grating, and said, 'Just as I suspected.'

'What?'

Pug motioned for his son to walk through the doorway with him, and once inside, Caleb saw they were in a vast basement, and that it was completely empty.

As the armed men arrived, Caleb said, 'Father, there's no one here.'

'No, and I suspect there hasn't been for quite a while.'

Chezarul said, 'Fled?'

Pug shook his head. 'They are days gone.' He looked at Caleb. 'I suspect they left right after your first attack, son. I think they left these wards in place so we would do exactly what we've done. Waste our time.'

'Then where is Varen? Where are the Nighthawks?' asked Caleb, frustration clearly marking his words.

Pug shook his head. 'Together, I think, but other than that . . . ?' He looked around and said, 'Chezarul, have your men search down here, and in the warehouses above. Have them mark – but not move – anything they find. I suspect the Nighthawks have left nothing behind, but perhaps they've missed something.'

He looked at his son. 'I wonder what your brother's doing now?'

Tal pulled himself up out of the muck, spitting out flavours he didn't wish to think about, let alone experience. The blast had taken him completely by surprise, and his ears still rang.

Standing still for a moment, he attempted to wipe off as much of the filth as best he could. As the ringing subsided, he could hear men approaching from down the tunnel, and he drew his sword.

When he was certain that the men were his, Tal motioned for them to follow, then hurried down the smaller tunnel to where Magnus had been. Tal could barely make him out in the gloom, but he moved as fast as he could, slogging through the sewage, and slowly overtook the magician.

Magnus stopped as the tunnel began to rise and when Tal finally reached him said, 'Sorry about the noise. Couldn't be helped.'

'A little warning?'

'No time,' said Magnus turning back towards the beckoning darkness. 'Are the men coming?'

'Can't you hear them?'

'I can scarcely hear you,' said Magnus. 'I had barely got a shield up when that trap sprang open – I didn't have time to consider the subtleties like being able to hear or see afterwards.'

'The men will catch up in a minute or two.'

'Let's wait for them. I'm done with surprises.'

In less than two minutes a company of thirty armed men reached them, and Magnus said, 'Everyone ready?'

Before anyone could answer, he had turned up the incline and trudged into the darkness ahead.

Tal motioned for men to light some lanterns, and just as the first was struck, light sprang up all around Magnus. Tal shrugged, indicated to the man holding the lantern to keep it alight anyway, then followed after the tall magician.

They came to a large opening at the end of the tunnel, blocked by an iron grating. The far side was piled waist-deep in debris. Above the gate was a vertical passage with several outflows emptying down it. A steady trickle of filth rained down on anyone standing before the grating.

'Is someone supposed to clean out this catch basin?' asked Tal.

'You'll have to ask the Imperial Keshian government's engineers about that, assuming anyone is responsible for this mess,' answered Magnus.

Tal said, 'It appears to be a dead end. Look at the rubbish, no one's passed through there in years, even if there was a way to move that grating.'

'Appearances are sometimes deceiving,' said Magnus.

He moved his wooden staff into his left hand and held his right hand outward, with his palm facing the grating. The air filled with the sound of tortured metal as the iron twisted. Dust and powdered rock filled the air as the metal ripped itself out of the stonework and fell forwards, releasing the mass of debris it held back. Those behind Tal moved to either side of the tunnel to allow the mass of rubbish to float by.

When the following water was down to a trickle, Magnus said, 'Now, let's see what's up here.'

They moved up an incline to a huge sump, full of foul-smelling sludge. Tal looked past Magnus into the tank and said, 'What is that?'

'Catchment basin of some sort, I should think,' said Magnus. 'Like on a farm, where they store all the manure so they can use it again for fertilizer.' He leaned out a little and looked up, straining his eyes in the dim light. 'I wonder what's up there?'

One of the men behind him overheard the question and spoke up, 'If I'm correct, we're right below one of the farmers' markets. Wagons from the farms unload up there every day.'

Magnus said, 'Sounds right. This mess smells different.'

The man behind them said, 'It's mostly vegetables and fruit that is thrown down here to rot to a pulp. A couple of good rain storms and it's washed away.'

'Rotting fruit and vegetables smell different from spoilt meat,' said Tal. 'Is there anything else?'

Magnus shook his head. 'There may be something hidden under this sludge, but I doubt it. I think we've been led on a . . .' His voice trailed off as something caught his eye.

406

'What is it?' asked Tal.

'Over there, can you see it?' He pointed.

According to Caleb, who had hunted with him more than anyone else, Talwin Hawkins possessed the best eyesight of any man alive. He could see a hawk on the wing a mile away or spot a fawn hiding in a thicket while others walked past. Once Magnus had indicated where to look, he saw it.

'I'll get it,' he said, stepping into the sludge. He sank to his thighs before hitting solid rock.

'Brave man,' said Magnus.

'I'm already a total mess,' said Tal, wading through the muck until he reached the object.

'What is it?' asked Magnus.

Tal reached down. 'I think it's some sort of a jar, made out of stone.'

As his fingers brushed the object, Magnus shouted, 'Don't touch it!'

Pain exploded up Tal's right arm as a blinding light filled the chamber. Magnus turned to the men behind and shouted, 'Run!'

They didn't need any further prompt, and fled immediately. Magnus turned to see blazing flames erupt from the vessel that Tal had touched and quickly incanted a shield spell cocooning Tal in a protective enchantment that would momentarily protect him from further harm.

But even in the blinding brilliance, Magnus could see Tal writhing in pain as he tried to stay upright. Stumbling backwards, he held out his right arm, which had been badly burned. Magnus could see the blistering flesh, charred black in places, and the small flames that still ringed the sleeve of his tunic.

His face was a mask of agony and Magnus knew he had only moments to get Tal out of there before the heat of the explosion overcame the spell and killed him. He reached within himself and attempted to contact Pug. *Father!*

Pug appeared next to him instantly and raised his hand to ward off the quickly rising heat. The sewage around the vessel was bubbling, crackling, and drying quickly enough that it was starting to burn.

Tal stumbled towards the two magicians. 'We've got to get him out!' shouted Magnus.

Pug closed his eyes, mouthed an incantation and suddenly the fire was gone. He and Magnus moved swiftly, ignoring the heat of the sewage as they grabbed Tal as he collapsed. 'Take him to the Island!' Pug shouted.

Magnus put his staff in the crook of his arm and reached into his robe. He pulled out a Tsurani orb and put his arm around Talwin's shoulders. Then suddenly they were gone.

Pug looked around the smouldering pit of garbage and moved to stand over the stone vessel in the middle of the room. The heat had burned away the surrounding plant waste and the item sat upon bare stone. He reached out and touched the object. It vibrated with magical energy, and the quality of that energy was disgustingly familiar to Pug.

He lifted it up. 'Got you!' he said softly with a note of triumph in his voice.

# CHAPTER 20

# VAREN

Tal gritted his teeth.

The pain was tremendous and the stench from the burned flesh of his right arm was sickening, but Nakor quickly applied bandages soaked in a solution made from powder that he had pulled out of his ever-present rucksack. Miranda arrived in the room set aside for Tal on the island, holding an earthenware cup. 'Here, drink this; it'll help ease the pain.'

Caleb helped Tal to sit up and drink. 'What is it?' asked Tal. 'Another magical potion?'

'Brandy,' said Miranda. 'I could give you something to knock you unconscious, if you'd like?'

Clenching his teeth, Tal's eyes ran with tears as Nakor finished putting the soaked wraps over his charred flesh.

'Wait,' said Nakor. 'Brandy?'

Miranda said, 'Yes.'

Nakor nodded to Pug, who put his hand over Tal's forehead, and the swordsman fell unconscious. Nakor then took the cup from Miranda and downed it. 'Thanks. Brandy's not good for him. Sleep is better. He'll hurt for a few more days, but it's the itching that will drive him crazy. Give him something for that.' Nakor put it aside and said, 'He will sleep for a while. We need to deal with other things now.'

Pug indicated agreement, and said, 'Back to Kesh.'

Nakor said, 'You go ahead. I'll be along shortly with Bek.'

Miranda motioned for Caleb and Pug to stand close and when they were all gathered around her, she moved them effortlessly back to a villa owned by the Conclave, which lay only a few miles outside of the city.

Caleb said, 'I need to get back into the city tonight. I've got three boys stashed away in a safe house –'

'Three?' asked his mother. 'Are you collecting them?'

'Long story. And Pasko and Amafi are also waiting for me.'

Pug said, 'Go later, there are things to discuss.' He motioned for them to follow him into a larger room, once used for galas, and now empty except for a few chairs and tables.

Once they were inside, Pug looked around the room. Besides his wife and their two sons, Chezarul also sat in the large main room of the villa, along with two of his most trusted men, who would act as runners if word needed to be sent into the city. Their horses were already saddled. Two adepts from Sorcerer's Isle patrolled the perimeter of the estate with a dozen of Chezarul's guards to ensure that no one approached undetected.

Pug said, 'I'm concerned by the fact that Caleb's first attack was anticipated, and that the Nighthawks seem to have fled the city. We either have a spy in our group or we are under some extremely subtle observation. I can rule out the second, as Miranda and I have used every art at our disposal to ensure this wasn't the case. Which means we have a spy.'

Caleb said, 'Who knew about the attack?' He pointed to Chezarul. 'He, I, a few key lieutenants and the rest of us in this room.'

'And Kaspar,' said Pug.

Perplexed, Caleb took a deep breath. 'But he was in the palace and did not know the time or location. They knew exactly when we were coming, Father, and Kaspar knew nothing about the raid today; we couldn't get word to him without exposing Amafi or Pasko to unnecessary scrutiny.

'So, if we have a spy, it's someone in this room.'

Chezarul said, 'These men are like sons to me. I stake my life on their loyalty.'

Pug nodded. 'I have no doubt.' He looked at the tall thin, dangerous-looking fellow named Donmati, and his heavily-muscled companion named Dahab. 'No man would rise this high in our company without being tested.'

Miranda said, 'Unless our spy doesn't know he's a spy.'

Pug's eyes narrowed as he regarded his wife. 'Explain, please.'

Miranda said, 'Caleb, where did you first obtain your information on the Nighthawks' nest?'

'From a man calling himself the Magistrate.'

Miranda asked, 'Did he know who you were?'

Caleb said, 'Only that we were men with gold.'

Miranda said, 'So he paid other people to gather information for you?'

Pug said, 'My love, where are you going with this?'

'Only that those who were watching Caleb, Kaspar, and Talwin may not have been aware of who, ultimately, was getting that information.'

Pug turned to Chezarul and said, 'How fast can you get a message to this Magistrate?'

'Hours, at the most. I would receive an answer from him by morning.'

'Then send a message and arrange a meeting. Give him whatever assurances and gold he asks for, I will not take no for an answer.'

Chezarul bowed his head and said, 'At once.' He motioned to his lieutenants and the three men left.

Pug said to Caleb, 'With Talwin injured, I need you to go to Pasko and have him get a message to Kaspar. Let him know the Nighthawks appear to have departed the city, but that we cannot be sure. They could be resting in a house down the road from here, for all we know, or they may already be on their way to another nation.

'Tell him that we still do not know where Varen is.' Then, more to himself than to Caleb, Pug

412

said, 'But if he's not skulking in the sewers, he's probably close to the seat of power. Kaspar will understand that as well as anyone. Should anything suddenly appear out of the ordinary in the palace, we need to know.' Pug reached into his robe and pulled out a small, silver object appearing to be little more than a charm. 'Tell him to keep this on his person at all times, and that if he needs to summon one of us, to break it.' He pointed to Magnus, Miranda, and himself. 'One of us can be there in an instant. Tell him it's also useful if he needs to leave in a hurry. We can get Pasko and him out of there quickly.'

Caleb said, 'Yes, Father' He embraced Pug, his brother, then his mother, and hurried out to the stable where a horse would be waiting for him.

'One thing about this troubles me,' said Magnus.

His mother dryly said, 'Only one?'

'There are other magicians in Kesh, besides Varen; some of them are on good terms with us and the Academy at Stardock, but not one word has come from the north warning us that Varen could be in Kesh.'

'Save for the evidence of the magical traps,' said Miranda.

Nakor said, 'Perhaps Varen hasn't used any unusual magic? There is nothing to prevent him from inhabiting the body of someone in a position where the practice would call no attention to him. There are a number of magicians and priests who frequent the palace from time to time.'

'Yes,' said Pug. 'Rumour suggests that Diigai has been using magic to prolong his life, as he is more than a century old. There could be more truth to that hearsay than we first thought.'

'Could Varen be the one giving the Emperor life-extending magic?' asked Magnus.

'No,' said Pug. 'We've already investigated the matter, and while the rumour abounds he's using magic, no one magician or priest has been alone with Diigai for years. That doesn't mean that one isn't coming to see him in secret, but we've talked to all our contacts in the Keshian temples, and we know that none of the more powerful priests is helping the Emperor. Even Varen could not possess one so highly placed and not be found out.'

'Then who?' asked Miranda. 'Whose life has he stolen?'

Just then Nakor appeared, Bek stood at his shoulder with one hand resting on it. Nakor said, 'I wanted to make sure he stayed out of trouble.'

Pug nodded. 'Ralan, go to the kitchen and find something to eat.'

The large young man nodded, frowning slightly at being dismissed, but saying nothing. When he was gone, Miranda said, 'We were just speculating about whose life Varen is currently living.'

Magnus looked at his father. 'I'm inclined to suspect someone in the palace,' Magnus said, 'Perhaps even one of the princes?'

'Possible, but unlikely,' said Pug. 'From what Kaspar and Tal have said, Varen exhibits erratic behaviour over time. He might go undetected for a while, but the princes of Kesh are scrutinized too closely for Varen to occupy one of them and not draw attention to himself. No, it's someone highly placed but not obvious. He might be inhabiting the body of anyone close to the Emperor, perhaps even one of his concubines.'

Miranda said, 'A woman who can influence the Emperor could be a possibility . . . though I don't know how likely it would be for him to choose a woman's body.' With a slightly rueful smile she said, 'You men seem to have certain inclinations which you are unlikely to surrender.' She paused, then said, 'I think he's likely taken hold of someone who can cause a great deal of trouble suddenly and without warning.'

Pug said, 'You've just named half the nobility of Kesh, certainly the men of rank among the Charioteers and Horse, as well as half a dozen highly-placed generals in the legion and Household Guard. At the right moment, a sudden attack . . .' Pug shook his head. 'He has so many places to hide.'

'But we know for certain that he's here?' asked Nakor.

'Yes, we do.' A sack sat against the wall and Pug now picked it up, opened it and pulled out the vessel Tal had found in the sewer.

Nakor held out his hand and Pug handed it to him to examine while Miranda said, 'What is it?'

Nakor said, 'Oh! It is Varen! He's in here!'

Miranda moved instantly, her dark eyes flashing

415

as she took two steps and plucked the object out of Nakor's hand. It was a simple earthenware jar, with a stopper fixed with a wax seal. 'There's no wards or other spells around it, are you sure?'

'The ward is inactive. If I hadn't acted, Talwin would be dead.'

'Do we destroy it?'

'Not until we find Varen,' said Pug. 'If we destroy it now, he'll know. His soul will return to whatever body he inhabits now and he will go to ground. Whatever plot he's hatching will be abandoned and he'll flee to safety, only to labour years and construct another plan before he risks confronting the Conclave again. Remember, this man has lived at least as long as we have, perhaps longer, and he can easily flee from body to body as long as this device is intact.'

'Where did you find it?' asked Miranda.

Pug told them how Tal had uncovered it and Nakor said, 'Brilliant. Absolutely brilliant.' He grinned. 'We could have dismantled this city one brick at a time, and it still may not have occurred to anyone to sift through three feet of vegetable sludge in a sewer. But Varen could go to the vegetable market any time he wished, and have the vessel rise up to him with a wave of his hand.'

'Which is why we need to hang on to this until the last possible moment of Varen's life. Had he not placed additional wards around the drain, we would never have found this.' He took the vessel from his wife and returned it to the sack. 'I could have been standing knee-deep in the filth a foot away and still not have discovered it. It was only chance that had Tal's sharp eye notice it.

'Had he not noticed it, all our efforts would have been fixed upon locating the Nighthawks' hideout and we might have thought that the current crisis in Kesh was over.'

Miranda said, 'So what do we do now?'

'We wait for him to give himself away,' said Pug. 'Whatever he has planned will go forwards. The Nighthawks are probably close. Something is planned for the Festival of Banapis, and we must stay alert.'

'The festival begins in less than a week, Father.' Magnus looked at his parents and said, 'If it is something monstrous like a wholesale attack on the Imperial family, or a move against another royal before the issue of the succession is settled, we can do nothing to stop the Keshian Empire from being thrown into disarray.'

Pug nodded. 'It's a risk. But we have the opportunity to destroy Varen, for once and for all, and that is more important. If we are vigilant, we may be able to divert whatever murderous plot he has set in motion, but as much as I wish to keep the Empire stable, finding Varen is our priority.'

Magnus nodded. 'Very well. I shall return to the city. With Talwin disabled, we need people with the ability to detect magic near the palace. What of you two?'

'We'll stay close,' said Miranda. 'The game is

coming to an end, and we will not risk being too far away from you to help.'

Magnus smiled, 'You mean you want to keep an eye on your boys, Mother.'

Miranda inclined her head and then smiled back at her eldest. 'I love my children, even when you were learning to make fire by pointing a stick at anything that burned.'

Pug laughed. 'What was he, three?'

'Not quite,' said Miranda. 'And you didn't think it all that funny at the time.'

'Because he nearly burned my study to the ground.'

Miranda gave her son a hug. 'Yes, even when we wanted to drown you and pretend you had never been born, we loved you, Magnus, as we love Caleb. So, yes, of course I want to keep an eye on my boys.'

Magnus put his arms around his mother and hugged her. 'I'm glad of the attention, this time, truly.' He stepped away and took his staff from where it leaned against the wall. 'You know how to find me if you need to,' he said, and vanished.

Pug said, 'Now comes the hard part.'

Miranda nodded. 'We wait.'

Kaspar nodded as Pasko finished reading Pug's message.

Caleb had gone to the safe house and told Amafi and the boys that things were under control, then he had taken Pasko aside and given him Pug's instructions. The old servant had gone to the morning market and made some purchases. When the morning rush of servants returning to the palace began, he merely followed them with goods his master had instructed him to fetch at first light.

Pasko handed the device Caleb had given him to Kaspar, who looked at it and said, 'Have you a small chain?' They were standing on an open balcony, in imitation of the precautions taken by Lord Turgan.

Pasko held up a finger. 'In my kit. A moment, m'lord.' He returned a few minutes later with a simple gold chain and said, 'Serving nobles like young Talwin, means one collects any number of things over the years. You never know when they might be useful.' He gave the chain to Kaspar, who threaded it through the small hole in the charm Pug had sent him. Then with Pasko's help, he fastened it around his neck.

'What is today's agenda?' asked Pasko, for he had not been inside the palace for two days.

'The usual receptions and parties, and the first big gala of the festival.'

'With Banapis but two nights away,' said Pasko, 'you fear Varen will move soon?'

Kaspar shrugged. 'When he lived in my citadel, Varen ignored almost all state functions, unless I specifically asked him to join us. He seemed oblivious to the social side of things. He's probably skulking around the lowest parts of the palace, dressed as a rat catcher or the midden-cleaner, setting magical devices that will destroy us in a single instant.'

'Caleb said that his father is convinced Varen is highly placed here in the palace, one able to quickly bring the nation to a crisis.'

'Pug may be wrong,' said Kaspar. 'He's a powerful enough man, and a bright fellow, but I'm sure he'll be the first to tell you that he's made his share of mistakes. No, for all we know Varen is a cook poisoning tonight's meal, and tomorrow, we could all be dead.' Kaspar tapped his chin. 'Unless—'

'Unless what, m'lord?'

'Unless he requires an audience to—' He turned to Pasko, 'Could it possibly be?'

'Could what be, m'lord?' said the old servant, looking confused.

'I have an idea. It's far fetched, but Pug should hear it. Have him meet me at—' He looked at Pasko again, 'Send word to Caleb that I need to see him. I'll be at his inn at midday.'

Pasko nodded and hurried into the suite of rooms and left Kaspar alone on the balcony, considering what he realized was probably the most preposterous of theories, but the only one he could come up with that met all the criteria they had discussed about Varen's purpose here in Kesh.

He stood alone for an hour, re-examining what he knew and what he feared, and the more he pondered the question, the more he knew he was right.

★　　★　　★

'You're mad,' said Miranda as Kaspar finished explaining his suspicions to her, Pug and Caleb.

'Varen's mad,' he answered. 'I may be wrong. There's a difference.'

Pug said, 'He would face the least amount of scrutiny, of all the people in the palace as long as he's fulfilling the functions of his office and not speaking to anyone suspicious . . . it is possible.'

Miranda said, 'I cannot believe it. Someone would have noticed by now.'

'Maybe someone did, but there are so many twists within turns in Keshian politics that should a spy go missing or a minor minister . . .' Kaspar's eyes widened. 'Maybe we've been making the wrong assumption about the Keshian nobles being murdered.'

Pug nodded. 'Perhaps they are not being murdered because they support Prince Sezioti, but because they noticed something.'

Kaspar said, 'I must get back to the palace and arrange to see Turgan Bey. I need to find out where those nobles were the week before each of them was killed.'

'If what you suspect turns out to be the truth,' said Miranda, 'We'll have the seven lower hells' own time, trying to prove it.'

'We can't prove it,' said Pug. 'Those who would believe us are already in our ranks. Those who oppose us might know, but they won't care, and those in the middle will think Kaspar is mad or a criminal.' He looked at Kaspar.

Caleb had been sitting quietly to one side, and he said, 'I understand some of the logic you used to come to this conclusion, Kaspar. But how can you be so certain?'

Kaspar said, 'The brothers' obvious love for each other. They may have had different mothers, but they are very close. The way they talk to each other, about each other . . . Warring factions are part of Keshian tradition, but the parties backing the princes seem to be ignoring the fact that neither would raise a finger in opposition if their father were to name the other as heir.

'If anyone raised a hand against Sezioti, Dangai would raise his sword to protect his brother and order the Inner Legion to join with the Imperial Guard. Sezioti may not be the warrior his younger brother is, but he would do the same for Dangai.

'No, I am convinced. Someone is weaving this rivalry out of thin air and killing those who may have suspected that something was wrong in the palace. I need to speak with Turgan Bey.'

Pug nodded. 'Take Magnus with you disguised as a servant. He's in the other room with Nakor and Bek.' To Caleb he said, 'I think it's time for you to send the boys back to the island. Once you've seen them safely home, return here for the festival. If, as Kaspar suspects, that's the day Varen makes his move – he'll want do it in front of as many members of the Gallery of Lords and Masters as possible.'

Caleb hesitated, and Pug said, 'What?'

'Father, I want to keep the boys here.'

'Why? It's almost certain to turn bloody in a hurry.'

'I'll keep them on the edge of things, but sooner or later they will have to be tested. They've done well so far, even better than I could have hoped for, but we're going to need every sword we can muster.'

'Even Jommy?' said Pug. 'I've not even met the lad.'

'He's able to look after himself. He may not have trained with a sword, but he's a brawler and keeps his wits around him. I'll make sure they know they're reserves, but I want them close.'

Pug conceded. 'You've taken the responsibility as their father, Caleb. It's your decision.' He smiled. 'Just be careful.'

Pug looked at Kaspar as he readied to leave. 'I hope you're right in your suspicions, for then we will have this over in two days, but I pray you are not, for so much will weigh on our ability to convince a palace of angry Keshian nobles we are protecting their nation. I will be close and you have the amulet. If I judge Varen correctly, he'll be waiting for me to appear, but he may not be ready for all of us. If we can provoke him into revealing himself before the entire court, we may yet save this nation, and this entire world.'

Kaspar said nothing as he left, but the grim expression he wore mirrored how Caleb, Miranda, and Pug felt.

Caleb stood up and said, 'I'll go and ready the boys.'

As he made to leave, both his parents hugged him and Miranda said, 'I wish you'd reconsider and take the boys to the Island, and you'd make me happy if you stayed with them.'

'Why?'

'You've a wife, now—'

'And three stepsons, apparently,' said his father.

Caleb smiled. 'Jommy will grow on you. He's a good boy.' He said, 'But you need swords with you, Father, and with Tal injured, I should be at your side. What was it Nakor used to say about magicians in battle? "One magician throw spell. Second magician counter spell. First magician throw second spell, second magician try to stop him. Soldier walk up and chop up first magician while he's trying to think of what to throw next."'

Pug laughed. 'It was something like that, but don't let him hear you imitating him like that, you'll hurt his feelings.'

'Kaspar will be there,' said Pug. 'And it won't be one magician facing Varen, but three of us.'

'And Nakor,' said Miranda, 'and that odd boy he has following him around.'

Caleb said, 'If you order me to stay at the Island I will, Father, but I would rather be here.'

Pug stayed silent for a long moment, before he said, 'I want you to stay on the Island.' He hugged Caleb again. 'But you're right; I need you here.'

Pug said, 'Miranda, keep an eye on things until I return, will you?'

'Where are you going?

'To the Island for a while. I think I might have an idea that might help us.'

Miranda kissed her husband, then he produced an orb and vanished. She motioned for her son and they left the room to fetch the three boys.

Final goodbyes were said, and Kaspar and Magnus left for the palace, stopping along the way to buy Magnus his disguise. Nakor bid the boys and Caleb good luck and after they and everyone had departed, he said to Miranda, 'Now?'

Pulling out a chair and sitting done, Miranda said, 'Now we order something to eat, and we wait.'

Ralan Bek looked at her and said, 'Is there something I can do?'

Nakor walked around the lad and put his hands on his shoulders. 'Soon, my young friend. Soon.'

# CHAPTER 21

# ANTICIPATION

Kaspar scanned the crowd.

The gala would be the centrepiece of the great Midsummer Festival of Banapis, the oldest known holiday in the world. Its origins were lost in antiquity, going back before the oldest recorded history. It was a day belonging to neither the past nor the coming year. According to legend, Banapis, known by other names in other nations, was celebrated over the entire world of Midkemia.

Kaspar had discovered that today, the Midwinter festival would be celebrated down in Novindus, and when it was midwinter here in Kesh and the other northern nations, it would be midsummer down there. He idly wondered if the extra Midsummer's Day that he experienced the year before in Novindus, really counted, and whether it truly made him an extra year older.

Both Pasko and Amafi were in attendance, as with Caleb elsewhere, Amafi had no further duties, and Kaspar had decided he could use an extra pair of eyes in the crowd. He knew that Magnus had secreted himself somewhere in the assembly, and

426

that Pug and Miranda were able to arrive at a moment's notice. He wished that Hawkins was recovered, for he knew his sword was irreplaceable. And where Nakor had got to was anybody's guess.

'This is the intimate celebration, Magnificence?' asked Amafi.

'It is if you're the Emperor of Kesh,' responded Pasko. 'Only his closest friends and dearest relatives are here.'

'All ten thousand of them,' said Kaspar dryly.

The plaza that marked the lowest edge of the upper plateau at the end of the palace proper, was as big as the entire inner bailey of the citadel at Opardum. Kaspar's entire army could assemble here without two soldiers rubbing elbows.

The plaza itself was divided into three levels. The Imperial family would sit upon the highest – a relatively small platform that could be reached from within the palace itself. There would be approximately five hundred personages of significant rank there with them. Had Kaspar still held the title of duke, he would be up there today. However, as a lowly suppliant he was relegated to the second platform, where the majority of guests would stand.

Along the entire edge of the second level a flight of six stone steps descended to the third level, but even without guards or barriers, those on the lowest level knew their place. The lack of guards was the Keshian gesture to the idea that during Banapis, rank held no meaning. In the Kingdoms of the

Isles and Roldem the king might mix with the commoners in the street upon this day, but in Great Kesh, it was simply the absence of a thousand white-clad Imperial Household Guards not barring the way that signalled this mythic day of equality.

Kaspar knew that to mount those steps to the second level without permission would instantly reveal to one where the guards were hiding, and to try to reach the upper platform where the Emperor sat would invite certain death. And at some point, Kaspar reasoned, *he* would be the one attempting to reach that highest platform. He glanced to either side of the raised area. Unlike the lower two sections, the imperial platform was high enough above the second level to effectively be a giant balcony, with a suitably impossible wall to climb. Easy access was only possible via the steps on either side, or by retreating into the palace proper, navigating up to that level, then somehow getting through the royal apartments or the Gallery of Lords and Masters.

The steps were guarded by a dozen white-clad Imperial Household Guards, and nothing short of a squad of trained soldiers would win past them. Kaspar turned to Amafi and Pasko and said, 'Seems to me if we're going to get up there, we'd best seek the back entrance.'

Amafi smiled. 'I know the route, Magnificence.'

'Let me guess,' Pasko offered dryly. 'You've assassinated a Keshian prince before?'

'Not quite,' said the former killer in his self-effacing way just as revellers started to hurry past them. 'I once was commissioned to remove a young courtier who was becoming a problem to a minor functionary here in the palace. The courtier was Trueblood, the functionary wasn't, and his wife was indiscreet. Sadly, the courtier choked on an olive pit during the celebration, up on that very plaza.' Amafi smiled. 'Truly one of my more subtle undertakings.'

Kaspar said, 'Well, the sun is setting and chaos will arrive shortly, so let's take advantage of it. I have noticed over the years that for the most part people do not bother you when you look as if you know what you're doing, so let us appear so.' He motioned for the two servants to lead on, and followed them as more and more people arrived in the middle plaza.

It took longer than he had anticipated to reach the entrance to the palace and as he had said, merely by looking as if they had a purpose to their movements, the guards at the main entrance let them pass without question.

'How long has it been?' asked Kaspar, already knowing the answer.

'Three hours, m'lord,' said Pasko. 'Almost three hours to the minute.'

'If we're late, he may not tarry.'

'If he won't spare you five extra minutes,' said Amafi, 'you didn't impress upon him the importance of the meeting sufficiently.'

'He has duties,' said Kaspar, picking up the pace. 'We're late.'

They arrived at a doorway in a hall, guarded by

two members of the Household Guard. As they hurried forward, Kaspar said, 'I'll have your hide if we are late, Amafi!'

For a brief instant the guard on the right of the door hesitated as an important-looking foreign nobleman and his two servants rushed through the portal. By the time he glanced at his companion, they had gone. The second guard shrugged ever so slightly, as if to say now it was someone else's problem.

Once inside the perimeter of the imperial apartment complex, no one challenged their right to be there. They circumvented the Great Hall and the Gallery of Lords and Masters, as those areas would be filling with the luminaries of the Empire and special guests who would fill the upper plaza as the night-time celebration commenced. Even now, jugglers, dancers, musicians and all manner of entertainers were performing for the assembled crowd. A great boulevard that separated the lower city from the palace itself was cordoned off. It would provide the route for a great parade, with elements from the legion, the great chariot companies and the cavalry all marching by, followed by exotic animals and finally, a great stage, on which a theatrical tribute to the Emperor would be performed.

Kaspar reached Turgan Bey's office as the Imperial Master of the Keep was rising from his chair of office. 'There you are,' he said as he saw Kaspar. 'I thought the message madness, for I wondered how you were going to get here.'

'Look like you know what you're doing,' Kaspar said, motioning for Amafi to keep a lookout at the door, while Pasko went to the open terrace.

Kaspar came to stand next to Bey and whispered in his ear. 'I know where Varen is, and I think I know what is to happen next. Who do you trust?'

'Right now, damn few people.'

'Who among the Inner Legion, the Masters of the Chariots and the Imperial Horse?'

'Even fewer. Why?'

'Who do you trust to save your Empire?'

'Kaspar, what is this about? Is our Emperor in danger?'

'Worse,' said Kaspar. 'I think the entire imperial family is at risk.'

'Tell me quickly,' said Bey.

Kaspar outlined the idea he had shared with Pug earlier and as he spoke, Bey's face drained of colour. When Kaspar was done, Turgan Bey said, 'Kaspar, I don't want to believe it. But what you suggest explains many things that up to now seemed without reason.' He sat back and was silent a moment, then asked, 'If you're correct, is there anything we can do?'

'I need you to get to as many as you can trust and let them know that when things turn ugly, the best thing they can do is to keep their swords sheathed, unless they see a direct threat to someone close by. Get a lot of drunken nobles running around with their swords out and people are going to die needlessly.

'The thing to remember is that we only need a few men close to the princes. They must be men you can trust, and impress on them . . . well, you know what to say. But I'll repeat this one thing. The Nighthawks did not flee the city; they are here in the palace, and tonight they plan to bring the Empire to its knees.'

'Kaspar, if you're right, you'll be made a prince of Kesh.' Then he looked him in the eyes. 'And if you're wrong, or if you've completely lost your sanity, we'll both be fed to the crocodiles.'

Kaspar's eyes reflected a hint of doubt. 'It's a risk, but we have no choice.'

'Where will you be?'

'I have to be on the dais, close to the Imperial family.'

Bey went to his desk and pulled open a drawer. He took out a small staff of ivory, with a single golden circlet around it. 'This is as good as an armed escort, Kaspar. No guard will question what you are doing if you're holding this.'

'Thank you.'

'Now, what next?'

'We wait,' said Kaspar. 'We can prove nothing until the Nighthawks make a move. And when they do, we will have to act quickly.'

Turgan Bey looked at Kaspar and said, 'May the gods protect Kesh.'

'And us all,' said Kaspar as the Master of the Keep left his office.

Amafi said, 'Magnificence, what now?'

'We wait,' said Kaspar, sitting in Turgan Bey's chair.

Nakor led Bek through the throng. 'Nakor,' said the large youth, 'this is wonderful! I've never seen so many people!'

Nakor nodded. 'Kesh is the largest city in the world, Ralan.'

'They are having fun, aren't they?'

'Yes, and so far managing to do so without hurting one another,' said the little gambler as he wended his way through the crowd.

'This is good?'

'Yes,' said Nakor. Every chance he had got he had been trying to inculcate Ralan with the concept of good, and while he knew he could never change the young man's nature, he thought he might alter his perspective a little.

A pair of burly city watchmen pushed through the crowd, shouting for the pedestrians to clear the route. Nakor grabbed Bek's arm and led him to the far side of the boulevard. 'Many years ago I came here with two men: Guda and Borric. They were fine fellows. We did the same thing then that we are going to do now.'

'What's that?' said Bek.

With a sly grin, Nakor said, 'Crash a party. Follow me.'

Bek shrugged, but the idea of arriving uninvited appealed to him, so he kept the little gambler's back in sight as they made their way through the crowd and headed to one of the many entrances to the palace.

Magnus stood quietly in a deep shadow, hidden by a colonnade from those nearby. From across the large boulevard, he had a direct view of the upper plaza, and he knew he could be there in seconds. He looked in vain for Kaspar or Nakor, and seeing neither felt a stab of apprehension. If Kaspar was correct in his surmise, this could be the pivotal moment in the short history of the Conclave of Shadows, for with a single misstep, their four most powerful practitioners of magic could be obliterated.

Pug and Miranda waited. Everything that could be done had been done and they could only sit and linger until the signal came, then they would act. Pug looked out of the window of the nearly empty house and thought how odd it was that he was never visited by a sense of home any more.

'What are you thinking?' asked his wife, softly, as the distant sounds of revelry reached them through the night air.

'Crydee, and being a boy,' he said softly. 'Sorcerer's Isle is home, but . . .'

'Home is where you were a child.'

He looked at her. In so many ways he felt incomplete when she was not near, and yet if they lived another hundred years together, he knew he would still never fully understand Miranda. 'Is that how our boys feel?' he said.

She smiled. 'When this is over, ask them.'

He looked thoughtful. 'I will. When this is over.' Then he stared out of the window again, waiting.

Kaspar quickly made his way through the press of the royal family, trying hard to get the attention of either prince. He caught Dangai's eye, and the Prince crossed over to greet him. He wore his formal attire as leader of the Inner Legion – black gartered sandals, a black kilt, black jacket and chest plate, and a massive helm which completely covered his head and was topped by a splendid horsehair plume, also dyed black. 'Kaspar. I didn't realize you'd be joining us.'

'I wasn't on the Master of Ceremony's list, I'm afraid.'

The Prince regarded Kaspar for a moment, then smiled. 'Well, it's not a formal state function, and everyone here is half-drunk already, so I doubt anyone will mind.'

Kaspar lowered his voice. 'How many units of your legion are close by?'

Dangai's eyes narrowed with suspicion as he asked, 'Why?'

'Because I believe there will be an attempt to take your brother's or your life tonight, possibly both of you.'

'Why was I not warned before this? And why must I hear it from a foreign noble?'

'Because your entire Imperial Intelligence Corps has been subverted,' said Kaspar frankly. After

435

conferring with the Magistrate in the morning, Pug and Kaspar had pieced together a picture that could mean only one thing: the reason their first attack on the Nighthawks had failed, and the reason that the Nighthawks had gone when they finally uncovered their nest, was that the assassins had been aided by Keshian spies.

Kaspar had taken the Emperor's warning about everyone having spies to heart. The Magistrate had openly admitted that, prior to his current accommodation with the members of the Conclave, he had sold information on the whereabouts of various foreigners to men he knew to be Imperial agents. It was the only explanation. The Conclave had been watched from the moment they had arrived in the city, and the only reason they were not all dead was that Varen saw an advantage in having Conclave agents in Kesh, fermenting trouble. If he could implicate them as agents of the Kingdom or Roldem, Kesh would go to war.

The struggle in the sewers and the warehouse district of the city had diverted Lord Bey's attention as well as the local constabulary and agents working for other factions in the government from the simple truth; that the real struggle was taking place in the palace.

'Something is going to happen tonight, and while it may look like a simple faction struggle between your supporters and Sezioti's, that is merely a mask. There are forces that wish to see the Empire plunged into chaos, even bloody civil war, Highness, and you must believe me when I tell you that I am here to stop it if I can.' Kaspar looked the Prince directly in the eyes and added, 'I will stake whatever honour I have left, and my life upon it.'

'What would you have me do?'

Kaspar glanced around. 'Gather as many men upon the Imperial platform as you can, but this is the difficult part; they must not be wearing the garb of the Inner Legion. The last time there was a confrontation between the Legion and the Household Guard, treason was the cause and it must not look like you're making a grab for power – that would play right into the hands of those behind this madness.

'They must be stationed where they can intervene and keep order. Something is going to happen, and I am not sure what it is, but when it does occur, it will be unexpected. Drunken men may think to pull blades first and consider the consequences later. The Imperial Guard will rush to defend your father if they think he is at risk, and it would only take one miscue for people to start dying.

'You must choose men you can trust, and if something goes amiss, they must prevent people from fighting. You'll need a hundred or more who can put themselves between those likely to want to kill one another. Can this be done?'

Prince Dangai said, 'You're certain there will be an attempt on my brother and me?'

'Perhaps more than that.' Kaspar said, 'I see both your wives and children in attendance, as well as

437

many royal cousins and other blood-kin. It's possible that if our enemies gain the upper hand tonight, the entire Gallery of Lords and Masters could be depleted.'

'You paint a grim picture.' Dangai motioned for one of his aides to come to his side. He gave him quick instructions and then said to Kaspar, 'Since my grandmother's time the Legion has not set foot within the halls of the palace, due to the conflict that eventually put my father on the throne. You realize that if you're wrong and I can't explain all of this to my father's satisfaction, I may be joining you and the crocodiles by this time tomorrow?'

'I wouldn't worry about satisfying your father,' said Kaspar. 'More than anyone here, he will understand what is at stake.'

'I shall speak to my brother,' said the Prince.

'Do so, and have his most trusted allies stay close at hand. I fear chaos is about to erupt and if so, we must throw sand on the fire before it turns into a conflagration.'

Dangai left Kaspar and Amafi came to his side. 'Were you believed, Magnificence?'

'I was. Either that, or in less than a minute a troop of guards will arrest us and drag us down to the dungeons.'

'Let us then pray for belief,' said the old assassin. 'My joints are too old to endure the cold and damp.'

Kaspar said nothing as his eyes scanned the room for the first sign of trouble.

★　　★　　★

By sunset, the festivities were fully underway with the parade below and the music and dancing in the streets beyond.

High on the imperial plaza, the nobles and influential commoners enjoyed the Emperor's largess. As darkness approached, two events were being anticipated, Emperor Diigai's arrival and the annual fireworks display.

Kaspar kept Amafi and Pasko moving through the crowd, returning frequently with information. As he had promised, Prince Dangai was also moving his own men throughout the area, positioning them so they could neutralize any outbreak of fighting; and as Kaspar had requested, they were all wearing festival garb.

Half an hour before the Emperor's anticipated arrival, Turgan Bey sought Kaspar out. The large man gripped the former Duke by the elbow and steered him to a relatively quiet corner of the upper plaza. 'I spoke to Prince Dangai, and he claims you're the one responsible for my guest list becoming shambolic.'

Kaspar said, 'Are all your agents here?'

'Yes,' said the Master of the Imperial Keep, 'but I have no idea what we are looking for.'

Kaspar said, 'It will most likely happen when the Emperor is seated. Prince Dangai's men will attempt to keep order, but it's the Household Guard that I'm worried about. If they see a threat to the Emperor, they'll kill anyone who gets near him.'

Bey nodded his head. 'I'm concerned, too. We have a lot of new faces in the guard this month.'

'New faces?' asked Kaspar. 'I thought it took years to join the guard.'

'It does, but a score of men were ready to retire and their replacements were already in the lesser ranks. The Emperor held a ceremony two nights ago, rewarding those stepping down with land and gold and elevating those who had served elsewhere in the palace to his personal bodyguard.'

'Is this unusual?'

'Yes. The Emperor usually waits until a month after Banapis to retire the older men.'

'Do you know these new men?'

'Yes,' said Turgan Bey. 'Each one has served in the palace for years.'

Kaspar lowered his voice. 'The Nighthawks are patient.'

Turgan said, 'Kaspar, these men have been hand-picked by the Emperor, after having served for at least five years, most longer. Each was recommended by his commander and all are veterans. Their loyalty can not be questioned.'

'That's what I fear,' said Kaspar.

'I must go,' said Turgan. 'I have a moment, only. What do you mean?'

'I have no time to explain. Have your men stay close to the two princes. And no matter what happens, have them protect all the members of the Imperial family.'

'Very well,' said Bey. 'But whatever happens—'

he looked around the festivities '– or doesn't happen tonight, you and I are going to have a long conversation tomorrow.'

'If we're alive tomorrow, I'll welcome it.'

Amafi returned and said, 'The Emperor comes, Magnificence.'

'I never thought I'd hear myself saying this,' said Kaspar. 'But I wish Talwin Hawkins was here.'

'His sword would be most welcome if it comes to a fight,' said Pasko, joining them.

Kaspar inclined his head towards a nearby knot of revellers laughing and drinking, several wives and consorts stood talking to noblemen, while children played underfoot. 'If there's a fight up here,' said Kaspar, 'a lot of innocent blood will be spilt. We must make sure that there isn't one.' Kaspar looked around and said, 'Have either of you seen Nakor or Caleb?'

Both men said they had not. Kaspar said, 'Now we wait. The procession will be starting in a few minutes.'

The three agents of the Conclave of Shadows stood as close to the entrance as they could get, given their lack of rank, and made ready.

Caleb moved with purpose, but slowly, along a darkening street, the three boys behind him in single file. With nearly everyone else in the city crowded along the great Imperial Boulevard, this broad street along the eastern side of the palace was effectively deserted. The massive building that was the palace turned the late afternoon street into a dark canyon, as the sun sank below the western horizon. This street was used primarily for carts and wagons carrying goods to the palace, while across the way the verge was lined with a clutter of tiny apartments, rising four and five storeys high. The only signs of human activity were the locked gates found every hundred yards, barring the way into the lower levels of the palace and guarded by members of the Household Guard.

The four of them stayed close to the buildings on the opposite wall, moving quickly enough to avoid close scrutiny but slowly enough to avoid raising suspicion. As they passed each gate, Caleb and the boys were subjected to a quick glance by the guards on the other side of the gate, but otherwise ignored. As long as they were not attempting to enter the palace, they were not troubled.

They reached a long stretch of deserted houses, all appearing well kept but very small and close together. Caleb whispered, 'This entire block is housing for servants who do not live within the walls of the great palace. Every house should be deserted, for every servant should be working in the palace late tonight.' He glanced around and suddenly movement in a window above caught his eye, then was gone. He moved back against the wall, holding up his hand for silence.

Caleb knew that only Truebloods were permitted in the great palace after sundown – the only exception to this rule was foreign nobility who were housed in a special quarter. That practice had been less rigorously enforced since Diigai had come to the throne with several key offices now held by non-Truebloods who resided in the imperial home. Caleb knew that on any other night but Banapis and a few other significant holidays, the apartments behind him would be full of inhabitants going about their business.

Caleb let out a long breath. 'I've got a bad feeling.'

Tad said, 'What?'

'Who's the sneakiest?' he asked.

'Zane,' said Tad.

'Tad,' said Zane at the same moment.

'I am,' said Jommy in concert with the other two.

The other three looked at him and Jommy said, 'Any of you live on the streets for a couple of years?'

Caleb smiled. The street ran northward for as far as the eye could see, but another street intersected from the east. Opposite that intersection another large gate could be seen.

'Can you get over there, close to that wall, and get a look at the gate without being seen from above?' he whispered.

Jommy glanced around. Softly he said, 'Shouldn't be too hard, but who am I hiding from? I don't see anyone.'

'Upstairs, second window. Someone watches.'

Jommy looked to where Caleb indicated and waited. After a moment, he said softly, 'I see him.'

'Do you think we've been seen?' asked Zane.

'If we had, someone would be down here,' said Caleb. 'Whoever he is isn't watching down here, but over there.' To Jommy, he said, 'So I need you to skulk around and see what he's watching.'

Jommy glanced around, then said, 'Too right. I'll be back.' He crept close to the wall until he reached the far corner, where he vanished from sight.

Long minutes passed, then suddenly the boy was back. 'Best I can tell,' he whispered, 'there's a gate into something that might be a marshalling yard – I don't know, 'cause I've not hung around this part of the city much. If not that, a place for deliveries to the palace. Anyway, the gate's closed and there's a pair of guards there.'

'Why would they watch that one gate?' asked Caleb quietly.

'Don't know, but there's one odd thing about it.'

'What?' asked Caleb.

'You know how those other gates we passed all had guards, too?'

'Yes,' said Caleb.

'Well, all those guards were inside the gate. These two blokes were outside.'

Caleb said, 'That's because those two aren't trying to keep people out; they're there to let people in.'

Zane said, 'What do we do now?'

'Some of Chezarul's men are going to be gathering at an inn not far from here, the Four Winds.'

'I know that inn,' said Jommy. 'It's only a half dozen streets east of here.'

'We were supposed to meet with them there. I think it might be better to bring them here.' He glanced at the sky. 'It'll be dark soon.' Looking at Jommy, he asked, 'Any place around the corner we can stay out of sight?'

'An inn, a few doors down.'

'Let's take a look.'

Moving purposefully, they started up the street, again attempting to move at a speed not likely to call attention to themselves. A small party of revellers rounded the corner, obviously well on their way to total drunkenness and shouted greetings to Caleb and the boys. Caleb said something vague in return and they rounded the corner.

They reached the inn, a nondescript door with a sign of a crocodile with an open mouth hanging above it. 'I expect this is used by those who work at the palace, for I can't see merchants staying here,' said Caleb as he opened the door.

He stepped into a room that was almost full of men and in a moment, swords were being drawn. For before him stood more than a dozen men, some wearing the black garb of the Inner Legion, while others wore the uniforms of the Household Guards, the Royal Charioteers, or the Imperial Horse. Caleb needed only a second to deduce what was in play. 'Nighthawks!' he shouted.

Zane and Tad had their swords out an instant after.

Jommy took one step away from the entrance, turned and ran.

Caleb backed out and said, 'They can only come through one or two at a time.'

Then the first swordsman struck out at him.

Positioned high on the steps of the large building opposite the palace, Magnus used his magic to increase his vision so he could see what was taking place on the upper plaza more clearly. He had already spotted Kaspar and saw that he, Amafi and Pasko were close to the entrance from which the Emperor's entourage was beginning to appear.

The imposing figure of the Master of Ceremonies entered, resplendent in his feather-festooned head-dress and leopard wrap. He swung his massive ivory-encrusted staff of office easily, like a walking stick, as a dozen trumpeters and drummers followed behind. When he reached the threshold to the plaza Household Guards ran to form a corridor to the steps leading to the throne, and the Master began to speak.

Across the vast hall, through the open door, the procession moved slowly. Nakor and Bek could hear the Master of Ceremony's imposing voice cut through the noise of the crowd, but his words were not clear. At the rear of the procession a massive sedan chair was carried by a dozen bearers, and upon it sat a very old man.

Nakor put a restraining hand on Bek's shoulder, for behind the chair stood a dozen armed Household Guards. 'We wait,' said Nakor softly.

'For what?' asked Bek.

'Something interesting to happen.'

Kaspar looked from face to face in the crowd, not entirely sure what he was expecting to see. Many of those nearby he recognized, even if he couldn't put a name to a face, for most had been in residence during his last state visit; others were people he had met over the last month here in Kesh.

The procession coincided with the parade on the boulevard below the palace. It was timed so that the Emperor took the throne just as the most exotic and colourful elements of the parade passed before his view, followed by a massive fireworks display. Then the revel would be in its full glory. Drunks would be passing out in the streets, fights would be crushed by the constables, babies would be conceived, and tomorrow morning the populace would return to life as usual.

Throughout the city the celebration reigned, but here next to the palace was the highest concentration of citizens, from the foremost to the humblest.

Kaspar looked around and realized that if things got out of hand, more damage could be done to the Empire in this location than at any other time or any other place.

The Emperor's sedan chair was carried through the door, and Kaspar absently put his hand on the hilt of his sword. He waited.

★　★　★

Caleb impaled another assassin, this one dressed as a household guard, when Zane shouted, 'Caleb! Behind us.'

Caleb risked a glance to his right and saw two swordsmen, dressed as Household Guardsmen, racing towards them. 'They must be the two from the gate!' he shouted. 'I'm busy!'

Zane and Tad turned to face the two newcomers while Caleb barred the door.

Zane said, 'I'll take the right!' Tad nodded, then charged at the leftmost guardsman. 'Idiot!' shouted Zane, then he leaped after his foster brother.

Tad's impetuousness proved fortuitous, for when he assaulted the swordsman on the left, the one on the right reflexively turned to help his companion. Zane suddenly faced a man who was turned away from him, his left side exposed.

The man realized his error a moment later, but died trying to pull back and face Tad.

Tad then turned his attention to the man facing Zane and saw his brother was holding his own well enough. He remembered what Caleb and the other instructors at Sorcerer's Island had said about two swordsmen who had not trained together being more inclined to get in one another's way.

He circled to the left, sparing a quick glance to where Caleb held the door and saw that he was being slowly forced back down the three steps leading into the inn. The more experienced swordsman had been easily dealing with Zane, but he saw Tad moving out of the corner of his eye and tried to circle away from the approaching second opponent.

Tad widened his circle, attempting to quickly get behind the man his foster brother faced and the man moved away from Zane, trying to keep both boys in his line of sight.

Zane was huffing from exertion and perspiration poured off his face. He was glad of the respite. The swordsman moved in a half-circle, trying to get his back to the wall of the building, so neither youth could move in behind him, but Zane moved too quickly on his right hand, and Tad too quickly on his left.

Zane motioned with his head and Tad nodded and suddenly they both ran as if trying to get behind the man, both to their left. The swordsman was faced with the instant choice of turning to face one of the boys and chose to stay with Zane, turning his back for an instant to Tad, who leaped forward and slashed across the man's exposed neck with his sword.

Before the man had hit the stones, Tad was rushing past Zane to stand next to Caleb, who was now down on the street, facing a swarm of assassins who were now coming through the door.

Caleb shouted, 'Run!'

Zane joined his brother and stepfather and said, 'No!'

Tad shouted, 'This way!' and started moving backwards up the street, away from the palace.

The three fell into line, stepping backwards as fully

twenty men came out of the inn. The three knew they would quickly be surrounded, but to turn now would invite being struck down from behind. The best they could do was retreat slowly up the street, moving fast enough to keep all the assassins in front of them.

As they reached a point two doors down from the inn, the assassins hesitated, and suddenly a figure with a thick thatch of red hair hurled by them, as Jommy appeared waving a club the size of a ham. He smashed it down over the protective thrust of one swordsman, crushing the man's skull, screaming like a madman in the process.

Then dozens of men were streaming past Caleb and the boys, and Chezarul's agent, Donmati, was standing next to Caleb. The thin dark man asked, 'Are you all right?'

'Yes,' said Caleb as he watched the assassins being overwhelmed by Chezarul's men. 'How many of you are there?'

'Fifty,' said Donmati.

'See if you can take any of these alive. They are all Nighthawks.'

Tad and Zane caught their breath and Tad said, 'Come on,' and followed after Chezarul's men.

Caleb nodded and charged after him, Zane at his side.

The outnumbered Nighthawks fought viciously, and to a man died, despite attempts to capture one. Suddenly it was silent.

Caleb motioned for the boys to come to him as

well as Donmati. 'I thought you'd run,' Caleb said to Jommy.

'Naw,' said the affable redhead. 'I just went to get some help.'

'It's a good thing you did,' said Tad, putting his hand on Jommy's shoulder. 'We'd have been done for in a few more minutes.'

Jommy shrugged. 'Looked like you were doing well enough when I got back.'

'Staying alive,' said Zane.

'There's no city watch,' said Donati.

'I didn't expect there to be,' said Caleb. He pointed at the far gate, opposite the street where they stood. 'Someone killed the guards there and put Nighthawks to guard the gate. The city watch are either dead as well, or they're over keeping order at the parade.' He put up his sword as he caught his breath. 'I need two of your men to search that inn. See if they can find anything that might prove useful. Then send another to carry word to Chezarul; we're going into the palace.'

'We are?' asked Tad.

'Whoever is orchestrating this night's mayhem expected this bunch' – he indicated the dead Nighthawks – 'to come up to the higher levels of the palace to start the killing.' With a half-smile Caleb said, 'Instead he's going to get us.'

Motioning for the others to follow, Caleb led the remaining swordsmen of the Conclave towards the now unguarded palace gate.

★   ★   ★

The sky exploded and the crowd cheered and laughed. Kaspar ignored the pyrotechnics and kept his eyes searching the faces around the Emperor. He noted that the two dozen young female 'attendants' who had surrounded the Emperor when Kaspar had played him at chess had quietly joined their master, slipping into various places that formed a circle around the dais – positions that would have gone unnoticed had Kaspar not been watching the Emperor instead of the fireworks.

Amafi came to stand close to him and Kaspar said, 'See those courtesans standing next to the House Guards?'

'They are lovely, Magnificence.'

'Yes, but how are they standing?'

'Not like playthings for the Emperor, but as if they are guarding him.'

The young women who had giggled and preened in Kaspar's presence all now stood with forced smiles on their faces, and their eyes moved restlessly around the plaza.

'Don't make eye contact with any of them,' said Kaspar, smiling and nodding as if telling Amafi something funny. 'Now laugh and look at the fireworks.'

Amafi did so and said, 'They are also searching the crowd. For what, Magnificence?'

'Perhaps they search for us,' whispered Kaspar close to Amafi's ear. 'Where's Pasko?'

'On the other side of the Plaza, as you instructed.'

'Good. Now, if we can—'

Before he could finish his sentence, the Emperor rose.

Seeing Emperor Diigai standing, the Master of Ceremonies struck the marble floor with the heel of his staff, causing it to reverberate through the throng. Years of courtly training took effect and within seconds the entire upper plaza had fallen silent.

Those below looked up and seeing the Emperor standing before his throne, they also fell silent. Within minutes the only sounds to be heard were coming from across the boulevard, too distant for the common folk to see what was occurring.

'Now!' said Kaspar. 'It starts now!'

# CHAPTER 22

# CONFRONTATION

Kaspar gripped Amafi's shoulder.
'Be ready!'
'What are we looking for?'
'I don't know,' said Kaspar as the Emperor lifted his arms.

'My people!' Diigai intoned, and his voice carried surprisingly well for a man his age. Kaspar had no doubt that everyone on the two plazas below him could hear their ruler. 'Today we celebrate Midsummer's Day, the Festival of Banapis!'

The crowd cheered and the Emperor paused for a moment. Kaspar grabbed the trinket around his neck Pug had given him and yanked the chain, easily breaking it from around his neck. He held it tightly in his left fist, while his right crossed over to the pommel of his sword. He was ready to respond with either.

Kaspar glanced to where the two royal brothers stood, amid their families. Both Sezioti and Dangai watched their grandfather with interest. The elder brother's face held an expression of mild surprise, as the Emperor was not scheduled to make an address tonight.

Dangai glanced around the plaza, and his eyes made contact with Kaspar, who nodded slightly. Then he noticed the Prince gently urging his young son to stand behind him as his hand moved to the hilt of his sword.

'We have much reason for rejoicing in the Empire!' shouted the Emperor. 'We are at peace and our harvests are plentiful. Yet, there is a reason for sorrow, as well.'

Immediately there was a hush from the crowd, for this was not what they had expected in the middle of the year's greatest celebration.

'In the heart of the Empire, amid all our bounty, are those who would see all our greatness reduced to ashes! There are those among us who seek to plunge the dagger of betrayal into the heart of Kesh. And even now those traitors stand among us!'

'Woe, Oh Kesh, that a father should confront such grief, for it is from those whom he loves most – from those he expects to reap the greatest joy – that this painful treason rises!'

The old man's bony arm shot forwards and he pointed at his two grandsons. 'There are the architects of madness, the betrayers of their line, they who would bring blood into the very house that sheltered them. They, my own blood grandsons, are the source of all the woes that betide the Empire.'

The two brothers stood stunned. Sezioti's expression showed he could scarcely credit his senses, and even though Dangai had been prepared for something going amiss this evening, his confusion was evident. 'Now, the madness that hangs over us will end!' shouted the Emperor. 'Take them!'

Several of the Household Guards hesitated, while two moved forwards instantly. Half a dozen armed men moved to intercept them, telling them to stand down. They were members of the Inner Legion and no matter what the Emperor ordered, they would not stand by and see the brothers taken by the Household Guard.

There was a tense moment and many nobles edged away from the confrontation while others tried to get closer to see what was happening. The situation was rapidly reaching a breaking-point and Kaspar gripped the summoning ward tightly.

Suddenly, the girls at the foot of the dais pulled short daggers from their kilts, and the Household Guards who failed to obey their Emperor found their throats slashed from behind. Blood fountained from the necks of over a dozen men, and in a near hysterical cry, the Emperor shouted, 'Murder!'

Amafi said, 'Magnificence, has the Emperor suddenly gone mad?'

'No,' said Kaspar, drawing his sword. 'He was mad a long time ago.' He stepped past his servant, nodded to Pasko, and took his place next to Prince Dangai.

'Take them! Kill them!' screeched the Emperor, and the two remaining Household Guards tried to take a step towards the Princes, but were quickly restrained by the legionaries who confronted them.

Members of Dangai's Legion were moving

quickly through the crowds above and below, urging people to remain calm, not to start more trouble and to let the drama between the Emperor and his grandsons play out. Kaspar could hear many voices urging those nearby to keep their heads, as more and more people began to express alarm. Many were fleeing the plaza, heading down the steps to the lower area and the street below, only to find their way blocked by those pressing forwards to see what was happening. The struggle between them was threatening to start a riot in minutes.

Kaspar reached Dangai's side, as the Prince shouted, 'Grandfather! What madness is this? There is no treason here!'

'You say no treason!' shouted the Emperor, and Kaspar could see the veins standing out on the old man's neck. At more than a hundred years of age, despite the sorcery that kept him alive, Kaspar knew his ancient heart must be close to exploding. His eyes were wide and his colour high, as his cheeks were flushed and perspiration beaded on his brow.

'Yet you stand next to foreign provocateurs! You say there is no treason here!' He pointed to Kaspar and the Prince and shouted, 'Kill them!'

No one moved for a moment, then the twenty young women from the Emperor's bedchamber swarmed forwards, shrieking and holding daggers high. The first legionaries who tried to block them were struck savagely and several went down, while others reeled backwards with deep, bleeding wounds.

'Defend yourself!' shouted Kaspar, and he stepped between the Imperial family and the closest girl. To Dangai he yelled, 'Get your children out of here!' Dangai took his youngest child, a boy of ten, and with his left hand moved him in the direction of his mother, while drawing his own sword.

One of the Emperor's concubines hurled herself at the Prince, who lashed out without hesitation, took her below the rib cage and with a twist pulled his sword out. 'Show no mercy! They are all bewitched!' he shouted.

Had Kaspar not recruited Dangai and his men before this moment, he knew it would have ended with the death of the two Keshian Princes and perhaps a dozen or more members of their family, but with the men ready, the girls, armed only with daggers, were killed swiftly. Not one retreated nor attempted to protect herself, so intent were they on attacking the brothers.

From behind, Kaspar could hear the sound of voices raised in question and others shouting answers. Then, seemingly out of nowhere, Caleb appeared and said, 'We hold all the entrances to the upper court.' To the Emperor Caleb shouted, 'The assassins who were to start your blood bath aren't coming. They're all dead.'

The Emperor's face contorted in rage, turning almost purple as he stared with wide-eyed astonishment at his dying courtesans, and then at Kaspar and Caleb.

Kaspar looked up and shouted, 'You'd better

sit down, or you'll burst your own heart . . . Leso!'

The Emperor howled a mad, gleeful laugh, and Kaspar dropped the charm Pug had given him, grinding it into the stone with his boot-heel.

Nakor could barely see over the heads and shoulders of those crowding the door. At least a hundred nobles had already fled the plaza, and more were departing by the moment. But many of them were still transfixed by the spectacle of the mad Emperor. They were creating a bottleneck for those attempting to flee back into the palace, and the jam was making movement in either direction impossible.

Nakor said, 'Bek, can you ask some of these people to move aside, please?'

The powerful youngster grinned, his eyes looking like two shining pools of light in the shadow thrown by his black hat. 'Love to,' he said as he grabbed the two nearest men standing in Nakor's way. 'Leave now!' he shouted, and if either of the men had been inclined to argue, they thought better of it as soon as they saw the demented grin on the youngster's face and started hurrying across the great hall.

Bek was like a force of nature, pulling men aside, irrespective of rank, and shouting, 'Run away!' After a few moments, the crowd around them decided to abandon watching the confrontation between grandfather and grandsons and they also left.

In just a moment, Nakor and Bek could enter the plaza. As Nakor looked up at the Emperor, he said, 'This isn't good.' Just then a flash of light announced the arrival of two figures – Pug and Miranda.

Kaspar said, 'Varen has taken the Emperor's body!'

'Oh, this is all too much,' shouted the Emperor. 'Just when I had things where I wanted them . . .' With a cry of pure aggravation, he drew back his hand and made a casting motion. From the palm of his hand erupted a blinding white ball of flame and it flew straight to where Pug and Miranda stood.

Instantly a wall of energy – bluish and pulsing – formed around Kaspar, Caleb, and the Princes, and quickly extending in a sweeping arc to protect everyone who stood watching the Emperor.

Blinding light played across the surface of the protective ring, and across the boulevard thousands cheered as if the spectacle were another display following the fireworks above.

A sizzling discharge of energy left the air thick with a tangy odour, as if lightning had just struck, and Pug stepped forwards and said, 'It's over!'

Leso Varen, in the body of the old Emperor, laughed. 'It's never over, Pug! Didn't I teach you that years ago? Kill this body and I'll find another. You can't stop me!'

Pug pulled the jar out from inside his robe and said, 'Yes I can!'

Suddenly the sorcerer's expression changed. His

eyes widened and he said, 'No! You can't!' The frail old arms moved like a musical master conducting minstrels and the air filled with a thrumming of energy that cause more people to flee. Those on the plaza below who had blocked the exit of those from above now sensed that something terrible threatened, and they also turned and fled.

Whatever this was unfolding before them, it had nothing to do with the normal world, and everything to do with evil sorcery. Battle-hardened soldiers stood holding their swords in hands without the inclination to use them, and others found themselves backing away like children confronted by a menacing street dog. Even some of the most decorated veterans of the Keshian army turned and ran.

Pug said, 'I can, and I will.' He smashed the jar on the marble floor and the mad sorcerer howled in impotent rage, as a foul green cloud erupted from the shattered jar. The cloud of smoke swirled like a whirlpool, and the funnel raced from where Pug had shattered the jar and straight at Varen.

Varen leaned forwards, and inhaled deeply, sucking the green miasma into his lungs. He straightened and as his body became fused with power, the lines in his face started to fade and withered muscles grew plump, and before the eyes of the assembled rulers of Kesh, he appeared younger by the minute.

'First you interrupt the party!' he screamed. 'Then you keep me from killing those two.' He pointed at the Princes. 'And, by the way, do you have any idea how hard it was to ensorcell those girls and get them to betray their masters? Without being caught, I mean? They were all trained spies! It took me months!'

Kaspar's instincts had been correct, for while the body belonged to another, the evil soul was undoubtedly Leso Varen's.

'And you, Kaspar,' shouted the sorcerer. 'It wasn't enough you had that thing kill me once, already?' He glanced around. 'By the way, where is it? I really need to get my hands on it. It would be ever so very useful for some other business I have planned.'

'Far from here,' said Kaspar. 'Very far from here.'

'Well, no matter. I have ages.'

Pug said, 'If you die now, Varen, it's over.'

Varen howled in delight. 'Do you really think so, Pug? Do you think I would be so foolish as to not have contingencies? You underestimate the respect I have for you and your . . . witch? Wife? What is it?'

Miranda said nothing, she knew Varen was goading her. Softly she whispered, 'He's gathering his power.'

Pug shouted, 'There is no place for you to flee to, Sidi.'

'Now that's a name I haven't heard in a long time.' The Emperor's body now looked as it had at the peak of his power. His hair was raven-dark and his skin smooth and shining with perspiration. 'Damn, it feels good to be young again!' Varen looked at the fallen girls from his private apartment and said, 'Pity. Do you have any idea how frustrating it was to sit there in that old body . . . well, never mind. I can find more girls.

'Now, where was I? Oh, yes, it's time to kill everyone!'

'Now!' shouted Pug.

Magnus acted. He had been slowly incanting as he watched his father and mother face the mad sorcerer and at the agreed upon moment he willed himself to his parents' side.

Varen raised his hands high above his head and waves of black energy pulsed downwards, rolling and curling like water cascading over rocks, yet flickering like flames across its surface. The evil magic surged, resembling oil burning on the surface of a wave of water. Yet the flames were without light or heat, consisting only of flickering darkness.

Pug, Miranda, and Magnus struggled to protect those around them, while Kaspar and the two Princes looked on in mute astonishment.

To the royal brothers, it looked as if the grandfather they revered had been rejuvenated to the powerful man they had known as children, yet he was twisted, distorted, and rendered alien to them by the madness and evil that poured from him. Both stood next to Kaspar, Dangai had drawn his sword, but was unable to move, rooted in place by uncertainty.

Pug shouted, 'Let none of his evil touch you! It will consume you like a flame!'

Kaspar looked on in disbelief and horror as those not protected by the shield of magical defence, were consumed. The black flame danced over their skin, and those still alive screamed in agony as their skin blistered, and the flesh blackened and turned to char. The liquid flames were unrelenting and even the bone was consumed after a few minutes.

What was most unnerving was that the black flames produced a chilling cold that threatened to suck the life from those behind the shield. It was a thing of despair and rage, this black flame, and the more Varen railed from his position atop the dais, the more insistent the flames became.

*Black liquid fire*, Kaspar thought, and the three magicians seemed to be using everything they could keeping it in check. Kaspar could see that while the three magicians had to act in concert and be mindful of those they protected, Varen was under no such constraint. He could lash out blindly in all directions and felt no concern over any other person's wellbeing.

At last Kaspar saw the face of evil, unadorned, unmitigated and without apology, and it caused him to feel hopeless. *How can we ever stand in the face of this?* he wondered and for a moment he was ready to concede the day.

Then he saw movement behind the throne, it was barely visible through the raging black flame beating against Pug's defences.

★ ★ ★

Nakor motioned for Bek to follow him. 'Stay close,' he said, holding up his hand.

Ralan Bek asked, 'What are we doing here?'

'Something good.'

'I don't care about good, Nakor.'

'Then something fun.'

'All right,' said the young man, a smile on his lips.

Everyone around them had fled and Bek could now see some sort of confrontation going on between the man on the dais and three figures at the edge of the railing that ran around the upper plaza. Then, something icy cold, black, and liquid seemed to burst around them, and Nakor held up his hands, as if warding something off from overhead.

A bubble of force, something unseen, kept the black flames from touching them. 'We must be quick,' said Nakor, as he mounted the steps behind the throne. 'I can't do this for very long. It's a hard trick.'

When they reached the royal seat, the man before it was shrieking like a fishwife, his words incoherent as he sent wave after wave of life-sucking energy at those cowering below. Only the three figures of Magnus, Miranda and Pug stood against him, using all their arts to protect those around them and on the plazas below.

Nakor kept one hand high above his head, then with the other touched Bek on the shoulder. 'Kill him, please.'

With a grin, Bek pulled his sword, stepped up

and drove it straight into the back of the possessed Emperor.

Suddenly the black, oily flames vanished, and there was silence. Kaspar could see Varen standing motionless, mouth open and his eyes wide in surprise.

The sorcerer looked down at the blade protruding through his stomach and said, 'Again?' Then he stumbled forwards a step as Bek pulled his sword free, and collapsed on the dais.

Suddenly the Emperor's body shuddered, and Pug and the other magicians turned. Nakor stood above the fallen sorcerer and he put one hand on Bek's chest and said, 'Back!'

A monstrous howl, like ten thousand years of rage, erupted from the body, and many covered their ears and grimaced in pain. A brilliant green flame sprang from the Emperor's corpse and through it a slender thread of green energy pulsed for a moment, then sped upwards into the night sky, and then north-east.

In an instant there was bedlam as most of those remaining fled from the upper plateau. By now there was also a wholesale exodus from the lower plaza, so that by the time Pug reached Kaspar and the Princes, only a handful of loyal soldiers remained.

'What was that?' Miranda asked her husband, as Nakor came hurrying down the steps.

Pug looked at Nakor and said, 'Varen's Death Rift?'

'I think so,' said Nakor.

'What does it mean?' asked Magnus.

Pug looked at his wife and son and said, 'Later. Right now, the Empire is safe and Varen is gone forever.'

Miranda didn't look happy at this, but nodded. She turned as Turgan Bey reached the princes. 'Highnesses, are you harmed?'

Sezioti came to his brother's side and said, 'We are fine, Bey.' He looked at his brother. 'Grandfather?'

Kaspar said, 'Your grandfather died over a year ago, Highness. That miraculous recovery when all thought him on his death bed was the sorcerer Leso Varen taking over his body. It was he who tried to plunge the Kesh into bloody conflict.'

'Why?' asked the elder prince.

Pug said, 'Highness, let us get to the Gallery of Lords and Masters and explain the situation to as many of them as we can. There is much to be done.'

Kaspar looked at the two Princes and said, 'And to start with, you two must decide how to rule your empire.'

Pug looked back and saw Magnus approaching with his arm around his mother's waist.

'Come,' said the Master of the Imperial Keep, 'get inside, please, Highnesses. We must restore order quickly.'

Pug followed the Imperial party to where over a hundred anxious nobles waited, and he knew that hundreds more would be gathering in the Gallery of Lords and Masters just a few minutes' walk away.

Dangai stepped to the fore of the group and shouted, 'Heed the words of your Emperor!' He turned to his brother. 'Heed the words of Sezioti, He Who Is Kesh!'

Miranda leaned in to whisper to Pug, 'Well, at least that's one problem we won't have to worry about.'

Pug nodded. 'But there are others.'

'Aren't there always?' she replied.

Hundreds of Keshian leaders sat in mute astonishment at the story that Pug unfolded for them. They sat in the Gallery of Lords and Masters, with Sezioti on the throne once occupied by his grandfather and grandmother. Dangai stood at his right hand, while Miranda, Caleb, Nakor, Magnus and Bek stood off to his left, at a respectful distance.

Pug stood in the circle of the vast arena, looking up at the galleries that rose on every side. He spoke calmly, slowly and tried to explain what he could about the century-long struggle between his forces and Varen's, but omitted any detail about the Conclave and their role in this. To the Lords and Masters of Kesh it sounded as if a small band of trustworthy magicians had hunted down a renegade of their craft and ended a threat. Most would have scarcely believed the tale that had been told to them, but they had witnessed its finale, and they were now inclined to believe any explanation that brought order out of the chaos they had just observed.

That the succession was apparently without

contestation was welcome, for the brothers agreed that Sezioti would rule with Dangai at his right hand.

After Pug finished, Sezioti said, 'My Lords and Masters, tomorrow begins the official mourning of our grandfather, for whatever may have occurred tonight, he ruled with compassion, mercy, and a strong sense of justice for nearly a century.' He let out a long breath as if he had been holding it, and Pug realized that the new emperor was a man feeling every day of his sixty-one years of age.

'We shall endeavour to uphold his legacy and rule as wisely.' He looked around the gallery. 'Please, return to your homes and spread the word: all is well within Great Kesh.'

Slowly, the mighty leaders of the Empire left the gallery, while Turgan Bey motioned for those on the floor to exit through the door behind the throne. Sezioti was the last to leave, and with an obvious expression of regret, he cast a look backwards over his shoulder.

As they moved through the hallway reserved for the Emperor's easy passage to and from the gallery and his private apartments, Nakor paused and when Sezioti reached where he stood, he said, 'Sorry about your father, Majesty. He was a good man.'

Sezioti's eyes widened. 'I recognize you! But . . . I was only a boy –'

'I'm older than I look,' said Nakor with a grin. 'I gave your grandmother that boy hawk so the line of royal falcons could be restored.'

The Emperor glanced at Turgan Bey who nodded and with a faint smile, shrugged.

'Who is this?' Sezioti asked as they reached the Imperial apartments. Two members of Dangai's Inner Legion stood at the door in place of the dead Household Guards.

'He's Bek,' said Nakor. 'He's coming with me.'

'Where are we going?' asked Ralan.

'Home for the night, then someplace else.'

Bek nodded as if Nakor's words explained everything.

Pug turned to Magnus. 'Go with Nakor and investigate the death rift site we found west of Maladon. If Varen has escaped again, we need to know where he went.'

Magnus said, 'Yes, Father.'

As he turned to leave with Nakor, Pug restrained him with a light touch on his shoulder. 'You did well, son. I'm proud of you.'

Magnus looked over his shoulder at his father, then smiled. 'Thank you.' Then he moved to Nakor and Bek and said, 'The night is young and we have work to do.' Suddenly the three of them were no longer there.

Caleb said, 'Father, the boys are with Chezarul and I should go and see to them.' He indicated with a small inclination of his head that he wished to be gone. Pug realized that the fewer of the Conclave's agents who were around to be questioned, the fewer the lies they'd have to concoct.

'You also did well,' said Pug and he watched as

his youngest child moved through the many servants and guardsmen in the hall.

Turgan Bey arranged a reception in the Imperial apartments with enough food, wine and ale to satisfy two hundred people. Servants were scarce, as many of them had fled, but a few of the most faithful remained to serve those who entered.

The Master of the Imperial Keep said, 'Majesty, I will have the Imperial Suites readied for you and your family in a few days' time.'

'There's no hurry,' said Sezioti. 'I'm comfortable where I am, and while this room may be suitable for one old man and a score of young girls, I think my wives might have opinions on what needs to be changed.'

The Emperor sat in the chair that his grandfather had occupied when playing chess with Kaspar. 'I heard every word you spoke, Pug, and I witnessed the insanity on the plaza myself just . . . what, two hours ago? But I still can barely believe what has occurred.'

'This is not a bad thing, Majesty,' said Pug. 'The sort of evil we face is . . . daunting, and most people are not even prepared to acknowledge it. Let the official history of Kesh record that your father died this day and that others died as a result of a . . . mishap. Some fireworks were faulty and unfortunately some people – the old Emperor among them – died as a result. Do not trouble your nation with secrets best left to we few.'

Dangai said, 'What of those who attacked us?'

Kaspar looked at Pug, who nodded at him. 'The Household Guard must be disbanded to the last man,' said Kaspar, 'and may I suggest that a watchful eye be kept on those who were serving closest to your grandfather, Majesty. Varen had years to prepare this mayhem, and many of those serving him were members of the Guild of Death.'

'Others,' Pug said, 'were enchanted, like the girls who died this night. Some of those may be redeemed by magic, others may be lost forever, but they must be identified. I can have magicians of Stardock come to see they are all found out.'

'How can we protect ourselves against anything like this happening again?' asked Turgan Bey.

Miranda said, 'My lord, for years my husband was a ruling lord of the Kingdom of the Isles, and he had the King's ear, as well as that of the late Prince of Krondor, Lord Arutha. Magicians were part of that court as a matter of course, and one of their tasks was to be vigilant against this sort of evil.'

Sezioti looked at his brother, who nodded. The Emperor said, 'Have you someone you might recommend to fulfil a similar function here?'

Pug bowed. 'I can send a reliable magician to your court as an advisor on things magical, Your Majesty. A Keshian,' Pug looked up and smiled, 'and perhaps even a Trueblood?'

Sezioti nodded and tried to smile, though his heart wasn't in it. 'Our thanks, magician, for all that you and your friends have done to save us, our families and our nation. What may we do to repay you?'

Pug was silent for a moment, then said, 'We ask no payment for doing what must be done, but we would ask you to consider two things. The first is to formally recognize what has been de facto for a century – that Stardock is an independent entity, belonging neither to the Kingdom of the Isles or to the Empire of Great Kesh.'

The Emperor said, 'It may be difficult to convince our Lords and Masters, given that Stardock is an anchor in the Vale of Dreams, but we shall endeavour to see it done. What else?'

'That in the future, should another threat such as Leso Varen menace Midkemia, you will think beyond your borders and be willing to render aid, even if Kesh's immediate interests are not apparent. Will you consider that?'

'Before, I would have had a great deal of difficulty understanding the wisdom of your request, Master Pug, but I now can imagine how the kings of Roldem and the Isles would feel with that monster sitting on my grandfather's throne, commanding armies unequalled in the world . . . yes, if you ever need Kesh's aid, send word and we shall heed you.'

'That's all I ask.'

Sezioti said, 'Then I think we are done. Let us relax as best we can, remember our grandfather for the good that he did, and try to blot out the horrors of this evening from our memory.'

'So says He Who Is Kesh,' intoned Turgan Bey.

The others nodded and then Prince Dangai said, 'Send for our families. I would have my wives and children close at hand.'

'And the grandchildren,' said the Emperor. 'Let us hear the sounds of joyous noise for a while.'

'It will be done,' said Turgan, bowing and motioning to a servant to carry word.

Miranda turned to her husband and said, 'What now?'

Pug smiled and said, 'We have something to eat. I'm famished.'

She returned the smile with a playful jab to the ribs with her elbow. 'I mean with the other things.'

Pug's expression darkened. 'We wait until we hear from Nakor and then we assess the damage. We've lost men here, over the last week, and some of our –' he glanced around to ensure he wasn't being overheard '– agents have been compromised. We'll need to shift some people around.'

'It never ends, does it?'

Holding her close, he said, 'No. But sometimes we win, and then we get to rest for a while.'

'Can we rest now?'

He put his arms around her and hugged her. 'For tonight, my love. For tonight.'

The early morning light barely cut through the lingering chill. Dew on the grass reflected the sun-like gems scattering the glittering light. Nakor, Pug, and Magnus hurried to the place where Nakor and Bek had found the tiny rift.

Pushing through the trees, Nakor said, 'There. It was there!'

Pug stood where Nakor indicated and said, 'Well, it's gone now.'

'Father,' said Magnus. 'Do you think Varen still survived?'

'I think all that bloodshed at Kaspar's citadel over the years was designed to give him a way out should his soul vessel be destroyed.' Pug looked at the place Nakor had indicated and said, 'I can't pretend to think like him, but I understand him well enough to know that no price would be too dear to him to escape final destruction. I wish I had returned sooner and put more time into researching this thing.'

'Even you can't be in more than one place at a time, Father.'

Nakor grinned and laughed. 'Don't be too sure, Magnus. It's just a trick he hasn't learned yet.'

'Let me see if there's anything still lingering here,' said Pug, closing his eyes.

Magnus and Nakor remained silent while Pug concentrated his energies and let his mind reach out, tracing the energy that had come from Opardum to this place then on to . . .

Pug's eyes opened wide and his face drained of colour. 'Varen!'

'What, Father?'

Pug looked genuinely shaken. 'I recognize a

component of this rift, Magnus, Nakor. I know where Varen has fled.'

'Where?' asked Nakor, his usually sunny demeanour fleeing before Pug's obvious concern.

'He fashioned this rift to be triggered upon his death. He has gone to Kelewan.' Pug looked at Nakor. 'Leso Varen is now somewhere in the Empire of Tsuranuanni.'

The three men said nothing more, for the most evil soul they had ever encountered was now loose on another world, in a nation three times the size of Great Kesh, and the search for him would have to begin over again.

Jommy stood blinking in astonishment. Marie hurried to greet Caleb and her sons. One moment Caleb and the boys had been in Chezarul's safe house in Kesh, and the next they had were standing outside the villa at Sorcerer's Isle.

Unlike his father and brother, Caleb had lingered a day in Kesh, conferring with Kaspar and Bey on what would need to be done next to reorder the Conclave's presence in the Imperial City. Magnus had carried word to Marie that Caleb and the boys were well and would be home at midday.

Marie finished kissing her sons and looked at Jommy. 'Who's this, then?'

Caleb smiled with a slightly guilty expression. 'I think it safe to say we've managed to pick up a third fosterling.'

The red-headed boy grinned and said, 'No

worries. I won't call you "Ma" if that's troubling you.'

Marie shook her head, smiled and said, 'I suspect I'll get used to it. Come along. I expect you're all famished.'

Caleb put his arm around his wife. Jommy began following the adults when Zane grabbed him by the arm. 'We ate before we left,' he said.

Jommy turned around, his brow furrowed and he said, 'But I'm hungry!'

'We'll be along in a while,' said Tad, grabbing Jommy's other arm. 'We'll show Jommy around the island.'

As they half-dragged him away from the large villa, Jommy said, 'This better be good, you two.'

'Come on,' said Tad, starting to run.

'Where are we going?' asked Jommy.

'To the lake!' shouted Zane, as he started to unbutton his tunic.

'The lake?' asked Jommy. 'What for?'

'For a swim,' answered Tad.

Jommy stopped. 'A swim! I don't want to swim. I want to eat.'

Zane turned, took a couple of steps back and grabbed Jommy's arm. Tugging on it, he said, 'Believe me; you want to take a swim.'

Just then the sound of female laughter could be heard in the distance as feminine voices shouted welcome to Tad.

Jommy's face appeared to light up in delight and he said, 'Girls?'

Zane said, 'There are some people you have just got to meet.'

Suddenly Jommy was off at a run, passing Zane who remained standing alone for a second, then he turned and ran after the boy from Novindus as the sound of splashing and laughter grew louder.

# EPILOGUE

# REDUX

Two black-clad men strode the field.

Both wore the black robes of Great Ones, the magicians of the Assembly. At first light they had been asked by the membership to investigate another reported rift, perhaps from the Dasati world.

'There,' said the one in the lead, pointing a short distance away.

He hurried, his taller friend behind him, and when they reached the object of their search, they both halted. The man in front raised his hands in a gesture of defence.

A rift had formed, no more than a hand's span in size, but most certainly a rift, and through it had come a creature. Both men looked at the thing and marvelled.

It appeared no larger than a baby in size, yet it stood upright and glared at them. Its shape was roughly human, with two legs, arms, and a head. The face was nearly featureless, two dark lines formed its eyes and there was a single slash where its mouth should be. The thing's head was completely round, a sphere with no other features.

It numbered three fingers on each hand, with opposable thumbs, and it was garbed in what appeared to be black trousers and tunic. It held a tiny metal staff in one hand, and with a defiant chirping sound, drove it into the ground before the rift.

'What is it?' asked the first magician.

'I don't know,' said the second, and for a moment his friend glanced at him, for his voice sounded strange.

'Are you well?' he asked, for his friend had been seized by an unexpected fever and had lain abed nearly three days before arising just the day before.

'I'm fine,' said the second man. The thing glanced in the direction of the morning sun, and shivered, though the day was already hot. It kept its face towards the sun, ignoring the two magicians.

'What's it doing?' asked the shorter of the two magic users.

'It seems . . .' the second magician paused, as if seeking the word '. . . fascinated by the sun.'

'If what we've heard is true, and this thing is from the Dasati world, their sun casts no light.'

'Oh, really?'

Again the first magician glanced at his friend. Then he looked at the staff and said, 'Look at this!'

The tiny staff was emitting sparks of purple which flew straight to the rift. Soon, tiny flows of energy, like purple-white lightning erupted from the staff and struck the rift.

'I believe it's drawing power,' said the second magician, his voice again sounding odd.

'Pug believed that the Dasati rifts were drawn here by the Talnoy. But he said he thought they needed a source of energy here to sustain them.' Then the magician's voice rose in alarm. 'We must destroy this now!'

As he started an incantation to obliterate the rift and the creature who stood before it, the second magician retreated back half a dozen steps. Then he raised his hands and two lances of green-white energy lashed out, incinerating the first magician where he stood.

The tiny creature turned its attention to the display and hissed like a snake warning an intruder to back away.

The second magician said, 'We can't have that, now, can we?'

He came and knelt down next to the creature, who had returned its attention to the sunlight.

As the morning sun climbed higher in the sky and the heat of the day rose with it, the tiny alien creature stood trembling. The second magician leaned in and said, 'Ah, you're not able to cope with all this yet, are you?'

The tiny creature trembled, and then the shaking became more violent until suddenly it erupted into flame. The flash left the magician momentarily blinded and he blinked to clear his vision.

'Well, that was interesting,' he said to himself. Then he looked at the staff that was providing the rift with power. 'So, someone wants to come and visit, do they?'

He reached out and plucked the staff out of the ground. As soon as he did, the energy flow stopped, and after less than five minutes, the rift vanished.

Sticking the tiny staff into his robe, the magician turned and said, 'Got to work on this language. Very different, and my accent just won't do.'

Humming a nameless tune, Leso Varen looked at the smouldering char that had been a Great One of the Assembly of Magicians. 'Too bad you sacrificed it all for the good of the Empire.' He knelt and lifted the man effortlessly, hoisting him across his shoulders. 'But at least you'll get a hero's burial, or funeral pire or whatever it is they do on this world.' He pulled an orb from his robe and depressed a toggle, and suddenly he was gone.

The morning sun beat down upon the grass and only a tiny bit of char revealed what had just occurred in the vast plains of the Empire of Tsuranuanni.